Bla...

Seer's Gambit Book 2

Shari Branning

Table of Contents

1

THE CHEF

Elf Rory Scout flicked the fur-lined hood back from her face and freed her aching ears from their imprisonment inside a wool cap as she stepped into the lodge. She rubbed their pointed tips and swiveled them around to restore circulation, but also to see if she could pick up any sounds that might hint as to why she'd been called in again so soon. She'd barely made it back from her last trip before one of the watch elves flagged her down and redirected her here.

Nothing stirred in the great hall, or any of the surrounding hallways, as far as she could tell. The familiar scent of peeled pine and rich soil welcomed her almost as warmly as her own home, and her feet sank into the moss that carpeted the entire lodge. Even in dead of winter, it remained verdant, damp, and warm in the lodge, and her soul cooed with pleasure.

For the place to be empty at three o'clock on a Rest Day afternoon was totally normal. Which begged the question, why was she here?

Slipping her pack off with a sigh of relief—it weighed half as much as she did—she leaned it against the log wall and went in search of Borden Captain and hopefully some answers. He wasn't in his office, but she followed the sound of murmuring voices down the mossy hallway, ducking a veil of lichen growing from one of the ceiling beams, and found the next office door open. She stopped in the doorway as Borden and another elf turned toward her.

Borden beckoned her inside. "Rory, good. We were hoping you would arrive soon. Come in."

"What's this about?" She glanced from the captain to the other elf, a man who looked familiar, but whose name escaped her.

"This is Taro Councilman. He's the council member who handles most of our foreign intelligence."

Ah. That explained why he looked familiar. Borden was her boss, but Taro was his boss, and one of the ten elven council members of Maireadd. Her mother was on the council as well, though her duties had more to do with tourism and public—human—safety. Why tourism was even a thing in a forest that had been cursed for the past five hundred years was beyond Rory, though she had to deal with it often enough.

"What's going on?" she asked.

"We're not entirely sure," Taro said, his eyes hawkish as he met her gaze. "You know about the situation in Barra. Their queen is a sorceress and she's driving the country into the ground, and taking the rest of the continent with her."

Rory nodded. "If Barra falls, everyone else's economy takes a trip down a wyrm den and doesn't see daylight for a very long time." Barra, their coastal neighbor to the west, controlled shipping and import and export for most of the continent. And thanks to being squished between the elves' cursed forest of Maireadd and the coast, it also had a high number of magicals living in it. Magicals that Queen Dianthe, the sorceress, and King Ebezer now considered resources rather than citizens.

"Not to mention unimaginable fallout to the magical community," Borden said, echoing her thoughts. "And we're not the only ones getting worried. Thyrus' president is getting downright twitchy. For good reason. He'll be the one taking the brunt of the economic collapse, as well as getting many of the refugees if things keep progressing." He didn't need to say that Maireadd would be getting the rest.

"So...what do you need me for?" Rory asked, looking between them. The humid warmth of the lodge had her sweating in her winter gear. She took off her gloves and unbuttoned her coat, but she still had a lot of layers on underneath it.

"Sorry to drag you in here directly from the trail," Taro said. "I promise we won't keep you long." He handed her a file from his desk. "The Thyrus government is asking us for a guide for one of their people crossing from Thyrus into Barra." He gave her a moment to read.

"Sean Leigh..." She scanned the first page, her black eyebrows rising toward her mussed hairline. "A...chef? What."

"Obviously that's a cover."

She snorted. "So what is he really? And why does he have a government endorsement to get him through Maireadd and into Barra?"

"They say the Thyrus president is pretty passionate about grilled eel. Maybe he's sending the man to look for recipes," Borden quipped.

Rory gave him a flat look, though her own thoughts weren't much more mature at the moment.

"Read the file," Taro said. "See if you can make sense of it. I have someone outside Maireadd with access to technology looking into him. They'll call us when they find something."

"What do you expect they'll find?" Rory asked, frowning over the small color photo paper-clipped to the file. Sean Leigh had red-blond hair, freckles, and a dimpled grin. He wasn't ugly, whether by human or elf standards, but he looked about as far from threatening as one could get.

"I suspect he's a spy, or worse."

"Really?" her forehead bunched again. That did not look like the face of a spy. Then again, maybe that was the point. "You're sure he's not just a chef hunting recipes for the president?" She flashed Borden a smile. The redheaded human might not look threatening, but Taro was right. This was so far into the realm of weird that it made a swamp troll look sane.

Taro shrugged. "I want you to find out. Whatever his mission is, I suspect it has to do with the situation in Barra, and that's a situation we can't ignore. Chances are, he and his president are on our side in this case, but we need to know what they're planning. We can't afford to have things blow up on our borders. If Thyrus and Barra come to open war, then, cursed or not, Maireadd is still stuck in the middle."

"I reserve the right to be skeptical," said Rory, shaking her head. "Though if he turns out to actually be a chef and nothing else, I may have to resign. At that point I'll have seen it all."

"Rory," said Taro as she was getting up to leave. "We're certain that Leigh's business is with Barra, not Maireadd, but just in case... be on guard. Don't let him slip away from you. And don't let anything happen to him. Thyrus is uncommonly protective of its people."

Rory stepped back out into the snow still clutching the file, her pack slung over one shoulder as she headed up the hill toward her tree house. Sounds of music and laughter filtered through the branches from other houses, and she hoped Angel had dinner cooked. All that talk about recipes and cooking had made her hungry. The agreement with her family had been that her sister Angel could live with her while she finished mage school, in exchange for taking care of the house whenever Rory was out on a mission. If having cookies and hot stew ready for her when she got home wasn't stated, it was implied.

Rory climbed the spiral stairs wound around the massive bole of her oak tree, and stepped out onto the planked landing. The house itself wrapped most of the way around the tree bole, leaving space where the stairs came up for a railed balcony. She pushed through the door into warmth and light, and kicked her boots off even before she dropped her pack.

"Roryyyy!" Angel squealed, flying out of the kitchen to collide with Rory, sending a puff of snow off her coat. "Welcome home! Supper's on. I expected you an hour ago though. I bumped into Iris Sentinel on my way home, and she said you'd passed the border of the city."

"Then she forgot to mention that she sent me right back to work," Rory said, shedding her layers and leaving a trail of clothes on her way to the kitchen. She waved the file before slapping it down on the table. "Another assignment already."

"Anything you can talk about?"

"You know I can't talk about my work."

"Well, does it have to do with the cute human?" Angel asked, peering over Rory's shoulder at the little photo of Sean Leigh.

"Something like that."

Rory ate while Angel asked questions about her last trip. She'd been escorting Elf Erinn Ambassador to Barra's capital after a visit home. Three days' travel either way on foot. Even though she'd been gone nearly two weeks, half of that time had been snooping around in the capital, not traveling. Angel understood that Rory couldn't talk about her work, but often she would tell about the places she'd visited or some of the people she'd met, or other odd things.

After dinner and a long bath Rory shut herself in her room with Sean Leigh's file and a plate of chocolate chip cookies—a weakness she'd discovered on one of her visits to Thyrus. Humans truly had some wonderful foods. Not that she'd ever admit that to her fellow elves. Or admit that she smuggled in bags of chocolate chips whenever she had to travel outside of Maireadd. Part of her hoped that Leigh was actually a chef. Maybe he could give her a few recipes.

The file was woefully short, extending only a few pages beyond what she'd already read. But Taro was right about things not adding up. Never mind the ridiculousness of Thyrus sanctioning a guide through Maireadd just for some random cook. The guy was his own enigma. Arrested at sixteen for... the file didn't say what. Junior sharpshooting champion. Won school medals in running track and martial arts. After getting kicked out of a military academy, he apparently dropped off the face of the earth for several years before popping back up as a chef in one of the cities. And he was only twenty-eight years old.

"Dragons' claws. Talk about weird. Who is this guy?"

That was all the information her own people had been able to dig up on him so far. The single page his own government had provided gave her absolutely nothing. Just a request for a guide and safe passage through Maireadd.

The biggest thing that stuck in her mind was the fact that they were sneaking him in on foot. If he were simply a tourist, even if by some chance he was a friend of the president, they would have just sent him over Maireadd in a chopper. She told Borden as much when she talked to him via magic mirror later that night. They had heard from their person in Thyrus, and didn't have any new information. She was to leave to go meet him first thing tomorrow.

She sighed. "And I didn't even get a chance to do laundry."

* * * * *

It took Rory three days to hike from her home to the Maireadd-Thyrus border. She and Mr. Leigh would be passing back through Maireadd less than a day's march from her home in the elven city of Tristini, since it was the narrowest point between Thyrus and Barra, and most of the main trails led through that way.

She waited at the edge of the forest on the evening of the third day, looking across a snowy field at the distant lights of one of Thyrus' little villages. Even from a mile's distance she could hear their chapel bells chiming a midwinter carol.

She bounced on her toes, puffing out a breath of fog into the dusk. Finally she gave up on trying to keep her toes warm while standing still, and knelt down to spell her boots for warmth. It wouldn't last too long without some kind of an anchor, just hopefully long enough for her to meet Leigh and start walking again so her feet would warm themselves. The council frowned upon excessive use of magic in front of humans, especially in their agents. They'd rather be underestimated, whenever possible. But Rory hated being cold, and it wasn't like it was a spell anyone could see.

A pair of headlights separated from the village and wound their way toward her in the gathering gloom. The car disappeared for a moment into a dip in the road, and then reemerged, pulling into the parking lot across the field. The road didn't reach all the way to Maireadd. No paved road did. From where they'd stopped the car, the road turned to dirt and gravel, and then dwindled to a narrow, rutted wagon track when it reached Maireadd.

Two figures emerged from the car and started toward her, slogging through unbroken snow. She could have gone to them, but this gave her a chance to study the two men before they reached her. The older one carried a flashlight, which annoyed her, as it blinded her every time it bounced across her face. Were human eyes really so weak that they needed a light already? It wasn't even fully dark yet.

"Elf Rory Scout?" the older man called as they came up. He was puffing a bit, which made his Thyrusian brogue almost incomprehensible. Leigh, the younger of the two, didn't appear bothered by the hike through the snow. Good for him. He had a lot more snowy miles to go.

Rory nodded once. "Yes."

"This is Sean Leigh," the older man said, shoving his companion forward without introducing himself. "Take good care of him."

Rory narrowed her eyes at the older man before turning to Leigh. "Did you get the information we sent?"

"Yes," he said, dimpling at her. Dragon scales. He was even cuter in person, human or otherwise.

"And you don't have any human technology with you whatsoever? No cell phone, no flashlight, nothing with batteries or electricity? No guns?"

"Nope."

"This isn't an arbitrary request. If you have anything like that, you need to get rid of it now. I don't feel like dying tonight if you bring something with you that the curse doesn't like."

"I'm clean," Leigh said, spreading his hands. "I promise." Somehow his accent, lighter and more precise than the other man's, made him even more appealing.

She nodded. "I always have to ask. Like I said, I don't feel like dying tonight." She eyed the older man again, looking back and forth between them. "You ready to go then?"

Her human charge nodded and stepped forward to follow her.

"Watch your six, Sean," the other man called before turning back toward the car.

"Who was he?" she asked.

"My...handler." Leigh glanced at her, flashed a dimple, and shrugged. "We both know that page they sent over with the request for a guide was a load of ogre crap."

Rory almost fell over.

"So you're not a chef?"

"I am, among other things."

She should have asked him what other things. Instead she caught herself by surprise when she said, "Can you make cookies?"

"Uhm. Yes?"

Now that they were under the trees it was dark enough that Rory couldn't see his expression, but he sounded surprised as well.

"I may have picked up a few bad habits in my travels," she admitted, surprising herself again.

He chuckled, but didn't say anything more, leaving them to walk in silence in the deepening night. If he wondered why they were hiking in the dark, he didn't say so, just kept up, walking at her side as though a stroll through a cursed forest at night was just another recipe to try out.

"What do you do besides cook?" she asked after the silence began to get oppressive, when she started imagining snapping twigs and squeaking snow out there in the trackless forest.

"You mean why do I have a handler?" he countered. Blunt, but his tone sounded more amused than guarded.

"Sure. You can answer that one if you want." She tried to make her voice sound light and the question inconsequential.

"Would you believe me if I said the president wanted me to spy out some new recipes?"

Rory snorted, and then burst out laughing. "No. No I would not."

"He really likes grilled eel."

She laughed so hard she had to stop and lean against a tree. Tears turned cold against her skin.

"I like to think I'm a funny guy, but even I'll admit it wasn't that funny."

She waved him off. "Context. Sorry I can't explain."

"Okay."

He waited for her to settle down, then walked in silence again. They must have gone a mile or more without speaking, and Rory became aware again of Maireadd's murmurs. The groan of trees in the bitter cold, the small clacks of twigs and branches brushing together, the squeak and crunch of some creature keeping up with them out there. She was fairly sure it wasn't the forest playing tricks on her this time.

"Do you dislike elves, Mr. Leigh?"

"What? No! Of course not. Why would you ask that?" He sounded startled, like his mind had been a thousand miles away.

"You've barely spoken."

"Well it's not for that reason. I'm just..." His coat rustled as he shrugged. "Elves are super cool. Magic and all that. Anyhow, if I don't talk I can't make a fool out of myself, right?"

That was unexpected. Again. This human was just full of surprises. Rory stopped and looked at him. She couldn't see much of his face in the dark, but he shifted, his boots squeaking in the snow. "Why are you here, Sean?"

The snow squeaked some more and his clothing rustled as he tried to stick gloved hands into his coat pockets. "I'm going to cook."

"You are the strangest spy I've ever met."

"You think I'm a spy?"

"Aren't you?"

The gap of silence that followed didn't tell her a thing.

"I'm a lot of things. But right now, mostly just a chef." He started walking again, then turned, waiting for her. Was he playing her for the biggest fool ever right now?

Rory sighed. She had a feeling this mission might turn out to be the strangest one she'd ever taken.

2

THE ELF WITH THE CUTE EARS

Sean knew the elves were keen to find out what his government was planning. Colonel Jacobs had informed him that the elf they'd be sending as his guide was thought to be an agent for the Council, though that hadn't been proven. What the colonel had failed to mention was that the elf was gorgeous, dangerous, and now probably thought him an imbecile. After talking to her, he felt confident in assuming Jacobs was right. The tricky part about the whole thing was that Maireadd's and Thyrus's interests lined up perfectly for his end game. But would they agree on how Thyrus planned to get there?

"Look, Sean..." the elf broke another uncomfortable silence. At least she'd gotten past calling him 'Mr. Leigh.' Thank goodness. "It's going to be a long few days if you can't figure out how to carry on a conversation. I'm not just saying that in hopes that you get comfortable and spill all your secrets to me. Maireadd is dangerous. That's why humans don't come through here without a guide. There are horrors in this forest you've never even heard of. Things that aren't purely physical monsters. Like hellhounds. Do you know anything about hellhounds?"

"Yes," he answered darkly. More than he wanted to know, in fact.

"They pop up out of the shadows when they feel your fear and tear you apart," she said, ignoring him. "It's not fear that draws them, though. Fear can just as easily signal courage. It's despair that brings them. Discouragement, depression, doubt, isolation. Those kinds of things. The things you feel when you give in to your fear. And no one's immune to those things. Not even me. So it's always better to have someone to talk to."

She left out the part about how they could appear anywhere—not just in Maireadd, and how they liked their victims helpless, desperate, and alone. How their claws carried a venom that inflicted horrific pain with just a scratch.

"Okay," Sean agreed, though he didn't know what to say. He had a lot of questions, but the elf seemed a bit prickly, and he wasn't sure she'd appreciate them.

Another long silence ensued, and she gave an exasperated sigh, obviously waiting for him to do the talking.

He stirred from his thoughts. "Um..." he tried. "Is there...I mean, do you always travel through Maireadd at night?"

"No!" she pounced on his question. "No we don't. Only when it's necessary. In this case, something has been stalking us almost since we started, and I don't want to camp in the open. That would just be asking to get our throats ripped out. If I was by myself, I'd find a tree to sleep in, but since I'm not, we're going to keep going until we get to one of our regular campsites. It's sheltered, and has permanent wards in place to keep the monsters away. We've only got another mile or so to go."

"Okay." He hitched his pack higher. Fifty pounds of sleeping bag and supplies, but no weapons. He had a pocket knife, but that hardly counted. They'd told him he couldn't bring any technology unique to humans, which meant no gun or carbon-fiber blades or taser or any of the gadgets he might normally have stashed away on his person. No one said anything about replacing them with something more old-fashioned, though, like a good old steel sword. He had an elf scout for protection after all. But he still felt vulnerable.

The campsite Rory mentioned ended up being a shallow cave hollowed out from a short rock ledge at the bottom of a ravine. Cozy and protected from the wind, but bitter cold with a lingering dampness in the air. Rory whispered a few words as they approached, and light crystals glowed to life in the branches of young evergreens surrounding the cave mouth. The air changed as well, the bitter edge giving way almost at once to a dry warmth.

"Wards are up. We should be safe now. Nothing short of a full grown dragon could get through these, and they'll keep the worst of the cold away as well."

"This isn't so bad," Sean said, dumping his pack on the ground and unzipping his coat as the warmth continued to build to a comfortable level. Evergreens grew at either side of the cave entrance, sharply fragrant and bowed with snow. The light crystals glimmered in the shadow of their branches like frozen fireflies.

"Don't get used to it," the elf warned him. "This is probably the most comfortable we'll be for the rest of the trip. Just hope whatever has been stalking us out there gives up tonight."

She pulled her hat off, and Sean couldn't help staring at her ears for a moment. Not that he hadn't seen elves, or their ears, before, but the sight always made him smile. They more resembled dogs' ears than humans.' Longer, pointed, and expressive, though not furry.

"What?" She fingered her ears and gave him a defensive look. "Are they frostbitten or something?"

"No, just cute." Troll turds. "Sorry. That was unprofessional."

"No, it's ok." Rory laughed while managing to look smug and delighted at the same time. "Elves are a bit conceited about their ears. If more humans paid them compliments, foreign relations would be twice as good as they are."

"Huh."

"You..." She looked to be struggling for a moment to choose her words. "You are cute as well. Is that an acceptable compliment for a human?"

"Um." Sean felt himself blush. "It's acceptable, it's just... well, more acceptable between friends, or romantically speaking."

"I see. That's why you said your compliment was unprofessional."

"Yeah. I mean, it just kind of slipped out, and your ears are really cute, but if I had meant to actually compliment you, like, in that romantic sense, I'd have said you're stunning. Because you are. But that's really unprofessional. Troll turds. I'm an idiot." He could feel his blush deepening, and swiped a hand over his face. What was wrong with him? His usual smooth tongue seemed to have stayed behind in Thyrus this time around. Or maybe it was the presence of the elf that had him flustered. Was she magicking him into being a bumbling fool? But she looked pleased.

"You humans are far too tight with your compliments. You're obviously very good at them, too, which seems a waste. Cute human." She reached up and patted him on the head as she swept past to begin building a fire.

Sean groaned. He turned to his pack and unrolled his sleeping bag, then found an energy bar to munch on, standing at the cave mouth and looking out at the black darkness beyond the fairy lights. Behind him, Rory whispered a word, and he heard the fire ignite with a whoosh. Warmth reached out and caressed his back, and a breath of air brushed the back of his neck. He pulled his hat off and ran a hand through his hair.

This is gonna be a long week.

* * * * *

Gray light and snowflakes waited for them when they broke camp next morning. Rory muttered under her breath as she left the warmth of the wards and scrambled up the side of the ravine they'd camped in. Sean sat on his pack at the cave mouth and watched her out of sight, waiting for her to scout around and see what had been following them the night before. He didn't have to wait long.

"We have a problem," she said a few minutes later as she slid back down the embankment. "Ice dragon."

Sean brought up a mental file on the creatures. He'd never seen one, but they were one of the predators he'd been required to familiarize himself with. They were wingless, with powerful hind legs that could run a man down in seconds. About the size of a large pony, their forelegs were short, but equipped with six-inch curved claws. They had double rows of teeth, and the ability to breathe super-cooled air that would cause a freeze burn on contact. Basically, they could turn your flesh into shriveled, frozen, dried-up meat. Like steak left in the freezer for too long.

"Did it give up?" he asked.

"It? No. She didn't. She's gone for now. The scouts are always female, and she just left to get the rest of her pack and bring them back for the hunt."

"Oh. Okay." That hadn't been in his file. He waited.

"This is a problem. Do you remember how I said these wards would hold up against anything but a full grown dragon? Well a pack of ice dragons amounts to about the same thing. I can call for backup, but it's not safe to stay here, and it'll take some time for anyone to reach us. We've got to get moving, and fast."

"Okay," Sean said again. He slung his pack onto his shoulders and followed her up out of the ravine. "Um, I'm assuming this is something you're typically prepared to handle."

"It's not."

"Okay."

"There shouldn't be any ice dragons here, for one thing. For another, even if there was, they shouldn't have ventured down from the tundra this early in the season. Winter's barely begun, and it usually isn't this cold or snowy this soon. Honestly, you're one of the last single parties we'll be guiding through for the year. We'll have tourists, of course, because of the skiing, but they come in groups, and have a full guard.

"So no, I'm not prepared to handle this. But the last thing you should do is panic. Excuse me. I need to make a call."

Sean hadn't been panicking. In fact, she seemed much more flustered than he was as she dug out a pocket magic mirror and demanded to speak with an "Elf Borden Captain."

Elves had an odd naming system. They took their position or job as a title, in place of having a family name. Colonel Jacobs had informed him his guide was an elf woman whose full name was Auralie, but the elves considered it rude to call someone by their full name if you were only given a partial. He doubted her title of 'Scout' was correct either. Not that he was one to talk.

"We have a situation," she barked at the person that appeared in her mirror.

Sean scanned the forest as she explained the problem to her captain. No doubt she would hear trouble coming long before he could, but he still felt the back of his neck prickle in the deep silence that only snow could bring to the world.

Rory finished her call and turned back to him. "In case you weren't paying attention, we're going to divert and head toward Tristini. They're sending out a patrol on horseback to meet us, but we won't see them until this evening. In the meantime, we get to hustle, and hope the dragon pack doesn't catch up with us before then."

"Okay."

* * * * *

The hours and miles stretched behind them as they 'hustled' toward the elven city, sometimes walking, sometimes jogging. Sweat prickled Sean's scalp under his hat and dampened his shirt, chilling him instantly when they stopped for a short rest and snack. But they didn't stay still long enough to get truly cold before they started off again. As afternoon came on the snow fell heavier. This close to the winter solstice and under the dense tree canopy, daylight didn't last very long. Only a few hours past noon, the gray winter light began to fade.

"Stop!" Rory hissed, throwing out an arm across his chest. "Hear that?"

"No," he whispered.

"They'll be on us in a few minutes. Leave your pack. All we can do is buy a few more minutes and hope the patrol gets here," she said, shrugging off her own pack and dumping it on the ground. Sean did so as well, and they ran. It felt like flying after lugging around the weight of the pack all day.

Rory glanced over as they sped through the trees. "Not that it'll do any good, but do you have a weapon?"

"These," he said, raising his hands. He hadn't actually meant it as a joke, but the flat look she gave him said she didn't appreciate it.

She drew a longknife from the layers of her winter clothes and tossed it to him. "I'll do what I can with magic, but you might as well go down fighting too."

He caught the knife out of the air. Too long for a dagger and too short for a sword, he swiped it through the air a couple times to get a feel for the length and balance. "Okay."

"And whatever you do, don't give in to your fear. Remember it's better to die by ice dragon than by hellhound."

Cheery, he thought. But he was still going to do all he could to keep from dying either way. He'd never fought an ice dragon before. He was kind of looking forward to it.

It only took a few minutes before he could hear the dragons crashing through the brush behind and to either side of them. They'd spread out and were trying to surround their prey. He grinned.

"What is wrong with you? Why are you smiling?"

He wiped the smile off his face. "What? No reason. I just love this time of year, don't you? The holidays coming, long nights, snow and stars and monsters chasing you. Makes you feel alive. What's not to like?"

Rory made it perfectly clear with her look that she thought he was a crazy person. Ah well. They only picked the crazy ones for this type of work.

Flashes of movement came closer through the trees and brush. Iridescent scales like mother-of-pearl. They'd left the trail when they turned toward Tristini, following the path of a stream instead. What little water was left in it after the summer was frozen now, crackling angrily under their boots.

"How many?" he asked as they ran.

"Six, I think," Rory replied. "Too many."

Maybe. He'd have to be fast. Faster than an elf. Was that possible? He stripped off his bulky coat and flung it away. Rory glanced sideways at him, but didn't say anything. He realized he was grinning again.

One of the dragons drew close on the bank above them, running on its two powerful hind legs, with its short, spindly forearms tucked against its chest, keeping pace effortlessly. Rory shouted a warning as it leapt toward him. Sean twitched backward and it missed him by inches, hissing as its teen snapped down on air. He never stopped moving, turning his momentum into a lunge. He wrapped an arm around the dragon's throat, flung himself onto its back, and stabbed the slender elf blade into the creature's eye. Steel slid into its brain, and it died with a hissing shriek. He leapt clear of it as it fell, taking the knife with him.

Rory had stopped, meanwhile, her hands raised as though she was about to conjure magic. Instead, she just stared at him, her dark eyes huge. Admittedly, it was an odd moment for him to notice the color of her eyes for the first time, but the rush of battle blazed in his blood, and every detail stood out in stark definition, even the smoked silver of Rory's eyes. Wisps of her black hair stuck out from under her hat, highlighting her pale face.

He raced toward her and the spell was broken.

"You can't be a cook," she panted as they ran.

"I am."

The stream bed opened up suddenly, and they slid to a halt, bumping into each other with the suddenness of the stop. The remaining dragons—five of them—surrounded them.

"Would you stop doing that!" Rory hissed.

"What? What am I doing?"

"Grinning like an idiot when we're about to get eaten."

She whispered a word into her palm, and then blew across it. A sudden rush of wind swirled around them, and in an instant they stood in the middle of a vortex of furious wind, a small stationary tornado that gathered snow and ice and flung it around them in a raging barrier.

"That won't keep them out for long," she shouted above the wind's roar as they watched the shapes of the dragons draw near outside their tornado cocoon, distorted and indistinct through the veil of flying snow.

"What's the plan?" he yelled back.

She eyed the bloody longknife, and chewed her lip. "Do you think you could do that again? I might be able to blind them, but I'll have to let the barrier go."

He nodded. "Do it."

"Don't get yourself killed. Our countries can't afford a war with each other."

He grinned.

3

ICE DRAGONS

Already the dragons were closing in. One of them poked its nose into her wind barrier as Rory took a second to make herself an ice blade. A foot long, an inch wide, and razor sharp, it had no handle because it would shatter on impact, and she didn't plan on wielding it with her hands. Next, she whispered the words to another spell, shaping it and then holding it for a moment as she looked over at the human. He had a maniacal grin on his face again, but he nodded that he was ready. She released her magic.

The wind barrier died with a sigh, and she got a good, close-up look at the dragon lunging toward her throat before her next spell activated and a dense cloud of ice particles and fog rose around them. She'd been trained to work with the elements on hand whenever possible, since conjuring a cloud of ice on a snowy day took far less energy and concentration than making and sustaining a fireball in those conditions would. She'd love to be able to hurl fireballs at these monsters—it just wasn't practical.

The dragon re-appeared out of the fog, only about two feet in front of her. She lunged to the side, feeling its icy breath blast past her, making her coat sleeve instantly freeze and crackle as she flung her arm out, directing her ice dagger at the dragon's open mouth. The blade caught the monster in the back of the throat, but didn't kill it instantly. She dove away again, nearly flinging herself into the claws of a second beast. Taking a cue from Sean, she used her momentum to swing herself onto the second dragon's back. Hooking a leg around its neck, she planted both hands over its ear holes and shouted a command. She wasn't capable of the kind of black magic that could stop a heart from beating, and wouldn't have used it even if she could, but there were many ways to kill without using a death spell. The air in the dragon's ear canals heated and expanded instantly under her hands, and she felt the tiny explosion in her palms when its eardrums exploded. It screamed, flailed wildly with sudden vertigo, and crashed into the first dragon. Wounded and confused, they clawed at each other while Rory jumped free.

Her ankle rolled on a hidden rock as she came down, shooting pain up her leg and dumping her in the snow, but she panted another spell, forming another handful of ice daggers, and flung them, one after the other, toward the two dragons' eyes until one struck home. The beast with the ear troubles collapsed. The other, still clawing its own throat, fumbled off into the fog.

She hadn't been able to keep track of Sean during her battle—couldn't even see him through the conjured fog. But now she heard a pained yell from him, and tried to run in that direction. Her ankle had other ideas though, and dumped her back on the ground.

Cursing dragons, their ancestors, progeny, and distant cousins, she formed another spell and *flew* herself toward the ongoing battle.

Flashes of movement, hisses, and Sean's hoarse breathing led her forward. Only a foot off the ground, she nearly bashed her injured ankle against a carcass. She passed a second dark, indistinct shape lying in the snow to the left and then crashed into the third and last dragon, bouncing back from its flank and losing her grip on her magic. She landed on her bad foot and rolled her ankle again. Her magical energy running low after using it on such a grand scale, she picked herself back up with a snarl and a blast of wind and settled onto her good foot, fully expecting the dragon to pounce on her. Before it could, Sean shot out of the fog and threw himself at the dragon's open maw. His longknife angled forward and up, he drove it into the dragon's mouth, up into its sinus cavity. He jerked his arm back, and Rory couldn't tell if it was in time to entirely miss those snapping teeth or not, but when the dragon bit down, it drove the knife hilt deeper, into its own brain. It fell with a soft whump into the snow.

Sean stood there panting for a moment, splattered in blood that dripped into the snow around him. He'd lost his hat and his bright hair stuck up in every direction over red ears.

"Are we done?" he asked finally, turning to her.

"I think so."

"Good." He dropped himself into the snow and lay back, clutching his left hand to his chest while he caught his breath. "That was fun, but enough's enough."

Rory released her magic, drooping with relief, and sank down beside him. Her ankle throbbed, and blood pounded in her ears. She hadn't thrown around and maintained that much magic on that big of a scale all at once since academy. Even elves, the strongest magical race, had a limit, and though she hadn't reached it, she could still feel the dulling effect of exhaustion setting in.

"What happened to that patrol that was supposed to meet us?" Sean asked.

"Ha!" she barked an ironic laugh and watched the puff of white breath dissipate. Their battle, though it felt like it had taken a lifetime, had only lasted a few minutes, and there was still plenty of light, though it was fading.

A soft huff of sound, somewhere between a whispered gasp and groan, got her attention, and she sat up and faced Sean. "You're hurt."

"So are you," he countered.

"Show me."

He held out his hands for her, wordless as she examined them. His right seeped blood through his glove. She pulled a much smaller knife from her pocket and flicked it open, carefully cutting the material away to reveal the gashes across the back of his fingers and palm. They were ragged, but not deep. Unfortunately, she didn't have anything to bind them, since they'd left their packs when they started running. She'd have to cut a strip from their clothes, but she left it for now, since he seemed to favor his left hand more.

She winced as she cut the glove away, already prepared for what she'd find, since the glove itself had been flash-frozen and then broken. Underneath, his hand looked raw and blistered, his skin cracked open in places, bleeding and discolored. She let out a breath.

"It could have been worse," she told him. "Your glove protected you."

"I know. Hurts like freakin' dragon fire, but at least I won't lose my hand."

"Dragon fire, dragon ice. Basically it amounts to the same thing. You killed four of them by yourself. You should be dead. *Anyone* should be dead. I don't even know of any elves that could fight three ice dragons at once."

He nodded, smiling softly, and closed his eyes, hunching over his hands. She noticed he was starting to shiver. With shock or cold she wasn't sure, since he'd dropped his coat back in the stream bed. Probably both.

She silently cursed her own injury, since it meant she'd have to use more magic to go back for their supplies, and she was already exhausted. But then, as she got ready to conjure a wind to carry her again, she heard a shout, and the sounds of horses coming through the trees.

A few minutes later a dozen riders appeared out of the dusk, pulling their horses up in a circle around them.

"Vasya," she greeted their captain. "You're late."

"So I see," he replied, surveying the scattered bodies. "What happened?"

"Exactly what looks like happened!" she snapped. Pain, worry, and fatigue had relieved her of any semblance of patience. She flung her hand toward Sean. "Get him taken care of, and send some of your people to get our packs. We dropped them when we had to run for our lives."

"What about the dragons? Are there more of them?"

"No. Maybe. There was one running around with an ice blade in the back of its throat. Probably dead by now, but you can keep an eye out for it."

At a few commands from Vasya, half the riders broke off and disappeared up the stream bed. The other half dismounted. A few of them went to examine the corpses, while Vasya and the medic grabbed supplies and came over.

"Do you have any injuries?" the medic asked her.

"I'm fine!" she snapped. "I just twisted my ankle. Get my human taken care of, before you start an international incident."

Sean, whose shivers had set his teeth rattling, visibly relaxed when Vasya wrapped a blanket around his shoulders and muttered a warming spell over it—air mingled with fire. He sagged in the snow, but still offered her a grin. "No one would miss me that much."

"I seriously doubt that. Especially now." She watched the medic clean and wrap the slashes on his right hand before turning his attention to the left. Sean flinched and cursed a blue streak while the elf rubbed salve across it and wrapped it. When it was done, he snatched both hands back to his chest and hunched in the blanket, silent. The medic examined Rory's ankle next, but there wasn't much he could do beyond bracing it.

Vasya flicked his gaze from the human to Rory, silently questioning what had happened. She shook her head.

When the rest of the riders got back, they distributed the extra packs among them, gave Sean his coat back, and then got him and Rory mounted up behind two of the scouts. Full dark had set in by the time they started toward Tristini. It would be midnight before they reached the city. She held onto the elf in front of her, thoroughly tired and miserable, her ankle throbbing with the motion of the horse. Not far away she could see Sean by the light of the crystals they carried, not holding on at all, simply balancing with his knees behind the saddle, keeping his hands to himself.

The dark trees, like the hours of their journey, slipped past in a blur. Rory kept nodding off, and once the elf she rode with had to catch her wrist to keep her from sliding from the horse.

"Sorry," she mumbled. "Long day."

He chuckled. They'd all had days like that. Even scouts, who spent prolonged periods, sometimes weeks at a time, camping and marching. Cold, adrenaline, and magic use sapped your energy, no matter how strong you were.

She straightened up, glancing over to check on the human. He still rode with his hands tucked safely in his coat, his posture slumped. He swayed with the motion of the horse.

"How far?" she asked, worried he might go to sleep or pass out and fall.

"We passed the first sentries ten minutes ago."

She barely held back a moan of relief, instead asking, "Borden is expecting us?"

"He and Taro Councilman are waiting for you at the lodge. We're to drop you off there."

So no chance of sleep any time soon then. Or at least not as soon as she'd like. She sighed.

Within minutes they were pulling up in front of the lodge. The elf she'd been riding with slid down from the saddle and then lifted her down, waiting for her to gain her balance on her good foot before he let go. Borden was there to meet her with a crutch and another elf healer, whom she waved off.

"We're fine for now. Let us get inside before you start hovering."

Vasya followed them into the lodge, but the rest of the patrol scattered to their homes. He and Borden had talked via magic mirror while they rode, so Borden and Taro were both up-to-date on what had happened, though Rory hadn't filled in all the details yet.

"It's a relief to see you alive," Borden said as they headed toward the councilman's office. "I was afraid the patrol would be too late."

"They were too late," she grumbled, struggling with the crutch on the moss floor. Sean plodded along behind them, looking half asleep on his feet and totally out of it while holding his hands awkwardly in front of him. They'd never found his hat.

When they arrived in Taro's office he greeted them with: "I'm sorry, Rory. We asked you to do a job, and then failed you. I know you and Mr. Leigh need your rest, so we won't keep you long."

"Thank you."

Taro shifted, watching her. She knew what he wanted, and sighed. "Mr. Leigh's safe travel through Maireadd was the mission you gave me, and as it's not complete yet, I'll take responsibility for his lodging for as long as he's in Tristini."

The words were a show for Sean. What they really wanted was to make sure she was still going to keep an eye on him.

"Thank you, Rory. Of course, we will happily take care of expenses, and Elf Bari Healer is at your service," he gestured to the elf woman who'd been hovering over Sean, twitching to take care of his hands with something better than a field dressing.

"We'd like to hear the details of what happened, as well," he continued. "Having ice dragons this near civilization isn't acceptable, so please come in as soon as you're able tomorrow."

"Of course."

Again, what they really wanted was her opinion of Sean Leigh. The ice dragons as well, certainly. But Borden would be handling that. Taro was more interested in the potential spy she was hosting.

They left the lodge, toiling up the hill to her house, where she called on her magic to lift her up to the balcony. She didn't think she could handle stairs at this point. Sean and Bari caught up a moment later. Angel met them at the door and pulled Rory into a hug that jammed the crutch into her ribs.

"Are you okay? What happened to your foot? Did you really fight dragons?" Her barrage of questions continued as they dragged themselves inside.

Sean sank onto the couch, looking as though he might become a permanent part of it. Rory extricated herself from her sister's concern and collapsed next to him with a groan.

"Thank you," he said quietly, looking over at her while Bari unwrapped his hands. He gave her a tired smile, not quite enough to dimple, but it brightened his face, bringing back a hint of his disarming boyishness. She'd seen his crazy dragon killing grin and his battle fury though, and wondered what secrets that innocent mask and lilting brogue might cover.

Bari stood, leaving his hands uncovered, and went to confer with Angel.

He winced as he flexed his fingers, his pain showing in his bright blue eyes. "I know your people don't like humans in their city, much less suspicious chefs. So thanks for taking me in." This time he gave her one full dimple.

She snorted and lifted a hand to wave him off, found she was too tired for such an extravagant movement, and dropped it back in her lap. "You were hardly in danger of getting left in a snowbank. When the Thyrus government requests a guide special for one of their people, we make sure we take good care of them. International incidents and all."

Bari came back with a basin of water and put a few drops from a vial into it, making the entire room smell of lavender and herbs. Sean winced as he lowered his hands into it, then sagged as the mixture eased the pain. He leaned his head back, and his lips parted almost instantly in sleep. He didn't react when Bari applied another salve and fresh bandages.

The healer turned her attention to Rory next, examining her ankle. She left another of her herbal brews to soak it in, and a wrap for it. "It's going to be a week or more before you can go running around the wilderness again," she warned before she left.

Angel saw the healer to the door, then flopped down in a chair across from them. She looked from Sean to Rory and raised an eyebrow. "Am I going to get the story?"

"Not tonight," Rory said, pushing herself up wearily. "Give me a hand."

Together they got Sean stretched out in a more comfortable position on the couch, careful to rest his hands across his chest without bumping them, and draped a blanket over him. He never stirred.

"I'm going to go do the same thing. The person that wakes me up before noon tomorrow gets a dagger up their nose."

* * * * *

No one bothered Rory, but nevertheless she crawled out of bed and a horde of bloody nightmares well before noon the next day. Sean still snored from the couch when she hobbled through to the kitchen where Angel had a fire going in the cook stove. Her sister sat at the table with one of her textbooks and a cup of tea.

"How are you this morning?" she asked.

Rory grumbled under her breath before she said, "I'd be better if I didn't have to leave the house today." She scrounged for something to eat, then went to find clean clothes. She'd collapsed in her wool under-clothes the night before, too tired to climb out of all her winter layers. With those goals accomplished and Sean still sleeping—she was more than a little jealous—she headed to the lodge.

"Are you well today?" Taro Counsilman asked when she swung herself into his office with the help of her crutch. He touched a round crystal sitting on his desk. It lit with a faint blue glow and he directed his next words toward it. "Borden, Auralie just came in. Join us if you would."

A few seconds later the other elf came in, nodding to both of them. Rory levered herself into a chair with a muttered apology. The others drew up seats facing her.

"You and the human are both well?" Taro asked again.

"Well enough. He was still sleeping when I left."

"Healer Bari assured us that he's in no danger of permanent damage to his hands. His left will take longer to heal fully, and there may be some scars, but he should be recovered well enough by the time you are that you can both continue."

Rory nodded, rubbing her gritty eyes. "She said it would be a week or more. Apparently I did a good job of twisting it. I hope Sean's mission wasn't time sensitive."

"That would depend on what his mission is. First though, tell us about the ice dragons."

Rory gave them the full story, starting with how she'd suspected something was following them right from the beginning, to how they'd killed all six of the dragons before the patrol showed up to help them. The others didn't ask questions until she finished.

"I hardly know what to focus on first," Borden said after a moment of silence. "The fact that however unlikely it is, it seems like the dragons targeted you and Mr. Leigh—or the fact that he killed four of them without any assistance. A human!"

"He didn't use any magic, correct? You can verify that?"

Rory lifted a shoulder in a half shrug. "I didn't have eyes on him the whole time, but from what I saw, it was all physical skill. He didn't act like he was trying to hide anything from me, and I didn't sense any magic use other than my own."

"Thyrus cracks down on sorcery more than most countries," Borden said. "I doubt they'd sponsor a magic stealer."

All of the races had gifts and abilities in different areas—for humans it was innovation and leadership, but they had no magical ability whatsoever, unless they stole it. Magic was in the blood of the other races, and stealing it required literally draining it out of them with their blood in a twisted ceremony that also called on other-wordly forces to bind it to the human soul. Magicals like Rory and the other residents of Maireadd both loathed and feared Barra's witch-queen.

"True," Taro murmured, frowning in thought. "I suppose it's possible he's just that good. It would explain why they sent him to do... whatever it is he's doing. Does he seem competent? What are your thoughts on his character?" he asked Rory.

This time it was her turn to hesitate. "I'm not sure. He seems a little careless sometimes, but I think he's also really smart. I don't know if the carelessness is real, or an act. If it's an act though, it's a good one. But there's something else. He doesn't fight like an elf."

"I would hope not." Borden chuckled. "The day a human fights better than an elf is the day that ogres fly."

Rory shook her head. "He killed four ice dragons. You really think he doesn't fight as well as an elf? What I said was that he fights differently."

"How's that?" Taro asked, glancing at Borden, who looked like he'd taken a bite of something sour.

"He's got all the skill that any of us have, from what I could tell. Maybe more, since that kind of speed and agility doesn't come naturally to humans, it means they have to work a lot harder for it. But he doesn't seem to have a decent sense of self-preservation."

"Explain."

"He wins because he throws himself toward risk. I watched him jump onto a dragon's back so he could stab it in the eye. He stuck his entire arm in another dragon's mouth so he could kill it. Do you know any of our kind that would do that?"

Since the answer was no, naturally her question met with silence. Elves were legendary fighters, their skills allowing them to keep their opponents at arms' length more often than not, or keep things quick and clean when they had to get in close. They didn't usually need to take risks, so they didn't. Their sense of danger and self-preservation was trained into them. The word "reckless" was almost a profanity in their culture. "If you can't kill, escape," her own instructors had taught her. Somehow, she didn't think that was a line that Sean had ever heard.

"Is he suicidal?" Borden asked.

"Not that I can tell."

"He sounds...dangerous."

Rory didn't reply. Sat and waited instead for more questions, or a change in her assignment. She agreed that Sean was most definitely dangerous, but there were many different ways to be so, and dangerous to someone—an ice dragon for instance—didn't necessarily mean dangerous to them.

"Keep watching him," Taro said after a long silence. "Try to get to know him better. See if he'll tell you about his assignment, or at least open up enough that you can guess. He seemed willing enough to admit he's not just looking for recipes—" a smile teased the corner of his mouth, "so maybe he'll drop some other hints."

"Oh, he was quite adamant that he is a chef," said Rory. "It's just not all he is. His mission might have as much to do with food as with politics. You never know." She smiled. She didn't believe that for a second, but the human had been so defensive of his cooking skills that she wouldn't be surprised if it was a side mission. At least a personal one.

"One more thing," Taro said as Rory rose. "We're going to look into why there were ice dragons where there shouldn't have been. But in the meantime, just be careful. When something unnatural like that happens, it begs the question whether there was an unnatural reason behind it."

She nodded.

Limping back up the hill toward her house, she considered Taro's ambiguous warning. Why would she or Sean be a target for dragons? And what on earth could influence them enough to leave their usual stomping grounds? They were dragons.

She was halfway up the hill when she heard Angel's screams.

4

UNICORNS AND SHADOW RATS

Sean woke up to the very particular scent of spiced elven tea. His muscles reminded him of yesterday's fight as he sat up and looked around, and a pink fuzzy blanket slipped down to pool in his lap. He pulled his hands free of the blanket and flexed them. He didn't remember the healer bandaging them again, but the wrappings looked fresh and neat, and though his wounds pulled, they didn't throb like they had last night.

Rising and wandering into the kitchen, he found another, younger elf that he vaguely remembered from the night before sitting at the table deep in study.

"Hi."

She looked up and smiled, and the resemblance to Rory was striking. Had she been introduced as a sister? His brain had fogged over in the hours after the fight, his memories a blur of exhaustion and cold. He remembered pain, as the elf healer treated his hands, but nothing much after that.

"Hi!" she said, closing her book. "How do you feel? Are you hungry?"

"Uh, ok. And yes. Sorry, what was your name?"

"Angel. I'm Rory's sister. She had to go in for a meeting, but she'll be back soon. Do you like eggs?"

"Sure. Eggs are great. What are you studying?" He sat down and flipped through the textbook she'd been reading, his hands partly immobilized from the bandages.

"It's a history of the Curse War, and how the curse affected the development of Maireadd and the culture and

39

economy of the rest of the continent. Human technology really took off after the curse, when elves became more secluded and reluctant to share their enchantments with other races."

"Hmm. Good stuff." He slid the book away.

Angel laughed. "Yeah, it's boring. But if I want a career like Rory's, I've got to get through it."

"Yeah? Just to be a scout?"

"Oh." She paled slightly. "Yes. Of course scouts have to have an intimate knowledge of the curse, if we're guiding tourists and checking on ogre populations and things."

"Ah." He flashed a smile at her. So Rory wasn't really a scout, just as he'd thought. Oh, she must be a scout as well, but also something a bit more...political. As expected. The elves weren't idiots. When his government requested for them to take him across Maireadd, with no real explanation, the only logical conclusion they could have come to was that he was a spy, an assassin, or something similar. So they'd sent one of their own to keep an eye on him. To try and figure out what he was up to.

Not that that bothered him. He liked Rory, despite her being a little prickly that first day. Not to mention she was gorgeous. Most elves had an other-worldly look about them that he found unsettling, with their metallic-looking eyes, and the ears. Somehow she made it look natural, if not entirely friendly.

Angel set a plate of scrambled eggs in front of him, then sat down while he ate and asked him about a hundred questions about their fight with the dragons. She was just taking his plate to the sink when she stopped, her ears swiveling.

"Do you hear that?"

He held his breath for a moment, listening. A faint scratching sound came from behind the door into what he guessed was the pantry. "What is it?"

"I don't know."

They both listened for a moment as the scuffling grew louder. It sounded like a thousand tiny claws scratching across the wood floor. Something scraped the door. He and Angel exchanged a glance, her expression just as puzzled as his own must have been. She got up and walked over to the door, pausing with her hand on the latch.

"I'm almost afraid to look."

He shrugged, but stood up. "Should we grab weapons? I don't know what kinds of things find their way into elven treehouses in the winter."

She laughed and pulled the door open. Half a second later her laugh turned into a bloodcurdling scream as a hundred rats with glowing red eyes poured into the kitchen. She leapt back, her elven agility carrying her across the room to where he stood. Together they scrambled onto the table.

"What are those things?" Twice as big as regular rats, with pitch black fur and those red eyes, he'd never seen anything like them, even in his monster studies.

"Shadow rats!" she shrieked. "Don't let them bite you! They'll drain your life energy. If enough of them get you, they'll kill you."

The back of his neck crawled as he kicked away a rat that made it onto the table. Angel, still screaming, blasted wind outward, temporarily scattering them. But they came right back, and he and the elf repeated the process of kicking and blowing them away as they swarmed up the table legs.

The front door banged open suddenly with a blast of colder air, revealing Rory standing there with her crutch raised like a club. She swore as half the rats changed direction and charged at her. Tossing her crutch aside, she summoned her own explosion of wind to keep them away.

"What the flamin' dragon butt?" she bellowed, forming a dozen tiny ice spears that she shot into the mass of inky black bodies. She repeated the process, limping further into the room. "Not going to help me out here, dragon slayer?" she called to Sean.

He sent another rat flying off the table. "Nope. I got nothing here."

The mass of wriggling black bodies diminished, a dozen at a time, until Rory stood in the middle of the kitchen, surrounded by bodies skewered by tiny melting ice daggers. Sean held his breath for a moment, scanning the room, half expecting some of them to get back up and start attacking again.

Rory picked up her crutch and pulled her magic mirror out of her pocket, glancing up as Sean and Angel climbed down off the table. "Call Borden Captain," she told the mirror as she went into the other room.

Sean picked up one of the shadow rats by the tail, its eyes still open and still red, though they no longer glowed. "Creepy."

"They're like hellhounds," Angel said, kicking a couple of them into a pile. "Part physical, part creature of shadow."

"How did they get in here? And why?"

The young elf crossed to the pantry door and peeked in. "Looks like they climbed through the trap door that we use for bringing up supplies. It wasn't latched, and they're big enough to push it open, if two or three of them did it together."

"So they come from..."

Angel shrugged. "We call it the shadow land. The realm of spiritual evil. No one really knows for sure what it is, or where."

That wasn't quite the question he'd been asking, since he already knew that much about shadow creatures, but he didn't clarify.

"What were they doing here? Why this house?" Call him paranoid, but this was the second time he'd been attacked in as many days, and Sean didn't believe in coincidence.

"I don't know," said Rory, coming back in and interrupting whatever Angel had been about to say, which was probably the same thing. "My boss is sending people over to clean up the bodies, and they're putting a guard on the house after this. Two attacks now is two too many."

Sean nodded. "No idea where they could have come from?"

"They're summoned creatures, like hellhounds, though they respond to a different set of negative thoughts. Greed, jealousy, malice. Someone brought them into this realm, whether intentionally or not. Shadow rats tend to like to stick around once they're here. They aren't intelligent like hellhounds, so they don't shadow travel. It's possible once they got here, they went on a rampage and this was the nearest target."

"Possible," Sean echoed skeptically.

"Possible," Rory said with a nod. "Not probable. Do you know of any reason why someone might be targeting you?"

"Me?" Sean raised an eyebrow. "Why not you? This is your house."

"Trust me, we're considering both possibilities. But if you know of someone who might be after you, that would help. Your safety is our responsibility while you're in Maireadd, and we take that very seriously."

Sean strolled over to the window to hide his smile. She'd gone all professional again, spouting off official lines. He did think about it though. There were people who'd like to see him dead, of course, but they were all either dead themselves, in prison, or didn't know his identity, much less where he was right now.

"No." He said finally. "I don't know of anyone."

Empty branches scraped against the other side of the window. Beyond them, the forest fell away down the hill, dotted with more treehouses, and a few cottages on the ground. Off to the left at the bottom of the hill was the lodge they'd stopped at last night, a log building that somehow looked like a living part of the forest, draped in winter moss, with seedlings sprouting from the roof. He spotted the cleanup crew already on their way up the hill.

"Maybe you should look to yourself, agent," he added quietly.

A soft intake of breath met his words. He smiled to himself. "So how long before we head out?" he asked before Rory could reply.

"Bari Healer tells me we should both be ready to travel in a little over a week. I hope your mission wasn't time sensitive, *agent*."

Behind him, he heard Angel squeak, and the sharp rustle of clothing as Rory likely elbowed her to silence.

His grin went wider.

* * * * *

The next morning it was Sean's turn to wake up early. He stretched on the couch, looking up at the garlands of evergreen boughs strung around the window frames. They were only a few days away from Midwinter, a holiday celebrated all across the continent by magicals and humans alike. The scent of the pine tickled his nose along with a lingering citrusy whiff of the cleaners the team had used to scrub away gooey black shadow rat blood the day before.

The house had that silence that comes with fresh snow, and a feeling of holiday in the air. He padded over to the window, looked out on a world almost blotted out by falling snow, and felt secretly glad that they weren't out there hiking in it today. Nor was he particularly eager to get to Barra, and the mess that was his assignment there. He turned away from the window.

Thanks to a good deal of magic and some ingenuity, elven tree houses featured most of the comforts he was used to in Thyrus; running water, indoor plumbing, heat. The wood burning cook stove in the kitchen wasn't what he was used to, but he could work with it. There was a neat little stack of firewood next to it, and he threw a few pieces in to get the fire built up while he gave himself a tour of the pantry.

His hostesses didn't have a bad selection of ingredients. Not bad at all. But not as good as home. Something could be said for the elves' course-ground grains. Folks in Thyrus would call them 'gourmet.' But they also had a disturbing amount of pickled and fermented items, from eggs to vegetables, to something he hoped was garlic and rosemary, though he wouldn't put it past them to replace the rosemary with pine needles.

Starting with a batch of yeast dough, which he set to rise on the back of the stove, he chopped veggies, whisked eggs, and made a pancake batter with the buckwheat flour. He had to pause there, because his hands were throbbing, but he'd made it that far, and it would look silly if he didn't finish, not to mention wasting ingredients.

Still with no sign of the girls, he put those things aside and gingerly rolled out the dough for cinnamon sticky buns, dousing the bottom of the baking dish in cream and maple syrup before he set the rolls in and put them back on the stove to rise again. And still no sign of the elf sisters as he tugged one of the bandages on his hand that was coming loose.

He cleaned up the flour and batter sprinkled everywhere, then started on a batch of cookies with one of many bags of chocolate chips he'd found stashed in a place of honor in the pantry. Those definitely weren't customary elven fare.

It wasn't till the sticky buns were coming out of the oven and filling the house with their maple-cinnamon scent that Angel and Rory found their way to the kitchen, blinking sleep out of their eyes.

"What is this?" Rory asked, surveying the rack of cookies, and the omelets and pancakes cooking.

"Breakfast. And a snack for later." Sean flipped a pancake and set the spatula aside to rest his hand.

The girls blinked at him. "You have flour on your nose," Angel said.

Rory went over and surveyed the rack of cookies, a longing look in her eye.

"Breakfast first," Sean said, grinning as he handed her a plate with her omelet and a stack of pancakes. Her eyes went wide with alarm.

"That's a lot of food."

Angel snagged a plate that he'd already loaded for her and took a bite. "Mm. It's not that much once you taste it." She reached for a sticky roll.

"You weren't actually lying about being a cook," Rory said after a few bites from her own plate.

Sean rolled his eyes. "What, a man can't have more than one skill set? You think all I'm good for is killing things?"

"Well not shadow rats, obviously." She raised her eyebrows at him as she bit into her roll.

He grinned. "Nope. You can have those all to yourself."

Angel left after breakfast for her classes, leaving Sean and Rory alone with the rest of the day ahead of them.

"Let's have a look at those hands," Rory said, settling onto the couch with a wince. "You shouldn't have used them so much this morning. Didn't they hurt?"

Sean shrugged. "Yeah. I can't afford to let them get stiff though, and have them pulling every time I make a fist. It only takes one flinch at the wrong time, and you're dead." He held them out for her to unwrap, meeting her eyes as she looked up at him. "I'm sure you know what I mean."

She didn't answer that—merely pursed her lips as the loops of cloth fell away, revealing cracked scabs that left red stains against the linen.

"You should be more careful. It was a wonderful breakfast, but hardly worth putting yourself in pain."

"If it wasn't worth it, then it must not have been that wonderful."

She looked up at him, holding his calloused, torn hands in her slender, cool ones. An uncertain smile played at the corner of her mouth. "Well, it was worth it to us, I'm just not sure it was worth it to you."

"I had your sister's version of breakfast yesterday. Trust me, it was worth it."

She laughed, still holding his hands. He wasn't sure why he noticed it. Perhaps because her fingers were so soft and slender, or because he wasn't used to holding hands with anyone, let alone an elf girl. She let go one of his hands to reach for the salve the healer had left.

"How do you come to know fighting as well as cooking?" she asked as she spread the salve over his hands, starting with the left one. It made his skin tingle and took away most of the pain.

"That question is in the wrong order. I've been fighting since I was four. I learned to cook later, because my mom's cooking is terrible."

Rory snorted a laugh before she caught herself. "Sorry."

"You should be." He grinned at her. "It was really awful."

She set the jar of salve aside and grabbed a fresh roll of bandages, carefully winding the cloth around his fingers and down over his wrist. "And who taught you to fight so young?"

"She did. She retired from the military after dad died and opened a dojo."

"Tough lady."

"She had to be. She had to deal with me all by herself." He chuckled, aware that it probably sounded rueful.

"How did your father die?"

"Equipment malfunction. He was in the military as well."

She finished with his other hand and released it. "I read the file your people were kind enough to send, but it didn't mention it."

"Ah. Well you know how those files are. They always leave the interesting bits out."

"It also mentioned that you were kicked out of military academy, so I guess you didn't get to follow the family tradition."

Sean hesitated. "Yeah. There was an incident." He didn't elaborate.

Rory's eyes gleamed, but she smiled. She must be itching to ask him, but that would have been too obvious, and she knew it. It was a complex dance they were engaged in, and the fact that they were both perfectly aware of it didn't diminish the game at all.

"How do the elves feel about this situation in Barra?" he asked.

"Concerned," she replied after a short hesitation.

"Aren't we all."

"Yes. But Maireadd could take the worst of the fallout, if it continues. We are the closest, and it is a conflict in magic, which more directly relates to us than it does Thyrus."

He leaned back in the corner of the couch and watched her. "It's too bad our respective governments don't trust one another enough to make a plan and work together."

"I can't say I disagree," she said cautiously. "Though elves have not always had good fortune in trusting humans."

"So here we sit, trying to get information out of one another, and ordered not to divulge secrets or missions, when there's every chance that we could have been allies."

Rory quirked a single black eyebrow at him, looking both startled and bemused, though she always tried to cover her expressions. "Your honesty is...mystifying. Anything else you'd like to share? Perhaps what you're up to, and what your plans are once you reach Barra?"

He grinned. "That would probably be irresponsible of me."

She gave him a long, inscrutable look. One that didn't end when she said, "Too bad."

"Yeah." He leaned forward a fraction, drawn by those smoked-silver eyes. He'd never noticed or read anywhere that elves' eyes were distinctly different from humans', but now as he gazed into them, he saw that her pupils were faintly slitted, like a cat's. Her irises glimmered with a metallic sheen. "Your eyes are incredible." He blinked and leaned back, feeling himself flush. "Sorry. That was unprofessional. Again."

"It's okay. You're good at compliments. And you also have very striking eyes. Blue is an uncommon color here among us elves."

"Um, thank you."

He stood and paced to the window, where snow continued to fall thick enough to almost blot out his view of the lodge at the bottom of the hill. He jumped when Rory joined him.

"My favorite view is from the other side of the house."

"Yeah?"

"Put your coat on."

"Uh, okay...?"

They both grabbed coats from the hook beside the door and he followed her down the short hallway, past the bathroom, to one of the bedrooms—he guessed it was hers. The treehouse, wrapped around the bole of the tree in an octagonal shape, had a hallway that followed the inside wall, connecting all the rooms.

"Not what I expected," Sean said, scanning the champagne pink and deep blue decor. She had a desk, a bookcase full of books and files, and another three shelves of different colored and textured yarns. Knitting needles and crochet hooks stuck out of a mug at the end of the shelf.

"Don't judge. Everyone has a vice."

"I wouldn't call it a vice," he said. "It just doesn't seem very...elven."

She shrugged. "Humans aren't all bad." She leaned her crutch against the bookcase for a moment so she could put her coat on, then led him out a sliding glass door onto another balcony. This one faced up the hill, away from the city. A little further up the hill from their tree, the ground dipped into a little dell with a pool not entirely buried under the snow. Brush and brambles hung over the water, while birch trees bowed down with their load of snow around it. The air smelled cleanly of snow and ozone.

"This is amazing," Sean said, his voice fogging in the cold.

"Places that are so beautiful like this make my heart ache. Like there's this longing to somehow become a part of the beauty. Days like this, the snow turns it into a different world. Or in the summer, early in the morning when the mists are rising off the water."

Sean didn't reply, caught off guard by her candor. Was this because of that weird moment staring into each other's eyes? Or was she playing at getting him to trust her and open up?

"What is that?" he asked suddenly. The bushes across the stream rattled, dropping snow. Rory tensed beside him.

The brush parted for a ghost of a figure. Pure white against the snow, for a moment it looked transparent before stepping to the edge of the pool and solidifying into the form of a horse. A pearlescent horn jutted from its forehead, pointed directly at them.

"Unicorn!" Rory breathed, straightening up. In her excitement she grabbed Sean's arm, squeezing it with both hands, though she didn't look like she was even aware she'd done it. "I can't believe it."

"I thought unicorns were a myth." Sean kept his voice low as well, feeling his own sense of awe reflecting what he heard in Rory's voice.

"They might as well be."

The unicorn pawed at the water, venturing out a few steps to where it could break through the ice to drink. It raised its dripping muzzle and watched them for a few moments, its big eyes far too intelligent for a beast. A sudden gust of wind drove a curtain of snow between them, and when it cleared the unicorn was gone.

They stayed out there for a few more minutes, not really expecting to see the creature again, but reluctant to go back inside. Neither of them spoke until they'd found their way back to the couch.

"I thought unicorns were a myth," Sean said again. "Now I don't know what I've heard that's actually true."

Instead of answering, Rory watched him for a long time in silence, until he shifted under her gaze. "What?"

"Unicorns are the antithesis of the shadow creatures. No one knows whether they come from the same place or if there are two separate realms beyond ours, one of darkness and one of light. Either way, they aren't from here. They appear and disappear like hellhounds do."

"Okay..." Sean said slowly. She was leaving something out.

She pinched the bridge of her slender nose. "I need to talk to my boss."

Sean frowned. "Um, okay, but why are you being so cagey? We just saw a myth wandering around on four legs, and you're not going to tell me about it? That's just cruel." He said it half jokingly, but with his curiosity raging, and Rory obviously hiding something, it wasn't far off the mark.

Instead of disappearing to make a call though, Rory stayed where she was, frowning. He let her have her space. As the minutes ticked by, he became aware of the faint tink of snowflakes hitting the window, and the soft groaning of the tree at another burst of wind.

"Would you say the Thyrus government is the highest authority in your life, Sean?" she asked after a good ten minutes had passed. "I mean, is there something more important to you than serving your country?"

He stammered in surprise. "What...? I... Sure. I mean, basic morality, fundamental right and wrong, is an absolute truth that the government can't change to suit itself. Otherwise Barra would be completely right in letting magic stealers go around slaughtering people. So yeah. My loyalty to Thyrus comes second to my loyalty to God, and is dependent on whether their orders comply with His. They know that. What are you getting at?"

"You never mentioned that."

"It never came up. It's not as though we're bosom buddies here, agent."

She shrugged off his jab without getting prickly this time. "So, you'd agree that there are some things that are more important than your mission? Things that transcend orders and duty and international peace and all that?"

He looked at her askance. "Please tell me you're not about to try and torture my secrets out of me."

"Why would I do that?" She sounded taken aback.

"I don't know! I just can't figure out where you're going with this conversation, and it's making me nervous."

She stared at him steadily for another long moment. "I'm asking you about your loyalties because I'm questioning my own," she said.

This time it was Sean's turn to pause for a good long while. "Does this have something to do with the unicorn?"

Rory nodded. "What do you know about them?"

"Not much. Just legends. That whole thing about being friendly to virgins, and something about making wishes."

She cracked a tiny smile. "They're seen so rarely that our information is limited, and even some elves don't believe in them. But if you still believe some of the ancient songs and texts, they say that unicorns only appear to those who are pure of heart. That's probably where the virgin thing came from, though it's not entirely accurate. And they don't grant wishes."

Sean felt himself blushing, and mentally rolled his eyes at himself. "So that whole 'the pure of heart shall see God' thing from the holy books?"

"Something like that. Some people think unicorns are the servants of God. No one really knows. But supposedly they appear before something momentous. Or at an intersection of choices. Sort of an omen, I guess."

"Okay..."

"Other stories put it a little differently. They say they're the sign of a promise—a blessing from God."

Sean hoped his face didn't give anything away as his heart twinged with hope. "Really? A blessing? What kind of a blessing? On what you're doing? Or on that choice that might need to be made?"

"I don't know."

"Okay. So this seems like it means something to you, even though you're confusing me. What are you trying to say?"

Rory sighed. "I'm really not sure. I suppose... I'm just contemplating if there's something going on here that's bigger than us and our respective missions and governments. Something more important than politics or loyalties or races. I'm honestly not trying to get you to spill your secrets. I'd just really like to know what's going on. First the ice dragons and shadow rats, now the unicorn. I'm afraid one or both of us may have a *destiny*." She said 'destiny' like it had a bad flavor.

"That's an interesting theory," Sean said, shifting in his seat. She couldn't know how much he'd been struggling with this assignment. Only a handful of people even knew about it, and none of them were aware of his qualms about it. How it was too big a job for a single person—they could hardly send in a team and risk being caught meddling in another country's affairs—how he feared the worst would happen, that he'd have to go through with his orders for the worst-case scenario. That he would fail. And what would the scope of that nightmare even involve?

"Sean?"

"Huh?" He realized he'd been silent for longer than he intended. "Sorry, just thinking."

She studied his face. "You look conflicted."

"It's nothing. Sometimes this job just...never mind."

She surprised him by putting her hand over his, a light pressure over the bandages. "I know. But unicorns don't show up like that for nothing."

He met her gaze. "I hope you're right."

5

MIDWINTER GIFTS

Rory kept an eye on the human after that. He seemed to lose some of his brash good cheer for a while, dropping into a thoughtful silence for most of that afternoon. Not that she blamed him.

The next morning she limped back down the hill to the lodge again. Sean had made another huge breakfast, and she felt stuffed. She'd rather have gone back to bed and watched the snow fall—it still hadn't stopped, with over two feet of it on the ground—than trek in to work to face more questions she didn't have answers to.

She wasn't even sure if she wanted to tell them about the unicorn. It seemed like a personal encounter. One she'd shared with Sean, and it connected them in a strange way. Human and elf, it had appeared to both of them, and for her part, it had sealed her trust in Sean, whatever his mission might be. He was one of the good ones. Though Borden and Taro were good men, they both had their noses buried in politics. In playing games, putting the Maireadd elves' interests above all others. Much as she loved her home and her people, their singular focus on looking after themselves bothered her more than a little at times. Hadn't God created all the races as equals, magical and non-magical alike? Then why their presumption that all things elf were unquestioningly the best?

But that unicorn—an omen of God's favor and direction—transcended race, culture and country. She really didn't know if Taro or Borden would understand that. Even Sean seemed confused by the encounter. But she wasn't. She didn't like the idea of being part of a bigger plan—a destiny. That often turned out painful for the players involved. But it also provided a measure of assurance and trust.

She pushed through the door into the muggy warmth of the lodge and shook snow out of her hair. A few elves greeted her on her way through. They were there decorating for the Midwinter celebration in a few days, and the entire place smelled sharply of pine. She shrugged out of her coat and headed for the offices.

"Have you made any progress?" Taro asked before she'd even sat down.

She leaned her crutch against the wall, buying herself a moment to gather her thoughts. "Nothing definite, no. He's solid, and smart. Oh, there is one thing."

Taro and Borden looked expectant.

"He can actually cook."

"Well that's..." Borden trailed off with a frown. "Irrelevant."

Taro chuckled. "You don't have anything definite, but we didn't really expect that. Any guesses?"

Rory chewed her lip. "I don't know what he's planning, or what his mission is. But he's smart and competent, and whatever he intends to do, he's going to get it done. Whether his plans align perfectly with yours, I don't know, but my impression is that he's a good man. I doubt he's out to harm Maireadd."

"I'm less worried about his own motivations than what his orders are, but that's good." Taro nodded. "Good work.

The question is whether the fallout from whatever his plans are could affect us, even unintentionally."

"That I couldn't tell you. But I don't think he would follow orders that he disagreed with. He's not the type." She paused for a long moment and they waited for her to go on, maybe sensing she wasn't finished. "I think there might be someone trying to kill one or both of us. Maybe with a soothsayer involved."

Both men drew back, exchanging a worried glance. "What makes you say that?" Taro asked.

"Because of the attacks." She drew a breath, debating to the end whether to tell them about the unicorn encounter. Somehow, she couldn't bring herself to do it. "The more I think about it, the more unnatural it all seems. Who would know where we were? And who would have a reason to kill either of us? I talked to Sean—Mr. Leigh, that is, and he says the only people who knew where he was being sent were his handler, the Thyrus president, and about two other people. High up officials. No way any of them could have been behind it."

"There's a lot we can infer even from that. He's highly trained, highly trusted, and whatever he's going to do, they're prioritizing secrecy. So it's big." Taro and Borden shared a grim look.

Rory shifted in her seat. "I have a theory. I don't know precisely why Mr. Leigh is being sent to Barra, though you're probably right that it's something big. The best way to stop that would be to kill him now. Which brings me back to the idea of a soothsayer."

"I don't know. That still seems like a bit of a reach, don't you think?" Borden said.

Taro held up his hand before she could respond, glancing at Borden. "It's a reach, yes, but perhaps not such a far one, considering the nature of these attacks. We'll have the guards keep watching your house. When you leave again, they'll accompany you."

"Thank you."

She left, using another wind spell to get her up the hill without plowing through the snow again, which hadn't helped her ankle on the way down.

Sean was stretched out on the couch when she got back. He cracked an eye open. "How'd it go?"

"I didn't tell them." She moved his feet from the end of the couch and sat down. His feet ended up on her lap. Somehow over the last day they'd gotten much more comfortable around each other. Even Sean, though he wasn't any more forthcoming about his business, seemed to accept the situation.

"Why not?"

She shook her head. "I don't know. I just couldn't bring myself to do it."

"Okay." He closed his eye.

"Are you going to sleep the entire week?"

"Maybe. When else am I gonna get a vacation?"

She shook her head. "How are the hands?"

"Getting better. How's the ankle?" He didn't bother opening even one eye that time.

"Getting better."

"What did you tell them?"

Rory grinned. "Wouldn't you like to know. Actually," she sighed, "I told them the truth, just minus that detail. Have you ever considered someone wants to stop you from doing whatever it is you're planning to do in Barra?"

He shrugged a shoulder. "Sure, if anyone knew. That's the nature of the business, isn't it, agent?"

"What if there was a soothsayer?"

At that his eyes popped open and he sat up, moving his feet from her lap to the floor. "Say what now?"

"It's just that I've been thinking about it... and it seems like someone wants one or both of us dead. Then there was the unicorn. Maybe there's a greater purpose going on here, and with every good purpose..."

"There's an evil one trying to counter it," he finished. "Interesting theory."

"Yeah. Just a theory. But watch your back once you get back out there in the big bad world."

He gave her a lopsided grin. "Too bad you can't come along and watch it for me."

And somehow with that remark they were staring at each other again, his blue eyes intense with color, but also with something more that she couldn't read. Unaccountably, her heart picked up its pace. And just as strange, she found herself glancing at his lips, wondering what it would be like to kiss a human. She shook herself and looked away. What in the name of all reason was that about? Perhaps she needed some space.

She got up and wandered into the kitchen. Whenever she got nervous or was trying to solve a problem she got snacky. But the sticky rolls and cookies Sean had made the day before were nowhere to be seen. *Angel, you little brat.* Her sister must have eaten them before she left for her classes, while Rory was in her meeting.

"Sean!" she called. "You need to show me how to make those cinnamon things!"

* * * * *

"Do you think it's weird having a human here for Midwinter?" Angel asked a few days later. "It seems a little weird." She kept her voice low, even though Sean was in the shower and wouldn't hear. Celebrations would be held that night, starting at dusk, but for now the girls were enjoying a quiet morning tea with a fresh batch of sticky cinnamon rolls.

"You say as you stuff your face with his baking."

Angel made a face at her. "You know what I mean. He's a nice enough guy, he's just... human. And a stranger."

Rory had ceased thinking of him as a stranger over the few days they'd spent together. He seemed more like a friend. A good friend, even.

"I feel really bad leaving you with him tonight," Angel went on. "You should be coming out to the celebration. Do you want me to stay?"

"Oh goodness no. I'll be fine."

"The family will wonder where you are."

"Mother knows I had an assignment. By this time she'll probably have pried most of the details out of Taro. Just go and have fun. Sean and I will be perfectly fine here. Besides, all that walking in three feet of snow. My ankle still needs a couple more days. Sean and Bari Healer would kill me if I reinjured it and had to wait another full week before we could leave."

Angel didn't look convinced, but she didn't press further. She still loved the Midwinter festivities with a childlike passion, whereas Rory loved them more quietly. She was truly just as happy to watch the lights from the window at home. Plus, there was a certain appeal in staying with the human. They didn't have many days left together, and in all likelihood they'd never see one another again, which seemed a shame.

Sean was quieter than usual that evening, other than to shoo her out of the kitchen while he got his pot roast into the oven and peeled potatoes. He came back into the sitting room to stand by the window and look out into the blue of dusk.

"You could have gone with them," he said with his back to her.

"Don't tell Angel, but I'd as soon watch from here," Rory replied. "Besides, I don't want to destroy my ankle again." Plus she was still supposed to be keeping an eye on him.

He nodded, watching the forest city. A fine flurry of snow was falling, not enough to accumulate, but it flecked the air, catching the light from the windows like drifting stars.

"Back home people would be out caroling in the streets by now."

Rory smiled at his back. "We elves wait for full dark to show off our lights and music. Do you miss home?"

"No. Yes. I miss my dog. And my kitchen."

She chuckled. "No family to celebrate with?"

"Not to speak of. Mom wasn't keen on the holidays after we lost dad. And the extended family is just...well. They're different."

"Ah."

He lapsed into silence again, standing like a statue with his hands in his pockets. Rory got off the couch to join him. Night fell fast over Maireadd, and already the twilight blue was darkening to midnight purple.

"Look!" she said suddenly. "It's starting." In the distance a light sprang to life, followed by a dozen more. "Come out on the balcony and watch with me?"

He nodded. "Wait though—I made hot chocolate."

He disappeared into the kitchen while she found a couple of blankets for them to wrap up in. She traded him a blanket for a steaming mug, and they slipped outside into the snow.

"What is this?" Rory asked, sniffing the contents of her mug.

"You've never had hot chocolate?" Sean sounded incredulous.

"It must be a human thing." She took a cautious sip and breathed out steam and excitement. "Oh. Oh, that's nice." She tried another sip. "That's amazing. It tastes like magic!"

Sean grinned a little, his dimple showing up in the glow of light from the windows. She wrapped her hands around the mug and bumped shoulders with him. "Thank you."

Instead of pulling away again, she leaned against his shoulder as they turned their attention back to the lights. Hundreds more had sprung up already, and they multiplied faster than they could keep track of as the elves of Tristini spread the twinkling golden lights through the branches of every tree in the city.

"What are the lights?" Sean asked.

"Crystals that gather and hold enough natural magic to light up and stay lit all night. Sort of like solar lamps, only with magical energy, rather than solar energy. They're the same as the ones inside that light the house, only much smaller. The crystals they're tossing into the trees are only fragments that chipped off when bigger lights were carved."

"I like them better than the electric kind."

The lights unfurled through the valley and up the hill toward them, and with them came the first hints of music. A thousand voices strong within their hearing, the melody clear and pure as the white crystal lights, delicate as the snowflakes, and deep as the valleys below the jagged mountains.

"Is it like this in the human cities?" she asked.

"Nothing is like this."

"But you have music and lights, don't you?"

He seemed hesitant to answer, too enthralled by the spectacle. "Candle light and electric lights, yes. Our music is merry like the firelight, but yours is pure and perfect like the starlight."

"There's a beauty in both," she said.

He glanced over at her, thoughtful. "Yeah, there is. I guess it's just easier to appreciate what you aren't used to."

She nodded. Of all the elves' celebrations, the Midwinter celebration of Light had always been her favorite with its symbolism. Lighting crystals or candles on the darkest day of the year in anticipation of the days becoming longer as God had come, incarnate, during the darkest point in history to bring hope and anticipation of all curses one day being broken.

The music thinned and fell to silence after an hour or more, though the lights would continue to shine until dawn. The elves had gone in to feast with their families. She and Sean went inside as well, their hot chocolate long gone and their toes going numb.

She set the table, going so far as to light a candle to put between them, while he mashed the potatoes and cut the pot roast. He'd made roast veggies as well as a pumpkin pie, and the scents tickled her nose.

"Mmm. So good. I'm going to miss you," she said after her first bite.

He dimpled but didn't reply, too busy shoveling food into his mouth.

After dinner they worked together to get the kitchen cleaned up before sitting back down at the cleared table. Rory had built up the fire in the cook stove and dimmed the lights. The candle light flickered across Sean's face as he rested his arms on the table so Rory could redo the bandages on his hands. They looked much better now. In another day or two he could leave them unwrapped. Of course, in another two or three days they'd leave for Barra.

"I really will miss you, you know," Rory said. "I never thought I'd have a human for a friend."

"It's not unheard of. We humans aren't that bad."

She chuckled. "That's not what I meant. It's just that borders are hard to overcome sometimes."

"Especially when they involve curses?" He raised an eyebrow.

"Exactly." She finished wrapping his hands and folded her arms across the table in front of her, finally meeting his eyes. "Thanks for tonight. And everything this week. You're by far the best house guest I've ever had."

His dimples flickered into existence briefly. "Just because I cooked for you?"

"Well, I saw a unicorn while you were here. That doesn't happen every day."

He grinned again a little bit. "This is usually the part of the night when people exchange gifts. At least it would be if we were in Thyrus."

She looked at him suspiciously. "I didn't get you anything."

"That's okay." He stuck his fingers in the front pocket of his flannel button-down shirt and drew out a chain with a thick man's ring at the end of it. "It's nothing crazy. It wasn't like I came into Maireadd expecting to spend the holiday." He slid the ring across the table to her.

Rory picked it up, curious. Etchings in the heavy, pale gold caught the light, and a thick oval sapphire flashed blue-black, also etched with an intricate knotwork pattern.

"It's a signet ring!" she exclaimed, looking up at him in shock.

He nodded. "If you ever get yourself in trouble, that might help you get out."

Already shaking her head she said, "I can't take this. There are only like two or three Families on the continent that still have enough influence from the old days to flash around signet rings. You might need it." She tried passing it back to him, wanting to add that this most definitely hadn't been in his file. Which of the Families did he belong to?

His lips quirked in a smile as he withdrew his hands from the table, leaving her holding the ring. "I never thought I'd have an elf for a friend, either, and I've got a feeling it's not something we should shrug off and move on from, especially if that thing about unicorns is true. As you said, things are going down out there in the big bad world. I don't need a ring to prove who I am, if I ever need to, and to be honest, I'm not even supposed to have it with me. Too easy to have my stuff searched."

She raised her eyebrows at him.

He shrugged and rubbed his nose sheepishly. "It would be moot if I was ever strip-searched anyway, and it still wouldn't prove I'm working for the government."

Rory snorted, trying to smother another giggle. A giggle, of all things. "You got a tattoo, didn't you? Of your family seal?"

"What can I say. We all go through a stupid phase. At least humans do. Anyhow, a tattoo is as good as having the ring, since it's illegal to do a tattoo of a family seal on anyone without proof they're who they say they are."

She tried really, really hard not to wonder where that tattoo was hidden, mentally smacking herself for even being tempted to wonder. Tattooing wasn't common among elves at all, and like many human practices, she had a strange sort of fascination for it.

"So if you get caught..." she paused, careful to try and word her question correctly, "...doing what you're being sent to Barra to do... will your Family still be able to protect you?"

His right eye twitched. "It's more likely they would never have the chance. If that were found on me, it might get me out of trouble, but it could also potentially blow my cover, or create an international incident instead, of saving my life. It represents a lot of power, but... not the right kind of power for this situation.

"But if you have it," he went on, "being an elf might put you in a precarious position in a different way—a position where having questions asked would be a good thing."

"I understand," she said, turning the ring over to study it. The power it represented aside, just the amount of gold and the size of the sapphire had to be worth a fortune. A bubble of discomfort formed in her chest. This was an unprecedented gift.

"Listen," said Sean. "There's a phrase that goes with it, in case you ever have to prove to the Family head your connection to me. He'll ask where you're from. You'll tell him, 'blood has no borders.'"

"Blood has no borders," she repeated, her chest tightening further. *Blood has no borders.* The unicorn, the attacks, their forced time together, and all along this code phrase had been attached to Sean. Perhaps it was not so unprecedented. Perhaps it was fate.

Across the table, Sean nodded to her.

* * * * *

A week later they stood at the edge of the forest, looking down into a long, sweeping valley twinkling with the lights of Barra's capital, Eyren, a city that sprawled for miles. Like a river, the heaviest glow of lights followed the curve of the land, disappearing beyond the mountain. But there were homes scattered along the slopes as well. The royal palace crowned the top of the mountain, a fairy-tale castle of towers, dungeons, thick walls and stained-glass windows. From this distance all they could see of it were pinpricks of light from those myriad windows.

"This is where we leave you," Rory said. They stood apart a little way from the other elves that had been sent along as a guard because of the two attacks.

"Yeah." Sean looked out across the valley, his face pensive in the starlight. He turned back to her. "Thank you." He chewed his lip, hesitating to leave. Rory felt the same.

"Here, before you go," she said, tugging at a cord around her neck. "I never did give you anything in return for Midwinter."

"You weren't supposed to."

She handed him the cord with her fairy light crystal. Chiseled in the shape of a crescent moon, it glittered under the stars. "To activate it, simply command it to shine. It will obey any language, as long as the intent is there, even if spoken by a human. Perhaps it will help you, if you ever find yourself in a dark place."

"Thanks." He slid the cord over his head, and then they gazed at each other for a moment. "I hope we see each other again sometime."

"Me too."

"Until we meet again," he said quietly, quoting the opening lines of an ancient farewell blessing. "May God above light your way beyond the sunset's end."

Her lips curled in a smile. "May the Redeemer grant you hope beyond your hopeless moments. And if we fail to meet again here..."

"I'll see you in the life beyond life." He nodded as though to seal the words as a promise, then turned and began walking. It started snowing again while she watched. A gust of wind picked up, softening his tracks, obscuring his form, and blotting out the lights in the valley. She turned and started in the opposite direction, joining the waiting elves under the eves of the forest.

"But hopefully in this life," she murmured.

6

THE ASSASSIN AT COURT

Five months later...

Sean gnawed the inside of his cheek, his pencil suspended over the order sheet. One case of lemons or two? If he served strawberry lemonade next week, they would need the extra. But he had made lavender lemonade for the last event. How much lemonade was too much?

He set down the pencil with a sigh and rubbed his eyes. If Colonel Jacobs had any idea how much time and energy it took to plan a banquet spread for court twice a month, maybe he would have come up with a different cover story for Sean. Not that he didn't enjoy the challenge, but the head chef had come down with pneumonia two weeks ago, so now Sean was organizing supplies and overseeing meals for the whole stinking palace, not just for court events. He was supposed to be playing at work here, not taking over other people's full time jobs.

"Two cases of lemons," he muttered to himself. "Three cases of broccoli. Cucumbers, zucchini, celery..." he glanced at his menu plan again. "And radishes. And that should do it. Flour, butter, cream..." he scanned back through the order. Somewhere beyond the closet of an office where he sat, and beyond the darkened kitchen, a bell tolled the hour. One o'clock in the morning.

He sighed. "This stinks." Even alone in the office he spoke in a flawless Barran accent, rather than in his native Thyrusian brogue, which he'd gotten rid of the second he left

73

Rory in Maireadd and set foot in Barra. Though Thyrus and Barra shared a common language, the accents on either side had become so thick as to be separate dialects. Thanks to his father's roots in Barra, he could use either of them without a trace of foreign accent.

Pushing the finished order aside, he stood with a groan and stretched the kinks out of his back. He traded his black chef's uniform for his black leather jacket and pulled his helmet from among scattered binders full of recipes and files full of invoices that spilled haphazardly over the shelf next to the desk. The head chef needed a secretary.

Snapping off the desk light revealed the darkness of the kitchen beyond. No one had remembered to leave a light on for him. Again. About to step out of the office, he paused at the sound of the kitchen door swinging open ahead of voices entering.

"Is it secure?" a man's voice.

"Of course. No one is here at this time of night. All the lights are off." The second voice was a woman's, and unmistakably belonging to queen Dianthe, who sounded annoyed.

Sean froze, his heart suddenly galloping.

"I'm the queen of Barra. I shouldn't have to skulk about in kitchens," she continued to grumble as her high heels clicked across the floor. "Why isn't there anywhere to sit in this place?"

"Kitchens are usually used for cooking, not sitting," the man replied dryly. "Besides, we won't have to hide too much longer."

Despite holding his breath and keeping utterly still, Sean couldn't hear a second set of footsteps, which meant the queen must be talking on her magic mirror, or her cell phone.

"We better not. Now what was so important that I needed to go wandering in the middle of the night?"

"I've heard from the spirits," said the man.

Sean, used to sneaking and keeping his silence, nearly let out an unmanly squeak of horror. Spirits? The man was a soothsayer? He gripped his motorcycle helmet tighter and started to pray, his hands suddenly clammy. What if they were spying on him right now?

"And what do the spirits say?"

"That your enemies are rising, and they are dangerous. You have a spy and assassin in your court."

"Who?"

Sean lifted his free hand to his mouth and silently chewed on his knuckle.

"I don't know yet. But there's a more immediate concern. The Seer is plotting something. He's throwing a gala at his mansion on the Isle of Selkies. You need to get some of your people out there. Your life and your rule depend on it."

"You're vague, as usual," the queen complained. Judging from where her shoes had stopped clacking she must be standing near the ovens, which would still be warm, even past midnight. She was probably trying to warm up, parading around in one of her scant dresses as she always did.

"How about this then—there will be someone there—a man—who will become a weapon, either for you or for your enemies. You need to either capture him or eliminate him."

"Now we're getting somewhere. Who is he?"

"I don't have a name, but they showed me his face. He's young. In his twenties. Blond, brown eyes, medium height and build. He'll be wearing black."

"And what's so special about him?"

"I'm not sure. I believe he is your most powerful opponent, aside from the Seer himself and that assassin, but don't be a fool and get hung up on him. You will have many enemies gathered there, and it is all of them that you should concern yourself with."

There was a pause. Sean felt like his skin was crawling, like the shadows might be watching him as he stood frozen in the office doorway, the helmet still dangling from one hand while he chewed his knuckle.

"I'll send Beck and Lyselle. Between them they should be able to handle it," said Dianthe finally. "But what about the assassin in my court?"

"You'll have to sort it out. I can't do everything for you." The soothsayer sounded contemptuous.

Dianthe snorted ungracefully. "In other words, you'll only help when it's easy. Or are you just worried about failing again, like you did over midwinter?"

"Be grateful the spirits have taken an interest in you. I pass along whatever they give me, but don't for a minute think it means I'm your friend or your servant. As for Midwinter, I did the best I could with vague information. With that meddling unicorn involved, it's no wonder I couldn't get a look at their faces. Though I don't understand how they got past the ice dragons. And if one of those two is in your court now, you better watch it, or you won't have to worry about the Seer or his weapon."

She gave a harsh laugh. They didn't linger to exchange pleasantries. Dianthe ended the call and Sean heard her sigh, followed by the clack of her shoes as she turned and headed toward the door. A moment later she ran into one of the work stations, rattling utensils and pans. She muttered something under her breath and a tiny light sprang up in her hand. He tensed, but she didn't look around, merely used it to find her way out of the kitchen without running into anything else.

The swinging door slapped shut behind her and Sean deflated. He leaned against the door jam, suddenly weak in the knees, and took a few deep breaths. After a moment he went back into the office and sat at the desk in the dark. He couldn't risk leaving too soon and running into Dianthe in the hall, and he had an irrational fear that any move he made, like turning on the light, might draw the attention of the soothsayer's spirits.

He rubbed a hand over his face, feeling vulnerable, and very alone. Even more alone than in all the lonely, long months since he'd gotten here. He was on his own here, and horribly outmatched—nothing but a desperate gamble by Thyrus to stop the collapse of a country, and with it, the continental economy. Not to mention the war that would likely follow.

And now he not only had to contend with the witch queen and all the resources she had at her disposal, but unseen foes as well.

His thoughts drifted to Rory. She had guessed there must be a soothsayer, even at Midwinter. It looked like she was right about that and the unicorn as well. He hoped so. And then he realized he missed her. The elf with the cute ears and the smoked-silver eyes. Had she run into any more trouble in Maireadd? Been sent on dangerous missions? He wished he could see her again, to tell her she was right and warn her to watch her back. But she wouldn't need the warning. He merely wanted someone to talk to. None of his own assignments had run this long before, and this one was nowhere near being over.

Almost an hour went by before he finally crept from the kitchen. There was no sign of the queen anywhere, and he managed to avoid sentries till he got to the door, but those knew him, and that he often worked late. He nodded to them.

"Fall asleep on the desk again?" One of them quipped as he passed. He snorted and waved them off without stopping. There was no reason Dianthe should question them as to employees leaving late...and no reason they should mention it, since they were used to it, but he still had to stifle feelings of paranoia.

The back parking lot was mostly empty when he left. His motorcycle waited between a couple of SUVs belonging to some of the night guards. Tonight he winced at the roar when it started.

Cruising down the mountain toward the city, his mind raced faster than the bike. Instead of turning toward the Leigh estate where he was staying with his father's family, he kept going down into the city and pulled up in front of an ancient stone church that had become familiar over the past few months. Even at two in the morning the windows glowed with soft light.

He removed his helmet and tucked it under his arm as he entered. The lingering scent of sacred incense tickled his nose, spicy and soothing.

"Hello?" his voice echoed among the empty pews.

"Coming!" came a muffled reply a moment before the priest emerged from the door leading to his study. His brown corduroy jacket looked rumpled, and his glasses sat crookedly on his nose.

"Did I wake you up?" Sean asked.

The priest rubbed at a red line down his face. "Oh, I may have nodded off on my books again. It's no matter. What can I do for you?"

Sean slid into a pew. "What can you tell me about soothsayers?"

The priest lost his pleasant smile, his face turning grim. "Why do you need to know?"

"I'd rather not say. But...how powerful are they? Is there a way to, I don't know, hide from one?" He knew their conversation wouldn't go beyond the chapel walls, but still it made him nervous asking so openly, and he glanced around as though the shadows themselves might be listening.

"The sacred texts warn not to study the ways of evil too closely. What I know of them is that they are evil, and often powerful, but not infallible. Those individuals have made a covenant and fostered a relationship with living evil, nameless creatures from the shadow realm that travel where they will and spy on whom they please, much as servants of God have made a covenant and built a relationship with Him. But, unlike God, spirits are not infallible. And they are also liars."

"Yeah," Sean agreed halfheartedly. The part about lying might be true, but it wouldn't do him much good if unseen forces were whispering his name in the queen's ear.

Recognizing what was probably a queasy look on his face, the priest offered, "Prayer is your best defense. Aside from that, the elves may have developed a way to prevent being spied upon. But I wouldn't know." He gave an apologetic shrug.

"Thanks anyhow." Sean stood, feeling the stiff ache from being on his feet all day and half the night. He needed to hit the gym, but he'd been working such ridiculous hours he hadn't had the chance since the head chef had been on leave. He turned back before he reached the doors. "Hey, do you know the Seer?"

The priest grinned. "Sadly, no. I would like to meet him some day, though."

"Yeah. Me too."

Back on his bike he flew toward the estate. The weariness of the long day battled with the excitement of the night, leaving him exhausted but still wired as he rode, his mind cycling through this new information, and how much of it he should share when he checked in tomorrow with Colonel Jacobs. He wondered who the weapon was that the soothsayer had talked about. But above all he wondered how he was going to get to the Seer's gala to check it out.

He left the old city center behind, cruising down quieter streets lined by ancient oak and elm trees planted at precise intervals with wrought iron street lamps between them.

A long, white gravel drive marked the beginning of the Leigh estate, his father's ancestral home. Here the trees were a bit less precise, and the wild grape vines and climbing roses a bit less tame. As he turned a bend the stone wall surrounding the mansion grounds came into view, mostly smothered by ivy and wild roses that weren't yet in bloom. A wrought iron gate slid open at his approach. He pulled up to the guest house and parked.

By that point he had no other thought than to get in and crash for a few hours before he had to be back to work. Probably wouldn't even make it out of his clothes. He tossed his wallet and keys on the counter and swiped a hand through his hair. It felt greasy after spending eighteen hours in the kitchen, but he couldn't bring himself to care.

He almost couldn't bring himself to care about checking the magic mirror stashed in a drawer in the bathroom, either. Unlike most magic mirrors that could pass for mobile phones, this one looked like a regular travel sized mirror—a plain oval with a cheap wooden back. The Thyrus government had an elf on the payroll that enchanted special items like it for them, rather than go through the usual method of shipping pre-made items in bulk into Maireadd to be enchanted and sent back. It made them harder to recognize as magical if they didn't match the thousands of others.

He did check the mirror... and it glowed briefly to indicate a missed message when he picked it up. Probably from his handler. Sighing, he took his mobile phone out of his pocket and removed the battery before going back to the mirror. It was almost impossible to monitor magical messages, whereas listening through a phone was a common hack. He never used the mirror without first disabling the phone.

The message wasn't from his handler. It was from Rory.

7

AN UNEXPECTED INVITATION

Rory had spent the past five months on typical winter assignments. Border patrols, mostly when things were slow, or escorting shipments of goods or the occasional group of tourists. She didn't see the unicorn again, though she often looked for it in the swirling snow or the misty spring mornings. She didn't have any more run-ins with dragons or shadow creatures, either, and began to wonder if Sean had been their target after all—a thought that was both a relief and a disappointment. There had been a small part of her that wanted a change. Wanted to be a part of something bigger. But life went on as it always had. Until the morning it didn't.

She was just getting back from escorting a shipment of miscellaneous enchanted items to the border, and playing with a frayed strap on her backpack as she walked, thinking she'd have to replace it before she went out again. She'd been walking since the first gray hint of dawn and had just passed the standing stone, chiseled with whorls and imbued with wards, that marked the edge of Tristini, when one of the sentinels hailed her.

"Rory!"

"Iris?" she stopped and squinted up into the foliage, but, backlit by the morning sun, all she could see was glowing green.

"Borden and Taro are waiting for you at the lodge. You're to check in with them before you go home."

"Both of them? Again?"

Iris's face popped from among the leaves down low where Rory could actually see her. "What did you do to deserve all these extra assignments from the higher ups? Tell me so I can avoid making the same mistakes." She grinned.

"Funny. That'll be the day, when they send a tree-dweller out to deal with swamp trolls and ice dragons," Rory said, returning her grin. Scouts and Sentinels had a longstanding tradition of exchanging good-natured jabs. She continued on her way with a wave, diverting toward the lodge rather than her own treehouse. The last time she'd gotten called in before she even reached her house had been when she was sent to meet Sean. She had a premonition that this meeting might also turn out to be unusual.

She had to pass the elven university of magic studies on her way, another lodge-like building, but far bigger than the meeting lodge, and prettier, too, overgrown with flowering blackberries and grapevines that twisted and arched among the tree limbs, shading the paths around the building. She wondered if Angel was in class this morning.

The usual damp warmth greeted her as she stepped into the meeting lodge. Today her sensitive ears picked up quiet voices and activity from the offices lining the hall beyond the front meeting room. She should stop and say hello to her mom while she was here. She'd been gone so much lately she had barely seen her family in months, besides Angel, and that was only because they still shared the treehouse. It didn't help her growing restlessness. And it also alarmed her a bit as she realized with a sudden shock that she had been spending more time thinking about Sean the human lately, wondering how he was getting on, than her own family.

"Rory, there you are," Borden greeted her as she stepped into the office. Taro was there as well, as Iris had warned her, and they both wore curious expressions as they watched her ease her pack off and lean it against the wall, putting her instantly on guard.

"Here I am," she said, settling into a chair with a stifled sigh. It felt good to be off her feet finally.

"This came for you," said Borden, sliding a big ornate envelope across the desk toward her.

She picked it up, frowning. The council didn't make a habit of censoring people's mail—it was just that there was no actual mail system for anything coming in from outside Maireadd. In the event someone in Tristini did actually get outside mail, it came to the offices because it was the only place for it to go.

Still, they both watched her hawkishly as she turned over the envelope, making her uncomfortable. But when she spotted the return address she realized why. It was from the Seer of Barra. Her mouth went suddenly dry.

Elf Auralie Agent

The honor of your presence is requested at a Midsummer's Eve gala to be held at the Mansion on the Bluff, Isle of the Selkies, and hosted by the Seer of Barra.

She read the invitation three times and still didn't feel it sink in. Wordlessly, she handed it over to Taro and Borden, who were practically drooling on themselves waiting to see what it was.

"What have you done to attract the attention of the Seer?" Taro asked, still staring at the invitation.

"Nothing," she replied, then rubbed her lips because they felt a little numb with shock.

"You're sure you don't know what this is about?" This from Borden.

She could only shrug and shake her head.

"Well, you'll have to go and find out, I suppose. One doesn't turn down an invitation from the Seer of Barra."

"Yes," Taro agreed, handing it back to her. "But Midsummer is a month off yet, which gives you plenty of time for your next assignment."

Rory sighed inwardly. It had been too much to hope that the Seer's invitation was the sole reason she'd been called in so soon. She loved her job, but all she wanted at the moment was to disappear for a week and stuff herself with those cinnamon rolls Sean had taught her how to make.

Borden pushed a file toward her across the desk. "Elf Erinn Ambassador hasn't contacted us in over a month, and we haven't been able to get her on the magic mirror."

Rory flipped open the file and her mouth went dry all over again. She had escorted Elf Erinn into Barra herself.

"You seemed to have developed a bit of a friendship with that Sean Leigh that you guided this past winter," said Taro. "We're thinking perhaps you can contact him. Do a little snooping around and see if you can find out what happened to Erinn. He might know something, if he's been at court. Even if he doesn't, see if you can talk to him and get a feel for what's going on there. If he'll talk to you."

Rory didn't reply for a moment. She stared down at the Seer's invitation, turning it over slowly in her hands, her mind suddenly crowded with too many thoughts and her heart with too many feelings. Excitement, anticipation, fear, hope. And a few other things she couldn't find names for. Why did the thought of seeing her human friend again turn her into such a mess?

"Rory?" Borden asked. "Is something wrong? Do you think the human will refuse to help you?"

She shook herself and looked up to find them watching her expectantly. "No. He'll help me. I was just thinking. When do I need to leave?"

"The sooner the better. Whenever you can be ready. We're going to send a few of the scouts with you. They'll take you as far as the border on horseback. Do you think you will be ready to leave by tomorrow?"

Her lips twitched in a weary smile. "Why not."

At least she would be able to ride most of the way this time. Horses were a commodity in Maireadd. The dense forest didn't lend itself well either to riding or to keeping horses, and hay and grain had to be brought some distance, so she was used to most of her travel being on foot.

Gathering up the file, invitation, and her pack, she nodded to them and slipped out, trudging up the hill toward home. Now that she was back outside she let herself reach for the signet ring on its chain around her neck, fingering the heavy gold and cool sapphire. The etchings in it had become familiar to her fingertips over the past several months. Now her heart fluttered annoyingly as she touched it, and a tiny shudder ran through her. Anticipation? Premonition? Fear?

It was nearly noon and her house was dark and cool after the muggy warmth of the forest, but also empty and lonely. After lunch she took a long bath, even though it was hot outside, carefully washing and re-braiding her hair. Then, magic mirror in hand, went out to sit on the back balcony.

Sean didn't answer her call, but then, she hadn't really expected him to. He'd been hiding that oddball magic mirror of his—she never would have known that's what it was herself if she wasn't so practiced in sensing enchantment—so she didn't figure he would be carrying it around with him.

"Sean, I'm going to be in Barra in a few days. I have a favor to ask. See what you can find out about Elf Erinn Ambassador...if you can do it without risk. I don't want to put you in danger, but I'm hoping there's a way we can meet while I'm there. I'll be coming on assignment, but I'd like to catch up with you. My cinnamon rolls aren't quite as good as the ones you made, and I need to find out what I'm doing wrong." She smiled into the mirror for a moment, but let it fall. "Anyway, I'll see you soon, maybe."

* * * * *

The next morning she was up and ready to go, with her pack restocked, by dawn. One of these times they needed to give her enough time off to catch up on laundry, but that aside, and in spite of yesterday's weariness, she felt restless and ready to travel again. Maybe it was the prospect of going into danger, or maybe it was the chance of possibly seeing her human again, but the desire to sit around and stuff herself with cinnamon rolls seemed to have evaporated with the early mists rising from the forest floor.

Vasya and another of the scouts were already waiting for her with a spare horse when she tromped down the steps of her treehouse. He tossed her the reins. "Let's go, agent. Daylight's wasting."

Since they were traveling by horseback this time, they got onto the main road leading from Tristini to the border of Barra and settled in for a long ride, though with the horses they would only have to camp once. Rory took her magic mirror out of her pocket and tucked it against the saddle under her leg where she could reach it in a hurry if Sean called her back. Vasya saw it and gave her a curious look, but she was saved from any snarky comments when the mirror chimed a moment later. Her heart jumped a little.

"Hey Rory." Sean flashed those dimples at her. Until that moment she'd forgotten how cute he was when he smiled. With that one smile everything came back in a warm rush. She missed his Thyrusian brogue, though. When he spoke, it was with a flawless Barran accent. "I guess there's no hiding from an elf that wants to track you down."

She grinned back. "Nope. Best not to try. How are you?"

"Busier than expected at the moment." He shrugged. Shiny white tile covered the wall behind him, and steam or smoke wisped around him. It looked like he was in a bathroom somewhere. Curious.

"I will be in Barra late tomorrow. Is there someplace that's safe to meet?"

He nodded. "There's an old stone church in the city center, down by the river with a cemetery behind it. The priest there is part of the Family. I won't be able to get there till late though. Probably midnight. In the meantime I'll see if I can find out anything about your ambassador. I remember her being at court when I first got here, but I haven't seen her in a month or so, I don't think."

"Thanks. Take care of yourself, alright?"

"You too." He swiped a hand over his face, turning suddenly serious. "I mean that. This city isn't a good place for elves right now. I hope whatever brings you here is important."

"Well, a missing ambassador seems pretty important. But I'll be careful."

"Do you still have my ring?"

For answer she pulled the chain out and held it up where the morning sun flashed against the etched sapphire.

He nodded. "Good. I'll see you tomorrow."

As soon as she ended the call Vasya whistled. "Is that a signet ring? Does Borden know you have it?"

"No," she admitted. "It wasn't relevant."

The other elf shook his head. "If that's not relevant, I'm not sure what is. Please tell me you don't *like* this guy. He's human."

"He's a friend," she retorted. Under her breath she muttered, "And about the best one I've got, too." It wasn't like she had the chance to cultivate many close friendships with her schedule what it was at the moment. She often worked alone, unlike the scouts who always traveled in pairs.

The horses plodded on toward the border where the scouts would leave her. Sean would be the only friend she had in Barra, and he wouldn't be able to risk being seen with an elf. Alone indeed.

8

THE SEER'S WARNING

Sean swiped a hand down his face and blew out a breath. First the Seer's gala, the soothsayer, and the queen sneaking around, and now Rory was coming here to investigate a missing ambassador. What else was about to get sprung on him this week?

The next day he had a sense of anticipation mixed with dread that he couldn't shake as he headed for the palace, then went through the motions of work that day. Good thing he'd already planned the menu and gotten things in order so he didn't have to do much actual thinking, cause his mind definitely wasn't on it. He planted himself in a corner and chopped celery to help clear his head and regain focus.

At five o'clock he stripped off his apron and chef's uniform and retreated to the office to change into formal wear, since that night was an open court and he had to play noble as well as celebrity chef. He yawned as he buttoned his dress shirt and fumbled with the bowtie.

The great ballroom was starting to fill up by the time he took up his usual post by one of the buffet tables of refreshments. He yawned again, letting his tired eyes unfocus for a moment—the glitter of jewels and brilliance of color and bright lights blurring and swirling together. But he had work to do tonight and needed his wits about him, so he shook himself and tucked away his weariness into a corner to be indulged later. Much later. He spotted Princess Calla headed his way and straightened. She offered a cordial smile and he bowed a half bow.

"It's Sean, right? Sean Leigh? Everything looks great tonight. You know the food is the only reason I show up at court every week."

They both chuckled politely.

"Have you seen Elf Erinn Ambassador?" Sean asked mildly. "The roast duck skewers tonight were inspired by elven cuisine, and I would love to get her opinion on them." He gestured to a platter of meat roasted on little wooden stakes.

"I haven't seen her. Not in quite a while, actually," Calla said, her brows puckering. Sean caught the glance she threw toward the queen.

"Ah. Too bad."

"Yes," she murmured absently. She excused herself and moved away.

The princess was an enigma, he thought as he watched her glide through the crowd. After five months in Barra he was fairly certain her loyalties were not with her father or her stepmother the queen. Rumor was that she was outspoken against their policies and favored the country's magical citizens. Yet she had seemed a bit subdued for the past couple weeks or more. He wasn't quite sure what to make of her, but even still she seemed to be the most stable of Barra's royals, and the one the common people loved the most. Her brother, Crown Prince Gaelan, had been graced with loads of charm, and that was about all Sean had been able to learn about him. He seemed to be lacking backbone, like his father. Though perhaps in the prince's case the issue was more about conviction than courage. Sean hadn't gotten to know either of them as much as he should, considering his mission was to determine which would be the best ruler, should he have to eliminate the others. Of all the times he'd been asked to spy on or kill someone, this was becoming the most difficult—in more ways than one.

Queen Dianthe, he would have no trouble ending. King Ebezer, as far as he could tell, was her puppet and nothing more. Judging by the king's usual vacant smile, perhaps he was more of a shell at this point than even a puppet. Either way, he felt no sympathy for the man. Whatever happened, Barra's hope for the future rested on either Gaelan, the charming waffle, or Calla, the enigma.

He caught sight of another young noblewoman he wanted to question headed down the table and gave her a friendly grin.

"Rylee, how are you tonight?"

She smiled, though it looked like her heart wasn't in it. Her jet black hair and slightly tapered ears were the only sign of her mixed elvin heritage, but she had been friends with the ambassador. The two of them always appeared inseparable.

"I don't see your friend the ambassador here this evening. I hope she's well."

The girl's eyes widened slightly before darting away. "I suppose."

Score. She knows something.

"Come to think of it, I haven't seen her in a few weeks. Has she gone back to Maireadd?"

Rylee shrugged one slender shoulder. "Perhaps. I really wouldn't know." She sidled past without meeting his gaze.

Much as he wanted to go after her and demand answers, he couldn't afford to draw that kind of attention, nor would she probably trust him enough to give it, so he watched, instead, as the young woman edged through the crowd toward Princess Calla, pausing to talk to her for a moment before she slipped out. Interesting. And dangerous. He shifted uneasily as the princess glanced toward him. He didn't dare ask any more questions tonight.

"Good evening Mr. Leigh."

Sean jumped and turned to face the elderly gentleman who had appeared, smiling, at his elbow. "Good evening. Mr...."

The little man just smiled, the chandelier light shining through his wispy white hair like a halo. "Don't worry about it too much," he said.

"Excuse me?"

"If you really want to know about the elf, you should ask Nigel. He lives under the Central City bridge."

Sean stared at him, speechless, his mind whirring.

The old man just smiled, then reached into his tuxedo jacket and withdrew a large, heavy envelope from an inner pocket. "This is for you. Please don't consider not coming. It's imperative that you do."

"Coming where? What?"

But the old man turned away with a wave, leaving him holding the envelope, and headed toward the dais where the king and queen had just entered and sat down not long ago. The crowd seemed to hush around him as he passed, and Sean groped for an explanation. Who was he?

The old man stopped at the foot of the dais and drew himself up to his full height of perhaps five feet. By that point he had the attention of the king and queen as well as everyone else nearby.

"You've led Barra to the edge of a precipice," he said without introduction. His voice carried through the room surprisingly well, and the hush deepened.

The queen leaned forward. "It's been two years since the last time you showed your face in this court. I see you're still preaching doom and gloom."

Sean's mouth formed a silent O. *No way. It can't be...*

"Last time, my warning was for the king. This time, it's for you, my queen," said the old man. "Stop this wickedness and you may be spared. Stop sacrificing people to feed your lust. Stop leading others to do the same. Stop turning a blind eye to injustice. Continue, and not only will you fall, but you could bring a curse down on Barra as well. A curse worse than that of Maireadd."

The queen leaned back and flicked her fingers at him. "Run along little man, before you start to annoy us."

Sean still held the envelope the old man had given him, and his fingers started tapping out a nervous rhythm on it. The Seer of Barra. He had to be the Seer. Which would make the envelope... He opened it hastily, glancing around to see that he was more or less by himself.

Mr. Sean Kerr Leigh.

The honor of your presence is required at a Midsummer's Eve gala, to be held at the Mansion on the Bluff, Isle of the Selkies, and hosted by the Seer of Barra.

"No way," he breathed.

He hastily tucked the invitation back into its envelope and then into his pocket, but when he looked up, the Seer was nowhere in sight and the queen was staring directly at him.

* * * * *

Sean slunk back to the kitchen as soon as he dared, escaping the eyes of the queen that he felt had strayed his way more than usual. The Seer was one of the good guys, right? Hopefully he knew what he was doing. If not, he might have just gotten Sean hanged.

"Leigh!" one of the sous-chefs called. "Good news for you! Peters is back in tomorrow!"

"It's about time!" Sean called back without stopping.

"Darn right!" the other laughed back. "You need your beauty sleep!"

All the food was out, the week's menus were planned and supplies ordered—which meant he could slip out early. Well. Sort of early. It was already eleven o'clock as he changed back into his street clothes and grabbed his helmet and jacket.

As he cruised into the city, he made a quick detour to a pawn shop that was open late. Thankfully they had what he was looking for—another motorcycle helmet. He paid the asking price for it without bothering to dicker and then headed for the chapel.

The ancient stone building looked the same as it always did, its stained glass windows casting rainbows of light over the sidewalk no matter the hour. It was just the butterflies flapping around in his stomach that protested that tonight was different. He reached for the worn wooden door handle and pulled it open.

Inside the church, a lone figure sat hunched near the front wearing a dark hoodie that covered her ears. His heart missed a couple beats as he slid into the pew behind her, and he started grinning like an idiot.

"Hey."

She turned. Her metallic eyes caught the light, looking alien and fearsome, but she returned his grin, her ears perked forward till they almost escaped the hood. "Hey."

9

TROLL'S TOES

Rory had to stop herself from diving over the back of the pew and hugging her human friend. It felt good to see any familiar face in this city, but his face in particular was especially comforting.

He must have been feeling the same, for he said, "Man, it's good to see a friendly smile. All those sharks at court are getting to me. How have you been? Seen any more unicorns?"

She laughed. "No unicorns. You're sure this place is safe?"

He nodded. "As long as we're the only ones here. The priest is solid. We've got a lot to catch up on." But despite his words, he didn't seem in a hurry to talk business. He asked how her winter had been, and soon they were sharing their adventures and laughing together. It didn't take magic for her to sense the weariness in him though, so she reluctantly steered the conversation back to business.

"You're going to the Seer's gala, right?" she asked.

He looked surprised for a moment, then his expression turned pensive. "You know about that?"

"Not much, only that I got an invitation, so I assumed that you had as well."

"Tonight. The Seer was at court. He was warning everyone that Barra would be cursed like Maireadd, only worse, if they didn't change. Which means I guess Queen Dianthe is influencing people more than I thought." He looked grim, which for some reason made her heart break a little bit, seeing him without the dimples and cheerful boyishness.

They sat in silence for a moment, Rory running her fingers over the pew back. The wood was so old that the grain stood out in raised ridges, stained dark by years and use. Finally Sean sighed.

"That's not all. You were right about the soothsayer," he said, then recounted the conversation he'd overheard in the kitchen only a few nights ago. "I've felt like I'm being watched ever since."

She smiled faintly. "Well, make sure you don't pick your nose then, even when you think you're alone."

His eyebrows shot up and he gave a surprised laugh. "Whoa now, wait a sec. Are you accusing me of being a closet nose-picker?"

"Of course not. Best not to start being one right now, is all. Then again... maybe you should. If anyone was watching they would hardly take you for someone dangerous." She wiggled her eyebrows at him and they both laughed. It eased her heart to see his good cheer return, even briefly.

"Anyway, I might have a couple leads for you on your missing ambassador. Rylee Annondale was a good friend of hers. She's like, a quarter elf? I asked her casually about the ambassador tonight and she got dodgy. I'm sure she knows something, and that she's afraid."

"Thank you. I'll find her."

"There's one more thing. Well, maybe. Something the Seer said to me, but I'm not sure... he kind of sounds crazy, you know? So I don't know if it's worth anything. But I thought maybe we could check it out together."

"What, tonight? You can't afford to be seen with me," she protested, even though she could almost weep with relief at the idea of having help. Eyren was a big city, and she'd been feeling overwhelmed since she'd gotten there.

Sean grinned. "No one is going to see either of us." He tapped the black motorcycle helmet he'd set in the pew beside him when he came in. "I've got another of these. We can go cruising all night if we want to. Just a couple faceless people out burning rubber."

"I've never ridden a motorcycle before," Rory said, eyeing the helmet with equal parts trepidation and excitement.

"Easy. You just hang onto me."

"How...scandalous. Hanging onto a human. Let's do it."

The night had gone cool by the time they stepped out onto the sidewalk. They'd been talking so long that midnight had long come and gone. Sean handed her a spare helmet, apologizing that it was a used one.

"As long as it doesn't crush my ears," she said.

With their identities safely locked away behind reflective face shields she climbed onto the bike behind him, awkwardly resting her hands on his waist.

"How hard do I need to hang on?" she asked, her voice oddly amplified and distorted in the confines of the helmet.

In answer he took her hands and drew them all the way around his middle till she was hugging him from behind, pressed against his back. He squeezed her hands briefly before letting go. Being that close made her feel odd and fluttery and a bit guilty.

He kicked back the stand, revved the motor, and then they were off down the street with the scent of exhaust lingering inside her helmet. Her stomach tried to crawl up her throat the first time they turned a corner, and then she was glad to be hanging on, even though they weren't going fast. She hadn't asked where they were going, too distracted by the idea of riding with him, but she watched the city pass by, taking note of the turns they made. She wasn't overly familiar with the city—she had only been there a few times—but enough to know they were headed into a seedier part of town.

Two rivers ran through the city, the smaller one behind the church where they'd started out, and the second one, wider, deeper, and dirtier. The two rivers converged to the north, outside the city limits, into a wide, sluggish behemoth of a thing that always ran muddy. But here, where it was still called Central River, it looked deep and fast. Sean slowed the bike as they neared an arching stone footbridge that had been built during better times. Refuse collected around the pilings like disgusting snowdrifts.

Whatever pleasure she'd had in riding around with Sean vanished in sudden dread as he set the kickstand and killed the engine. "This is where the Seer said to look?"

He shrugged. "Supposedly someone lives here. Must be a homeless person."

"Must be," she said, looking around. They were parked in an abandoned lot on the riverbank, where weeds grew up out of cracks in the pavement. An old warehouse loomed out of the dark a few blocks down, but other than that there wasn't much to see, even if it had been light out.

Together they walked to the edge of the lot, leaving their helmets on, and looked down on the dark river. Then they turned and headed toward the bridge and the piles of garbage that Rory was beginning to be able to smell over the dank scent of the river.

"Anyone home?" Sean called, not too loudly, as they neared the bridge.

One of the heaps of trash stirred.

Rory jumped and grabbed for the knife she usually wore on her belt. Since she was trying not to draw attention in the city, she hadn't worn it. Magic tingled in her fingers.

Sean put his hand in his pocket. "Hello? Nigel?"

Garbage shifted and cascaded around a broad pair of shoulders and a shaggy gray head that rose up from the shadow of the bridge. The figure turned to face them and Rory let out a squeak.

"Troll!"

The big, craggy gray face split into a grin, and the big, flat eyes glowed faintly green in the dark. "Elf!"

"Whoa," said Sean. "Take it easy, folks. Nigel? The Seer sent us."

"Hm." The troll lumbered out of the shadow of the bridge and into the weak light of a nearby streetlamp. Nearly seven feet tall, he wore tattered flannels and filthy jeans, and his gray skin did its best to appear shadowed, even in the light. Thick gray hair, more like fur, tufted out around his head like a mane. "Do I know this seer?"

"I don't know?"

"Trolls are immune to magic," Rory hissed at Sean. It was the main reason why elves hated and feared them.

"I know," he whispered back with a hint of amusement in his voice.

"Well, what did he want?" asked the troll.

Sean extricated his arm from her grip—she had no idea she'd grabbed it—and strode forward. He took his helmet off and tucked it under his arm.

"We're looking for Elf Erinn Ambassador. The Seer said you might be able to help us."

"Ah, the pretty little elf lady without any magic to meddle with." The troll actually looked a bit sad for a moment.

Rory frowned. "She had magic."

"Not any more. Come. I'll show you where she is."

She exchanged a glance with Sean as they followed the troll across the bridge into what had once been a little park. Now, in the dark, it appeared wild and overgrown, and almost as dark as Maireadd without any street lamps nearby. Long grass tangled around their feet as they neared a small copse of willows.

The troll stopped in the blacker shadow beneath one of the biggest, oldest weeping willows she'd ever seen.

"This is where I left her."

"Here? What do you..." Rory stepped forward, but her foot sank into freshly turned soil, and suddenly she understood. She pulled off the motorcycle helmet and dropped to her knees to run her hands over the mound of fresh dirt. A choking feeling rose up in her throat and her stomach turned bitter and heavy.

"Please, tell me what happened."

"I don't know what happened," said Nigel. "Pretty little elf rode the river down to my bridge. She had no more magic, and she looked sad, so I buried her here, because elves like trees."

Rory worked for a moment to harden herself enough to be objective, to find out what she needed to know. But it took a few tries to get the words past the knot in her throat—a question she already knew the answer to.

"What do you mean she had no magic?"

"Someone stole her blood. No more blood, no more magic." The troll shrugged his big shoulders. "Not even an elf deserves that."

"How do you know it was the ambassador?" She pushed.

Nigel stuck his hand into his pocket and pulled something out. It was too dark to see what it was, but he handed it to her and her fingers touched the unmistakable cool surface of a light crystal. She whispered to it, commanding it to glow, and soft white radiance filled the little copse. The crystal was cut in a perfect circle with the ambassadors' seal engraved on both sides. The seal that should have guaranteed Elf Erinn's safety in any country.

Rory closed her fist around it till only a little light leaked out. Enough to see the troll's toes sticking out of a hole in one of his boots. The sight seemed so incongruous, given the circumstances, that she had to stifle a hysterical laugh.

"When was this?"

The toes wiggled as Nigel thought about it. "Not quite a moon cycle."

"Three weeks?" asked Sean. "It's been about that long since I remember seeing her at court."

He nodded. "It might be that. I don't keep track of the weeks."

The others fell silent as Rory continued to kneel in the soft dirt, the chill of the night seeping through her, hardening her grief into something physical and tangible as she started to shiver. Sean touched her shoulder, the living warmth of his hand like a lifeline.

He helped her to her feet and they walked back to the bridge in silence, where Rory turned to the troll. "Thank you, Nigel. Perhaps someday our races need not be enemies."

The big shoulders shrugged. "I am no one's enemy unless they choose it."

"Yeah. I'm starting to see that."

As they walked back to the motorcycle Sean asked, "Where to? The church? Or is there someplace you're staying where you'd like to be dropped off?"

"The Sunrise B&B," she answered absently. The B&B was run by nymphs and was known by the elves to be a safe haven for magicals in the city. When they were getting ready to leave though, she touched his arm. He paused and looked back at her, the blank visor of his helmet reflecting orange light from a streetlamp.

"Sean, can we... I just want to drive around for a while. Would that be ok?"

He nodded.

She wrapped her arms around him and leaned her head against his back. For once she didn't question how comforting it was to just to hold someone—even a human—and have him occasionally squeeze her hands. It was enough to lose herself in the whir of the pavement beneath the wheels and the lights of the city flashing past like shooting stars.

10

HUNTED

Rory didn't know what time it was when they got back to the B&B and she finally crashed in bed, but it was near dawn. Sean hadn't said a word when he dropped her off, just squeezed her arm as he steadied her getting off the bike, then waited to make sure she got safely in the door. She felt bad. He'd looked tired in the evening, before they went to see Nigel, then spent the whole night driving her around, and she hadn't even told him thank you. Thank you for being there. Thank you for practically doing her job for her, tracking down the fate of the ambassador. Thank you for being her only friend.

She knew where Elf Erinn Ambassador was, and what her fate had been. Now she just needed to find out why and how. And once again, Sean had come through with the other lead he'd given her. Today, she would track down Rylee Annondale and find out what she knew.

The B&B offered breakfast to their guests, either in the big dining room downstairs, or delivered to their rooms. Gracie, the nymph proprietor, recommended the second option to her non-human guests—particularly elves.

"The situation is sticky right now," she'd told Rory as she checked her in and showed her to her room the day before. "Our queen isn't the only sorceress in the country, or even in the city. But there is hostility growing even between magicals and regular humans, thanks to her and those she's helped into positions of power. It's even worse for elves though. Not only are you the most powerful race as far as magic, but people see one of you and assume you're from Maireadd, and think you're either spying or somehow tainted by the curse, or goodness knows what. The elves that did live in Barra are fleeing to Maireadd every day because they're afraid. There have been killings on both sides and not much justice or truth as to who's doing it. If a magical is killed, no one cares. If a human is killed, a magical is accused. And once accused, they disappear."

"Sounds grim."

"We aren't completely without help." The nymph had said, her dark, chubby cheeks dimpling in a secretive smile.

This morning when Sean dropped her off, Rory crashed on the bed for a couple precious hours before Gracie's gentle tap at the door woke her. She stumbled over to open the door, brushing wisps of hair out of her face and straightening her rumpled clothes.

But the nymph didn't seem appalled at Rory's appearance. Her skin, such a cool, deep brown it was almost black, crinkled in a warm smile. Her silver-sprinkled hair was pulled back in a bun, making her the perfect picture of a grandmother. She had a tray of omelets and toast and elvish tea in a little silver teapot.

"You look tired, dear. Shall I make you an energy smoothie?"

"No, thank you. But maybe you could help me with something else. I'm looking for the Annondale residence. I think they're minor nobles, maybe? Do you know where it is?"

"Ah." Gracie's smile turned a bit more careful. "They are a part of the court. I'm not sure for how long, with the mixed elven blood. And you'll want to be careful. Wait till dusk, if you can, and keep your ears covered."

Rory wanted to protest, but the nymph was probably right. Plus, she was still too exhausted and heartsick to care much about going back out yet. With directions for later and breakfast for now, she retreated back to bed, and once she'd eaten, went back to sleep.

* * * * *

At dusk Rory took a taxi cab to the heart of the old city, where narrow, cobbled streets were shadowed by stone arches and tall row houses that seemed to form one continuous labyrinth of stone alleys, narrow passages, and open balconies. It was beautiful, in its own way, with planters overflowing with flowers at nearly every windowsill and every corner, but Rory had never seen so much stone and brick in her life.

She paid the taxi driver and pulled the hood tighter around her ears as she turned and started up the street. This part of the city seemed to have been built haphazardly, one street, one house or shop on top of the next, with blind alleyways, dead end corridors, and stone stairs set in narrow passages between buildings.

"This is ridiculous," she muttered. "How does anyone find their way? Would it have killed them to at least build in normal city blocks?"

Gracie had said to watch for the brick house standing on its own. At the time, Rory had been skeptical, but now, as she came to the end of a row of connected townhouses, she saw the next building set apart from those around it, the red brick standing out amid gray stone. It even had its own tiny yard. Well... not really a yard. Just a bit of a flower bed out front beside the stoop.

She looked around quickly before climbing the few steps to the door. For a moment she thought she saw a dark figure lurking in one of the crazy little passages between buildings, watching. But at a second glance, the place appeared empty. Her scalp pricked as she grasped the brass knocker and gave the door a couple good thuds.

A butler opened the door, thick eyebrows turning down over a hawkish nose as he took in her casual appearance and distinctive elven ears covered by her hood. His frown deepened when she asked to see Rylee, but he showed her into a small sitting room just off the main hallway and went to get the noblewoman. A big bay window took up most of the front of the room. Rory padded over to it, her boots sinking in green carpet almost as thick as the moss that carpeted the lodge back home. Outside, the street was growing darker by the minute, but once again she thought she saw a flicker of movement from the corner of her eye.

"You shouldn't be here."

Rory turned, instinctively moving away from the window so she didn't have her back to it. "Rylee?" she asked. The young woman was around her own age, somewhere in her mid-twenties, with dark hair and eyes, her ears lightly pointed and perky, but far more human than elven. She wore a lacy blue babydoll blouse with a knee-length skirt, and was barefoot.

"They are watching this house," Rylee said, glancing from Rory to the window and back. "The only reason we are still safe here is because we have so little elf blood that we barely have magic to go with it. But they've been waiting for you."

"For me?" Rory said, stepping further into the room, her neck prickling.

"You're from Maireadd aren't you?" Rylee asked. "You're here for your ambassador. She's dead."

"I know."

They watched each other for a moment in silence, measuring one another. The young noblewoman looked pale, with dark circles under her eyes and a nervous, jittery way of moving, like a bird constantly startled.

"Can you tell me what happened?" Rory asked.

The other woman left the doorway with a sigh and perched on the arm of an uncomfortable-looking gold-colored parlor chair. "Not really. Erinn was nervous. She told me she thought she was being followed. Two days later I went to see her—she had a townhouse not far from here—and the place was trashed, like a pack of wild animals had been in there. There were scorch marks on the walls, and the shadows..." she paused and shuddered. "The shadows in there were moving. I ran away."

"Did you report it to anyone?"

"Of course not!" Rylee snapped. "I'm part elf myself. You know what happens to magicals who report crimes? We become the criminal, is what. I ran away and never looked back. But Erinn never came back either, and ever since then someone has been watching me. That's how I know she's dead. They must have killed her, and they knew Maireadd would send an agent when she didn't check in, and that eventually the agent would find their way to me... and here you are. They'll kill you next."

"Who is 'they'?" Rory asked, forcing her voice to remain calm and measured, though her heart rate was picking up and her palms starting to sweat.

Rylee shrugged but said nothing.

"You're barely a Barran citizen at this point. You can't possibly be protecting these people."

"I'm trying to protect myself!" Rylee lunged off the chair's arm, her little fists clenched.

Rory paused. "Come back to Maireadd with me then. The elves would welcome you."

She curled a lip at her. "Says the elf who is going to be dead within a day. No thanks. If I need to get out of the city, I'll ask Princess Calla. She's about the last friend we magicals have at court... and she doesn't parade around trying to get people killed." She smoothed her skirt, turning and walking to the door. "You should leave." Then she was gone.

Rory stared after her, her cold anxiety turning to hot fury, both at the situation and at Rylee herself. After a moment she pulled her sweater hood back up over her ears and followed the other woman out of the room. There was no sign of the butler in the hall, so she slipped quietly out the door into the darkening night.

Her mind was busy with the little information Rylee had given her—questions upon questions. But she also kept a close watch on the shadows around her as she retreated up the sidewalk. This old part of the city was beautiful during the day, but now, with the night upon it and a light fog descending, it gave her the creeps. There were so many blind corners! Each one she passed she half expected something to jump out at her. And what about the moving shadows that Rylee had described in the ambassador's house? Had there been hellhounds? Here in Barra? It wasn't unheard of—not as if they were exclusive to Maireadd—but it could signal just how bad the situation here was getting if they were popping up now.

A werewolf howled somewhere close by and Rory froze.

Standing still on another odd corner where three streets converged, she listened and thought. Werewolves didn't normally howl—they were just people, after all—unless they were signaling to one another. Like if they were hunting. But in the city? What would they be hunting? Her? Why would they hunt an elf?

Rylee hadn't specified who was watching her, but werewolves weren't magicals in the traditional sense. Of course magic gave them their ability to shapeshift, but they couldn't wield it, so their power couldn't be drained with their blood and stolen from them by sorcerers or witches. Was it possible that whoever had killed Erinn had somehow convinced the werewolves to work for them?

Another howl sounded, this time from the opposite direction. Then a third. They were converging on her from each direction.

Magic tingled in her fingertips.

11

CRAZY PEOPLE

Sean woke after a scant couple hours of sleep to someone pounding on his door. The clock beside the bed told him it was eight in the morning. He snatched yesterday's pants off the floor and hopped-tripped to the door while putting them on. Through the window he could see his cousin standing on the tiny porch looking bored. She was a teenage socialite who lived for flirting with young nobles and buying shoes, and showed no interest in getting a real hobby, much less a job. Normally he pitied her. Not today.

He pulled the door open. "What's up, Lina?"

Her gaze scanned over him, from his tousled hair and wrinkled shirt to his bare feet and half buckled belt. "Eew. What happened to you?"

"Spent the night cruising around, visiting homeless bridge trolls."

"Okay, whatever." She wrinkled her nose, flipped her blonde ponytail over her shoulder, and produced a small envelope from her pink designer sweater, which she handed over. "This came from the palace for you this morning."

"Okay, thanks." He shoved it into his back pocket and started to close the door.

"Aren't you going to open it?" She protested, curiosity getting the better of her attempt at being cool.

"It's probably something to do with work. Not that exciting."

"It had the king's seal on it."

"Did it?" Sean's heart picked up its pace, but his hand remained steady as he pulled the envelope out of his pocket, glanced at it, and put it back. "So it does."

Lina stared at him for a moment, but when all he did was shrug, she turned with a huff and stomped off the porch. She had to pass the in-ground swimming pool on the way back to the main house, and he kind of hoped she'd fall in. She didn't.

Alone again, he opened the envelope and found inside an invitation to join the royal family for a 'small gathering' that evening for dinner.

"Hmm." He tapped the card against his leg. Since he was the one who had been planning meals at the palace for the last few weeks, and he hadn't been told about this, he guessed it must be a last minute thing, which made him nervous as he remembered the queen watching him the night before when the Seer gave him his own invitation. His sudden popularity was a bit unnerving, given the circumstances. He retreated back into the house and closed the door with a grimace.

He went to work that day long enough to go over the menu plans he'd made with the head chef, newly back to work after his bout with pneumonia. The other chef was aware of the dinner gathering that night and had been told to prepare for a party of seven.

"That's the royal family plus three," Sean said.

"Two," the chef corrected him. "The king's mother will be there. They specified no corn, and she's allergic."

"Right."

So, the royal family plus himself and one other. Should be interesting. He had a sinking feeling in his gut as he drove back home.

Taking the battery out of his phone once again, he locked himself in the bathroom in the guest house and got out his magic mirror. Feeling extra paranoid, he turned on the shower to run in the background.

"Call Colonel Jacobs."

The colonel's red face and gruff voice filled the mirror. "This ain't the scheduled check in, kid. What've you got for me?"

"I'm not sure yet, sir. But there are some things you should know, in case..." Sean cleared his throat, suddenly a bit awkward. "Well, just in case."

Jacobs' face pinched. "Spill it, then."

So Sean told him about the queen and her soothsayer, about the Seer and his gala and the invitation, and about the elves' murdered ambassador. He wrapped up with the dinner invitation for that evening. "I don't know why they've invited me, but I have a feeling it has something to do with the Seer's invitation. It's got me nervous."

"It's a good opportunity, though," Jacobs said. "Get an idea what's really going on in that family, and who the successor needs to be. Just watch yourself. I don't have an abundance of people with your skills to send in as a replacement if you get yourself offed."

"Yes, sir.

"This seer can see the future, right? He wouldn't invite you to this gala of his if you were going to get yourself killed before then."

"I'd hope so, sir."

"Well then. Let me know how it goes tonight."

"Yes, sir."

Sean climbed in the shower while it was still running, but by that time the water was getting cold. He hurried to clean up and shave, then dug through his clothes for something casually dressy. Or as his mom would have said, "Something respectfully schmoozy that you can still throw punches in." He went with a bright blue dress shirt and charcoal pinstripe trousers. His black string tie was a favorite. It was a bit old fashioned, maybe, but he'd used it to kill someone once. It went with the faint white scar on the underside of his arm.

He fingered the light crystal that Rory had given him for a moment, then tucked it under his shirt where it usually stayed. If anyone ever asked, it was merely a trinket he'd picked up in his travels. But having it on him somehow gave the illusion that he wasn't as alone. Where was Rory now? Had she found out more about her ambassador's murder? Would he see her again before she went back to Maireadd? The horror and pain in her smoky eyes last night as she knelt on the ambassador's grave still haunted him, and he paused long enough to offer a silent prayer for her safety in a city full of enemies. Then he finished brushing his teeth and left the house.

At the palace, a butler met him at the entrance, took his invitation, and led him through plush halls carpeted in red, with rich walnut wainscoting, and into the library, where Princess Calla, Crown Prince Gealan, and a stranger were already gathered. Plus another man who lurked in a corner watching both the princess and the room.

The prince, sprawled across a satin-cushioned purple loveseat, beckoned Sean in with a jovial greeting.

"Don't tell me you finally escaped the kitchen! I thought we were keeping you chained up back there."

"I was starting to think that myself, your Highness." Sean gave him a polite bow and took a seat in one of the uncomfortable purple-striped parlor chairs that matched the prince's loveseat.

"This is Alard, another of our nobles who's come into the area recently," Gealan introduced the stranger. Alard looked a couple years older than Sean, perhaps in his mid thirties, with dark hair and eyes. He seemed pleasant enough, but Sean felt uneasy as they shook hands. Who was he? Was there significance to his presence here, along with Sean?

Calla, standing by the bookshelves deeper in the room, glanced up from a book and smiled, then went back to reading. The princess wore stylishly ripped jeans and boots and had her blonde hair in a ponytail. She was a cute girl, twenty-three to her brother's twenty-six, and not at all what he'd pictured for a princess before he got to Barra. Calla the enigma.

"Don't feel bad. She doesn't talk to the rest of us, either," Gaelan said, drawing Sean's attention back.

Sean flashed an easy smile. "Who can blame her? You all must get tired of the events and obligations."

"It's not so bad when you're used to it. How are you holding up in the kitchen?"

"Yes, where did you study?" Alard chimed in. "And why on earth would you work so hard when you don't have to? You are of the nobility, aren't you?"

"Sure," said Sean, leaning back and propping an ankle over his knee. He refrained from squirming to get comfortable in the miserable chair. "The Leighs have been nobility in Barra for centuries. I just like the challenge. I've been all over the continent. Studied in Thyrus for a while, went down south to Mardhe. Came back to Barra. Got bored. Figured I'd move back to the family estate with my uncle and see what the capital has to offer. I've always loved cooking. It's a form of art—one you can experience with so many more of your senses than just your eyes."

"We don't see your uncle or aunt often at court," said Gaelan. "Not since my father married Dianthe, I don't think." His and Alard's gazes rested expectantly on Sean, who lifted his palm in a halfhearted shrug.

"Uncle's gout, probably. His favorite nymph healer moved to Maireadd, and he's been grousing about it ever since."

"We've lost a lot of our magical workers," Gaelan said, looking almost thoughtful for a moment. "Dianthe has that ban on magicals working in government now, but they're leaving the private sector as well."

"Can we trust them even there?" said Alard. "Imagine if they turned on us, with their powers."

"That's a consideration. There's been discussion as to whether they're even people." Gaelan shrugged noncommittally.

"I guess you royals have to think of all the angles, right?" said Sean, grimacing internally. Was the prince really this misguided? Was he confused? Or did he just not care? Or was everything he did an act here tonight, as it was for Sean? He'd been watching Gaelan for months now, and though the prince often acted flippant and was unfailingly charming, once in a while Sean caught a flash of cunning in his eyes.

"Sure we do—as long as we settle on the angle that won't get us ousted by the nobility," Gaelan replied with a chuckle. Alard joined in.

Sean scratched at the back of his head. "That's another consideration. I don't envy your position, Highness," he said. Looking up, he found Calla watching him from over her book. She diverted her gaze back to the book.

"Excuse me," said Sean, rising. "It seems inexcusably rude not to at least say hello to your sister."

Gaelan dismissed him with a wave, while Alard's gaze snapped up, pinching and flashing with something not-so-friendly. Jealousy? Again, Sean wondered what his part in this was as he turned his back on him and tread over the thick white carpet to the princess, who was studiously ignoring everyone.

"Your Highness." He offered a shallow bow. "May I ask what you're reading?"

She jumped, then laughed. "You're a silent one." She closed the book. "It's nothing too interesting. History, some engineering." She tucked it back on the shelf and shifted so she was blocking the title. "It's good to see you enjoying yourself for a change. We've all certainly been enjoying your culinary artwork."

Sean grinned. At least someone here recognized the artistry of good food. "Thank you for the invitation."

"That was Dianthe's doing," she said. "She thought we'd like to get to know you and Alard better, since neither of you have been in the capital long."

"Ah. Generous of her." Was that the reason? Or did it have to do with the Seer's invitation?

Calla shrugged. "I guess." She didn't seem particularly enthused, though she kept a polite smile.

"You know, for being a library, your chairs here aren't very comfortable."

She laughed, the sparkle returning to her eye. Good. People were more apt to open up when they were engaged, or in good humor.

"I hear you opened your own bookshop. Do you have a favorite genre or author?"

That won him a real smile, and soon they were talking books, history, and writing.

They drifted toward the sitting area as they talked, and Sean glanced back to catch the title of the book she'd been reading: Sanctuary, a Fascinating look at the Safehouses and Tunnels of the Curse War. He also noticed the lurker in the corner drifting after them.

"My bodyguard," Calla explained, when she caught Sean watching him.

The princess brought her own bodyguard into the palace? Interesting. What Sean wouldn't give to have a word with the man. Or rather werewolf, judging by how he wore his hair unfashionably long, the top part tied back. He had a single tiny braid that started at his left temple, signaling undivided loyalty to someone, whether his community or a gang or an individual person. The princess, perhaps. He stayed within three paces of her at all times.

They'd just wandered back to the sitting area when the butler poked his head in to announce that they could gather in the dining room.

Sean found himself following the princess and her werewolf down the hall, and watched as her motions and the set of her shoulders grew more tense as they neared the dining room. Gaelan displayed no such discomfort, at least not outwardly, as he continued to chat with Alard.

They entered a modest room, less grand than the rest of the palace, with a tiled floor in warm colors, a cherrywood dining set, and antique accent pieces around the room. The long table was set in white and crystal. They took their seats with Alard positioned next to Calla and Sean across from him, sitting next to Gaelan. The grandmother came in and sat on the other side of Calla, patting her hand. A moment later the king and queen arrived. Everyone stood while they took their seats at the head of the table, then sat back down.

"Wonderful that you were both able to come this evening!" The queen beamed at them from her place at King Ebezer's side. She wore one of her famously scanty dresses, a plunging, green, sleeveless thing with crystals glittering at the base of the daring neckline, strategically placed to draw the eye toward her assets. Her auburn hair caressed her bare shoulders. She continued, "We love getting to know everyone at court, don't we, darling?"

"Of course," King Ebezer replied brightly. He had the same empty smile pasted on his face that he always wore at court. Compared to the dazzling queen he looked drab and faded in his plain green dress shirt. The colors matched. But while Dianthe was vibrant and drew the eye with almost animal intensity, Ebezer seemed to repel notice, his eyes vacant, skin and hair graying.

Calla ducked her head, but not quite in time to hide her eye roll. Gaelan glanced at his father and then away, his lips flattening briefly.

"Calla, dear, did you really need to bring that thing to dinner?" The queen flicked her fingers toward the werewolf bodyguard, who had taken up a position against the wall behind the princess.

"Jamie goes where I go," Calla answered shortly.

"It's uncouth to bring animals to dinner."

Calla turned to her grandmother, a pleasantly plump little woman who exuded classy poise. "Gramma, would you mind terribly moving down a seat?"

The older woman gave her a sly smile and moved down.

"Jamie, come join me." Calla beckoned him over to the table. He came instantly and sat down between her and her grandmother. The guy was good. Not even a twitch marred his bland expression.

Icy silence followed for a few beats until Alard cleared his throat. Turning to Calla he smiled. "How has your bookstore venture been going? Do you get much business?"

"It's nice to be useful," she answered after a pause. "And business has been good."

"I'd like to come see the shop sometime. Perhaps we could have coffee together."

"Lovely Idea!" Dianthe smiled her radiant smile at him as though things hadn't been awkward a moment ago.

"We're open from eleven to nine every day," Calla said, and left it at that.

But Alard wasn't to be put off politely. "What days are you there?" he pushed.

The princess shot him a perplexed frown. "I'm there every day. I live there. If you're asking when I work in the bookshop, it varies."

Dianthe pursed her lips at the girl, but said nothing. Gaelan looked like he was trying not to smile. The grandmother had yet to say anything at all. And the king... Ebezer continued to eat with that stupid, vacant smile.

Aware suddenly that he was being watched, Sean looked up and met Jamie the werewolf bodyguard's gaze for a moment across the table. His cool, dark stare didn't give much away, but Sean got the impression of his disgust with the conversation, and of challenge. Would Sean step up and divert attention away from the princess, or would he add to her discomfort? But Sean was more interested in watching the family dynamics, which were proving to be educational as well as fascinating.

"What about you, Mr. Leigh?" Dianthe said, and at once he was the center of attention anyway. "You've barely told us anything about yourself."

Sean flashed a smile. "Not much to tell. I like to cook. And eat." He gave his empty plate a wry look. He'd finished before anyone else.

"I couldn't help but notice you talking to the Seer the other night. Well, he calls himself a seer. Crazy old man. I hope he didn't bother you too much."

"Nah, he's cool. I like crazy people."

Dianthe blinked. "Yes. Well. That's... admirable. He didn't say anything interesting?"

Sean shrugged and shook his head. "He was just rambling. I can't even remember what about."

The princess looked across at him with a puzzled frown.

Alard suddenly frowned as well, glancing at something in his lap—presumably his phone. He picked it up a second later, apologizing profusely, and hurried out of the room. A moment later he came back in with more apologies.

"I'm so terribly sorry, but there's an emergency that's come up that I have to deal with. It can't wait. Please forgive me." He bowed, then turned to address Calla. "Perhaps I shall stop in to see you this week. I would look forward to it. Would that be all right?"

"We don't tend to turn customers away."

"...Right." Looking perplexed and a bit annoyed, he bowed again and left. The queen didn't look particularly offended, and of course, the king didn't react. Calla seemed relieved. Gaelan frowned slightly but didn't say anything.

"You're from down south a bit, aren't you?" Dianthe asked once Alard was gone, looking at Sean. "Brookside, was it? Is that where your mother lives?"

"No, just another branch of the Leigh family, I'm afraid. My dad married a commoner. It's sort of quiet down there, and I got restless. Guess that's what travel does to you. So here I am." He flashed a grin.

He wasn't entirely lying. The Leigh family did have extensive properties down in Brookside, and he'd been there several times and was on good terms with his cousins. The Leighs were clannish, and though they didn't know about Sean's work, they would still cover for him in a heartbeat, if anyone asked whether he'd actually been living there. None of them liked Dianthe, as there were quite a few of them that had married magicals.

"Oh, I'm afraid I'm still learning about all of our nobles. I was a commoner too, once." She gave him a sly smile.

Sean raised his glass to her. "To marrying our betters."

She actually giggled. Sean smiled, rolling his eyes inwardly. Princess Calla didn't bother to hide her eye roll.

The rest of the dinner passed in stilted conversation. The queen found a way to bring up the Seer again, fishing for hints about his intentions, and connections to Sean. The king remained silently smiling—it started creeping Sean out long before the end of the evening. The grandmother didn't say much, but she appeared to dote on Calla, who also didn't say much. Gaelan and Sean chatted the most. The prince was effortlessly charming and easy to talk to and always found a reason not to have an opinion about anything.

Sean excused himself around nine, after the king and queen had made their exit, and headed home.

He was already piecing together bits of information and conjecture that he'd gleaned from the evening, prepared to report to Colonel Jacobs when he walked in his door. He was looking forward to calling in his report and then making it an early night. But when he grabbed his magic mirror and found it already glowing with a missed message, his heart sank.

Rory's face filled the small glass, dim and outlined in shadow. She spoke all in a jumbled rush. "Sean, I'm in trouble. I know you can't help, but if I don't make it... if I don't make it, talk to Rylee Annondale. You were right. She knew about Erinn, but someone was watching her—she said they were waiting for an agent from Maireadd to show up to investigate, and now they're after me. There are werewolves, and a sorcerer, I think. But listen. Rylee said something about the shadows in Erinn's house—it made me think of hellhounds. I think Barra is in deeper trouble already than you thought."

The mirror shook and she looked away for a moment, then turned back. "I'm sorry. You're the only friend I've got here, and I know you were sent to do something about this. Someone needs to know. If I don't get back to Maireadd, find a way to tell the council, if you can. I'll call again if I can. Thanks for everything."

The mirror went blank and Sean swore.

12

THE GORGRIM

As Rory stood on the corner where three streets converged, she looked around. This was a quiet section of town, mostly residential with a few shops. There were no bustling crowds to run into to throw off pursuit, if indeed it was she that the werewolves were after. No way would Rylee Annondale welcome her back into her home for shelter. What she wouldn't give to be back home in the forest.

No obvious escape presented itself across the intersection, so she turned back the way she'd come and ducked down a narrow opening between two buildings. It wasn't big enough to be called an alley—it was more of a passageway that ended in a set of steps up to the next street which was a full story higher than the intersection. This place was a nightmare! She bounded up the steps and flattened herself against a back wall of one of the buildings where she could peer back down the passage with one eye around the corner. Sure enough, a moment later a slinking figure on all fours entered the narrow passage.

Rory blew out a breath and turned away from the corner to survey this new street. There were a few shops up here, but it was past the dinner hour, night was coming on, and most of them were closed. One tiny cafe still had its door standing open with light spilling across the sidewalk. She sprinted toward it. A broad, middle aged woman in a green apron was filling napkin dispensers at the long counter when she ducked inside.

"Please, do you have a back door?" Rory panted.

The shop owner took one look at her and grabbed a broom from behind the counter. "Get out!" She stomped toward her, shaking the broom at Rory like she was a stray cat. "You and your filthy elf magic aren't welcome here. Out!"

Rory backed out hastily, nearly tripping over the threshold. As soon as she was through the door the woman slammed it closed, followed by the unmistakable snick of the deadbolt.

Her heart thundering in shock and fury, Rory turned and faced the werewolf. It stood a few paces away, watching her, its lips pulled back in an amused grin.

"Well, what do you want?" she said.

Werewolves couldn't really talk in wolf form, but he turned his head slightly, looking from her to the left of her as though directing her gaze. She glanced over to see another wolf turn the corner onto the street. There was at least one more of them around here somewhere—maybe more. In the cafe's big picture window the fat woman stood watching, still holding her broom.

"Will you let me pass?" Rory asked. Magic sparked at her fingertips.

The nearest werewolf bared his teeth and gave his head a little shake.

"Okay then."

Summoning her magical energy to her hands, she spoke a word and drew back her hand. The fireball formed at her fingertips as she released her throw. It lit the street in dramatic orange as it arched toward the wolf, who leapt out of the way almost in time to avoid it. The fire grazed his side, igniting some of his fur. He yelped and dropped down to roll it out. Rory didn't stick around to see whether he succeeded. She sprinted past him toward the passage she'd come through, but instead of taking the stairs back down to the street below, she directed her magic to her feet and muttered a few words to boost her leap toward the roof of one of the buildings along that lower street. It wasn't too far of a leap with her magic and with the incongruous difference in levels between the streets, but it was a tricky bit of magic, and left her crazed with adrenaline when she landed on the gentle slope of the tiled roof. She dropped to a crouch and looked back.

In the few seconds it had taken her to get onto the roof, a car had turned up the street and came to a stop in front of the cafe where the two—now three—werewolves had gathered. The light in the cafe turned off, leaving the street lit only by streetlamps and the last glow of dying daylight. A man got out of the car, standing by the opened door to talk to the werewolves. He wore a suit, as though he'd just come from a high powered office job or a fancy dinner party, and a mask, of all things. One of the wolves pointed his nose in her direction, and the man turned to look.

Rory's skin crawled as she met his gaze, even though she couldn't see his face. She rose and sprinted to the far edge of the roof, then dropped down to the lower street, using her magic to cushion her landing with a puff of wind. She turned blindly up the street and started running. It wouldn't matter which way she went now. She was positive that man had been a sorcerer. The question now was, should she spend the time and energy to try to hide—masking her scent and whatever else it would take to conceal herself—or should she conserve her energy in case it came to a magic duel?

She ducked down another alley and onto another street, this one lower still, silently cursing this haphazard, nonsensical neighborhood.

The hard part when fighting a sorcerer was that she had no way of knowing what kind of power she might be dealing with. Fighting another magic user was pretty straightforward and came down to skill and ingenuity most of the time. But a sorcerer might be either very weak or ridiculously overpowered, depending on how many people they'd slaughtered and stolen magic from. She was willing to bet this sorcerer wasn't one of the weak ones.

On the other hand, now that they had her scent and knew she was nearby, it would be next to impossible to escape without help. They knew the city. She did not. And if the woman at the cafe was any indication, she couldn't count on finding help.

Slipping into yet another narrow alley, she pulled her mirror out of her pocket. "Call Sean Kerr Leigh," she demanded. The mirror glowed faintly for a moment before going dark. She hadn't really expected him to answer, so she sent him a message instead. If the worst should happen, someone needed to know what was going on. And Sean was her nearest friend... perhaps her only true friend, she thought ruefully, since she spent so much time away from home. At any rate, he was the only one who might be able to follow up on the information here in Barra, and he would find a way to get word to the council if he had to as well.

That done, she slunk back to the mouth of the alley and looked around. She'd made up her mind while leaving the message. She wouldn't waste her energy on trying to hide. She was more than willing to fight. But she wasn't going to sit and wait for them, either. If she could keep going downhill, eventually she'd end up at Central River, and she had an idea that if she made it that far she'd have a chance to get away after all.

Darting across the street, she made for another dark slot between a couple more row houses. This time the passage dumped out into an open square with more shops and restaurants and a fountain burbling in the middle.

As she stood there, a pair of headlights flashed across her face. She flinched and ducked back. A werewolf's warning growl stopped her from turning and running back the way she'd come. He was nothing more than a shadow in the dark alley.

Rory took a long breath. *Easy. You've trained for this.*

Somehow it wasn't the same though. This wasn't Maireadd. And it felt wrong to battle werewolves. They should be on her side.

The sorcerer parked on the street leading into the square and got out. He didn't bother to stop and talk, just slammed the car door and strode toward her. Another werewolf appeared from another alley. Rory was well and truly surrounded.

Whispering in the sacred elven tongue, she summoned the elements to her, holding her magic ready in her fingers so that she'd only need to speak a word or two to command it. The elements were the simplest to wield and took the least energy. Elves might be the most versatile magical race, but they did have one slight disadvantage. Where most of the other races used their magical abilities, whatever they may be, on an instinctive, psychic level, elves commanded it using words and motion to shape their intent. Or they could use physical objects or substances to create an enchantment, like with magic mirrors. Sorcery operated much the same, but with stolen magic.

Turning suddenly, she cast a fireball at the wolf behind her. Fire was always a good bet against anything with fur. The werewolves hadn't learned anything from her last fire attack, either, because once again it caught the wolf in the side as he tried to dodge, igniting his fur and lighting up the alley. She didn't have time to see what happened to him though, as she barely jumped aside in time to miss a fireball aimed at herself. This sorcerer wasn't wasting any time.

She ducked back into the alley with the yowling, rolling werewolf and pulled a wooden handle from her pocket. After the ice dragons last winter, she'd decided she needed to be a bit more prepared. She recited the words to activate the spell she'd placed on it. A long, thin blade of ice stretched out from the hilt to form a sword. She slid her hand along the blade, murmuring an additional spell over it. Now it would deliver an electrical shock as well as a cutting edge.

She blew on her other hand and spoke a word, creating an invisible shield of air pressure that moved with her arm like a buckler.

Thus armed, she activated one last spell in her shoes that boosted her leap into the open to a soaring arc that took her halfway to the fountain in the middle of the square, and overtop a dual attack of fire and wind that the sorcerer hurled at the mouth of the alley the instant she moved. Unfortunately, her booster spell was only good for one leap. She landed in a crouch and sprinted toward the sorcerer, who conjured another fireball and accompanying blast of wind. She dodged the fire, but the wind pushed her back for a moment, blasting against her shield like a hurricane gale. It whipped the hood back from her face and howled in her ears. She shouted a command and the shield re-formed into a wedge shape, allowing her to cut through the wind toward her enemy.

A flash of movement to her right warned her of another attack by the second werewolf. She brought her ice sword up as she spun and met the wolf mid-leap with a slash across his chest. He dropped to the cobblestones bleeding and twitching. But the sorcerer used the distraction to launch a bevy of fire lances. Rory leapt over one, blocked another with her shield, and swept the last one aside with her blade, raising a hissing cloud of steam as fire and ice collided. She plunged through the steam toward him and at the last instant dropped and rolled and felt something pass over her head. A spell of some kind. He was trying to wound or capture her, not kill her. Her magical blood was no good to him if she was already dead.

From the ground she took a swipe at his legs, which he jumped back in time to escape. She rolled back to her feet and for a moment they were face-to-face. His gaze was dark and angry and he hadn't stopped chanting all during their brief battle, his voice eerie from beneath his mouthless mask, but it took till that moment for her to catch the words. He was summoning something.

He finished his spell and for a moment the square was eerily silent as if frozen in time. A few faint tendrils of mist hung above the fountain. The third werewolf, his side singed black from her earlier attack, limped quietly into view, then paused, waiting.

The earth beneath Rory's feet trembled.

"You didn't," she said. "Bastard!"

Without waiting for more she flung herself into a back flip that landed her on the lip of the fountain. Not a second too soon, either. The cobblestones where she'd been standing cracked and buckled upward and a ghastly whitish tentacle slithered up, groping along the ground for something to grab onto. Half a dozen more of the abominable things erupted as Rory sprang backward again, like the ever reaching arms of an octopus. Only instead of suckers these were covered in fine little fleshy fingers that rippled and undulated like the legs of a centipede.

One of the tentacles found the unfortunate werewolf standing by and wrapped around his paw, the fingers gripping and digging in, holding him fast. With a sudden crack the wolf's leg snapped as the monster yanked him down, pinning him against the ground. He let out a screaming howl as another tentacle emerged and wound around his body, pulling him down into the cracked earth.

Rory turned to sprint away, but the ground heaved up at her feet, throwing her off balance. A tentacle whipped out and wrapped around her ankle while another reached for her other leg. She slashed at the first one, severing it, and the ground shook with a monstrous subterranean shriek as she scrambled up and bolted away.

She heard the crackling, singing roar of a fireball and ducked, never slowing her sprint across the square as the cobblestones buckled and flew up around her, the monster keeping pace under the ground beneath her feet. Behind her, she was vaguely aware of the sorcerer chanting and swearing as he ran after her. The dark mouth of another alley presented itself and she raced into it, only to realize it ended in a brick wall with nothing but a dumpster squatting in the corner next to an overflowing heap of trash. She would have cursed her luck, but she didn't have time. Screaming a spell of her own, she cast her hands out toward the wall in a quick motion, never slowing her pace. A few paces from the wall she leapt up, her feet touching down on a shelf of pressurized air. She motioned and leapt again, higher. If she could make it to the roof...

A long, white tentacle snaked up, reaching for her. It brushed her foot as she leapt again, and distracted her enough not to realize the sorcerer was preparing another spell. A gale of wind struck her from behind halfway up, throwing her forward against the brick. Stunned, she fell.

13

HOLDING VIGIL

Sean gripped the mirror so hard for a moment he thought it might crack before he got a handle on himself and set it down.

Rory must still be in the old city center where Rylee lived. At least that was his best guess. For one wild moment he almost grabbed his helmet and went racing out there after her. But the message was from several hours ago already, and he couldn't afford to blow his cover...not for a single person. Not even a person he cared so much for. Instead he picked the mirror back up.

"Call Jack Kerr."

It took a moment, but the old man's voice and face filled the glass, sleepy and irritated until he saw Sean. Then his expression melted into concern.

"Sean? You in trouble, boy? Where are you?"

"Hey grandpa. I'm okay. But I have a friend who might be in trouble. Remember the elf I told you I gave my ring to?"

"The cute little agent?" Grandpa's bushy brows went up. While the rest of his hair had gone stark white, those eyebrows remained as black as the queen's soul.

"That's the one. She found some trouble in Barra's capital. I don't know exactly what's going on..."

"Is that where you are? In cussed Barra? Is that why you have a Barran accent all of a sudden?"

All Sean could answer was with a shrug and shake of the head, eliciting a grumble. His grandfather knew exactly what kind of work he did, but never where he was, or what his assignments were.

"Well, what do you want me to do about it?"

"Nothing, unless someone contacts you. Probably all you can do is verify the signet is real and wasn't stolen."

His grandfather clicked on a light next to the bed, momentarily blinding Sean. "You're determined to worry me into the grave, aren't you? First this job as a—"

"Don't say it."

"And now you're giving out your signet ring to elf girls," Grandpa said without missing a beat. "You know people usually only give those away to their lover."

"She's not."

"But you wish she was?" He held up a placating hand before Sean could protest. "What I'm getting at is, exactly how much does this girl mean to you? What lengths do I need to go to make sure she stays alive, if it falls to my hands?"

Sean paused, suddenly questioning his motives. Grandpa had a way of throwing him off like that, making sure he was thinking in the right direction.

"She's special," he finally admitted. "But not just to me." Quickly he recounted the incident with the unicorn, the Seer's invitation, and Rory's own admission that her loyalties were to a higher call than just her country. He kept it vague, and left out some details, but he hoped it was still enough to convince the Family patriarch.

"So what you're telling me is, the elf can't be allowed to die."

"Not if there's anything you can do to stop it at any point."

"And what about you? Do I have to look forward to getting you out of trouble too? Or having you sent home in a body bag?"

"If I mess up, I doubt anyone is going to send my body home," Sean admitted with a dark chuckle.

"You there alone?"

"Always."

Grandpa scowled. "I'm going to have to have a talk with the president. One of these times they're going to send you in alone to do a job that's meant for two men."

"Or ten," Sean muttered.

"They need to find you a new partner."

"I never had a partner," Sean countered. "Not since Academy, and that doesn't count."

"'Course it does. You need someone to watch your back."

Sean wouldn't know what to do with someone watching his back. But now, suddenly, he felt the isolation of his position pressing on him again. Seeing his grandfather's face struck longing through him like a blade.

After the brief conversation he put the mirror away, feeling more heartsick and alone than ever.

Someone to watch your back.

Sean shrugged off his dark thoughts and turned his mind back to the situation at hand. Of course his grandfather would have done anything in his power to honor the Family's signet ring anyway—otherwise why bother having one. But having his assurance that it would be honored and furthermore, that he would treat Rory's safety the same as he would have Sean's, should the need arise, was something, at least.

It must have been midnight before he gave up pacing and grabbed his helmet. He drove out to the little stone chapel by the river and pulled his bike up behind the building, in the shadow of the shrubbery bordering the graveyard. Inside, the priest, in his usual rumpled corduroy jacket, stepped out of the office to greet him.

"What can I do for you tonight, my friend?"

Sean dropped into the front pew, facing the altar, with a weary sigh. "Fix everything that's wrong with the world."

"I'm afraid that's a bit beyond my job description," the other man said, pushing his glasses up.

"Yeah. Too bad. How about a candle?"

"A candle?"

"Back home, there's this tradition. If someone you love is in trouble, you light a candle and hold vigil for them until it burns out."

The priest brought out a candle and a matchbook to light it, setting it down on the altar. He took a seat beside Sean. "God hears even a single prayer, you know. You don't have to spend the night begging Him."

"Oh, I know." Sean rubbed at his eyes, which were starting to feel gritty. He hadn't had much sleep this week. "That's not the point. It's like... a show of solidarity, you know? You don't want your friend to be alone, but you can't be with them, so you hold vigil and they know that somewhere out there someone hasn't given up on them. Or maybe they don't know, but God knows, anyhow."

The priest gave him a quizzical smile. "Maybe I should get two candles."

They sat in silence for a long time until the priest asked, "Is this about your elf friend?"

Sean nodded slowly. "I'm afraid," he admitted. "For both of us. And for a lot of other people. But yeah, tonight it's mostly her. This city is so full of evil. And she's out there, and I can't help."

"You aren't entirely alone, you know. There are other people out there too, fighting the darkness. Lighting their candles, so to speak. It can feel lonely, but you're not the only one."

"There might be one less, after tonight," Sean replied, unable to shake his grim mood, or the shadows that seemed to crowd his soul tonight. He hadn't realized how much it meant before, knowing Rory was out there somewhere with a *destiny*. He smiled a little, remembering how she'd reacted to seeing the unicorn—full of wonder and dread—and how she'd said the word destiny like it was a curse.

"Keep your despair in check," the priest warned. At Sean's sharp look he explained, "When you leave here, I mean. The city is full of evil, as you said. There are rumors of shadow rats in the streets, and worse."

"Hellhounds. I heard the rumor. Do you know anything more about it?"

"No. Only the rumors, for now. Don't worry tonight though. This is a sanctuary, is it not? Such things are not allowed to tread on holy ground. So if you ever feel despair, bring your desperation here and leave it."

"Right." A flicker of a smile touched Sean's face. He rubbed his eyes again and leaned back in the pew. On the altar, the candle burned steadily. It had hours left before it burned out. He let his gaze lose focus.

"It's ironic," the priest said, startling him out of a near doze.

"Huh?"

"Everything happening here in Barra now. It's so similar to the Curse War. Humans and magicals distrusting one another, and that distrust turning to hatred. Only instead of Barra, Thyrus, and Maireadd, all at odds, this time it's all internal, here in Barra. The hatred, the black magic, the politics..."

"Yeah." Sean blinked at the candle flame, thinking. It was during the Curse War that the Kerr family had risen to power in Thyrus, when they overthrew their king and made peace with the elves of Maireadd. Barra, with its high population of magicals, had been tearing itself apart, half the country—the humans, mostly—supporting Thyrus, while the other half—the magicals—were sympathetic to Maireadd. The country had nearly been destroyed, and even after five hundred years those hostilities hadn't entirely been erased. Now Queen Dianthe was fanning the embers, it seemed.

His mind flashed back to the book Princess Calla had been reading earlier that evening, about safe-houses and tunnels during the Curse War. Apparently the priest wasn't the only one making the connection. Were any of those old tunnels still around? And why had the princess been trying to hide what she was reading?

The candle flame guttered and began smoking as the door to the sanctuary opened, admitting a small figure in a dark hoodie. Sean almost leapt up and ran to the person, thinking it was Rory, but then she threw the hood back, and he sank down in his seat. It was a fae woman, not an elf. She shivered as she looked around for the priest, pausing when her gaze fell on Sean to give him a wary look.

"Leah?" The priest hurried to her. "What is it?"

"Something is attacking the city." She brushed a lock of plum purple hair out of her face. Another wary glance at Sean and her hair faded to a more natural brown. "I don't know what it is. It keeps shooting these—these tentacle things out of the ground like some kind of giant octopus. It's in Market Square down in Central City. It's already made a building collapse, and anyone that goes near it..." she paused and took a breath. "It pulls them into the ground. The police are there, and the military, but no one seems to know how to stop it. I can't get hold of Calla, and I didn't know where else to go."

"Well, sadly I'm not going to be much help fighting a monster—" the priest shot Sean a concerned glance "—but we can pray, right? Come back into the office and we'll get you some tea."

"They're saying an elf summoned it," the girl said as they passed Sean's pew. "You don't think that's true, do you? What would it mean? That Maireadd is declaring war? Or is it more lies?"

"Best not to rush to assumptions in these times," the priest reassured her.

As soon as they had disappeared into the office, Sean slipped out. It was still dark outside, but dawn couldn't be many hours off. He rolled the bike out of the shrubbery and had a moment's debate with himself before setting off through the dark streets.

He went home first, where he traded his helmet and jacket for a long-sleeved T-shirt, knit hat, and a pair of big biker's goggles that he never wore. But they would make a decent low-key disguise, as long as his hair stayed covered and no one spotted his bike. The helmet would have been nice, but it was too bulky and cut down his range of vision too much. He tucked his handgun into his waistband. Then he left the guest house and sneaked over to the manor.

Everyone was still sleeping, thankfully, when he let himself in. His boots were silent on the thick, expensive rug in the hallway, and he even managed to avoid bumping into the little antique table that served no practical purpose other than to display an equally antique silver tea set. There was a little door in the paneling under the stairs that looked like a closet, but it led into the basement, which had been quite the interesting place once upon a time. It had a cell and guard room off to one side, the iron bars rusty and pocked with age. The other side had been a root cellar not quite as long ago—it still smelled faintly musty like potatoes. Now his uncle used it to house his historic weapons collection. Crossbows, spiked clubs, even war hammers and battle axes. All Sean was interested in were the swords.

It was still dark when he got back on his bike and headed for Central City. He could see emergency lights flashing against the cobblestones long before he got to market square, and stopped, wheeling the bike into one of the tiny passages between buildings where it was unlikely anyone would notice it, especially before dawn.

The sword slapped him in the leg as he walked toward the commotion. Emergency vehicles lined the streets, flashing their lights. Huge floodlights had been set up around the square, and the whole thing was cordoned off several blocks away, with a crowd of gawkers standing around. He took advantage of a few unguarded alleys to get past the blockade.

The fairy had been right. One of the buildings around the square had collapsed, but there were no rescue workers around it, digging for survivors. The whole place appeared deserted, with the fountain in the middle cracked and broken but somehow still pouring water. Red and blue lights gleamed eerily in the stream and reflected in the surrounding puddle. Cobblestones had been thrown around, the ground broken up here and there.

Sean knelt in the shadows next to a bakery and placed his hand on the ground, palm flat. A faint tremor tickled his fingertips. The back of his neck prickled, but he grinned. The gorgrim was still here then.

He stood up slowly, surveying the square and the buildings around it, thinking.

A low, keening sob broke into his calculations, coming from the direction of the flattened building. It was a woman's voice, pleading wordlessly into the night. No one ran to her rescue.

Sean drew the ancient sword he'd borrowed from his uncle's collection. It was a plain one, but sharp, and the leather-wrapped grip fit nicely in his hand. *Jacobs is gonna kill me*, was his one thought as he stepped from the shadows and strode toward the fountain in the center of the square. He kept his steps measured and unhurried, adjusting his goggles so they didn't interfere with his range of vision. He must look ridiculous. He cracked another grin.

And maybe half mad.

"Hey, you there! What are you doing?!" a panicked shout from one of the police officers chased him across the square. More shouting followed, but no one dared try to stop him.

14

MONSTER SLAYER

Sean was halfway to the fountain when he felt the earth shudder under foot. "Going to come out and play?" he said, tapping the sword tip lightly on the ground as he walked.

Another shudder.

He stopped and crouched down, placing his free hand on the stones. They were vibrating. Keeping his hand where it was, he tapped the sword's pommel against a cobblestone, giving it a couple good raps.

"That's right. I'm right here."

The vibrations grew to a tremble. He drew a long breath, let it out slowly. When the tremble had turned to a rumble and become audible, he threw himself backward in a roll, flinging out his arm with the sword as he moved. It sliced cleanly through the white tentacle that burst out of the ground where he'd been standing an instant ago, drawing a subterranean screech.

"It's about time."

He let his roll carry him to his feet without ever stopping, dancing back and slashing at another groping arm that whipped out of the ground at his feet. This one had already been severed near the end and bled a pinkish ooze. He chopped the stump down even further. Another tentacle followed his footsteps, again an instant behind, and he sliced that one off too.

"We can dance all night," he called, "But you're going to run out of arms."

Three of them erupted at once this time. Whipping around him, brushing against his legs as he spun away. His sword shortened one of them while he grabbed another with his free hand, holding it back so it couldn't latch onto him and suppressing a gag at the sensation of its little fleshy fingers wriggling in his grasp. He ducked under the third as it snapped over his head. A fourth tentacle erupted suddenly and wrapped around his sword, yanking it out of hand and flinging it away.

"Bastard." He dove away, rolled, and then ran, the white tentacles snapping and curling at his heels.

The sword had come to rest against the curb by the sidewalk. He swooped to grab it without slowing, running straight at the wall of the bakery where he'd started. He took a running leap, planted a foot on the wall, then another, using his momentum to run straight up for one glorious second before shoving off in a back-flip that carried him over top of half a dozen frantic appendages. Landing squarely on his feet, he watched the building shake as the gorgrim smashed into its foundations below ground. It was coming up higher. Not long now before it broke the surface.

He swiped, almost lazily, at the nearest tentacle. The monster seemed dazed, taking a few seconds to recover from its collision, but having another arm chopped off woke it up. The ground shook. Sean backed off a few paces. It was coming up. Sooner than he'd figured, too. He adjusted his grip on the sword and reached for the pistol with his other hand, but didn't grab it yet.

A crack ran up the bakery wall, then an instant later the sidewalk buckled as a mound of pale flesh shoved upward.

Several screams rang across the square, reminding Sean that he had an audience. Not how he preferred to work, but it couldn't be helped. He backed away a few more steps.

The gorgrim broke through the ground like a breaching whale, tossing rocks and coming to rest with a belly flop in the open, in all its hideous glory. Searchlights swept over the mottled flesh—Sean hadn't noticed that they'd been joined by a helicopter—casting even more hideous shadows across the square.

The beast had no eyes. Shaped roughly like a squid, its dozen or so tentacles swarmed around a gaping central mouth while the rest of its blob of a body quivered like half-melted gelatin. Worst of all, its hide was translucent, allowing him to see its insides and what it had recently ingested—in this case, half a dozen humans.

Heat flashed through Sean, followed by cold. He was almost sick right there on the spot. But stopping to puke would have meant he joined the others, distorted and half digested.

The beast's hide had to be a lot tougher than it looked, to be able to move as fast as it did underground. Best not to try killing it that way. Its lack of eyes was disturbing, too. He couldn't put a bullet or stick a blade through an eye socket that wasn't there. He'd have to go directly through its mouth, which meant getting past all those lashing appendages swirling around it like a nest of worms. At least some of them had been severely shortened.

If the gorgrim hunted by sensing vibrations in the ground, then it could likely sense them in the air as well. Since he was standing perfectly still, it hadn't made a move toward him, even though he wasn't more than a few steps away.

"Whoo. Here goes."

He ran and swung the sword in a powerful arc that sliced through two more tentacles, but a third whipped out and cracked him across the stomach like a club, knocking the wind out of him and sending him flying. His head smacked against the stones, stunning him, and for a moment he lay there disoriented, struggling to pull in a breath. It came finally, in a half strangled gasp, and then he was panting and coughing and grappling for the sword that had fallen from his hand. Shouts of dismay and calls of encouragement from the crowd rang across the square, surreal in the awful moment. The stink of dirt and rot stung his nose.

His hand closed around the sword's hilt at the same second a tentacle wrapped around his leg. It jerked him backward, scraping across the broken paving stones toward the gaping hole of a mouth. The sword clanked along with him, gripped tightly in his fist.

Twisting sharply, he swiped at the tentacle gripping his leg. The angle was all wrong and he couldn't cut it off without flaying his leg open, but he managed to sheer off dozens of its gross little fingers. The gorgrim screeched its rage and suddenly Sean was whipping through the air, flung upward and about to be brought down and cracked open on the stones in another second. He hacked viciously at the coiled tentacle around his leg and this time cut through—he felt the bite of the blade along his shin a half second before it dropped him. Twisting in mid air, he landed on his knees on the gorgrim's head and drove the sword into it. The thick hide resisted at first, as he'd thought it would, but the blade was sharp and once he brought his full weight to bear it pierced through. He pulled the sword free and leapt clear as the monster bucked and screamed. It wasn't paying him much attention now, so this time he walked right up to it, pulling his gun, and put all fifteen rounds into the open maw. A tentacle whipped past his head and he ducked, but the beast was done. Its thrashes were those of a creature dying.

Sean turned and walked away.

By the time he made it back to where he'd parked the bike it was dawn and he was limping. His leg and his head were both bleeding and throbbing, though neither was bad.

He took off the hat and goggles and packed them in the saddlebag. Then he pulled out a bandanna to quickly bind around his pant leg. On the way home he stopped and tossed the hat and goggles into the river. Then he stood there and watched the sunrise for a moment, as it turned the river's oily black surface to sparkling gold. The best time to enjoy a sunrise was always after a battle, when he felt truly alive. This morning, though, the effect was dampened as he thought about the gorgrim and its belly full of bodies. Had Rory been one of them? Would he ever know? Was he truly alone, now?

It was fully light by the time he slunk home, praying no one noticed. He cleaned the sword first thing and stashed it under his mattress. He'd have to return it later. Then he cleaned his leg and wrapped it properly. It had mostly stopped bleeding, as had his head. The hat had sopped up most of the blood. The rest washed out in the shower. He had the beginnings of a bruise right at his hairline, but there wasn't much he could do about that. Thankfully today was his day off. He fell into bed and passed out the second his face hit the pillow.

Five minutes later someone banged on the door.

Sean whimpered into the pillow. It did nothing to stop the racket. His whole body protested as he dragged himself out of bliss and scrounged a pair of jeans off the floor. They might have been from two days ago.

He yanked the door open so hard it wrenched his bruises and he swore, then snarled. "What?!"

"Geez. Don't bite my head off," Lina said. "What's wrong with you?"

"I have people banging my door down when I just went to sleep. So whatever you need, please..." he gestured for her to speak.

She scowled. "Dad sent me over to get you. He said you'd want to come watch the news with him this morning. There was some craziness last night. An elf summoned a monster that attacked Central City. You gotta see it."

15

THE SIGNET RING

Rory woke up levitating.

She screamed and flailed, only to find that she'd been gagged and cuffed, and was hanging above the dumpster where she'd fallen. She must have grazed her head against the side of it.

"Hold still or I'm going to drop you," the sorcerer warned. "Trust me, you don't want that."

Wide-eyed above the gag, she stopped struggling and took stock of her situation.

The sorcerer had bound and gagged her during the few seconds she must have been dazed. Now he was levitating her out of the dumpster. More alarming were the half dozen white tentacles thrust up through the ground around them, waving impatiently. Somehow he was keeping the gorgrim that he'd summoned in check as well.

Without her hands or her voice Rory couldn't access her magic. All she could do was wait until the sorcerer settled her on the ground. He grabbed her arm and hauled her upright, then shoved her along in front of him. The gorgrim trailed them, making the ground tremble and sending up expectant tentacles through the earth, waiting for its chance. She held her breath until they got back to the car and he pushed her roughly into the back seat. She wanted to ask about the monster as they drove away—was he just going to leave it to terrorize the city?

Twisting around in the seat as they pulled out, she saw the tentacles in the light of the streetlamps, like eerie, bony fingers thrust up from someone's grave. They sank back into the earth as they drove away. Her guts clenched.

"Call Queen Dianthe," the sorcerer said as he drove. He must have a magic mirror up there. A moment later a woman's musical voice filled the car.

"Well? I hope it was worth it, leaving in the middle of dinner like that. It was very awkward."

"It was worth it. I'm bringing you a prize. An elf."

The queen fairly purred. "All is forgiven, then. Best not to bring her directly to the palace, though. Take her to the military base. I'll meet you there. I'm sure she's a spy anyway."

"As you wish, my queen. There was one small glitch."

"Oh?"

"My werewolves failed me. I had to summon a gorgrim to get her."

"Your wolves failed you? You mean you have no idea how to actually fight a magic duel and hold your own." She laughed, and it wasn't a nice sound. "All that magic, and you barely know how to use it."

"She's well trained, my queen."

Not well trained enough, Rory thought ruefully, jerking against the cuffs. *It would have been useful if they taught me how to pick a lock without magic. I'll bet Sean knows how to pick locks. Stupid elves.*

"No matter. We can use that to our advantage too. We'll just blame the gorgrim attack on the elf."

A few minutes later they pulled up to a high chain link fence topped with razor wire, and two guards came up to the windows, shining lights into the car. Rory blinked and squinted.

"I caught this elf prowling around the city," the sorcerer said without removing his mask. He jerked a thumb in her direction. "She summoned a gorgrim before I could stop her. I've contacted the queen, and she's supposed to join us here."

One of the guards shined a light on Rory, then on the masked sorcerer. "We'll get you an escort."

Ten minutes later they were marching down a dingy hall in the bowels of the base. Two guards took charge of Rory, while the sorcerer was escorted into another room. They took her into a little room with a single chair and a mirror—no doubt an observation window—and nothing else. Fluorescent lights shone dully on cement block walls. The female guard searched her thoroughly, tossing the few items she had on her person into a bin. Rory cringed when they took Sean's ring, but perhaps it would help her. It was about the only hope she had for getting out of here alive, unless she caught a lucky break somehow and could figure a way out of her handcuffs or gag. Either one. Didn't even need to be both.

The woman replaced her handcuffs with zip ties, keeping her hands secured behind her back. Then she took the bin with Rory's things out of the room while her partner took up station by the door, his gun trained on Rory, who returned his gaze silently. She tested the zip ties. They had even less wiggle room than the cuffs. No doubt that was the idea. She tried the gag next, but it was thick and tight and there was no wiggling it loose, either. So she sat and waited, and prayed.

A short while later the door opened and a woman strode in, accompanied by a senior officer. With her signature auburn curls, stylish dress, and predatory gaze, Rory recognized queen Dianthe.

"Well, look at you," the queen purred. She turned to the man. "Take her gag off, colonel."

His lips tightened briefly, but he strode over and began working on the knot in her gag. "Answer her Majesty's questions, and nothing more. If you whisper, or your lips so much as twitch, my sergeant over there will put a bullet in your brain. Understand?"

She nodded.

The gag fell away and she tried to work the moisture back into her mouth without looking like she was mumbling a spell. The colonel stepped back and nodded to the queen.

"You're from Maireadd. No question there," Dianthe began, smirking. "So, did you find your ambassador? I assume that's what you were here for."

"Yes. I found her."

The queen's sculpted eyebrows twitched upward briefly. "And what other kinds of information were you looking to bring back to your council?"

"None."

"Who did you talk to while you were here?"

Rory didn't respond.

The queen drew near. "You're an elf mage, so you know what I'm capable of with just a little bit of magic." She murmured under her breath and reached out to touch a single finger to Rory's neck.

Pain arced through Rory, so fierce and so sudden it took her breath away. And then it was gone—too quickly to even scream. She huddled in the chair, gasping and disoriented.

"That was a tiny sample of what I'm capable of, so you'd better tell me the truth, elf. Who did you see while you were here?"

When Rory still didn't respond, the queen slapped her across the face. She didn't even use magic. Just a good old-fashioned slap.

"Answer me!"

Rory didn't. She looked from the queen to the young sergeant covering her with the gun, to the colonel. The colonel looked stoic, but his young officer seemed uncomfortable, chewing his lip.

Dianthe turned away and spoke to the colonel. "I will send some of my people over to get her in the morning. We'll deal with her at the palace."

That didn't sound good. Rory twitched involuntarily against the zip ties.

The colonel cleared his throat. "Your Highness, remember the signet ring we found on her. It might be wise to be cautious about—"

"She's an elf and a spy. I don't care who's protecting her. And I don't appreciate being questioned."

The colonel nodded, but she was already clacking out the door on her ridiculous high heels. He turned back to Rory and replaced her gag, wearing a pucker between his gray brows.

"Sir?" the young sergeant ventured once the door had slammed shut behind the queen, "What happens now?

That's a bad thing, isn't it? Hurting someone that's protected by one of the Families?"

"It's bad," the colonel admitted with a sigh. "Probably even worse than killing an elven ambassador or blaming Maireadd for a gorgrim attack."

"What are we going to do? Just let Her Majesty get us into a war?"

"Mm. We'll see. Keep an eye on our elf."

The colonel followed the queen out, leaving Rory and her guard to stare at one another some more.

Rory was tired. Her head ached dully, her mouth felt dry and her jaws sore from the gag Her arms hurt from being held behind her, and she smelled like the dumpster. She wanted nothing more than to go to sleep, but that wasn't going to happen any time soon.

The door opened suddenly behind the guard, making both of them jump.

The colonel was back. This time it wasn't the queen who accompanied him, but a younger woman. Her blonde hair was pulled back into a hasty ponytail and she wore ripped jeans and an oversized hoodie. Princess Calla, if Rory wasn't mistaken. Another man followed her in. Her bodyguard, perhaps. She stepped right up to Rory and removed her gag.

"Your Highness," said Rory.

"That's right. And you are?"

"Rory Scout, of Maireadd."

"What brings you to Barra, Rory?"

"Looking for our ambassador."

The princess stuck her hands in the back pockets of her jeans and leaned back a bit. "Did you find her?"

"She's dead. I was trying to find out what happened. I didn't summon that gorgrim."

Calla's lips flattened briefly. "My people tell me you're a spy."

Rory didn't comment on that. She watched the other woman while following the bodyguard with her ears as he paced. He was a werewolf, she guessed, and after her recent encounter with others of his kind, she couldn't feel comfortable with him prowling around the room. Perhaps it spoke well of the princess, that she was willing to hire a magical, and also trust him to protect her. Or perhaps he was another mercenary, willing to work for anyone, be they a sorcerer or a princess.

"You were also carrying a signet ring from one of the most powerful Families still in existence."

Rory's heart fluttered a bit—that must be why they had called the princess here, rather than just wait for the queen to send her people—but she only shrugged.

Calla sighed and rubbed her head, glancing at her werewolf. "All right then. Tell me why I should let you go and not let Dianthe have you."

"The elves haven't been enemies to Barra in a long time," Rory answered slowly.

"They haven't been friends, either."

"But do you want them for enemies? Because that is the path you're walking now. Anyway, I've heard about you, your Highness. They say you aren't like the others, and that you believe in your people, whether human or magical."

"You're not one of my people," Calla countered.

"The ambassador should have been under your protection, and now she's dead. Maireadd will only stand for so many insults."

"And the Kerr family for even fewer, it seems," Calla shot back. "We verified the signet ring you carry. The Family patriarch was adamant that we let you go *or else*. What is your connection to them?"

"I can't say."

Calla replied with an annoyed sigh. She opened her hand, which she'd held closed since she came into the room, and let a gold chain slide through her fingers. Sean's ring dangled, swinging, at the end of it. Rory could almost feel the familiar, comforting weight of it, the delicate pattern etched in the stone, and her fingers twitched to hold it again.

"You're in an interesting position, you know," said the princess. "A Maireadd spy carrying the Kerr family seal. As you said, Barra is flirting with hostility between ourselves and Maireadd, which should make you an enemy. But since you've also been claimed by the Kerrs, you're not only under their protection, but you speak for them, as well. Meaning that every insult or act of aggression you commit is done in their name, as well as Maireadd's. And every insult or act of aggression done to you is done to them. It's sort of like tiptoeing around a war with two countries at your back, not just one. Are the elves and Families allied now? Are they conspiring to stamp us out?"

"Not to my knowledge, Highness," Rory answered, her heart fluttering. Had Sean really handed her all of that, when he'd given her his signet ring?

Calla gazed at her for a long moment. "Perhaps we can help one another."

* * * * *

Calla had to confer with the colonel, but soon Rory was free and following them out into the cool night. The fresh air had never smelled so sweet, even tainted by asphalt and exhaust fumes. Somewhere in the distance a chorus of sirens wailed. None of them said much as they piled into Calla's tiny sports car and left the compound.

"Have I put you in danger?" Rory asked when the silence stretched.

"No more so than usual, I don't imagine," Calla said as they drove. They'd reached an older section of the city by then. "I was just thinking. Dianthe will come looking for you as soon as she knows we got you out. You won't be safe till you're back in Maireadd. But there was something I was hoping you could help us with before you left." She slotted the car into a spot in a back alley, killed the engine, and turned to face Rory. She had to lean around the bodyguard, who sat in the middle, and whom she'd introduced as Jamie. "Here's the thing. We have a sorcerer in the city—you met him, I think—and he's got werewolves working for him. Scent trails have become an issue, and he goes masked and has figured out how to block his own scent, so we can't identify him. If you are able to create a spell that can mask your scent like he can, and would be willing to help us, then we can hide you here for the day. If not, then you better not get out of the car. We'll drive straight to Maireadd tonight, and hope Dianthe hasn't already heard that you're missing and called in roadblocks."

Rory tensed at mention of the sorcerer. Well, she wasn't the only one having trouble with him then. At least Calla would have fewer werewolves to worry about now. Which reminded her of the gorgrim the sorcerer had summoned. Was that the reason for the sirens and commotion out there? She was afraid to ask.

"I can do scent blocking," she said finally, rubbing Sean's ring as she thought. "I'll need a few things if you want a spell that lasts, though."

After a bit more discussion, and after Rory had blocked her own scent, they got out and hurried to the shop.

"I'll let you clean up a bit, as long as you make it quick," Calla said as she unlocked the back door and let them in. "Then we need to get you hidden. This is the first place Dianthe will look for you."

Rory got a glimpse of the shop as they hustled her upstairs to Calla's apartment. They stayed only long enough for her to get a fast shower and for Calla to gather a bundle of food and water for her, then it was back downstairs, between rows of books of every size and color lined up on elegant wooden shelves. Calla led the way down into the basement, where she moved aside a pile of boards and some shelving and opened a door that had been invisible in the brick wall. She and Jamie left Rory there and hurried back upstairs, where Dianthe's people were already arriving.

Alone for the first time in what felt like a week, Rory settled back against the cold brick wall of the tiny hidden room. She couldn't help feeling like she'd traded one prison for another, but this time at least she was free of guards and able to use her magic. She summoned a light so she could make sure she wasn't sitting with any spiders, and caught her breath for what felt like the first time all night. She wasn't out of danger yet, for the queen would still be looking for her, and then there was her promise to Calla and Jamie to help them with their werewolf problem. But for now she was content to rest and nibble on the snacks Calla had given her.

The hiding place was barely big enough to stand up, and only a few paces long, and she could stand and touch both walls without extending her arms all the way. There was an old trunk in one corner with surprisingly clean blankets, so rather than spend magical energy she might need soon by warming the room, she contented herself with wrapping up in a blanket and hunkering down in a corner. Then she pulled out her magic mirror, which Calla had returned.

"Call Sean Kerr Leigh."

16

THE SEER'S GALA

"What happened to you?" Uncle Arden asked as Sean sank gingerly onto the couch.

"Laid my bike down last night," he lied, touching the new bruise on his head.

"You're going to kill yourself on that thing." Arden turned back to the television. Clearly the continuous news coverage of the monster downtown was more interesting than Sean's supposed minor motorcycle accident. "Get a load of this. They've been replaying it all morning." He turned up the volume as video of Sean's battle with the gorgrim began to play. It switched between aerial footage from the helicopter and some captured from the ground. Thankfully both were too far away to be good quality.

"This guy is crazy," Arden said, leaning forward, his gaze glued to the screen.

Sean's hand tightened on the arm rest of the couch as he watched himself on television. He did look crazy in the video. And kinda awesome.

"Who is he?" he asked, wincing as he watched himself get knocked down and bash his head on the ground. It looked like it hurt, and he held his breath waiting for himself to get back up again as a tentacle groped toward him.

"No one knows," his uncle said. "But he's got a sword. Can you believe that? I don't know if that makes him brilliant, or an idiot. Oh here. Watch this."

Sean was watching, reliving the battle as a spectator. It was a new experience, and surprisingly stressful.

"They're saying an elf summoned the monster. I don't know why an elf would want to, though. The military is saying it could be an act of terrorism. Maireadd trying to restart the war. I don't know why they'd do that. But I guess they've never been friendly to humans."

"Did they say what happened to the elf?"

"No, nothing on that. Man, look at this guy fight."

The video was replaying again. This time in slow motion.

Sean brooded mostly in silence as his uncle gave commentary on the commentary. The anti-elf spin the media was putting on the event worried him. Even his uncle, who wasn't anti-magical, was getting his feathers ruffled. The priest was right. This was turning into the Curse War all over again.

And where did that leave him, and the job he was sent to Barra to do? What good would it be to eliminate the witch queen or any of their corrupt rulers, if the populace was already turning against itself? But that was the whole point, wasn't it? Dianthe saw the elves as enemies. As non-people. If she could make everyone else see them that way as well, then no one would lift a finger to stop her. She could offer a bounty for them and other magicals, even. Would she eventually invade Maireadd itself, and collect elves to use as magic batteries?

He excused himself as soon as he dared and slunk back to the guest house. Even with everything he had to be worried about, he fell into bed, passed out again almost instantly, and didn't wake up until late in the afternoon. By that time his bruises were stiffening. He did a few light stretches and then checked his phone and mirror for messages.

One message waited for him. From Rory. His pulse raced in his ears as he waited for it to play.

"Hey, Sean, I just wanted to let you know I'm okay. I'm with Princess Calla right now. She's got some kind of hideout in her basement." Rory paused. He could see the dimly lit brick wall behind her, but her eyes held his attention. They were deep and mercurial. "You saved my life tonight. It looks like the Barran military is far more concerned about earning the ire of Family Kerr than that of Maireadd. I'm not sure how to feel about that, honestly. Calla said some interesting things about having a signet ring... things you forgot to mention, apparently. Anyway, the princess asked me for a favor, so once that's done I'll be headed back to Maireadd. I'll see you soon, at the gala. I wish we didn't have to wait that long. And thanks." She stared into her mirror for a moment before deactivating it.

Sean held his mirror in his hands, even after the message ended and it went blank, thinking, and wondering why his heart hurt. Slowly he replaced the mirror in the drawer. The gala was only a few weeks away now. Did he even dare go? Dianthe was already looking at him suspiciously just for talking to the Seer at court.

This new twist on Princess Calla was interesting, too. She cared enough to sneak an elf away behind her stepmother's back, and even had a secret room in her basement? He remembered that book she'd been looking at in the library, about Barra's hidden tunnels. Perhaps there was more to the princess than he'd thought—which was great. But her family couldn't be entirely ignorant of her divergent views. And that meant he had better not get too friendly with her or her werewolf, since he couldn't afford any more suspicion.

* * * * *

During the next few weeks Sean kept his head down, worked hard, hit the social scene more than he'd like, and counted the days till the gala, praying nothing would blow up in the meantime. Colonel Jacobs saw the news coverage of the gorgrim attack and guessed that the "Monster Slayer," as he was being called, was Sean, and reamed him out thoroughly. Sean and Rory found little excuses to leave messages for each other every few days, even though they shouldn't.

On the morning of the gala he started for the coast early, arriving in time for the afternoon ferry over to the island. There was no sign of Rory on the ferry, and his heart sank. But there were other boats crossing the channel. He just hoped she'd been able to make it through Barra again without incident.

The ferry didn't land at the island's southern coast, which faced mainland Barra across the channel. That side was all jagged rock shores and steep sandstone bluffs, though there were a few private docks there. Instead it circled to the east, where the beach was gentler, and docked by the Isle of Selkies only town—a little seaside village that catered to tourists. A battered pickup truck—again, likely the only thing of its kind on the island, since the residents mostly used ATVs—was there to shuttle guests to the gala. Sean rode in the bed of the pickup with a couple of selkie guys and a fairy who all looked at him suspiciously.

They bounced along gravel and dirt roads back toward the south side of the island where the Seer's mansion perched on the edge of the bluff overlooking the channel. The pickup dropped them off, then turned around and headed back for the last few guests. Sean stood on the broad gravel path that led around the mansion toward a garden patio off to the side and tugged his sleeves straight, touched Rory's light crystal that rested on its chain under his shirt, then headed for the house.

He made a couple laps around the patio and saw nothing of Rory, so he went in. Glass patio doors stood open to a vast banquet hall and adjoining ballroom. Still no sign of Rory. He saw no one else he knew in the growing crowd, either, and by that time most of the guests had arrived, so he wandered into the banquet hall where there were fewer people. A little bell chimed in the other room and the low murmur of conversation stilled as someone spoke. He caught a bit of it. Enough to know it was a greeting and an invitation to head to the dining room.

There was no seating directory, so mild chaos ensued as everyone circled the room, looking for their places. Most of them laughed and smiled as they maneuvered around one another, and the crowd's edgy energy loosened into general merriment. Sean wandered through the room longer than most looking for his table, and was beginning to suspect he had somehow been forgotten, when he finally ventured near one of the circular tables that was set a little apart from the others, semi-isolated behind a big planter with a bunch of ferns. Princess Calla and her werewolf were seated there, along with another woman he didn't know, and he was going to walk past and make another round, but the princess waved him over.

"You're with us tonight, Mr. Leigh," she said.

He approached the table and bowed. "Your Highness."

"Just Calla," she corrected.

"Jamie." They exchanged a nod.

The other woman introduced herself as Kiah of Lomasi, heir to the Lomasi selkie clan matriarchy. Kiah was a dark, sunkissed and curvy beauty, with kind eyes and an open, friendly smile. Sean's attention was drawn away halfway through the introductions, however, when he spotted Rory at long last. For a moment he didn't recognize the elf—used as he was to seeing her dressed casually or for the outdoors. Tonight she wore a silvery gray gown, almost the exact shade as her eyes, that shimmered as she moved. A long slit up one side of it showed off a generous amount of her thigh every time she took a step. Her black hair was done up in some kind of elaborate braid like a crown around her head, showing off her expressive ears.

Her gaze went around the table, snagging a moment on Kiah before she nodded to Jamie and Calla, then finally catching Sean's eye. Not a flicker of expression hinted at recognition, except that her cheeks flushed slightly before she looked away.

Sean could only hope he looked that indifferent, with his heart racing and his stomach squirming.

Once Rory sat down, Calla said, "It looks like we're just waiting on Mr. Blaine, whoever he is."

Sean glanced at the place card beside him. Who was he, indeed? The Seer had placed the princess, the selkie heir, and two secret agents from two different countries all at the same table. Since it was the Seer, was it somehow intentional? And if so, what was special about Dylan Blaine?

"Maybe this is him," said Kiah.

A young man approached, in his twenties, maybe, dressed stylishly in black slacks and a black dress shirt. He had darkish-blond hair and brown eyes, and he looked nervous.

Sean started drumming his fingers under the table. Twenties, blond, brown eyes, dressed in black... *He's the weapon.*

The guy didn't look like much. Medium height and build, reasonably athletic, probably decent looking if you were into guys. So what was his secret?

Dylan gave Calla a half bow before sliding into his seat between Sean and Kiah. He didn't quite meet anyone's gaze as they made the final round of introductions, and his anxiety was so palpable it even made Sean feel jumpy.

"Mr. Blaine, please tell me you're one of the publishing empire Blaines," the princess said.

A conversation about books and authors ensued, mostly between Kiah and Calla grilling the stranger. But being a writer or publisher didn't seem like something that would bring this man to the soothsayer's attention. Or maybe it was, depending on what he was writing. Sean watched him doubtfully. He didn't seem like much of a revolutionary.

Rory caught his eye and furrowed her brows slightly, shifting her gaze between him and Dylan as though to ask why he was studying this stranger so intently. Sean raised his brows in return, and suddenly became aware of Dylan watching them. He cleared his throat, tried to think of something to say, and drew a blank.

"Did you have trouble traveling from Maireadd?" Calla asked Rory, and thankfully the conversation and attention diverted.

The first course of their meal came out, a delicate chowder with crab and halibut that must have been caught that morning. Creamy, but light—suddenly he found himself wishing he could meet the Seer's chef. That desire only grew with each course. It wasn't often you found food good enough to calm anxiety and bolster goodwill, but between courses the volume of laughter and conversation kept getting louder. He wondered idly whether, if he were to serve good food on the street corners of Barra, it would have the same effect.

"Does anyone know why we have our own private table in the corner?" Jamie asked when dessert had finally been served, his gaze fixed across the room where the Seer was going from table to table greeting people.

"I assumed it was because of the princess," Rory said. One of her ears kept swiveling, following the Seer's progress through the room.

Sean glanced from Calla to the Seer, who was nearly to their table. Would he explain what all this was about?

"Don't look at me," Calla protested. "I didn't request this. And I'll be furious if I find out I was singled out, again. Politely furious, of course."

"You could always ask him," Kiah said as the Seer approached. But they all fell silent.

"Good evening, my friends." The Seer beamed at them. "I hope you're all enjoying yourselves."

"It's lovely," Calla said. "Though I believe we all have a few questions."

"I've been told I raise more questions than I ever answer, and that it's infuriating, so ask at your own risk." He held up a hand. "But let me make proper introductions first."

"But we've already..." Calla began.

"Met, yes. I know. And shared pleasantries. But that will not be enough to get each of you through the coming months."

"What?" said Calla.

Sean shifted uncomfortably, sharing a glance with Rory.

"Princess Calla, for instance," the Seer went on, smiling fondly at her. "You own a bookstore, an act of rebellion against your father and step-mother, whose policies you vehemently disagree with. From there you organize escapes for citizens who are in danger from the witch-queen's thirst for power."

Calla blushed and sputtered.

"Jamie Quinn is a bit of a vigilante. How many magicals have you rescued now? Congratulations on making the queen's most wanted list, by the way, and nice touch working for the princess under her nose."

The Seer, unaffected by Jamie's fierce scowl, moved on.

"Sean Kerr Leigh."

Sean barely had time to get nervous before the Seer called his name. His full name, no less. His heart dropped into his stomach. "Please don't."

17

CONFESSIONS

"What Mr. Leigh doesn't want you to know is that he's a spy and occasional assassin, Thyrus's last answer against a war with Barra which, frankly, would be catastrophic. He's been keeping an eye on things for several months now, and is another one working under the queen's nose, even as she searches for his identity."

If there had been silence around the table before, now it was a silence that was a physical weight. Sean could feel their gazes on him—especially Princess Calla's. Nothing like announcing he'd been sent to murder her family. He stared straight ahead, afraid to meet her gaze, as his stomach tried to tie itself in knots. Was this the end of his assignment, then? That he'd have to go home in failure? And could they even send in a replacement after this?

The Seer didn't leave him time to stew, fortunately, before he moved on to his next victim.

"Elf Auralie is a spy as well, for the elf council. And a guide, of course. She and the council have had eyes on Barra for a while now as well, and with good reason. Last time something like this happened, Maireadd was cursed and the world hasn't been the same since."

Rory seemed unconcerned that the Seer had spilled her secrets. She wore a faint smile as she glanced at Sean.

"Kiah of house Lomasi."

Kiah jumped.

"Kiah doesn't have many secrets. Heir to her clan's matriarchy, she's a princess to her own people. She also made a bet with her sister tonight. Dylan, you might want to ask her about that." When Kiah groaned he said, "I'm sorry, my dear. I couldn't resist. And I gave you a very nice advantage here with the seating arrangements. I hope you appreciate it."

"Far be it from me to question your wisdom, oh embarrassing one!"she laughed.

The Seer turned lastly to Dylan Blaine, and Sean forgot his own problems for a moment to see what the man's big secret might be.

"Dylan Blaine," the Seer said more gently than he had to the others. "I would never have brought you here if I intended harm. There are difficult times coming for everyone at this table, including you. But you can help. The time for hiding is past."

Dylan shuddered visibly.

"Dylan Blaine of Blaine Publishing Group. You may also know him by one of his pen names. Shannon Whittaker or Darren Anderson."

Well, that tidbit of information certainly excited the girls, but it didn't help Sean much. So the guy was secretly a writer. Had he misjudged? Was there someone else here tonight that fit the soothsayer's description? But the Seer wasn't finished.

"That's not the secret he's so terrified of anyone finding out though. Dylan is an empath."

Sean sucked in a silent gasp. There it was. He let the conversation flow around him for a moment, half listening as he mulled over this new information. An empath could indeed be considered a weapon. Especially a powerful one. And there were only three or four of them born to every generation in the entire world. Unfortunately for them, their insights were so valuable and sought after by rulers and really anyone else that they were often enslaved or blackmailed into serving others. There was a high suicide rate among them. If Queen Dianthe got her hands on Dylan, it would be bad for the country and even worse for him.

The Seer moved on from their table after advising them all to exchange contact information. He left behind an awkward silence.

Then Rory laughed. "I wonder if they have to take lessons for that. Like, to be an official seer you have to learn how to be infuriatingly vague first?"

That helped ease a little of the tension around the table. Till Calla turned to Sean and said, "Please tell me you weren't sent here to assassinate my family."

"Uh..." Sean cleared his throat awkwardly. "No, Princess. Assassinating your family is not my mission—at least not for now. It was only ever to be considered as the absolute last resort. And even then...Well, it's your step-mother Dianthe that's the witch. It's been a matter of debate as to how many of the bad policies coming down are hers alone, or whether she has your father in her thrall."

Calla was silent for a time before she sighed and said, "You saw him at dinner a few weeks ago. It's like my father isn't there anymore—and I have no idea whether whatever she's done to him can be undone. It's been so long..." She drifted into silence. No one at the table spoke for a long moment, but Dylan was watching her intently. "Well, empath, what do you see?" she asked suddenly, turning to him.

"I don't see things," he retorted. "That would be the Seer's realm of expertise. What I *sense* is the loss of your father and brother—I'm assuming to Dianthe's influence—and your fear that it's too late for them. Well, for your father. You seem more hopeful about Prince Gaelan. You resent the thing that's made you feel the loss of their love, again I'd guess that would be the queen." He turned to Sean. "But she's not mad at you, so relax."

"You got all that just from my emotions?"

Rory, who was watching this curiously, said, "The elf council would love to get their hands on you."

"So would everyone else," said Calla.

"He's dangerous," said Jamie, the first he'd spoken for most of the evening.

Sean caught Rory's eye while the others' attention was diverted. She sat at the place next to him, yet still seemed infuriatingly out of reach. Since the Seer had spilled their most dangerous secrets, did it matter any more whether the others knew that he and Rory were friends?

Apparently she was thinking along the same line, for she smirked at him. She found his hand under the table and gave it a squeeze.

Sean felt himself blush.

"Who else knows about you?" she asked Dylan, turning back to the conversation as though nothing had happened.

Sean missed whatever the answer was, too busy studying the wisps of black hair at the nape of her neck that had escaped her braids. She was facing Dylan and the others, but had her ear swiveled toward Sean.

When Dylan excused himself to get some fresh air a few minutes later, Calla turned to Sean. "What are your plans?" she asked bluntly.

"I'm not sure yet." They watched each other, while the others at the table watched them. Could he really trust them all? Did he have a choice now?

Rory squeezed his hand under the table. "Remember the unicorn?" she said. She recounted their encounter at Midwinter for the others, and how they'd been hunted briefly.

"You were right, you know," Sean said. "There was a soothsayer. He must have seen something about us, but he still doesn't know our identities, or at least not mine." Then in turn he told them about the conversation he'd overheard several weeks earlier.

Calla looked the most grim with the news. "We're all in danger then. Especially Dylan. And you, Sean, if they figure out what you are. Goodness knows Dianthe is already out to get me, one way or another. If she sent both Beck and her sister Lyselle, you'd better believe she's serious. How long do you plan on staying in Barra?" she asked him. "Or should I say—how long until you finish your mission?"

Sean shrugged and shook his head. "So far I've just been keeping an eye on things. Thyrus is prepared to do anything within its power to shift the political crises they see coming to Barra. I've been looking for some way to do that. If all else fails and it's the only way, I will..." he paused, struggling to get the words out into the open. "I will kill whoever I need to."

Silence followed his confession. Calla chewed her lips, her face turning a bit blotchy as though she was fighting tears. They waited until she regained control.

"I understand," she said finally, her voice steady. "But you do know that Dianthe won't be easy to kill."

"I know."

When Dylan came back a few minutes later and announced that he'd seen Beck, the queen' assassin, lurking outside, the mood around the table, already subdued, became somber, as this confirmed so many of their fears.

"They'll be suspicious of anyone that was invited tonight," Jamie said.

"Probably." This from Rory. "But it seems like most of the people here are just here for a fancy party. It might look suspicious because of who's hosting, but if there's nothing going on, beyond our little meeting back here, then there's not much for them to find out. We're just six more guests."

"There are a lot of magicals here," Kiah pointed out.

"I should think that would be expected. He is a seer, after all."

Sean shook his head. "If they're suspicious of him to begin with, then even normal activities would be suspect. They'll be trying to read intrigue into everything he does, no matter how innocent."

Silence settled over the table, even while music struck up from the ballroom. Through the wide doors they could see couples waltzing across the dance floor.

"Your assassin has a weakness," said Dylan. For a moment Sean thought he was talking about him, but the other man was watching the dancers. Beck, then.

Following his gaze, Calla's brows crinkled. "A fae?"

"Look, the Seer is right," Sean said. "Things have been getting bad, but they're going to get a lot worse. We all need allies. Normally I'd be the last person to say it, but we were brought here for a reason. I'd guess we've all been feeling pressure lately, and if we're going to get through whatever's coming next, we need to trust each other. Am I wrong?" He looked around at each of them.

Dylan broke the following uneasy silence. "People tend to think empaths are invading their privacy, just by being what we are. And we're not infallible. Not to mention you'd have to trust me in order to trust my opinion on something. All that to say that I'm wary of making myself useful. But if you all want to know what I've been picking up from everyone..."

Sean nodded for him to continue.

"From what I can tell, we all have our own motivations when it comes to helping Barra. Some of them lean toward altruism and loyalty, while others are more personal or professional. But from everything I've sensed from the five of you tonight, I think you're all trustworthy. At least I hope so, since my life depends on it."

"And mine," said Sean. "So what do you all think? Exchange contacts? Who's got phones and who's got magic mirrors?"

They exchanged information, then Dylan and Kiah slipped away to the dance floor. Rory rose as well.

"I'm going to see the Seer's gardens. It's a beautiful evening." She glanced at Sean meaningfully, then turned and sashayed toward the open patio doors.

"Better go after her, Sean *Kerr*." Calla said, raising an eyebrow at him.

He sighed ruefully. So much for hoarding any secrets tonight.

18

MEANT TO START HERE

Rory heard the princess's remark as she headed for the open patio doors, through which she could already feel a tantalizing breeze. Apparently Calla had just put together whose signet ring Rory carried. If Sean answered her, it was lost to the murmur of the crowd as Rory stepped out into a small courtyard adorned with more decorative trees, grasses, and flowers, and a small fountain in the center. It wasn't dark yet, and wouldn't get fully dark here till after midnight, but there were paper lanterns hanging in the tree branches and from an arbor off to the side. Stone benches lined the courtyard at intervals. As she stood there admiring the beauty her ear picked up a familiar light step at the door behind her.

"I've never seen anything like this in Maireadd," she said without turning. "Our land doesn't like to be tamed. We plant gardens, but even they somehow become a bit feral."

"Was that part of the curse?" Sean asked.

"I don't know."

They had the courtyard all to themselves while everyone was inside either dancing or finishing their desert. Rory wandered toward the arbor, overshadowed by a couple of weeping cherry trees and nearly swallowed up by a flowering clematis. Sean followed. She was sharply aware of his presence tonight, and how closely he walked at her side, brushing arms with her at every step. It made it seem natural when he touched her hand and then held it lightly, his callouses, earned from hours with a chef's knife, feeling warm and rough over her knuckles. They were thick with muscle, too. Such human hands. But she liked them.

They stopped beneath the warm light of the lantern under the arbor and faced one another. Neither spoke for a few minutes. Rory fiddled with the chain that held Sean's ring, hidden beneath the neckline of her gown. Now that they were here, after so much had happened, she didn't know what to say. She didn't even know how to classify their relationship anymore. Were they just friends, or had something changed? Their still-clasped hands seemed to suggest that it had.

She was still contemplating this when Sean touched her face, startling her as he gently tilted her chin up till they were eye-to-eye.

"Are you all right?" he asked. His blue eyes looked gray in the lamplight.

She frowned. "Why wouldn't I be?"

"Dianthe almost murdered you. You had to fight a sorcerer, and now you're being blamed for the gorgrim attack on the city."

"All part of the job, right?" she shrugged and looked away. When he didn't say anything though, she relented. "Fine, yes. I feel like a colossal failure. First you did my job for me, tracking down the ambassador—"

"—With help from the Seer," he reminded her.

"Then I got my butt handed to me by the sorcerer. Do you know that elves aren't even trained to pick locks without magic? You can probably get out of handcuffs in your sleep. Then it was your ring that saved my life... and if that wasn't enough, you had to go clean up the mess with the gorgrim. I don't know whether to be disgusted with myself or with elves in general. I never thought I was a bad agent before."

"I can't navigate a cursed forest," Sean said. "I'd have gotten lost and eaten by hellhounds without you. We all have our strengths."

Rory felt her eyes prickle. "Do we? All I seem to be able to do lately is fail. And I don't know whether to admire you, or be terribly jealous."

"Neither? You can't do it all—you're just one elf against long odds. We handled the ice dragons together. That was a pretty big problem that the council never prepared for...and given the situation in Barra, they never should have sent you alone."

"Thyrus sent *you* alone, and you seem to be handling everything okay so far, including saving my butt."

A shadow seemed to pass across his face. "All I'm doing so far is watching and listening. I don't know if I will be able to do the job they sent me for, when I need to do it. I might be able to kill Dianthe—maybe—but she's already spread her ideas through Eyren. Will ending her even help?"

"I guess that's why we're here, right? 'Cause the Seer saw that we'd need help, even if our governments are under-prepared?" She smiled at him, trying to offer the encouragement that he had given her a moment ago.

"I'm just glad they sent me to you."

"Me too."

They stared at one another under the flickering orange light of the paper lantern. The warmth of the color made Sean's red-gold hair look like it had originated in the flame.

His eyes were shadowed though, darker, and more intense. He had a dusting of freckles across his nose that she found herself studying now that they were only inches apart.

"Would it be weird if I kissed you?" he asked. His fingers had found her face again, his thumb stroking her cheek softly. The scars from last winter's dragon attack had faded to thin white lines across the back of his hand.

"Probably," she said, her heart thundering as her attention moved to his lips and her face heated up. "But maybe it would be a good weird."

"Don't know till we try," he said, leaning a bit closer.

"That's true."

Her hand was on his shoulder, her fingers playing with his collar for a moment before she slid it around to the back of his neck, his bright hair brushing her skin and sending shivers through her. It felt like having goosebumps inside. Very weird. But definitely good weird. She liked it. And she did like him a great deal, even if he was a human. She shifted forward till they were nose-to-nose. His other hand went around her waist and they stood there like that for a long, silent moment.

A thousand thoughts chased each other through her mind as she looked into his eyes. If she kissed him right now, it could change everything. Not just their friendship, but also potentially their work. Would the repercussions reach beyond that? When the future of Barra could rest, at least partly, in their hands?

"Maybe it's meant to start here, with us," Sean said.

Startled, Rory's gaze flicked up to his eyes, only inches away. "What is?"

"Closing the rift between humans and magicals."

"With a kiss?" she asked without moving.

He smirked. Then he leaned down, closing the gap, and kissed her softly. They parted for an instant, then he kissed her again. Rory's fingers slid up and tangled in his hair as she returned the kiss, and it didn't feel weird after all. It felt right. It felt like hope.

And sadness.

She drew away. "What are we doing? This can't go anywhere. You know that, right? I mean, look at us. Neither of our lifestyles are exactly conducive to any kind of stable relationship. And I... I refuse to be someone's fling."

Sean raised an eyebrow at her and smiled a little. He reached over and tugged on the chain at her throat till it pulled out from the collar of her gown, revealing his signet ring dangling at the end.

"You think I'd give my family's seal to a fling?"

Rory flushed. "You never told me... I mean, I knew it was a big deal, but the way Princess Calla talked... would the Kerrs really go to war over..." she gulped a little. "Over me?"

"Oh. Yeah, about that. Usually we only give those out to... uh..."

"A spouse or a lover?" Rory guessed, feeling her blush deepen. Should she be angry? Flattered?

"Yeah. A spouse or a lover. With all the power and responsibility that anyone born into the Family would have." He dropped the chain, letting the ring thump back onto her chest, outside her gown this time.

"And is that what you were envisioning for our relationship when you gave it to me?" she asked, still taken aback a bit, but also curious.

"No, I..." Sean ran a hand over his head and rubbed at the back of his neck. "Not really, no. I just knew that our friendship was special. We fought ice dragons together. And shadow rats. And then there was the unicorn. And elves—well, elves never offer friendship to humans. You were—are—the closest thing to a friend that I have."

Rory closed her hand over the ring, feeling her heart pounding under her fist. "And what about now? I don't know what to think about this." She used her free hand to gesture around them. "Or us. If there even is an us."

"I don't know what to think either. It's just that..." he huffed a sigh and ran a hand over his head again, his shoulder muscles bunching against his shirt. "I don't know what the future looks like. I'm good at what I do, and I do love fighting monsters," here he grinned sheepishly, "but I don't want to look back at my life in twenty years and see nothing but a string of dead bodies, you know? Taking evil out of the world is important, but it kinda seems meaningless if you're not building something, too. Does that sound crazy?

"Anyhow... I guess what I'm trying to say is that I'd like to build something with you, I think. Maybe we'll just be good friends. Maybe someday we can be something more..." He drifted off and averted his gaze.

"Maybe I'd like that," said Rory, and with a sudden surge of tenderness toward her crazy, monster-killing human, she leaned up and kissed him again, bold enough this time to bury both hands in his soft hair. One thing could be said for humans—their ears didn't stick out and get in the way of hair stroking like elves' ears did.

He seemed happy enough to return the kiss, turning it into something more this time. A non-verbal communication that came close to saying, silently, "I love you." By the time they parted again she was breathless.

Whether it was a faint noise, or perhaps a flicker of shadow at the corner of her eye, she didn't know, but as they stood there mesmerized by one another she knew suddenly that they weren't alone anymore. She jerked away from him, looking around.

"What is it?"

"Someone's here." she searched the shadows, swiveling her ears to catch the faintest sound or the smallest movement, and still nearly missed seeing the man standing in the dark against the wall, watching them. The only reason she did was that a sudden gust of wind set the lanterns swinging, and the light caught his eyes like those of a cat, reflecting green.

She summoned her magic so quickly and forcefully that it sparked at her fingertips before she could even get out the word for light. At the same moment the man ducked away, so the sudden, brilliant light that flared to life above Rory's hand revealed only his profile as he slid behind a potted tree and disappeared.

"Did you see him?"

"No. It was probably Dianthe's man. He was here tonight. And we knew it." Sean sighed. "That was stupid."

Rory squeezed his arm, letting her light fade slowly. Dread and guilt settled like a ball of iron in her stomach. "I'm so sorry."

He shook his head. "Not your fault. I started that."

"I wonder..." she said tentatively. When he looked at her questioningly she went on. "I mean, the Seer had to know the queen's assassin was here, right? He even came in and danced with that fae girl for a while. Do you think... Oh, I don't know. But it doesn't seem like the Seer would have orchestrated all this if it was going to get you killed."

Sean gave a rueful snort. "He didn't tell us to run off and make out at his party, either. Besides—do you really think he sees everything?"

"No, of course not. He's not God. I was just—I'm afraid for you."

He found her hand and squeezed it. By unspoken agreement they headed back inside. He paused right before they went in though, tugging her to a stop.

"I'm sorry," he said.

"For what?"

"If it sounded like I blamed you, or regretted kissing you. I don't."

She squeezed his hand and then let it go. "I know."

The others were gathering back at their table as well, getting ready to leave, though many of the other guests showed no sign of stopping the party any time soon. It was after midnight.

They all looked at one another, that feeling of somber expectation weighing on them all as they prepared to part ways.

"Until we meet again," Sean began.

"May God above light your way beyond the sunset's end," Calla said, taking up the next line of the ancient farewell blessing.

"May the Redeemer grant you hope beyond your hopeless moments," said Rory, looking at Sean and the new haunted look in his eyes.

No one finished the last line—at least not out loud, though they were probably all thinking it. *And if we fail to meet again here, I'll see you in the life beyond life.*

They went their separate ways after that. Kiah and Dylan, who'd been making eyes at each other all evening, walked out together. Sean parted with Rory with a long look and a nod, rushing to catch a ride back to the ferry before it left for the mainland, since it wouldn't be back that night. That left Rory alone with Princess Calla and Jamie the werewolf. They stood there awkwardly for a moment, with too many revelations between them.

"I'm glad you made it out of the city safely," Calla said at last.

Rory nodded, fingering Sean's ring out of habit. "Thanks to you both. I hope you didn't pay too dearly."

Pain flashed in the princess's face. "This is war. A silent one, but a war nonetheless. Something tells me we'll all pay dearly before the end." Rory's stomach twisted. Before she could reply though, Calla went on, "Jamie and I are taking the chopper back to Eyren tonight. If you'd like, we'll give you a ride. We can drop you off somewhere outside the city, or get you to one of our tunnel safehouses again, and you can get home that way. It would be a safer trip for you."

Rory considered for a moment. It was true. Taking a helicopter ride would cut off half a day of travel, since she was going to have to take the ferry back over the channel, then hire a car to drive back to the border. She'd been lucky the council was able to get her a ride out there with a selkie trader. Getting back was going to be a little trickier. And a short stop in the city should pose little risk if she was with the princess.

"Thank you," she said.

"Good," said Calla. "We should say goodbye to the Seer, and then we'll go."

But the Seer was already coming their way again, like he'd been summoned by Calla's words. "It looks like I've already missed the others. Oh well. I would like to have spoken to your young man before he left," he said to Rory, clasping her hands in his gnarled, warm ones. "Don't feel badly about earlier, my dear. There is more at work here than you know. And don't cling too tightly to your failures. He will need you before all's done."

Dazed and full of questions, Rory could only stammer unintelligently before he moved on to Calla, pulling her aside where they talked earnestly for a moment. When she came back, they left.

"The pilot is one of my people. He's solid." Calla said as they were crossing the mansion grounds toward her waiting helicopter. "Once we get there though, you'll want to hide your ears until we get to the car."

They planned to drop her off at the B&B where she'd stayed during her last visit to the capital. Once there, she wouldn't have to leave the house. She could take the tunnel that started beneath it all the way across the border into Maireadd. Calla had a couple little things she was looking for magical help with, and hoped Rory would stay the extra day. Rory was more than willing, since they wouldn't arrive in the city until early that morning, and she had no desire to spend half the day walking after being up half the night.

It was around three in the morning when their chopper set down on the roof of one of the buildings in the same military base where Rory had been held for questioning. Anxiety and bad memories fluttered through her as she pulled her hoodie on over her evening gown and cinched the hood around her face. Luckily it was a cool night, so she wouldn't stand out too badly. Even Calla had put on a sweater and raised the hood as they climbed down so that her hair was protected from the whirlwind from the chopper blades. They descended flights of metal-grate stairs in an unwelcoming gray stairwell and exited into a mostly empty parking lot. Someone brought their car around—a big, black SUV with tinted windows—and then they were on their way again. Rory sighed in relief when they were past the razor wire fences and the gate had rolled closed behind them.

"What does the elf council think about your invitation to the gala tonight?" Princess Calla asked presently, as city lights flashed past outside.

Rory stirred and turned from the window. "Curious. Worried. Hopeful that the Seer would provide some insight into our current situation. They're always greedy for news, or for an edge that will protect us against..."

"Barra," Calla finished for her.

Rory nodded.

"What will you tell them?"

"As much as I can without betraying everyone's secrets." Rory sighed. "Apparently my loyalties are not what they used to be. I feel like I should be angry with the Seer for taking advantage of that."

"Having doubts about your council?" Calla's eyes were sharp in the dim light of passing street lamps.

Rory knew she wasn't obligated to answer. This was a conversation, not an interrogation, but she also knew that the Seer was right. They needed to trust one another.

"No... I'm no traitor to my people. But I disagree with some of the council's assumptions about what's best for Maireadd. We've been closed off since the Curse War. We allow trade and travel and even tourism because we must. But we haven't formed an alliance with anyone in all that time. We don't learn from anyone else." She looked down at her hands, clasped together in her lap. "I don't even know how to pick a lock without magic. In our pride, we've made ourselves vulnerable, and it scares me."

"I think we're all feeling vulnerable," Calla said quietly.

Jamie stopped the car in front of the B&B, and after brief goodbyes, Rory jogged inside, where Gracie, the nymph proprietress, was waiting to show her to her room.

* * * * *

Rory hadn't been asleep for more than an hour or two when her magic mirror started chiming from underneath her pillow, dragging her from an exhausted nightmare. She drew it out sluggishly, squinting against the blue glow of the glass.

"Kiah?" she asked stupidly, trying to blink the blurriness out of her eyes. The selkie looked panicked. "What's wrong?"

"This!" the image in the mirror jerked and turned, coming to focus on the crumpled form of Dylan Blaine, the empath they'd met just last night. "He ran into Lyselle, I think, before he got to his charter boat. I'm guessing she tried to put a subversion spell on him, then sent a kraken after him."

"Dragonfire!" Rory swore. She called up a light off to the side while Kiah launched into her story. Basically, Dianthe's witch sister, Lyselle, who had been at the gala, though Rory hadn't seen her, had tried to subvert the empath to her will. A spell that would turn him into a walking shell. It was the nastiest kind of spell out there, and one that was expressly forbidden in the sacred texts. It was one of the spells that had been used during the war centuries ago that had resulted in Maireadd's curse.

But from Kiah's story it sounded like the empath was fighting it, somehow. Empaths were so rare, even Rory knew very little about what they were capable of. She did know about subversion spells, however. They were aggressive—and terrifying. There was debate among scholars, but the prevailing thought, because of the wording of the spell, was that it actually summoned a spirit from the shadow realm to bind the victim and sorcerer together and actively subdue and subvert the victim's will. Those who'd been subverted and released—which was incredibly rare, since sorcerers weren't known for being merciful—were never the same afterward. Broken, haunted, and often outright mad.

Rory sent up a silent prayer that that would not be Dylan Blaine's fate as she briefly explained the situation to Kiah—leaving out the part about the shadow spirit.

"So basically, it's killing him," said Kiah. She had let her light go out, so it was hard to see her in the dim twilight of the early morning, but even still she looked stricken.

"Yes. The spell itself is like a poison—sort of."

"What can I do?"

Rory fell silent again as she thought about it. She could remove the spell herself, of course, but it would take over an hour, at the least, to get out there, by the time she contacted Calla and got a chopper, then made the flight. By the looks of the empath, he wouldn't last that long. Which left it up to Kiah. But selkie magic was purely element-based. They were connected to the sea, and could wield the elements associated with it; water, wind, and even light. But they couldn't conjure spells or enchant items like elves could. Elements were the fastest and easiest even for the elves, and that's what Rory was mostly trained to wield going into battle. Even many of the enchantments they performed involved combining and binding the elements. But that wouldn't help Kiah. Given the situation, there was only one thing that came to mind.

Rory figured that Dylan must be blocking the curse on his own, somehow, keeping it from taking over his spirit and his will, though she'd never heard of such a thing being possible before. But because of the sentient nature of the curse, since it couldn't get to his mind and heart, it was attacking his body. What he needed was a shield to block the curse physically, and not just mentally and internally. Selkies did have one thing that could do that. Their coat.

Selkie coats were like their own personal magical fingerprint, or coat of arms, that manifested as a unique pattern of markings across their shoulders and back. They exchanged coats when they got married, binding themselves forever to their partner through magic. It was a fascinating process, and the effects still weren't entirely understood, but in essence, once they'd given their coat to their spouse, it acted as a kind of shield and protection against all others' magic but their own. Selkies—married selkies—were notoriously immune to magic attacks. That just might work for Dylan.

But it would also mean they were married, by selkie custom.

"I might have a solution, but I don't think you're going to like it."

Kiah didn't like it.

"Don't freak out," said Rory.

Kiah was totally freaking out. "I'm not." Her eyes darted between the mirror and something off to the side, presumably Dylan.

"I mean, the whole thing about exchanging coats, it's more of a traditional thing, right? It doesn't mean you're actually married to him," Rory said, grimacing.

"No—that's kind of what it means."

"Can't you just think of it as... I don't know. An unbreakable alliance or something? I mean, unless you consummate it. I guess then it would be marriage."

"Rory!" Kiah hissed. But in the end, she agreed to do it.

"If anything... well, just let me know how it turns out, okay? Not that each life isn't precious, but we could really use an empath on our side."

"I will. Thanks. Guess next time we talk I'll be a married woman."

Rory snorted. "Might want to see how he feels about that before you go advertising it. Or acting on it."

Despite her glib words as they ended the call, she was worried. What if her solution didn't work? Then not only would they lose their empath, who was a potentially powerful ally, but Kiah's future would be drastically altered, with no coat to give away to any future lover. If a selkie's mate died, their coat didn't return to them. Once Kiah gave hers to Dylan, it was, indeed, forever.

Rory lay there staring up at the darkened ceiling, and whimpered. Then she called Sean.

19

EMPATH AT COURT

The little bell above the door chimed as Sean pulled it open, greeting him a moment before the scents of coffee, ink, and new book glue. A display table near the door was set up with stacks of Darren Anderson thrillers, which made him grin.

"Hi there! Welcome to Princess Books! Let me know if I can help you find anything."

Sean did a double take at the girl behind the coffee bar. She looked familiar, but it took him a moment to place her. "Leah, right? The fae?"

She wore her hair plain brunette today, and looked stricken when he called her a fae. "How do you know me?"

"The night of the gorgrim attack. You came into the church while I was there."

"Right." She flushed, a bit of plum purple creeping into her hair.

"I wondered if Calla might be around this evening."

"She had business at the palace today. She should be back any time though. You're welcome to hang out and wait, if you want." She gestured toward the bookshelves with her cleaning rag.

"Thanks."

Sean hadn't had much time to read in a long while. Out of curiosity, he picked up one of Dylan's Darren Anderson books from the display table and thumbed through it. He was still standing there when the door blew open moments later and Calla came in followed as always by Jamie, one step behind her. Something flashed in her eyes when she spotted Sean, there and gone too quickly to identify, and then she smiled.

"Mr. Leigh. Good to see you again."

"Your highness."

"Have you been finding everything you need?"

"Oh, I'm just looking around. Now that the head chef is back, I have time to do some reading, finally." He held up the book.

"Good choice."

"Yeah. I heard something about the author recently. Someone told me this morning that he had a bit of a health scare."

Calla blanched. "I hope he's doing better."

"Haven't heard any more. I was hoping maybe you had."

"Oh. Well... can I treat you to a cup of coffee, since you're here?"

The three of them settled into a corner table in the cafe area, and Leah brought over a tray of coffees, cream and sugar. It wasn't fancy, but the bookshop served the best coffee in the city, so it didn't need to be.

"What's going on?" Calla asked, once they were alone. She had dark circles under her eyes, and looked like she'd gotten even less sleep than he had.

Sean filled them in on his call from Rory that morning. He'd spent the remainder of the night last night in a little town along the coast before driving back to the capital. He'd only gotten back home an hour before, then stopped for a bite to eat before coming to the bookshop.

"I was hoping you had talked to either Rory or Kiah today," he said, his voice still lowered. "You think the Seer would get us all together just to have one of us die right away?"

Calla flattened her lips. "We got in early this morning, and then spent most of the day at the palace. Unfortunately. Let's hope Rory's solution worked."

"If the selkie had the guts to go through with it," said Jamie.

"Let's just hope the cost isn't any steeper than it's already been... for any of us." The princess gave her werewolf such an intense look that Sean shifted uncomfortably, feeling like he was intruding on a moment. But then she turned back to him. "You need to be careful. Dianthe practically interrogated me today about the gala. She knows you were there."

The iron ball of dread that had been riding around in his stomach since last night settled in even heavier. "How much does she know?"

Calla could only shrug and shake her head. "That you were there, and that you sat with me, which is pretty incriminating by itself, given my reputation. Why? Did something else happen?"

"I think Beck saw Rory and I together outside. Uh... talking."

Calla's eyebrows shot up. Jamie snorted.

Sean felt his face heat. He cleared his throat. "Anyway."

Silence fell between them. He played with his half-empty coffee cup, pushing it back and forth across the table in front of him and watching the steam roll around it. He was tired.

"The night of the gorgrim attack," Jamie said suddenly. "Was that you?"

"Huh?" Sean looked up. His mind had been wandering.

"Did you kill that gorgrim in Central City?"

"Oh." He grinned sheepishly. "It could have possibly been."

Jamie whistled. "I wondered who was crazy enough to take that thing on. That was... spectacular."

"Well, I figured it's not every day you get an opportunity to battle a gorgrim. I couldn't just pass it up."

"...Right."

"What made you suspect me? No one else had better figure it out. My CO would kill me if I got outed because of that."

"Lucky guess, mostly," said the werewolf. "Body type and movement matches. And you mentioned fighting ice dragons before. Your hands have calluses and from knifework and swordplay."

"I'm a chef."

Jamie just smiled wolfishly. "Do you chop veggies with both hands?"

Sean glanced down at his hands, moving them from the coffee cup to study them. The scars from the ice dragon still showed on the back of his right hand. "No."

Calla smiled tiredly. "Sounds like we owe you thanks already."

Sean went home soon after that, crashing in bed despite the late coffee and the worries souring the back of his mind, for a long, exhausted sleep.

* * * * *

That week Sean avoided the palace as much as he could. When he did have to go in to work, he kept his head down and prayed he'd go unnoticed, hoping that the gala excitement might blow over before Dianthe had a chance to corner him. His strategy seemed to be working, till the night of the next open court.

He and Calla and Jamie had managed to bump into each other a couple times during the week, and they kept him updated. Dylan had survived Lyselle's subversion spell, thanks to Kiah's coat, which made them legally married according to selkie custom. That had to be awkward. Calla brought the new couple to the capital to see if Dylan could help her with Gaelan, and to identify one of the sorcerers that had been plaguing the city. The same one Rory said had summoned the gorgrim. Supposedly Dylan and Kiah were coming to court that night. Sean wished they wouldn't. He had a bad feeling, and things were still too stirred up since the gala.

On the other hand, he had his own reasons why he hoped Dylan could get a good read on the crown prince. If Dianthe suspected Sean, then he might need to take her out before she, in turn, had him arrested—or worse. But with the king under her sway, and Prince Gaelan's questionable loyalties, he just wasn't ready to make his move. Not to mention the growing divide between humans and magicals in the city, which the queen was fostering. Her death wouldn't necessarily stop that from worsening at this point. She wasn't the only one who despised magicals. There were other political forces at work that could easily twist her murder and pin it on the magicals—that might happen anyway, but he felt like the situation was just too ticklish right now. At least Jacobs wasn't breathing down his neck pushing him forward. Yet.

What they needed was someone to step up and start bringing humans and magicals back together. Someone to lead. Perhaps Calla, but so far she hadn't stepped up to influence the nobility or the general population.

Once he had the evening's refreshment preparations in order that night, Sean locked himself in the office to change out of his chef's coat into a suit. He situated his lucky string tie at his neck—the one he always grabbed when he was nervous. If he could go invisible tonight, he would. With a last tug at his collar he left the shelter of the dumpy little office, crossed the kitchen, and stepped out into the hall.

The kitchen was situated behind the big ballroom where they held court every week, and opened into a modest hallway mostly used by the staff. A few steps brought him to the one of many doors standing open to the ballroom. Each door had a double guard posted tonight—which was one guard more than usual. Even this door, usually left clear for the servers to come and go without tripping over anyone's decorative lance, had its two men stationed just on the inside.

Sean got a queasy feeling in the pit of his stomach as he stepped between the guards into the ballroom. This couldn't be good. He started to turn around, thinking he'd pretend he forgot something and slip back into the office to call Dylan or Calla and warn them, but the queen's voice stopped him.

"Mr. Leigh. Good to see you this evening."

Sean pasted a carefree smile on his face and turned back, bowing. "Your Majesty."

Dianthe wore one of her cleavage-baring, glittering evening gowns that made her look like an expensive hooker. Maybe it was just the way she wore it.

"Everything looks wonderful tonight, as always." She lifted her bejeweled hand and fluttered her fingers toward the buffet tables. Were those diamonds on her fingernails?

"Thank you, your Majesty. It's always an honor to be allowed to show off for the court." He grinned as though his heart wasn't pounding in his ears. The queen responded with one of her tinkling laughs, flicking auburn curls over her shoulder.

"How do our culinary offerings compare to the Seer's, I wonder? You were there for that gala—what do you think?"

"His chef is an inspiration, but I hope you aren't asking me to compare him to myself."

Another tinkling laugh.

"Tell me," said the queen, and the words signaled a subtle but powerful shift of energy. "Why did the Seer invite you? What was his purpose?"

Sean found himself leaning toward her, suddenly eager to share all kinds of interesting things. Which meant she had laced the words with compulsion. He wanted to talk. It was like an itch that demanded attention. Before he could blab all his deadly secrets, he bit down hard on the side of his tongue. The sudden sharp pain jolted his mind back, and for a moment he couldn't work his tongue even if he still wanted to talk. He tasted blood. The Thyrus government had made sure he knew that trick, since it was still the best human and non-magical defense against magical manipulation. Unfortunately.

Sean faked a coughing fit to cover his pause and watering eyes, then when he got his tongue working again excused himself and said, "I don't know. Like you said, he's a crazy old man. I have no idea what his motivations were... but it was a nice party."

She regarded him through narrowed eyes for a moment. "I wonder why he would suddenly decide to host such a grand event out of the blue."

"Lonesome, maybe. He lives alone out there on that island with no one but the selkies for company."

"Perhaps." She smiled faintly, though the sharpness never left her eyes. "Well, enjoy your evening. I'm planning something a little special tonight myself."

"Oh?"

"It's a surprise." She winked at him.

Sean watched her walk away, then swore. "Son of a stony spiked lizard." He touched a fingertip to the end of his tongue and drew it away with blood on it. "Yours is coming," he muttered toward her retreating form.

The ballroom was filling up fast. Usually Dianthe let people mingle and chat for a good half hour or longer before she and Ebezer made their grand entrance. Sean assumed she'd gone out so she could make a more grand and visible entry later, which meant, hopefully, he had a few minutes to find one of the others and warn them off. He didn't dare call from his phone. Not here. Someone talking on their cell phone during court would stick out like a troll at a pixie convention, plus there were too many ears.

He edged his way through the crowd, surreptitiously scanning for any of his allies while nodding and smiling at acquaintances. Several people cornered him to chat, making it impossible to slip away without arousing curiosity. And with the queen already suspicious of him, curiosity was one thing he couldn't risk. So he smiled and exchanged small talk, and then excused himself, all the while looking for his friends. He finally spotted Dylan with Calla and Jamie—and Gaelan and Alard.

He must have been radiating panic, because Dylan looked over and met his eye. The empath muttered an excuse to the others and started angling toward the drink table rather than heading directly toward Sean. They met behind the ice sculpture—this week it was of a dragon breathing fire. Kiah had managed to come along as well.

"The queen is planning something tonight. You have to get out now," Sean said without preamble.

Kiah sucked a tiny breath, losing a few shades of color from her normal golden-brown.

Dylan looked at the doors, with their double guard, then toward the staircase that the royals always used for their grand entrance. "Too late."

Sean bit back several choice curse words as Queen Dianthe, King Ebezer, and another woman—Lyselle?

—descended the grand staircase. He slipped away while Dylan and Kiah hurried back to Calla. Taking a chance that she hadn't yet ordered the guards to keep anyone from leaving, he strolled toward the nearest set of doors, nodding casually at the guards as he passed. They made no move to stop him. Thankfully this door led back toward the kitchens, so they were used to him coming and going this way and wouldn't remember it as unusual. He stopped in the hallway just outside the kitchen doors. No one was in sight either way. The guards stood on the other side of the doors into the ballroom, and had their backs to him. They wouldn't turn around unless there was a commotion.

From his post outside the kitchen, he could hear the dull roar of conversation in the ballroom, and he could hear when it quieted as the royals took the dais.

"My people," said the queen, her voice carrying distinctly. There was a pause. "I've been informed that we have a special guest here this evening. A very special guest, in fact. The kind that might only show up every few generations here in Barra. I can't express how pleased I am with my dear sister for bringing word before an opportunity like this had a chance to escape."

Another pause. Sean felt the hairs on the back of his neck prickling and caught himself holding his breath. He wasn't the empath—he could only imagine what kind of chaos Dylan must be picking up from the crowd. But the nervous energy rolling out of the ballroom was almost palpable.

"Come up here, Dylan Blaine of Lomasi," the queen said. "Barra, may I introduce you to our very own empath."

Shocked gasps filtered out into the hallway, and even the guards at the door shifted uneasily.

"Don't be shy. Come up here, Mr. Blaine."

She put a magical compulsion into her command. Sean felt himself lean forward before he checked himself. But then he took a few steps toward the door anyway, curiosity drawing him closer. He could just see Dylan, Kiah, and the others standing at the edge of the crowd. Dylan, who'd been the target of the queen's compulsion, hadn't budged.

"Dragon scales," Sean whispered appreciatively under his breath.

"Mr. Blaine, don't you think you've avoided your destiny long enough? Come up here and join me. You have a lot to offer your country and the crown."

"No."

The atmosphere in the ballroom seemed to compress. Kiah was looking around frantically at the exits. Sean caught her eye when she looked toward him, and nodded. She whispered to Dylan.

Dylan spoke to the queen. "My loyalties and my destiny are with Barra and the royal family. Not with you, sorceress."

Tension crackled in the room.

Dianthe gazed at the empath for a long moment, an evil smile growing on her face. "Guards, seize him."

Dylan thrust out a hand toward the guards and they faltered.

"Seize him!" Dianthe ordered again, once again lacing her words with enough compulsion that Sean could feel it. The guards jerked forward like puppets.

Dylan flung his hands out wide, and a wave of fear rolled off him like the cold breath of death itself. Sean sucked a gasp and instinctively dropped into a half-crouched fighting stance before he caught himself. A second later, every single person in the ballroom lost their mind. Some of them attacked the guards or one another. Others ran.

Sean flattened himself against the wall as a horde of crazed nobles dashed through the door, now unguarded. Dylan, Kiah, and Jamie were among them. Sean stepped out and jogged along with them.

"What was that?" he said.

"Desperation," Dylan panted.

Sean motioned them down the first hall they came to. "Yikes. This way." He ducked down yet another hall, and they followed. "Where's Calla?" he asked Jamie, who jogged along in back.

"With her brother."

A final turn brought them to a narrow utility hall. No one was in sight.

"I can't take you any further," Sean said, nodding toward a security camera installed at the corner. "If I'm seen with you, my cover will be blown, and... well it wouldn't be good, and not just for me. I'm sorry. If you take a left at the end of this hall, you'll be in one of the storerooms with a loading dock that you should be able to slip out. It's guarded, but that doesn't seem like it will be a problem for you."

"Thanks." Dylan clasped his hand briefly. "Till we meet again."

"God keep you," Sean replied. "I'll find you later, if I can." He nodded to Kiah and Jamie, then turned and sprinted back the way they'd come till he could join the rest of the crowd and slip into the kitchen.

Apparently Dylan's wave of fear had hit the kitchen as well. Pots, utensils, and spilled food were scattered over the floor, and a small table had been turned over. The dish washer and the head chef were huddled together on the floor under the oven, one of the sous chefs had disappeared, and the other was clutching a bloody towel around his hand.

"What happened? The chef asked.

"Queen Dianthe found herself an empath and thought she'd cornered him," Sean said, headed for the office.

"The queen made that... that panic?"

"No. The empath did." Sean ducked into the office and closed the door, letting out a breath and allowing himself to deflate for a moment. He sat down behind the desk and ran his hands over his hair. God grant them all protection this night.

20

SECRETS

Rory squirmed in her seat facing Taro and Borden, even though they weren't looking at her. An hour ago Calla had called, asking to speak with the council. Dylan had been outed at court and forced to flee, and he and Kiah needed asylum. His secret was no longer a secret. No way would Taro turn down doing a favor for an empath. What made Rory nervous was the greedy glint that had come into Taro's eye when she explained the situation and called the princess back on her mirror so he could talk to her.

Rory dug her nails into the chair's armrests. Calla had sounded subdued when she talked to her earlier. She didn't say what had happened, exactly, only that Kiah and Dylan were at a safe house in the city, and would use one of the tunnels to get to Maireadd. She mentioned starting once Dylan woke up, if he was all right. So *something* had happened. But what? Had they tried to curse him again?

"Did you hear that?" Borden asked, interrupting her thoughts. "You're going to the border. We'll send Vasya and his scouts with you. You'll leave today. Whatever happens, you keep that empath alive."

She nodded with more confidence than she felt. Despite several successful missions since she'd escaped Barra, that defeat still stung. And her secrets were piling up. She wouldn't be able to conceal her relationship with Sean—not only a human, but a foreign operative—forever. As far as the elf council knew, it was Calla alone who had come to her rescue when she'd been captured. She still hadn't told them about the signet ring.

Sure, they had encouraged her to befriend him, to get information. But carrying his ring and kissing him under arbors was most assuredly not what they had in mind. And she hadn't told them about Dylan. It was Calla who dropped that bomb during her conversation with Taro. For now, he assumed Rory hadn't known. Another strike against her. She cringed inwardly as she left the lodge to repack and get ready to leave.

Was she doing the right thing, keeping these secrets?

But there was that greedy light in the other elves' eyes when they heard about an empath coming to them.

That afternoon she left for the border with a dozen scouts to act as guards, Vasya among them. They would have to camp that night, and would arrive midday the next day. It should only take three days on horseback, both coming and going. Three long days, with Vasya teasing for information and the scouts bantering among each other and ignoring her. She hadn't had that kind of camaraderie with anyone since her days at the academy.

Late in the day her mirror chirped at her again.

"Probably Kiah," she muttered, wrestling to pull it out of her pack without stopping and dismounting. Vasya was walking his horse alongside her—and watching curiously when Sean's face popped up. He raised his eyebrows.

Blushing, Rory waved him on, slowing her horse till the others had passed her, leaving her walking at the back of the group. Vasya kept twisting in the saddle to watch her. She frowned at him and fell further back.

"Sean. You're okay."

"For now." He grinned at her, flashing dimples, but his eyes didn't quite light up like they usually did.

"What's happening? I'm on my way to meet Kiah and Dylan now."

"Yeah. Keep them safe, huh? That soothsayer wasn't lying when he said Dylan is a weapon." He explained what had happened at court, how they'd escaped from the heavily guarded palace.

"But what about you? Do they suspect you at all?" she asked, shooting Vasya another dirty look when he slowed his horse, obviously trying to eavesdrop.

Sean's expression pinched. "Dianthe questioned everyone afterward—the whole court. We were there for hours. She's already suspicious of me because of the gala. But for now I'm okay. For now."

"I wish I could be there with you," she said, then blushed. "I just... you seem really alone."

"Calla and Jamie are here."

"But you can't risk talking to them."

"Yeah." He stared off to the side, seeming for a moment almost vulnerable. The monster-slaying assassin-spy. The lighting there—it looked like he was sitting in the bathroom again, with a tile wall behind him—made him look a little paler than normal, his freckles a little more pronounced.

"What about Beck? He hasn't said anything to Dianthe or anyone yet about us?"

He could only shrug and shake his head. "Not that I know of."

"That place is evil. Eyren."

"Ever since Dianthe had that conversation with the soothsayer I keep imagining I'm being watched," he admitted. Then gave a rueful huff and shrugged again. "What about you? Do you think things will be okay there, with Dylan?"

It was Rory's turn to shrug and grimace. "The council will keep him safe, for sure. Whether he ever leaves Maireadd—that's another question."

"Take care."

"I won't let anything happen to him."

He smiled briefly. "I meant take care of you. I wish I could be there. You seem alone too."

When Rory ended the call she found Vasya hovering at the back of the group, his horse just ahead of hers and his ears swiveled back toward her, trying to catch whatever he could of their conversation. She gave him a withering glare as she urged her horse on past him.

"That doesn't look good, you know," he said, catching up. "Trying to hide things from me."

"From you? Who's the agent and who's the scout here?"

"Do agents blush at their secret missions?" he called after her as she kicked her horse into a trot, passing the rest of the group.

Rory spent the rest of the day with a sinking feeling she couldn't shake.

* * * * *

They got to the tunnel entrance midday the next day, but there was no sign of Kiah or Dylan. Rory was familiar with all the tunnel entrances that opened in Maireadd, but she's never known where they ended on the Barra side. This one opened up only a hundred yards or so from the border where the forest, and the curse, began, as did most of the others. Kiah had called an hour ago to let them know they would be there, and now they weren't here.

Dismounting, Rory pushed aside the vines and shrubbery that concealed the tunnel entrance and activated her light crystal so she could peer into the darkness. Nothing. Before she could panic, however, her ears picked up the shuffle of footsteps through the underbrush, and she turned as the two of them emerged from between pine trees.

"There you are." She ran over and gave Kiah a hug. "I'm so glad you're both all right. After everything..." She shook her head, looking between them.

Dylan looked rough. His face was whiter than usual, making a stitched gash in his forehead stand out starkly below his hairline. He had dark circles under his eyes.

Kiah, on the other hand, was blushing.

Rory suddenly wondered if the Seer had called them all to the gala for more than just the future of Barra. Had he been matchmaking? Kiah and Dylan were technically married now.

"We're still alive. A little worse for wear," said Kiah.

"Are you up for going a bit further? We'd like to get as many miles behind us as we can tonight. We're hoping with the horses we'll be able to make Tristini by tomorrow evening."

Dylan and Kiah both nodded, despite him rubbing his head.

Once they were mounted on the spare horses the scouts formed up around them as a guard. Rory rode in the middle beside Kiah.

"Sorry about all this," she said quietly to the selkie as they rode. "When the princess called in a favor and told the council about Dylan, they went a little crazy."

"Mm," Dylan grunted.

"This isn't going to be an issue, is it?" Kiah asked.

Rory paused, resisting the urge to glance at Vasya. "No," she said quietly. "We'll make sure it's not."

* * * * *

The next day they made it to Tristini by evening, despite everyone's apprehension. Judging by Dylan's jumpiness and the way he kept watching the shadows, they were still being watched themselves. The soothsayer, perhaps? But nothing happened, and Rory got them settled in their treehouse without incident. The council were really outdoing themselves. Guests were almost never given their own house to stay in by themselves in the elven city, much less their own tree house.

After she got them settled in she went to check in with Borden, filling him in on how they'd been watched the whole way home. He wasn't happy about that, and posted extra guards around the city for the night.

Rory went home to an empty house. Angel wasn't around, and there wasn't any food made. She ate a stale cookie from the pantry, took a bath, and called it a night, crashing in bed with her magic mirror. She called Sean. He didn't answer, of course. He never kept his magic mirror on him. But she told him about their trip, how Vasya was getting suspicious of her, and how Dylan suspected the soothsayer was watching them.

"I wish you were here," she admitted. "I miss your cinnamon rolls. And that macaroni casserole thing you made over Midwinter."

Mostly she missed him. She missed having a friend. The easy affection Kiah and Dylan displayed had set her longing more than her own loneliness. She used to think she was good at her job. That the missions she took for her country made it worth it to come home to stale cookies, or to be snubbed by the scouts that she often worked with. But was it? And what kind of agent got herself captured by a sorcerer, blamed for letting a monster loose in a foreign city, and had to have an operative from a different country track down the information that she was supposed to find? What kind of an agent fell in love with a human?

"I'm not in love," she said, tucking the mirror under her pillow. She snuggled in and pulled the blankets up, staring at the rafters. "I'm not in love."

* * * * *

Next morning her mirror chirping under her pillow woke her up. The council wanted to meet Dylan and Kiah. Of course. She pried herself out of bed and got dressed, grabbing another stale cookie for breakfast as she headed out the door.

First she stopped in to see Dylan and Kiah to give them a heads up about the council meeting, and caught them in the middle of some kind of flirtatious tickle-fight. Apparently they were getting along well. Then she backtracked to the office to check in with Borden. Other members of the council were already gathering at the lodge, milling about, deep in discussion as she passed through. Her mother was there, and gave her a concerned look as she trotted past. Why?

"Auralie," Borden greeted her when she stepped into the office. "Close the door, would you?" Once she had, he continued, "How are our guests faring? You've made sure they're comfortable and don't need anything?"

"They're doing as well as could be expected, under the circumstances."

"Of course. And what about you?" The older elf's dark gaze drilled into her as he leaned forward on his desk.

"What about me?" Rory asked, with the beginning of nerves stirring in her belly.

"How have you been? We're keeping you busy lately. Are you holding up?"

What is this about? She wondered. Out loud she said, "I'm fine. I could stand to do some laundry though."

A smile flickered on his face, there and gone, and not enough to activate the crinkles around his eyes. "Have you spoken to the Thyrus operative Sean Leigh recently?"

"We keep in touch, when possible."

Borden nodded. But instead of pressing her with more questions, he smiled and dismissed her to bring Dylan and

Rory to the meeting. She had the sinking feeling as she left that she hadn't heard the last of the conversation.

To make things worse, when she got back to Dylan and Kiah, they greeted her with the news that they'd had a visit from Beck, the queen's assassin. An assassin. Here in Tristini. Lyselle had Dylan's family and was holding them to use as leverage against him, per the queen's orders. Beck was supposed capture Dylan and take him back to the capital, but he hadn't. He'd struck a deal, instead.

"He must really love that fae," Kiah said, glancing over at Dylan, who stood by the window brooding, while she filled Rory in on what had happened. "He was supposed to kill me, but he's worried about the queen getting her hands on his lady friend, whether to steal her magic, or to use her against him. He wants us to get her out of the country. My life for hers." She touched her throat and blinked a few times.

"Thank God he has at least one weakness," said Rory. She didn't know what else to say. They'd already had so many close calls, poor Kiah must be a mess. But the selkie was holding it together, somehow. Rory turned to Dylan. "You're going to want to leave right away, aren't you? I know I would. Look, no matter what happens with the council, I promise I'll get you out of here."

"You don't think it will come to that, do you?" Kiah asked.

"No, at least I don't think so. But they will do everything they can to delay you and get you to stay."

They made their way in silence back to the lodge, where Rory slipped into an unobtrusive corner to watch the proceedings. The energy in the room was high with anticipation as Elf Korin Councilman stood up to greet their guests. He was so excited he stumbled over his words.

"We uh... would like to officially welcome you to Tristini." He beamed at them.

Dylan glanced over at him, twitched one eyebrow, then went back to stoically staring at nothing, leaving Kiah to address the assembly. Rory wondered what kind of emotions he was picking up in the room. Whatever they were, he didn't look impressed.

"Thank you," said Kiah. "We are so grateful for your help and hospitality. And we're sorry that we must leave so soon."

"Leave?" squawked the flustered Korin. "You can't leave!"

Rory reached for Sean's ring on its chain around her neck. *Oh no.*

"Pardon?" Kiah raised an eyebrow at the elf.

Taro stood and held up his hand to forestall more awkward stammering, smiling at Kiah and Dylan. "Forgive us. Let me start again. I'm Elf Taro Councilman, and welcome. We truly are honored to have both of you here. First of all, is there anything at all that you need? I cannot imagine being in the situation you both are, and we would be pleased to do anything we can to make you more comfortable here."

"Thank you," said Kiah. "I'm afraid we won't be able to stay long enough to get comfortable, though. Something's just come to our attention this morning, and we'll need to head back to the coast right away."

"I see," Taro said, looking a bit sour. "We'd hoped you might be persuaded to stay with us for a time."

"You honor us," she said, shooting Dylan a look not unlike Rory had seen mothers give their children when they thought they might be misbehaving. But the empath was innocently studying a spot on the wall just above everyone's heads. "We would love nothing more than to be able to rest and enjoy the elves' hospitality, and I hope that one day soon we will be able to. It's been too many years since the races, magical and human alike, welcomed and worked with one another. To that end, perhaps you would have an interest in forming an alliance."

Rory's fist clenched around the ring as she leaned forward.

"Alliance?" Taro glanced around at the other council members. "The elves of Maireadd have not allied themselves with any outsider since the curse."

"Yet you hoped to be able to claim my consort, the empath, as a resource that you might be able to use," said Kiah placidly.

Uneasy silence settled into the room. Finally Taro smiled. "It did seem prudent to offer our friendship and help to someone of such potential value."

"Then why not make it official?" Kiah said.

She said something else, too, but Rory didn't hear, as someone bumped into her arm and whispered "You must be happy about this."

"What?" She turned to find Vasya standing at her shoulder, looking smug.

"Agreeing to an alliance with your friends."

"We would be stronger for it." Rory turned back to the proceedings.

"Elves are the best mages in the world. Magic, skill, physical agility. We don't need a human, or selkies," he whispered, apparently not done with the conversation.

Rory rubbed her fingertips together, wishing she could cast a spell of silence on him. She wanted to hear what was going on.

"Oh wait, I forgot, your boyfriend is human."

She flattened her lips. "I'm trying to listen."

"Is he your lover, too?" Vasya wagged his eyebrows suggestively.

Rory turned on him with a silent snarl. "Back off," she hissed.

He raised his hands, grinning. "Hit a nerve there, did I? Well, I just came to tell you that Taro wants to see you after the meeting. You'll take our guests back to their house and then come right back."

Rory didn't respond.

"Did you hear me?"

She sneered without turning to him. "I heard."

He walked away, thankfully, but by then Kiah and Taro had finished their discussion, and Rory's belly was crawling with nerves. The meeting broke up a few minutes later, and she escorted Kiah and Dylan back to the treehouse where they were staying.

Returning to the meeting hall, Rory paused in the doorway, listening to the low murmur of voices from inside. The council were all still here, not just Taro and Borden, her bosses. And they'd returned to their seats round the circle in the big hall. *Oh, this can't be good.* She clutched Sean's ring for a moment, then tucked it away under her shirt before she stepped into the room. They would still be debating Kiah's proposed alliance before they agreed to make it official. But they wouldn't be still sitting around the circle to do that. Rory knew how these meetings worked, and normally they would dismiss and talk among themselves about any important decision before reconvening later in the day. Were they waiting for her?

Borden's questions that morning, then Vasya's smug and vaguely threatening conversation, and now this. Dread slithered through her as she approached Taro's seat from outside the circle. He turned at her approach and beckoned her toward the empty chairs that Kiah and Dylan had just vacated. He wasn't smiling anymore.

Rory sat down facing the ten members of the council, including her mother. A few other elves, Borden and Vasya among them, stood outside the circle as well, watching. Rory clasped her hands loosely in her lap, resisting the urge to reach for the signet ring, and returned their gazes.

21

LOYALTIES

"There are a couple of things that have come to the council's attention that we would like to discuss with you," said Taro. When Rory didn't respond right away, he cleared his throat and continued. "Uh, first, the matter of our new friends, Dylan Blaine and Kiah of Lomasi. Some of our scouts who accompanied you from the border reported that you seemed friendly with them, like you knew them before you met a few days ago. Did you?"

"Yes," said Rory. "I'd met them at the Seer's gala. We sat at the same table." Where were they going with this?

"Did you know Mr. Blaine was an empath before he came here?"

Rory paused to steel herself. Wherever this was going, it wasn't going to be good. This wasn't a discussion. This was a trial. "Yes. The Seer revealed several dangerous secrets of the people who sat with us, in confidence."

"And you didn't see fit to tell us any of this?" Taro looked stern and cold, and Rory had a good idea that this wasn't going to be the worst question they pulled out.

"It was in confidence," she repeated. "The Seer had a purpose for bringing us together that night, and it wasn't for the benefit of giving the elven council a new toy."

Wow, tactful, she chided herself silently. Someone in the room drew a sharp breath, and silence descended for an ominous moment.

Korin spoke up. "Did you forget that you happen to work for the elven council? Should we remind you of your job description?" A small elf, he was practically vibrating with rage. "What purpose could possibly supersede your loyalty to your own nation and race?"

Rory spread her hands on her lap, once again pausing for a few beats to collect the right words. "If you could go back in time and stop Maireadd from being cursed, would you?"

Silence.

She went on, "According to the Seer, there's a curse coming on Barra, because of the Witch Queen and the evil she's spreading. The Seer's purpose was to bring together a handful of people who could potentially help stop it. I don't know how, or why, but I was one of them. So yes, to me that seemed of greater importance than my duties to the elf council."

"Dragons take Barra," someone muttered.

Rory met the gaze of her mother, who looked pale, sitting with her lips compressed, her slender, elegant hands trembling in her lap. Rory wished she could pull her aside, to tell her how sorry she was to embarrass her or cause her grief. At the same time she had a sinking feeling. If her mother was worried for her, then she was probably in real trouble.

Taro cleared his throat. "Moving on, for now," he said, mercifully taking back the interrogation before the council got sidetracked arguing. "It seems there's another important piece of information you neglected to tell us. When you befriended the human, Sean Leigh, this past winter, he gave you his signet ring."

"Yes," said Rory simply, when Taro paused and waited. Her heart skipped a couple beats as she reached up and slowly drew the chain and ring out and let it fall outside her shirt. More murmurs spread around the circle.

"Can we assume that your relationship and knowledge of this human, a foreign operative and possible assassin, I might add, are more than you led us to believe?"

"I didn't lead you to believe anything," said Rory, her pulse thumping painfully in her ears. "He's a friend, and also a member of one of the Families. He gave me his seal because he values our friendship."

"You're not lovers, then? Usually those rings are only given to a spouse."

"We're not." Rory felt her face flush, and couldn't help glancing again at her mother, who wore an inscrutable expression, something between a grimace and a wince.

"Do you know more about him and his mission that you've told us?"

"Yes."

Silence. They wanted her to elaborate, but Sean's secrets weren't hers to tell, any more than Dylan's had been. She clenched her jaw and balled her hands and said nothing.

"You might want to make this easier on yourself," Taro said gently. "It looks bad enough keeping secrets. You'd do well to answer our questions now."

"Sean's identity and mission are not a threat to Maireadd."

"Should we believe you?" Korin snarled. "You haven't told us the truth about anything else."

"Really, Korin?" Rory's mother sighed. "Try to keep it civil, at least, would you?"

"I suppose you support your daughter's treason, then, Mara?" Korin turned on her, like an angry lap dog.

Mother arched an eyebrow at him. "I've hardly heard anything worthy of being called treason so far. Why don't we let Auralie continue?" Turning to Rory, she said, "What I'm hearing is that you've been serving both the Seer and the Council. You've made friends outside of Maireadd, and are trying to honor their trust by not divulging their secrets. That does put you in an awkward position, since in essence you are placing their interests above ours."

"It does," Rory admitted. "Maireadd is my home, and the elves are my people, but I have to follow my conscience, before God. Who am I, or what honor do I have if I don't?"

"So now you're saying that the Council isn't honoring God?" Korin butted in again. Taro raised his eyes to the ceiling and a couple of the other council members sighed.

"It seems to me that the Council usually serves the Council first, and only worries about serving God when His directives align with theirs."

Korin's face turned red with rage, while Mother winced.

Again, Taro jumped in before things could get out of hand. "Auralie, are you aware of what it means to bear a signet from one of the powerful Families? That you speak for them, and they for you? They will protect you as their own, and back you as their own."

"Yes, I know."

"It seems you have another claim to your loyalty, then."

"I hadn't considered it so."

"Do you think that kind of power goes only one way? Should they ever call on you to help one of their own, or fight one of their battles, you must answer."

Rory thought about that for a moment. She hadn't considered it before, but Sean had meant the ring as a gift, not a contract, otherwise he would have said something. He knew her position as an agent, with obligations and loyalties that couldn't be lightly set aside. She would never have agreed to any favors, no matter who asked, if they were detrimental to Maireadd or to her conscience. And that wasn't the point of the signet rings, anyway. Sean was honorable, and it was a gift given in honor. But the council wouldn't understand that. They would question whether that had been his purpose all along—to divide her loyalty.

"If that's not treason, then it's tiptoeing the very line of it." Korin emphasized his point by jabbing his finger in her direction. "The girl has sold herself to so many masters, she can hardly count them. And is she really telling the truth about her relationship with the man? The humans might be fools, but even they wouldn't give away that kind of power to someone who couldn't pay them back. Since our little agent isn't exactly a political prize, I can only assume he's getting it in favors of another kind."

Outraged magic sparked at Rory's fingertips, but she remained seated and kept her voice calm. "If the Council brought me here to slander my character and gossip about my personal reputation, then I think my time would be better spent elsewhere."

"All our time would be better spent elsewhere," grumbled someone else.

Taro frowned at his fellow council members. "Korin, let's not all turn into screeching pixies, shall we? Rory, we're not here to attack your personal life, but these are questions that need to be addressed. Do you have anything else to say on the matter?"

Well I don't know, it sounds like you've got me all figured out, Rory wanted to snarl. Instead, she said, "You set me to a task too big for one elf, and then accuse me when I accept help. You wanted me to befriend a human, but now you don't want me to actually be his friend. You failed to anticipate dangers that I only survived because of my human friend. If it wasn't for this," she held up Sean's ring, "I'd have been sacrificed to Queen Dianthe. If not for Sean himself, I'd have been eaten by ice dragons. And if he hadn't stopped that gorgrim attack on Barra, which I'll remind you was being blamed on us, all of Maireadd could very well be at war right now. He helped *you*, without coercion or even thanks. You assume that because we are elves—the best mages, the best warriors—that there is nothing to be gained or learned from other races, but I almost died because of that assumption. You wanted me to spy on the Seer and find out what he knew and how it could help us, but you didn't want me to actually engage with the Seer and listen to his advice. You say 'dragons take Barra,' but if Barra falls, we all suffer for it. Yes, I've kept secrets. Because of all this." She spread her hands in an appeal. "So what is it that you want from me?"

Taro drew a long breath. "I see."

"Thank you," said Mother. "We'll discuss this. If you'd like to go and rest, since you'll need to leave early tomorrow to take our friends back to the border..."

Rory nodded to her, then stood and walked out without another word. She met Vasya's eyes as she passed. She hadn't a single doubt that he was the cause of all this, but he wasn't worth her ire. Brushing past, she stepped out into the muggy summer afternoon warmth and hiked up to her treehouse. Only once she had locked herself inside did she collapse onto her bed and let the tears come. Eventually she fell asleep there with a damp, wadded handkerchief in her hand.

She woke late in the afternoon with puffy eyes and a face stiff with dried salt tears. Angry and ashamed of herself, she went to shower away evidence of her breakdown, and not too soon, for when she emerged from the bathroom she found Mother sitting on the couch waiting for her. Rory sat down beside her and Mother wrapped her in a tight hug.

"My strong, amazing girl," Mother murmured into her hair. "I am so proud of you."

Rory pulled away with a sigh. "Truly? For what? Ruining my own career? Getting myself exiled?"

"There won't be any exile. Not even Korin could convince anyone that that's warranted. The worst they agreed to was taking you out of the field for now and transferring you to border patrol."

"Wonderful." Rory scowled and rubbed her prickling eyes, determined not to give in to any more tears. It could have been worse. But it could have been much better, too. Stupid, stubborn Council. And where did that leave her? The chances of seeing Sean or the others ever again while stuck on patrol looked well nigh impossible. What use could she be to them now? She could quit altogether and do freelance mage work, perhaps, but that had never appealed to her.

"Don't give up," said Mother, tilting Rory's chin up like she used to do when she was a tiny elf girl. "You ruffled feathers today, but you're an excellent agent, and you've got connections now that they can't ignore."

"I'm not so sure I want to go back to being an agent... or a scout." Rory looked away, turning from her mother's soft gray eyes. "They were at least partly right, you know. When you wake up one day and realize that your only friends are the people who are your assignments, or who could be your enemies, it makes you question... things."

"You didn't fail the Council, they failed you. Perhaps all of us did. Just because you were an agent didn't mean that you needed to be isolated or under-prepared."

"It doesn't matter much now, does it?"

"It does matter. You held onto your honor and your convictions before God, Whose truths don't change with the shifting whims of politics or popular opinion, and that has carried you through this far. Suppose another agent without honor or conviction was sent out alone and tasked with the impossible? Would they sell us out or switch sides once we failed them? The council is upset, but if we don't learn from this, then we really are fools." She leaned back in the couch and blew out a breath, looking suddenly old and tired. "Sometimes I think I would like to give up my seat on the Council. You saw them in there today. Imagine having to work with Korin regularly."

Rory snorted. "He's like your own version of Vasya."

"Oh, honey, Vasya is a puppy who only thinks he has teeth." She laughed, and in a moment Rory was laughing with her.

And then instead of laughter it was sobs, and Rory clung to her mother and wailed, "I don't know what to do! Everything is ruined, and I've failed, and I think I might be in love, and it's all wrong, wrong, wrong!"

Mother pulled her close, rubbing her back and stroking her hair, whispering little hushing sounds. "Peace, my elfling. Your story isn't over yet."

"It feels like it is," Rory sniffled, collecting herself once again. She pulled back and scrubbed her eyes.

"Wash your face," said Mother. "The Council has agreed to Kiah of Lomasi's proposed alliance. You must go tell her. And in the morning you must leave again."

Rory nodded and rose without saying anything further. What was there to say? That evening she checked on Kiah and Dylan again, and in the morning, they left.

* * * * *

A day's ride brought them to the edge of Maireadd, miles to the north of Barra's capital. A rusty barbed-wire fence marked the end of Maireadd, and beyond it, open farmland leading to the road. Rory left the small band of accompanying guards and walked with them to the eves of the forest. She'd said nothing to them of her own troubles. With Dylan's family being threatened by Dianthe's sister Lyselle, and trouble on the Isle of Selkies, they didn't need her problems on top of their own.

"There's your road. Sorry to bring you out in the middle of nowhere like this, but it's probably the safest."

Kiah hugged her. "Thank you. Till we meet again."

"May God above light your way beyond the sunset's end," Rory replied, returning her embrace. "I hope next time we meet it's over hot chocolate and Sean's cinnamon rolls, and we're laughing over all of this." It was an impossible hope, a far-flung wish, but she wished it with all her heart.

"Me too."

Rory watched them start across the field, hand-in-hand, and her heart throbbed painfully. She returned to the horses and the waiting elves, and together they turned back toward Tristini. They would push on for another hour, until it got dark, before stopping for the night.

None of the other elves spoke to Rory as they rode and later made camp, and she didn't try to break the cool silence. It wasn't worth the effort. Anyway, summer nights in Maireadd were all but deafening, especially since they'd made camp near a bog. Insects, frogs, and wind in the trees, added to intermittent owl screeches and passing bands of wolves or werewolves. Rory rolled into her sleeping bag and cast a mild sound dampening spell in her tent, more to muffle the voices of the other elves than the sounds of the forest.

She pulled her magic mirror out of her pack and held it in her hands, debating for a moment whether to call Sean. When had it become her first instinct to share her heartaches and joys with him? But this time was different, since he was at the heart of the falling out with the Council. Would he take blame upon himself for it, if she told him?

Perhaps she should wait until her own heart wasn't as raw. But she wanted to see his face again so badly, and if she left him a message, he would surely call her back, eventually. In the end, she fell asleep with the mirror clutched in her hand.

The mirror's frantic chiming awakened her the next morning. Rory's heart sank when Kiah's face appeared in the glass, streaked with blood and tears.

"Lyselle's taken Dylan."

22

A JOB TO DO

Sean jumped when one of the sous chefs dropped a spoon and it went clattering across the floor. He chuckled at himself for the benefit of anyone who might be watching, and it was a good chuckle. It didn't sound fake, or convey any of the nerves that were making his stomach squirm. He pushed through the swinging doors and stepped into the hallway. Tonight, the doors to the court stood open with the usual number of guards, though that wasn't particularly reassuring. Open court wasn't supposed to be until next week. Dianthe had called everyone together early, just a few days after Dylan and Kiah's escape.

Sean wasn't the only one with jitters tonight. The second he stepped into the grand ballroom he noticed the noise level was lower than usual, even though the room was packed. People stood clumped more closely together, spoke more quietly. Glances darted. There was a rumor that something was happening tonight, though no one knew what it was. Even the kitchen staff was wondering what was going on. They had asked if he knew. Why the last minute change? He told them he didn't know. That was a lie.

He'd checked the messages on his magic mirror right before he came in that afternoon, and found the one a panicked Kiah had left earlier in the day.

Dylan Blaine had been taken.

Rory had escorted Dylan and Kiah back out of Maireadd, and they had returned to the coast after Beck tipped him off that Lyselle was holding his family. Dylan, apparently, had hoped he could persuade her to let them go. Which she had. But she'd taken him, instead. Kiah hadn't gone into the details, but as far as anyone knew, Dylan was back in the capital right now. The queen probably had him stashed here at the palace somewhere. Thankfully, he was too valuable to be killed. Judging by the flying rumors, she was probably planning on showing him off tonight like a prize pony.

Sean smiled and greeted a few acquaintances as he made his way through the crowd looking for Calla and Jamie. He spotted them toward the back of the room. Calla stood against the wall, for once not swarmed with schmoozing nobles—probably because Jamie stood a step in front of her, glaring like he might eat anyone that came too close. Sean caught her eye. She beckoned him over, then touched Jamie's shoulder lightly. The werewolf relaxed—sort of—dropping his aggressive stance as Sean approached.

"Mr. Leigh. How are you?" She smiled and offered her hand.

He bowed over it. "Fine, Your Highness. Thank you. Yourself? You look lovely tonight." Which she did, wearing one of the little black dresses that she favored, with a pair of little black heels. Her blonde hair was swept up into an elegant twist. Jamie scowled at him. He needn't have. Sean would much rather have seen Rory dressed up and sparkling in the light of the chandeliers.

"What's happening?" he asked under his breath.

"I haven't been able to learn anything. Only that he's being held in the old tower keep. The guards aren't letting anyone anywhere near there, either. Not even me. Only Dianthe, Lyselle, and Beck, have been in that whole wing of the castle all day." She rubbed her arms. "I feel sick."

Trumpets blasted their obnoxious message that the royals had arrived. The whole room hushed as the royals descended their grand staircase, the king looking as vacant as ever while his queen flashed a hundred karat smile and even gave a little wave.

"This can't be good," Jamie muttered.

Tonight, Dianthe didn't even bother to pretend to let King Ebezer greet the court. She directed him to his throne where he sat down and smiled his benevolent, stupid smile at everyone.

Sloppy, Dianthe, Sean thought. But sloppy was not a good thing. Sloppy meant that she didn't care. That she didn't need people to believe her lies anymore.

"Welcome, everyone!" she called happily. "After our little snafu last week, I can promise you that tonight will more than make up for it. Tonight is going to be special, my friends."

Sean touched the string tie at his neck. He and Calla exchanged a look as the excited introduction continued. At last the queen subsided and looked to the side door that led from the dais to a small anteroom. The kitchen staff had been ordered to bring refreshments back there before court. Now the door opened, and Dylan Blaine stepped onto the stage.

The whole room seemed to draw one collective breath in a gasp.

"May I present Dylan Blaine of Lomasi—Barra's very own empath. I don't think he's going to be running off this time."

About the only recognizable feature was the empath's dirty blond hair. His face was a mess of blood and darkening bruises, with one eye swollen shut and a long, thin slice down one cheek that oozed blood. His nose looked blobby and discolored, and blood had gushed out of it at some point, then been smeared everywhere. His shirt had been torn open and his chest and arms worked over with fist and knife, leaving welts and long, shallow slashes. His hands were cuffed in front of him. He looked like he could barely stand.

Beside Sean, Calla let out a distressed whimper before covering her mouth. Even stoic Jamie looked taken aback.

Dread settled in Sean's gut like a yawning cavern. Had they already tortured Dylan for information? Who had he given up? Or was the queen just softening him up for this moment?

"What is this, Dianthe?" Prince Gaelan demanded, interrupting whatever she was about to say. He stormed toward the dais with the crowd melting back out of his path. "You've gone too far!"

The queen held up a hand. "Relax. Don't you want to see what our empath is capable of?"

"He's my friend." Gaelan looked like he was going to strangle his stepmother.

"And I'll return him in one piece, once we've had our fun," she replied, exasperated. "As long as he cooperates. Don't make a scene in front of everyone, dear."

She turned back to the crowd, drawing a little vial from the bosom of her dress. Its contents were so blue they seemed to glow.

"This can't be good," Jamie muttered again under his breath.

Dianthe smiled, still putting on her show. "Truth potion. You've no doubt heard of it—the elves make it. It renders anyone who takes it incapable of lying. So whatever our friend here says, you can count on it being the honest truth." She gave one of her tinkling little laughs and tossed the vial to Lyselle, who'd come in behind Dylan.

"Really, Dianthe?" the prince protested as he stepped up to the foot of the dais. "Is all this necessary? What are you hoping to achieve here?"

"I'm going to find out who my enemies are!"

Sean felt the bottom fall out of his stomach. He touched his string tie again, then shoved his hands into his pockets. Murmurs rippled through the crowd. Calla had her fists clenched, her face mottled red and white. For the first time, Dylan showed real signs of life. He drew himself up suddenly as Lyselle stepped toward him with that vial of potion.

"Wait." His voice carried over the crowd, strong in spite of his injuries, though his broken nose made it sound nasally. He held out his cuffed hands to Lyselle. "I'll take it. I won't be lying to anyone today."

"Dylan, man, you don't have to do that," said Gaelan.

Sean was casting his own desperate looks toward the doors. They'd all been shut. The guards stood at attention. He looked over at Jamie and met his eyes. The werewolf gave him a fraction of a nod. They were in it together if this went any farther south.

Dylan took the vial from Lyselle and tossed it back like a shot of alcohol. He threw the empty vial down at Dianthe's feet.

"Actually, I do," said Dylan to the prince. "Truth is important. And who would stop the sorceress from having her way, anyway? Certainly not your father. He sold his will to this witch years ago, and I doubt there's anything of the real man left. The king is long gone." He paused, then grinned savagely, making fresh blood trickle from his split lip. "Wouldn't you know. The truth."

Dianthe slapped him. "Speak when I tell you to."

"Or you'll torture me again, or try a subversion spell, like your sister did, yes I know. What I wonder is if I'm valuable enough to keep you from killing me outright."

Dianthe actually hissed. Like a snake. "You're trying to goad me."

Dylan shrugged, then winced.

"It won't work."

"It already has," he replied. "Oh look. More truth."

Sean's stomach squirmed, whether in horror and dread or in glee, he couldn't say. He kept holding his breath.

"Yes, truth. And here's the part where you pay for it." Dianthe brought her hands in close, muttering over them under her breath. Then she reached out and touched Dylan.

His back arched and he went rigid as though he'd touched a live wire. And he screamed. A raw, agonized scream that wouldn't end. The kind of sound that no human being should ever make.

Sean took a step forward, even though there was nothing he could do. He was gasping in shallow breaths now himself, his throat aching, as though something in his stomach was trying to claw its way up and out.

The queen let Dylan go and he fell, just folding up and hitting the floor. But at least the screaming stopped. His chest rose and fell in shallow breaths, while the chandelier light glistened in the gore coating his face. After a moment he stirred, then rolled to his knees. He stayed hunched there for another long moment, coughing a few times before pushing slowly to his feet. His face, beneath the blood and bruises, had turned gray.

"Don't goad me," Dianthe said smugly.

"Or you'll do it again. I get it." Dylan said, somehow pulling himself upright and standing tall once again. His voice was wrecked. "Like a shock collar for your dog, right?"

"Damn," Jamie whispered.

And that was more articulate than anything Sean could come up with. His fear had just transformed into something like hero worship. In that moment he knew to the bottom of his soul that no force on earth could compel the empath to betray any of them.

The queen regarded her prize for a moment. "You're going to tell me who my enemies are here today. Finally, I'll know who is really loyal to me."

"You do know that I'm an empath, not a psychic, right?" Dylan said. "Also, you're paranoid. That's a bad trait in anyone."

"But you still know. You can tell who's afraid of me. Who feels guilty."

"Everyone in this room is afraid of you. Come to think of it, that's probably a pretty good reason for you to be paranoid."

"Except you, perhaps?" she shot back. "You don't seem afraid. Fool."

The empath merely shrugged. He scanned the crowd, meeting Sean's gaze for a moment before he closed his eyes.

Dianthe snapped her fingers under his nose. "Come now, empath. Stay with me here, unless you want another lesson. It's time to begin. You'll start with him." She turned and pointed to Prince Gaelan, of all people, who still stood at the foot of the dais. Gaelan's face went white and his eyes wide. He hadn't been expecting that.

Dylan looked at the prince, then at the queen. "You're right to be paranoid, Dianthe. Not because of the prince, or the princess, or the elves or the selkies or any of the Families or the nobles here today." His voice rose as he listed off the factions. "Because of all of them. You want to know who your enemies are, who is loyal to you—but when have you ever deigned to befriend anyone, or to reward loyalty? Since you've subjugated and destroyed the king, loyalties aside, Prince Gaelan is the rightful ruler of Barra. You could assassinate him—you could execute everyone in this room—but there would always be others. Someone will always be against you. You are evil, and as long as you live there will be good people who are brave enough to stand against you."

Dianthe's face went white. "Have a care, empath. Your usefulness only goes so far. You will cooperate, eventually."

"No, I don't think I will. Kill me, if you like. It'll be less embarrassing, and save you time. But I won't be your puppet. Ever."

"You'll change your mind." She reached out toward him again.

Sean took another involuntary step forward. "No, no, no, no," he muttered under his breath. He could feel the blood draining out of his face, his heart tearing apart in his chest.

But this time when she touched Dylan, he reached out first and grabbed her wrist with his cuffed hands. And then somehow she was the one screaming. She collapsed to her knees, Dylan's grip the only thing still keeping her up as her screams became raw and rasping and then fell silent. He let go and she slumped to the floor.

No one moved in the whole ballroom. No one even breathed. Not until Dylan stepped back away from the unconscious queen, his gaze sweeping the crowd. Then Lyselle motioned and the guards rushed forward to seize him. More guards and servants rushed to the queen as they hauled him toward the door.

"Courage," he said over his shoulder, just loud enough to carry over the rising chaos. A moment later the feeling hit. Courage.

Everyone else felt it too. Everyone seemed to pause for just a moment—even the guards as they were hauling Dylan out.

For Sean it felt like he could breathe again. Like he was invincible. For one insane moment he considered going up on that dais and snapping Dianthe's neck while she was unconscious, right there in front of the whole court. He didn't have much time to dwell on that foolish thought though. A moment after Dylan left, followed by Lyselle, Dianthe revived. Her face was a ghastly chalk color and she didn't even spare a glance for the court, for whom she'd been putting on the show just a few minutes ago. She exited into the anteroom, leaning on one of the servants. A moment later, once pandemonium had taken over the room, a man slunk up onto the dais and slipped through the door after them. He was wearing a dark cloak, of all things, and for some reason Sean, who was still watching, felt his skin crawl.

"Did you see that?" he asked. It was loud enough in the room that Jamie, with his sensitive ears, was the only one who heard him. He nodded, looking uneasy.

"You should go," Calla said, touching Sean's elbow. "I don't know what's going to happen tonight." When he started to protest she said, "If there's anything you can do, we'll call you. But you're not going to get anywhere when we can't—not without endangering yourself. And we're going to need you." She looked grim.

Sean raised his brows.

"Someone needs to kill that witch."

"Right."

* * * * *

Sean couldn't go home. Not after tonight. Instead, he drove to the little stone chapel by the river, lit another candle—the priest had them sitting out on the altar now—and settled onto the front pew. If ever there was a night to hold vigil for a friend, it was tonight.

Someone needs to kill that witch.

The job he'd been sent to Barra to do. He'd killed his share of monsters and men, but she scared him like none of the others ever had. Whatever torture spell she'd used on Dylan, she could do to him as well, and probably a hundred others like it. Did he even stand a chance? And what would happen if he failed?

He felt queasy.

Leaning back, he closed his eyes and recalled the raw courage that Dylan had sent out over the crowd an hour ago. It had felt like... freedom. Did the empath even know what he'd done tonight? Not just with manipulating the emotions of the crowd, but with standing up to Dianthe. He'd been crushed and broken and still, somehow, utterly fearless. And in being fearless, refusing to cower and be beaten, he'd stripped Dianthe of her power. And it had been glorious.

"She'll kill him for it," Sean said quietly to the empty sanctuary. He sent up yet another silent prayer for his friend's life.

The door leading back to the office creaked open and the priest poked his head out. "Ah. I thought I heard someone come in." He joined Sean, trying to tug his rumpled corduroy straight as he sat down. He noted the candle and asked, "Who's in trouble this time?"

"Another friend. It's bad."

The priest nodded. He stood back up and lit a second candle, then sat back down, bowing his head in silent prayer. They sat together in silence for a long time.

"I have a job to do, and I don't know if I can do it," Sean said presently.

"Is it resolution you lack, or skill?" asked the priest.

"Neither. It needs doing, and I'm good at that kind of thing. But this situation is different. I'm afraid it might be too big for me."

"God did say that it's not good for man to be alone. You can ask for help, you know."

Sean stared into the steady candle flame. "Maybe."

"This city is tearing itself apart," the priest said, for once opting to turn the conversation himself. "Whatever kind of trouble you and your friends seem to always find yourselves in, I hope it's the kind that will do some good."

"What have you heard?"

"Humans and magicals distrust one another more than ever. Violence is getting more common. And my people are talking about hellhounds here in the city. There are masked sorcerers haunting the streets.... This job that you need to do—I hope you can finish it soon."

"Yeah. I wish it was that simple."

23

AS GOOD AS DEAD

Three days passed before Sean heard anything more about Dylan's fate. Calla never contacted him to mount a rescue mission, even the news reports were suspiciously quiet about the whole affair. So he'd gone on with his routine as though nothing had happened, even though it was eating him alive. His day off came and went—he snuck into the weight room in the manor and spent most of the day working out and practicing forms. On his way out he paused to watch the news with his uncle for a few minutes. They were talking about a big storm happening over the channel and the Isle of Selkies. A magic-fueled storm. Commentators were blaming it on the selkies, though as far as he knew no one had ever heard of a selkie controlling weather on any kind of large scale. Their realm of power was the sea.

Back at work the next day, the kitchen staff were still buzzing quietly, whispering things like "Furious," and "Escaped." He didn't dare ask, but let them whisper until productivity suffered, then chewed them out for gossiping instead of working.

The next day he got a text from Calla telling him to stop by the shop because she had a new book by his favorite author, which could only mean they had news about Dylan. He intended to stop in before work, but Lina cornered him after his workout and demanded he tell her what had happened at court, because all her friends were talking about it. Then his uncle wanted to show him more news

248

footage—this time of some kind of attack in the city. Mutilated bodies were being found in the slums and on the streets. Magicals were to blame, of course.

By the time he extricated himself it was too late to stop. He drove to work in frustration, only to find the head chef out sick again, leaving him in charge. Which meant, since tonight was the night the next week's food order needed to be placed, he wouldn't get done any time before midnight. So much for this not being a real job.

No one remembered to leave the lights on for him—again. He turned the light off in the office and stepped out into the darkened kitchen, pausing for a moment to let his eyes adjust while half expecting Dianthe to come prancing through again, or worse. Being in the palace at night gave him the creeps lately, and tonight he could practically feel evil brooding in the shadows. Everything was dead silent, and there was an eerie, indefinable quality to the night that made his hackles rise. Suddenly he wanted nothing more than to get out of there.

Tucking his motorcycle helmet under his arm, he crept through the kitchen, stepping quietly so his sneakers made no sound on the tile, and touched the doors. Nothing. No sound. So why did he feel like something was incredibly wrong?

A muffled shout followed by a thump drifted down the hallway. About to push the door open, Sean's hand stilled and he peeked through the crack between the swinging doors just in time to see Queen Dianthe stride past. She was chuckling to herself, her head held high, and passed by not more than two feet away. He jerked back.

After a moment holding his breath, Sean eased forward to peer between the doors again. No sign of the queen or anyone else out there. He cracked a door enough to get a better look and verify that the hall was clear. More thumps, followed by a crash. He approached the ballroom cautiously. Cracking the door first, he took a quick look, then stepped silently into the room. He stood in the shadows with his hand on the door, ready to make a quick exit if needed.

Daylight had gone from the skylights, and the chandeliers were darkened, leaving the room semi-lit by strip lights along the base of the walls, and dimmed decorative lamps in the alcoves. The middle of the huge room was shadowy and he had to let his eyes adjust again, after being in the brighter hallway. It took a moment for him to understand what was happening.

Crown Prince Gaelan crouched awkwardly near one of the marble pillars, clutching his side with one hand while holding the other outstretched toward one of the buffet tables, which hovered in front of him like a shield. Levitating. He was using black magic. Trying to defend himself against...what?

A shadow. It took a moment for Sean to spot it, and then for an instant he thought it was a hellhound. But the movement seemed wrong. Then it passed in front of a light, where he could see the silhouette. A panther?

But not a panther, either, because as he watched, the form seemed to flicker and hesitate, and for just a moment, it was a man.

Then it was a panther again. But not. It was too dark. The lights, dim as they were, didn't gleam in its fur. Instead it spread shade around it, dimming the light even further. And its eyes were glowing a soft golden-green.

Sean's lips parted in a silent curse. What the blue dragon fire was that thing?

Better question—should he let it kill the corrupted prince and save himself the trouble later?

The panther thing paced, forcing Gaelan to move the table to keep it between them. It crouched, and for a moment Sean thought it was going to jump right over top of the floating table. Instead, it disappeared. Gaelan, shielded behind the table, couldn't see it—until it rematerialized in the shadows beside him.

Sean acted without thinking. He couldn't help himself.

"Hey!" He took a step into the room and chucked his helmet at the beast. Gaelan and the panther both turned. The beast's form dissolved into shadow and became a man. One that Sean recognized, but took a moment to place. "Beck?"

For a moment they all looked at one another, frozen in tableau.

Sean stepped closer. The assassin's form blurred, becoming shadowy around the edges, then solidified again. Gaelan dropped the table.

"I suggest you run, Prince," growled Beck, without turning to look at him.

Gaelan shoved to his feet, still clutching his side. He looked from Beck to Sean. "I messed up," he said. "I'm sorry." Then he turned and ran for the nearest exit.

Beck twitched. The shadows wrapped around him again, blurring his form as he whipped back toward the fleeing prince. "Not fast enough," he said, his voice gravelly and inhuman as he resumed his shadow panther shape.

"What the...?" Sean dove after panther Beck, catching him in a flying tackle that slammed them both to the floor hard enough to rattle teeth. "I thought you were on our side now," he gasped, wrestling two hundred pounds of pissed off panther as it heaved to its feet with him still hanging on. Gaelan disappeared through the door. For a moment Beck paused.

"I'm not on anyone's side. Not yours. Not his." He resumed bucking and wiggling, his paws scrabbling toward the door after the prince. "Definitely not on that bitch Dianthe's side." He freed himself with a kick to Sean's face. Fortunately his claws weren't out, but he still snapped Sean's head back and left his chin stinging. Beck bolted.

Sean scrambled after them. "I'm really confused."

Instead of picking a door that led into one of the many hallways, Gaelan had run for the one that opened onto a balcony overlooking the palace gardens. Sean came through the doors just in time to see panther Beck's tail vanish over the stone railing. He slid to a stop and looked down. It was a full story down to the courtyard below. Grumbling, he backed up to get a running start and leapt, planting one foot on the railing to boost himself into a somersault. He flipped outward in a drop that only lasted a second and ended in a shock and a rolling tumble. Next second he was back on his feet and sprinting after them again.

Up ahead something crashed. A sculpted stone birdbath flew past his head as he came around the curve in the path. Beck tumbled into view next, coming to a stop sprawled in the walkway. Gaelan stood in the shadows between a rose-covered arbor and an ornamental cherry tree, his hand still outstretched and chest heaving as though he'd thrown the great hunk of stone himself. Blood glistened darkly down his arm. He looked at Sean wide-eyed.

"I messed up," he said again. "I just wanted to stop her, but Dianthe knew it. She summoned him..." He looked at Beck, who stirred and started to rise.

Sean dug his bike key out of his pocket and tossed it to the prince. "Get out of here. Maireadd. Find Rory."

"I'll never make it," Gaelan said, catching the key out of the air. "The shadows are coming for me too. I messed up."

Wondering what he was talking about, and thinking he must be losing it, Sean glanced at the shadows around them. He jumped and swore. Gaelan wasn't crazy. The shadows were alive, writhing and reaching. The prince gave him a rueful smile.

"I'm as good as dead."

Beck stood, taking his human form and looking around. He started to growl. The shadows danced back away from him, but they continued to move and solidify. Sean strode past the assassin, stepped over a quickly solidifying shadow, and slapped Prince Gaelan across the face.

"Run, idiot."

24

SHADOW PANTHER

Shocked, Gaelan stared at Sean for a moment. Then he turned and ran.

Sean spun back in time to collide with Beck. He hauled off and punched him before he could resume chasing the prince. Beck snarled, his attention finally snapping away from his prey. He dropped into a fighting stance and struck out, still moving like a predator. Sean blocked a blow that would have blinded him, and another that should have broken his nose. He jabbed a quick kick toward Beck's knee, but the assassin flowed away. It was like trying to fight with water.

Beck was a predator. Lethal, graceful, and quick as a striking snake. But Sean was fast and powerful and moved without thought. They danced around one another, trading strikes and blocks too fast to see, fighting on instinct rather than sight, while around them the shadows took form and glowing red eyes blinked to life.

Sean swatted away a jab from Beck aimed at his throat, then jerked back as a dark shape launched toward him from the side. Red eyes. Claws that just caught his leather coat sleeve on the way past, shredding it. The newly materialized hellhound missed ripping his arm off by an inch, landing between him and Beck. They both stumbled backward. It lunged for Sean again.

He jumped back with a yell. The monster's paws raked across his chest, slicing open his leather jacket like tissue paper, and skimming shallowly across his skin. Unnatural pain ignited from the scratches. Massive jaws snapped shut a hair's breadth from his throat, slapping him with flying drool. He kept stumbling backward with the hound snapping and clawing after him till his back hit the arbor. Throwing an arm up to protect his throat, he fumbled with his other hand toward the cord around his neck that held Rory's light crystal. The hellhound's paws hit him full in the chest. The jaws started to close on his arm...

And then it was gone.

The weight left so fast that he sagged forward for an instant, even as he pulled the crystal free of his collar.

"Light!" he gasped.

Sudden white light blazed out like lightning across their corner of the garden, instantly dazzling and revealing. Beck had caught the hellhound by the scruff and hauled it back, yipping and whining like a puppy. His form blurred into shadow for a moment, then vanished, taking the hound with him.

Sean stood there, panting and blinking in the light, clutching his chest. He was still staring around stupidly when Beck re-materialized and stepped out of the shadow of the cherry tree. Sean tensed and dropped into a defensive stance, but the assassin just frowned at him. He was alone. No hellhound.

"Put that light away before someone sees it."

Sean let the light fade and tucked it away, keeping a wary eye on the other man. "What did you do with the hellhound?"

"Took it back to the shadow world. There were two others though. They went after the prince. He's gone, so they'll probably head into the city now."

"He's gotten away gone, or dead gone?"

"Got away. I don't sense him nearby anymore, but he's still out there." For a moment the assassin stared out across the garden, and his eyes seemed to light up from within, glowing like they had when he was a shadow panther. "We should probably find those hounds before they kill anyone."

"You have wheels?" Sean asked.

Beck growled. "No. I was summoned." He brushed past and started walking back toward the palace.

Sean followed, mentally going through files of information on every non-human person, creature, or entity he'd been forced to study. Finally he asked, "What are you?"

Beck glanced back, his face shadowed and unreadable. "What I am has not been named in Barra in over five hundred years, and I won't name my kind now. I'd like to know how Dianthe figured it out."

They stopped under the balcony from which they'd jumped earlier. Sean looked around, searching for a way up to it. "You're going back in?" he asked, thinking of the incriminating bike helmet he'd left in the ballroom.

"I need to erase the security cameras, and make sure they don't record us leaving. Neither one of us want our secrets getting out, do we?" Beck grinned a predatory grin at him, his pointy incisors gleaming in the light from intermittent solar lamps along the path. He took a couple steps running start, then used one of the stone lovers' benches as stairs, his foot hitting the seat, then the back rest, then making an inhuman leap up to grab the floor of the balcony. He used the railing to haul himself up and over, disappearing inside an instant later.

Sean was still eyeing the distance and calculating whether he'd be able to do the same thing when Beck reappeared and tossed his helmet down to him.

"Meet me in the parking lot." He disappeared again, leaving Sean alone in the garden.

Sean rubbed the growing pain in his chest. "Well this has been monumentally weird." But he couldn't turn back now. He needed answers, and not just to satisfy his raging curiosity. Beck knew way too much about him. Sean needed to find out what he planned to do with that information, and who else knew.

Picking his way through the garden, he examined the slashes in his coat, and the four thin scratches beneath. They weren't deep, just enough to stain the edges of his torn shirt a bit, and to deliver a small amount of their venom into his bloodstream. He grimaced. Hellhounds' teeth and claws carried a unique type of venom that inflicted pain on their victim. It wasn't necessarily deadly, by itself, unless the person had a weak heart. But it would cause horrific pain. The more venom, the more pain. Even these small scratches burned like he'd been slapped with a smoking hot fry basket. Worse, other hellhounds were drawn to the marked victim. There was no cure for it, that he knew of, other than to let it work its way through his system for the next few hours, or days.

One of the lights had blown out in the employee parking lot. Given Beck's apparent gift for vanishing and reappearing in shadows, it probably wasn't the best place to hide, but it galled Sean to linger out in the open, so he stuffed himself into the shrubbery bordering the dark area of the lot and waited. Looking around, his motorcycle wasn't where he'd left it, so at least Beck must have been right, that the prince got away. Hopefully that wouldn't come back to bite him in the butt later.

Five minutes passed before the assassin slunk into view. He scanned the area and headed right toward Sean.

"It's where I would have hidden," he said when he got close enough to speak quietly and still be heard. He nodded toward a big black SUV with tinted windows. "There's our ride." He started toward it.

Sean didn't budge.

After a few paces Beck turned back. He studied Sean silently for a moment before he said, "I think we'd both agree that a conversation would be mutually beneficial right now."

"Yeah," said Sean, stepping out of the shrubbery. "I just don't feel like trading punches in a moving vehicle."

"I have no reason to try to kill you," said Beck.

That might or might not be true. Sean really had no idea what was going on, but the assassin had been going after Gaelan, and showed no interest in Sean until he got in the way. On the other hand... what in the blazing inferno was going on tonight?

He nodded finally and got in. "Any idea where those hellhounds went?"

"You'll make good bait with those scratches. And I can track them."

"Of course you can. Cause that's perfectly logical."

Beck glanced over as they drove past the guard shack and out the gate. His eyes glowed faintly, which was dang creepy.

"My people are flesh and bone and we live in this world, but we're also spirit and shadow, and can walk in the other world as well—parts of it. I can sense when creatures of that realm, like hellhounds, are nearby. My kind were created, or maybe hybridized or cursed—who knows—to prey on evil creatures. We can be summoned and set against witches and sorcerers, hellhounds, soothsayers. But once someone summons one of us—me— and sends me after a target, I'm a slave to it. Compelled. I have to either kill the target or be killed. We've worked very hard to erase the memory of our existence."

"Interesting." Sean responded. He wasn't sure what else to say, since his questions had just multiplied rather than diminished. Should he believe all this? But he'd more or less seen it for himself.

"I'll go after the prince again—my nature and Dinathe's meddling will drive me to hunt him down eventually, but for now, as long as he's not nearby, I'm in control."

"So... because he stole magic and became a sorcerer, binding himself to evil, Dianthe was able to sic you after him?"

Beck's lip curled. "Something like that."

"But she's way worse. She's killed—who knows? Maybe hundreds—to get her power. Yet you were working for her."

"Gotta pay the bills. I'm good at killing things. And as long as no one knew I could be summoned and controlled, I was safe."

"Hm."

They left Royal Boulevard and took a turn onto a cracked and darkened side street that led to the warehouse district. Sean grimaced and rubbed at his chest again.

"And you're going to swear on your honor that you will never tell anyone—human or magical—what I've just told you. Nor will you seek a way to summon me or any of my kind."

Sean studied the other man's profile in the dim glow of the dash lights. He showed no emotion, yet somehow radiated an intensity that was palpable. He'd just spilled probably his deepest secret—and that made Sean more than a little uneasy.

"You have my word," he said.

"Good. Otherwise I would hunt you down and kill you and everyone you love... including that pretty little elf." Beck's pointed canines gleamed for a moment when he smiled.

Sean said nothing. He wouldn't want this guy for an enemy. But if he was telling the truth, then he also understood why he was demanding secrecy. Either way, he would stand by his word.

"Now that that's out of the way..." Beck pulled off the street and stopped in front of a deserted furniture warehouse. Grass grew through cracks in the pavement, briefly spotlighted by the headlights before he flicked them off. "Your next question will be whether I've told Dianthe about you. I haven't."

"What about me?"

"You're an operative sent here from the Thyrus government, and your assignments are usually the kind where people end up dead. You're like me—good at killing things. Which means that Thyrus wants someone at court to die. Probably Dianthe. What I don't know is whether your people know about your affair with the elf."

Sean didn't bother pointing out that kissing under an arbor didn't constitute an affair. Instead he said, "Impressive. And since you've been working for Dianthe, the reason you didn't tell her all this is...?"

"Dianthe is a rabid dog. She needs to be put down—the sooner the better."

"And the reason you don't do it is...?"

"I was working for her voluntarily until a few days ago." He started drumming his fingers on the steering wheel—the first sign of anxiety or discomfort he'd shown. Was he actually that afraid of the queen? He killed the engine and cocked his head as though listening for something, then said, "She has a soothsayer."

"Yeah, I know."

"Don't let him near you. Don't try to kill the queen when he's nearby, either. And don't let him or Dianthe touch you." Beck rubbed at the side of his neck, as though trying to brush away a phantom itch. Maybe a phantom memory.

"What about Gaelan?" Sean asked. "You got away from Dianthe—whatever your motivations were—but then Gaelan stole magic, which allowed her to summon you back and activate this curse, or whatever it is, that's going to drive you to hunt him down. Am I getting all that right? So you'll kill him, then?"

"Eventually. Maybe in the next few days, or a couple weeks at most. Unless he finds a way to kill me first—or to remove his black magic."

"Is that possible?"

The other man was silent for a long moment before he said, "Yeah. It's possible. But not without help."

"Who? Or how? Maybe Calla or Rory can find a way to tell him?"

Beck scowled, suddenly tense. "Let Gaelan die. He deserves it. There's only one guy I know of who can or would help him—but last time he took magic off a witch, it almost killed him. Listen, you need to hurry up and kill Dianthe. She figured out how to get me after Gaelan, and she's already tried to have Calla killed. One of these days she'll succeed. And one of these days she's going to figure you out, too, and then you'll wish you were dead. Best get it done before that happens."

Sean shifted uncomfortably in his seat. The silence in the vehicle pressed on him. Beck wasn't the only one afraid of the queen and her soothsayer.

"I didn't tell her about you, but that doesn't mean she isn't suspicious," Beck said. "Watch your back, and don't wait too long." He cocked his head again, then opened his door and jumped out.

Easier said, Sean thought, wincing as he followed.

25

BEING STUPID

It took a moment for Sean to spot the black shapes and two pairs of glowing red eyes slinking along in the shadow of the warehouse. Beck, catlike even in his human form, prowled to meet them. Sean followed, allowing a bit of distance and clutching Rory's light crystal in his hand, waiting to see what Beck would do.

The hounds stopped as Beck approached, sidling back a bit and spreading out. The assassin stopped as well. One minute he was standing there staring them down. Next minute, he was gone and his shadow panther form had one of the hounds by the throat. The panther and his prey vanished in the next instant, leaving Sean alone with the remaining hellhound.

The light crystal bit into his hand, ready to flood the parking lot with brilliance, but he waited, looking into those red eyes as they took a step toward him. They were mesmerizing, pulsing. The pain of the scratches across his chest seemed to rise up and pulse in time to those eyes, growing worse with each beat.

Beck reappeared behind the hound, but the beast was too focused on Sean to notice until it was too late. It only took a few seconds for the panther assassin to drag it back to wherever it had come from and then reappear as Beck. He nodded to Sean.

"You kept it occupied so it didn't run off. Thanks."

Sean let go of the light crystal and wiped his sweaty palm down his pants. "Sure," he panted as they walked back to the SUV. "Got a plan now?"

"Since I'm technically a fugitive in a stolen vehicle, I'm gonna disappear for a while. I'll take you to the border so you can get your bike back. If Gaelan was smart he ditched it before Maireadd. Since he's not dead yet, I'm assuming he was smart."

"You can tell where he is?"

"Oh yeah."

It didn't take long, once they were out of the city, to reach the place where the road ran out, becoming a faded dirt track that dwindled before disappearing into the eaves of the cursed forest. Sure enough, there was his motorcycle lying on its side, just at the foot of the first line of trees. Gaelan was nowhere in sight, though as they approached, Beck tensed up, drumming his fingers on the wheel again. He let Sean out without a word, turned the vehicle around, and took off, throwing dirt. Sean walked over and righted his bike.

"Could have used the kickstand," he grumbled.

The forest loomed before him, dark and watchful, with a seething malevolence in the whisper of branches without a breeze. This close to Maireadd, his thoughts turned to Rory. Where was she right now? Somewhere near?

"Alright, I'm going," he said to the forbidding line of trees guarding the border like sentries, and put his helmet on. He wheeled the bike up the path a ways before starting it up. Its roar shattered the night, and the feeling of watchful hostility increased behind him, raising the hairs on the back of his neck. He gunned it and sped away, relieved when the tires hit pavement. Though going back into Eyren was probably no less dangerous. There was no safety for him now—not unless he forsook his mission and went home, and even then he'd have to cross Maireadd to get there. No, now it was either succeed or die. And more immediately, there was the matter of the hellhound venom burning his chest, which would draw the creatures to him until it worked its way out of his system.

He was bone-weary as he cruised through the quiet streets, and wanted nothing more than to go home and go to sleep. But he imagined more hounds finding him there, alone, and tearing him apart. Instead, he turned once again toward the chapel by the river.

Despite that it was around two in the morning the priest came out to meet him as usual, automatically lighting a candle to set on the altar.

"Who is it this time?" he asked as Sean sank down in one of the pews.

Sean huffed, half sigh, half chuckle. "Gaelan. Barra. All of us." Then, "Don't you ever sleep?"

"One could ask the same thing of you."

"Yeah. Hellhounds can't come here, right? Is it okay if I just stay here tonight?"

"Hellhounds?!" The priest's eyes, which he'd been rubbing tiredly, widened.

Sean brushed aside his jacket to reveal his tattered shirt and scratched chest. "It's been a long day."

The priest sucked in a sharp breath. "You haven't even cleaned them. Don't you know the venom will clear out faster if you do?"

"I haven't exactly had the chance."

With a nod, the priest hurried back toward his office, leaving Sean alone in the shadowy sanctuary with the dimmed lights and the lingering smell of incense. A moment later he came back with a blanket and a handful of paper towels soaked in antiseptic, which he handed to Sean, who shucked his jacket and eased out of his T-shirt. The antiseptic brought a cold burn all its own to the inflamed scratches when Sean blotted them with it. He hissed and had to stop halfway through to let his vision clear.

"Are the hellhounds here in the city?" the priest asked.

"They're gone," Sean replied through clenched teeth, finally setting the towels aside. He pulled his jacket back on, willing his hands not to shake, and stretched out on the pew with the blanket. "Thank you."

The priest nodded. "It's why this is called a sanctuary, after all." He shifted and made to rise, but stopped when Sean spoke again, quietly.

"I'm afraid."

"The venom weakens your mind to fear and despair while it's in your system."

Sean nodded. "I know. But hellhounds... I've always been afraid of them."

"Most rational people are. But you don't seem to fear many things. Why them?" The priest settled back into the pew in front of Sean, twisting sideways so he could see him.

Sean lay on his back, staring up into the rafters. The pew was narrow, and the cushion meager. He wiggled a little to get comfortable, then cringed when the motion set off the fire across his chest again.

"The academy used to send us out on training missions, only after a while, they weren't fake anymore. They'd be real missions, with real danger. I was paired up with my buddy when our last mission went sideways. We were both hurt, him worse than me, and freaking out, hidden away in this crap-hole bar with a pile of dead bodies, and the hellhounds cornered us there." He sighed and rubbed the area over his chest.

"You survived," the priest prompted quietly. "Your friend didn't."

"No."

Silence settled into the room, till Sean became aware of the quiet sputter of the candle in a draft, the low purr of a car passing outside, the ticking of a clock hung on the wall opposite the pulpit.

"What else?" the priest asked. "You're one of the most stable people I know. You don't fear without reason. You don't cling to your pain or loss like many do. You don't take blame on yourself out of guilt, or things you can't control. What was different about that time? Surely it wasn't the only time you lost a friend, or saw someone torn up by hellhounds."

"No. Except they didn't tear him up."

Hesitating, with a tug on his perpetually rumpled corduroy, the priest ventured. "You didn't..."

"Kill him myself? No. I filled out my report, plus I had injuries from the hounds... I talked to the academy shrink... they all said I was lying. That I either killed him and hid the body for some reason before the attack, or the hellhounds ripped him up and ate him, and I blocked it from my memory. They said I was lucky. Well, they were right on the last part. Backup came before the hounds got me." Sean stopped and snorted a humorless laugh. "Listen to me evading. You want to know what happened? Those hellhounds opened this—this hole. A hole in nothing, right there in the air in front of us. It was all dark on the other side of it, and there were voices, sort of, whispering through. The hounds dragged him in there, or through there, or wherever the hell it was, and I heard him scream, right before the hole closed up."

"The shadow land," said the priest, his eyes wide.

"I guess so," said Sean, studying the patterns of shadows from the rafters. No one at the academy had believed him, but they couldn't prove he'd murdered his friend, either, so they kicked him out. Someone saw his report and believed him though, because the next week he got a call from some of the president's people.

"I've never heard of hellhounds dragging someone to their own world still alive," said the priest.

"Probably because no one ever comes back. But what happened to him? That's the part I can't shake."

The priest regarded Sean silently for a long moment. "Death is only death. For anyone whose soul has been entrusted to the care of God the Redeemer, there is only life to look forward to after our bodies are killed, be that here or in the shadow realm. Not that being torn apart by hellhounds sounds like a particularly peaceful way to go."

Sean snorted. "No. No, it does not."

The priest stood. "Get some rest. Nothing will drag you away to the shadow land while you're here. Wherever God's presence is, is holy ground, and evil creatures can't set foot there. Remember that."

"Thank you."

* * * * *

A few normal days passed while Sean mulled over the situation with Gaelan. He had to report in soon, and still had no idea what to tell Jacobs, or what his plan was. Gaelan's timing for deciding to go sorcerer stunk. And as for assassinating the queen... well. He should probably plan his own funeral before he tried it.

He'd gotten back from a run one morning and then holed up in the disused weight room to finish training—lifting weights and running through forms. Today he'd confiscated a couple of matching rapiers from his uncle's collection to practice with, just for a change of pace. Instead of following the fighting forms he'd memorized so long ago, this time he created his own, dancing and spinning around the room, putting together his own series of moves with the two blades. Gotta have fun once in a while.

He worked at it till the sweat was dripping in his eyes and running down his back, and had just completed a flawless and complicated set of blocks and thrusts when he heard a giggle behind him, and a girl's voice.

"The heck, Lina. You never told me your cousin was hot. And ripped."

Sean froze.

"Ew. 'Cause he's my cousin."

He turned slowly to face the girls. "Something I can do for you?"

"I can think of a few things." Lina's friend batted her eyelashes. She might as well have been Lina's twin, with her preppy clothes and too-mature makeup. And she couldn't have been more than sixteen. Ew indeed.

Lina elbowed her as Sean put the knives down and wiggled his shirt on over his sweaty 'hot' muscles. Gross. She elbowed back, and a bout of whispering ensued.

"What's your tattoo?" the Lina-twin asked. "I love tattoos. My dad won't let me get one."

He wasn't about to tell her it was the Kerr Family seal that he carried on his shoulder.

"It's some mythic thing," Lina said, oblivious. She elbowed her friend again and then handed Sean a copy of the city's popular tabloid. "You're friends with the princess, right? We want to know if this is for real, or if they faked it."

Sean took the paper with some trepidation and looked at it. Someone had caught Princess Calla and Jamie making out. Their picture took up the whole front page with the caption "Royal scandal! Princess Calla in an affair with a werewolf!" splashed across the bottom.

Sean snorted, and then had to smother a laugh.

"It's in the regular paper, too." She handed him the morning newspaper, which sported the same front-page picture, with a caption that was only mildly toned down.

It wasn't funny... not at all. But he suddenly wished he could show these to Rory and hear what she had to say about them. *At least we're not the only ones being stupid.*

He scanned the story and handed it back with a mostly straight face. "First of all, that's a kiss, not an affair." He thought of Beck's similar assumption about him and Rory and mentally rolled his eyes. Was it the racial thing that made everyone default to the most scandalous accusation? "And second, what's it matter if it's true or not? It's Calla's business who she wants to kiss. Not yours. Or mine."

Lina looked uncertain for a moment, but her friend gasped in horror.

"But he's a *magical*. That's *gross*."

"Why? They're people too."

"No, they're *not*." Lina's friend actually pulled a shudder. "My dad said she could get cut off for this. Disinherited. Even with Crown Prince Gaelan missing. He said that's the worst they'll be able to do to her, but that it should be worse. He said since she's a public figure, they should make a public example and execute the werewolf."

"Whoa! That's pretty extreme, don't you think?"

"No." She didn't even blink.

"So what makes werewolves not people? They can think, and reason, and love, obviously." He gestured at the papers in Lina's hand. "They have a conscience and know right from wrong. Sounds like a real person to me."

She made a disgusted sound and spun on her heel, whipping her perky ponytail around as she flounced out of the room. Sean raised his eyebrows at Lina.

"You agree with her?"

His cousin squirmed a little. "I'm not sure. It's kinda weird... but he looks just like a human, and I wouldn't want someone to tell me what boys I can and can't kiss. He is pretty cute." She glanced at the picture. "One of our maids used to be a nymph, but she got scared and left the city a few months ago. She was always really nice to me, even when no one else was."

Sean picked up the knives and wiped his sweat off them. "Yeah, I remember her."

"That was pretty cool," she nodded at the knives as they left the room. "I thought you were just a cook."

"What, I'm not allowed to have hobbies? Cooks gotta be good with knives, right?"

She rolled her eyes at him, but laughed anyway. "Whatever. See you."

"Yep. Lina?"

She paused, about to head upstairs, and looked at him expectantly. He hadn't really meant to speak, and debated for a moment what he could afford to say.

"Folks like to agree with the people they admire, or that they're trying to impress. It doesn't make them right—it just makes them followers instead of thinkers. All the people saying nasty things, they're just following the queen. Don't be a follower, huh?"

She looked at him for a long moment, then turned and bounded up the stairs.

Sean put the knives back and went to get ready for work. He wasn't laughing anymore. Things had just gotten a lot more complicated.

26

PLANS AND PRAYERS

Rory answered her mirror expecting Sean. Instead, it was Princess Calla's face that popped up.

"I hope I'm not bothering you at a bad time," she said. She had her hair pulled into a sloppy ponytail, and there were dark circles under her eyes.

"No, Princess."

In fact, no time was a good time at the moment. After the debacle of a trial before the council, when Rory returned from escorting Dylan and Kiah to the border, they'd stripped her of her name and her career. She was no longer Auralie Agent to anyone, but merely Auralie, or Rory, Scout. Her cover identity had become reality, and now she was riding border patrol with the partner assigned for her. Tarha, an elf ten years her senior with a big smile and a habit of hovering around watching Rory like she was a toddler about to get in trouble. The woman had no sense of personal space. There was no point in Rory slowing her horse, or speeding up to give herself some privacy, because the other woman wouldn't take the hint, So Rory stopped altogether, swung down, and walked away.

"What can I do for you?" She asked once she had a few paces between her and her nosy partner.

"We need to meet. All of us," Calla said in the mirror. "I messed up, and Gaelan..." she stopped, pressing her lips together and swallowing. "Things are getting bad here. Is there any chance you can come through the tunnels and meet us? We're meeting at the church."

"When?" Rory asked.

"Within the week, I hope. When can you get here?"

"Day after tomorrow?"

"Then that's when we'll meet. Be there at dusk."

They ended the call, leaving Rory staring at her own reflection in the mirror. She studied herself for a moment, thinking. Her eyes looked a little sad, staring back at her. *The world is full of sorrow. I lost my career, Kiah lost her coat, Dylan was tortured, Calla lost a lot of her books...*

"We're going to win this, right?" she whispered.

Turning, she called Borden as she walked back to her horse. He didn't look happy to see her.

"Auralie. What do you need?"

"I just talked to Princess Calla. She wants to meet with me and the others the Seer brought together. Day after tomorrow. I'm not sure what's going on, but it sounds bad."

"We'll send someone," he said.

"No," Rory replied, feeling her fury rising again, but checking it before it showed on her face or in her tone. This was her mission, her friends. "The invitation was to me. *I'm* supposed to meet with them. The five other people that the Seer specifically called together. You think they are going to let some elf they don't know come and listen in on them? I am going to that meeting. This is just a courtesy to let you know that you'll need to send someone to finish the patrol with Tarha. And because I am still concerned with the interests of Maireadd, despite what Vasya's been whispering to you."

Borden scowled. He wasn't liking this one bit, but he knew she was right. "Fine. Go. This doesn't mean that you're getting your job back. And I'm sending someone with you."

She raised an eyebrow. "Who?"

He hesitated. "Vasya. He's shown an interest in becoming an agent."

She snorted. If he thought Vasya was going to be allowed to meet Calla or any of the others, he was going to be sorely disappointed. Especially if he expected Rory to vouch for him.

"He better be at the tunnel entrance by noon, day after tomorrow, or I'm leaving without him."

With that call out of the way, Rory informed her babysitter of the change in plan, and they adjusted their route accordingly. Despite the increasingly desperate circumstances, anticipation bubbled up in Rory while they rode, and a little bit of smug satisfaction. The council might hate her guts, but they couldn't deny her connections.

Calla had said everyone was to be at the meeting, so did that mean Sean, too? Would it be a risk for him to be there with the rest of them? Selfishly, she hoped he would be able to come. They'd been talking every few days for the past month, and their friendship seemed to be teetering on the edge of something... more. At least if the squirming in her stomach at the thought of seeing him in person was any indication.

The next day passed slowly, but they made good time, and when they camped for the night they were only a couple hours ride from the entrance to the tunnel leading into Barra. By midmorning the following day they arrived at the tunnel entrance, and then had to wait a couple of hours for Vasya and the elf that was to replace Rory on patrol. After lunch, Rory and Vasya headed into the tunnel, leaving their horses with the others, who would camp in the area and wait for them to return, probably late the next night or early in the morning.

For herself, Rory had no intention of staying overnight in Barra. Once the meeting was over, she would walk back to Maireadd, even though it would take half the night. Vasya could do whatever he wanted, for all she cared.

"How's your human boyfriend?" he asked after a couple hours of icy silence.

Rory glanced over. His face looked sharp and leering in the odd shadows cast from their light crystals. The illusion didn't help her opinion of him at the moment. She sighed and looked away.

"He's my friend."

"He's a foreign operative and a human."

"And you're an elf, which means you should be a friend and an ally, but you're not. You've destroyed my career. Be content with that, Vasya, and stay out of my life, or I'll start to take it personally."

"Is that a threat, Scout?"

She barked a disbelieving laugh. "Does it really need to be?"

They went back to their silence.

There was no way to tell the time in the tunnel, but Rory guessed they must be getting close to the end, judging by how long they'd been walking, and the amount of brick used to build the walls. Toward Maireadd, the walls and ceiling were shored up with rough stone and ancient, blackened wooden beams. But under the city, it was brick and crumbling mortar.

Sure enough, a few minutes later they came in sight of a set of narrow wooden steps, some of them polished with age, others recently replaced with new lumber. The door at the top was of simple wood paneling, built to look like part of the wall, though it was also overhung on the inside by a decorative tapestry depicting the interlocking three-pronged star symbolizing the Trinity. The door slid back noiselessly and Rory peeked out to make sure no one was in sight. They stepped out into the hallway between the office, to the right, and the priest's private quarters, to the left.

"How do we know this isn't a trap?" Vasya whispered.

"Because we're not surrounded?" She gave him a peevish look and headed for the office.

Jamie, Calla's werewolf, met them at the door. His dark eyes flicked from Rory to Vasya. "Who's this?"

"Vasya, my babysitter. The council doesn't trust me to come alone anymore."

"Vasya the snitch?" Sean's voice rose from behind Jamie and set her pulse racing a moment before he appeared at the door. He flashed her a dimpled grin before turning to Vasya, who suddenly looked uncomfortable.

"Human," he said stiffly.

Sean eyed him distastefully. "Anyone who snitches on one of their own people would snitch on us without thinking twice. He can wait in the sanctuary."

Vasya turned an offended shade of red and started to protest. Jamie interrupted.

"I don't know him. He's not going near Calla."

"There you go. Sorry elf-boy." Sean grinned.

Vasya shoved forward past Rory, puffing out his chest. "I'm here representing the elf council!"

"The elf council wasn't invited," Jamie answered dryly. "Rory was."

Rory scratched her nose, hiding a smile. Sean winked at her.

Vasya wheeled on her. "The council is going to hear about this. Don't be surprised when your name goes from scout to traitor."

Suddenly Sean loomed over them. He was so solidly muscular that Rory had never really thought of him as particularly tall, but the few inches he had on Vasya seemed to expand until he towered over him.

"Keep it up, representative of the council, and your council is gonna find itself offensive to both Barra and Thyrus, not to mention the Kerr Family. You really don't want that."

Vasya shut his mouth, shot Rory a withering glare, and marched away.

Sean and Jamie exchanged an amused look. The werewolf slipped back into the office, but Sean stepped out into the hall and hugged her—a little tighter than just friends normally would. At least among elves.

"I'm glad you made it," he whispered into her hair.

She nodded, her face buried in his chest, suddenly and inexplicably wanting to cry. She'd been keeping it together for so long—been alone for so long—that finally having someone to cling to nearly broke her. Shuddering, she drew a deep breath and pulled back, swiping at her eyes. "Thank you."

He kissed the top of her head. "If you want me to make elf-boy disappear, just say the word."

She snorted, and then started sobbing and laughing at the same time. Sean pulled her close again and held her, shushing and rubbing her back till she calmed down. One of his hands found her ear and his fingers caressed the tip of it. With her other ear pressed against his chest, she could hear his heart hammering.

"They're all waiting for us, aren't they?" she said without moving.

"No one is going anywhere. Take your time."

She drew back, sniffing and wiping her face. "I'm good. Let's go."

He gave her a look with enough tenderness to make her heart do a little surprised thump, casually wrapping an arm around her shoulders as they walked into the office.

The office wasn't big, but they had managed to fit six chairs in a circle around the room. The priest had gone to let them have their privacy, so it was just the four others who greeted her as she and Sean stepped into the room. She almost started crying all over again. Here, she wasn't alone. Here, all of them had suffered loss or grief of some kind. They all knew what they were fighting for.

Dylan's ordeal was perhaps the most obvious in the discolored bruises and healing cuts visible on his face and arms as he turned when she came in. He nodded slightly to her, no doubt understanding perfectly her overwhelmed feelings. Beside him, Kiah clung to his arm as though she might lose him if she let go. Calla still had dark circles under her eyes and her face looked drawn. Jamie, stoic as ever, sat with his arms crossed over his chest, but once in a while he would cast little, agonized glances at the princess. None of them were unscathed.

Kiah and Calla both stood and welcomed Rory with hugs before she sat down between Sean and Calla.

"Thank you for coming. I know it wasn't easy," Calla said. She turned to the others. "For any of you. But a lot has been happening, and I thought it was time to see where we're all at, and make a plan, if we can, or at least come up with some options. The six of us are supposed to be saving Barra, and so far..." she trailed off and looked around at them. Jamie snorted. Dylan touched one of his scars thoughtfully. Sean looked worried.

"At least we got rid of one problem," Kiah muttered.

Calla pointed to her. "That's a good place to start. I don't think any of us have actually heard what happened to Lyselle, Dianthe's sister."

Kiah glanced at her husband and squeezed his arm. "Dylan took away her magic. She's powerless now. Just a regular human. She's been staying with the Seer."

"Wait, really?" Sean leaned forward suddenly, staring at the empath. "You can do that?"

"Apparently." Dylan rubbed his chest, looking a little sick.

"It almost killed him," Kiah supplied. "If not for my coat, I think it probably would have."

"That must have been what he meant then..." Sean said, half to himself, leaning back and glancing at Calla. His ruddy face suddenly looked a little pale. She motioned for him to continue, but he didn't right away, sitting there chewing on the inside of his cheek.

Instead it was Dylan who spoke, glancing over at Sean sharply. "Oh, no..."

"What?" Calla looked between them.

Sean said, "I'm sorry. I haven't had a safe way to contact you these last few days. I was warned that Dianthe is getting suspicious of me, and I... I'm not at liberty to tell the whole story."

"Not at liberty? What story?"

Sean sighed. "What you said about Dylan being able to remove someone's stolen magic... well. I know why your brother is missing."

Rory thought Calla was going to jump out of her chair and strangle the answers out of Sean before he could draw breath to continue.

"Gaelan stole magic."

He might as well have dropped a grenade in the room. Calla threw her hands to her mouth with a wail. Kiah gasped. Jamie swore, then turned to try to comfort Calla. Dylan just closed his eyes and pinched the bridge of his nose. He looked like he was going to be sick.

Even Rory cringed. Sean slid his hand into hers and gave it a squeeze. She could feel the tension in his hands, and see it in the rigid line of his shoulders and the way his face pinched when he glanced over at her. She slipped her hand from his grip and rested it on his arm.

Calla's face had gone death-white and she shook. Her breaths started coming in gasps. Dylan rose silently and crossed over to kneel in front of her, meeting Jamie's gaze briefly before taking her hands and bowing his ruined face over them. They stayed like that for a few long moments, and Rory, sitting next to them, was probably the only one who saw the tears that splashed across Calla's hands as Dylan held them. Gradually her shaking eased into stillness, and a little of the color returned to her face as her breath steadied. She whimpered, though, her eyes growing red-rimmed.

Rory moved her chair closer and put her arm around the princess, while Kiah and Jamie surrounded her on the other side, comforting her Sean cleared his throat and continued recounting his story, his voice steady and quiet.

"Dianthe was able to send a hunter after Gaelan. Something about him using black magic made it so she could curse him. So this hunter can track him, no matter where he runs, until either the hunter or... the prince, is dead."

"Who's the hunter?" Jamie asked.

Sean shook his head mutely. "I'm sorry. I gave my word that I would keep his identity and kind a secret. He wasn't any happier about being cursed to hunt the prince than anyone else. But he said the only way to get out of it, other than one of their deaths, would be if Gaelan lost his black magic. He said that might be possible, that there was someone who could help him, but he wouldn't say who."

"Whoever this hunter is somehow knows about what happened to Lyselle, then," said Kiah, exchanging an inscrutable look with Dylan.

"And this hunter is the person who told you that Dianthe is getting suspicious of you?" Rory guessed.

Sean nodded.

"So there might be hope?" Calla asked, sitting up a little straighter. Dylan unobtrusively moved back to his seat.

Sean shrugged and grimaced. "If your brother can stay ahead of the hunter, and if he somehow knows enough to get to Dylan, and if Dylan is up to helping him. He was hurt when he got away. I don't know how badly. I'm sorry."

Calla nodded, brushing at her eyes. "Thank you for your honesty. And thank you for giving my brother a chance." To Dylan, she said more quietly. "And thank you. I hope..." her voice trailed off.

"How did you do that, exactly?" Rory asked Dylan. "Remove Lyselle's magic, I mean. You didn't kill her, so it's not the same as her stealing magic from one of us, I take it. I mean, can you use the magic you took from her? I apologize if this is off topic, but I thought I knew most of what there is to know about magic, and I've never heard of that."

"I just pulled it away from her, like I'd do with pain. I don't know if I'd have been able to use it or not. I kind of think that to try would be really, really bad," said Dylan. "Worst experience of my life, and that's counting Dianthe's torture spell and Beck's knuckles."

Rory grimaced.

"Gaelan's disappearance leads to our other big problem," Sean said, shooting Calla another apologetic look. "Thyrus is breathing down my neck about getting rid of Dianthe before she figures out who I am. But..."

"But with Gaelan gone, there's no suitable heir," Calla finished for him. She looked like she might burst into tears.

Surprised, Rory looked from Sean to the princess. "Why not you?"

"Someone got lucky with a camera. Right place, right time," Jamie spoke up for the first time. "Now the princess is having an 'affair' with a werewolf, and the entire court is calling for her head."

"It was just a kiss. But they'll never stand for me as their ruler now," Calla said. "Not that I wanted that to begin with."

Rory glanced over at Sean. He met her gaze and smiled ruefully.

"If I were to renounce all support for magicals and fire Jamie, they might be appeased..." Calla looked up at Jamie with so much pain that Rory wanted to cry for her. "I could go on helping the magicals even more secretly, but... but that still feels like it would be a betrayal. I don't honestly know if I'd be able to go through with it. Or whether it would even be worth it."

"No," said Kiah suddenly. "They won't let it go, as long as popular opinion is against us. If you back down, they'll smell weakness like blood in the water and just keep pushing until they have you hanging yourself with your own rope. I say, if you're going to date a werewolf, then own it."

Calla looked pensive, and Jamie unconvinced.

Kiah went on, "Hear me out here. Remember that Shannon Whitaker novel that was so popular last year?" She glanced at Dylan with a twinkle in her eye. "It was about a couple forbidden to be together, but they fell in love anyway, and—it was so romantic. It was at the top of the bestseller lists for months. So, what could possibly be more romantic than the princess falling in love with her forbidden werewolf bodyguard? Find a way to play that up."

Calla's face went from pale and drawn to bright red as she sputtered—trying and failing to find words.

Rory snickered before she could stop herself. She muttered an apology and slid her chair back to her place closer to Sean.

"I have a few connections at one of the national newspapers," Dylan put in. "I could pull some strings and make that story happen. For that matter, I could sell it in a direct connection to the books. I could probably even get Shannon Whitaker to write a guest piece for the paper."

"That's probably the best idea you're going to get," Sean said. "We need to start turning public opinion. Dianthe has such a strangle-hold on her people's hearts and reason right now, and that's what makes her dangerous. Not her magic."

Calla and Jamie exchanged a long look. He had a gleam in his eye, and she, a tiny smile to match it. Finally she nodded. "Do it. It's a gamble, but it's one I don't have to sell my soul for."

There was a short silence in the room, as though everyone had paused to catch their breath.

"Rory," Calla asked, "Is there anything we should be aware of happening in Maireadd?"

Rory frowned. "No... if there was, I likely wouldn't hear about it, since I'm not technically an agent anymore. But I know the council isn't happy. We've had more and more refugees flooding in, and it's making them twitchy. There was talk of closing the border, but I've been on border patrol for the last week, and so far nothing has changed."

"That would effectively trap anyone who's in danger or running from Dianthe here in Barra," Calla said. "Unless they have the resources to charter a boat, or cross the mountains."

"The elven council cares only for the interest of elves," Rory replied. "And even then, only Maireadd elves.

"They're trying to protect their own," Calla said. "As much as I would like to fault them for that, I can't."

Rory sighed. "Yes and no. Maireadd isn't lacking resources or space. We could take a third of the population of Barra before we felt much strain. They just don't believe anyone else is worth helping—which is why I'm now a scout instead of an agent, more or less. If Vasya has anything to say about it, I won't even be that."

"What would they do to you?" Sean asked.

Rory shrugged. "Banish me, worst case. But I don't see that happening. They need border control right now, and even though I offended them by placing conviction and honor above my duty to them, they don't truly think I'm inclined to commit treason. My mother is on the council, after all. And the Seer has taken an interest in me, with his invitation to the gala. They can't ignore that any more than they can ignore my friendship with Calla and with Family Kerr."

Sean squeezed her hand.

Calla nodded. "I had one more idea that I was hoping Rory and Dylan might be able to help with. Sean has already mentioned the need to get people's attention, and get them thinking, rather than blindly following Dianthe's lead, and I had already had a similar thought. Only I was thinking about history."

Rory frowned. She met Dylan's gaze briefly, wondering what on earth Calla had in mind.

"It's been five hundred years since the curse war, and Barra isn't remembering so well these days. Many of the history books dealing with it have been destroyed. Even after the Seer came and warned us, and so many of the same things are happening, with humans and magicals against one another. I thought maybe it would be a good idea to revive that history."

Dylan cleared his throat. "Uh, what does that have to do with me and Rory?"

"Well... you have the skill to make it interesting. People don't care about history, but they do care about stories."

"Ah."

"And Rory," Calla turned to her, "I know the elves kept better records than we did. We're losing our own history. I'm afraid we've nearly lost Maireadd's part in that war, beyond generalizations and blame. Perhaps you'd be able to dig up your people's side of the story—the side of the magicals, and help Dylan with that?"

Rory nodded slowly. "Yeah. I could do that."

Dylan looked a bit incredulous. "That's... a lot of research, and not much time. Better hope I don't have to go on the run again."

"The Curse War was when Family Kerr came to power," Sean said. "I think grandpa Jack still has some pretty detailed records about that. Contact him if you need more resources. He's the Family head."

"You really think this'll help?" Rory asked, scratching one of her ears. She noticed Sean watching her.

"I pray it does. I pray something does," said Calla.

And they did pray. The six of them. Burly Sean and Jamie, Beautiful, loving Kiah, hurting Princess Calla, Dylan, who carried the burdens of everyone in the room, and Rory, lonely and longing. They prayed for hope and for their lives. Then they said their goodbyes, lingering, hugging, crying. Wondering if they would all see one another again. Finally they parted.

Sean pulled Rory aside as the others filed out into the sanctuary. They would leave at different times, so as not to draw attention.

Alone in the hall, neither of them seemed to know what to say. Rory stepped forward and wrapped her arms around him, and he held her.

"I don't know when I'll be able to call again," he said. "I'll try to... but it's probably not a good idea to do it regularly anymore, if Dianthe is watching me. Who knows what ways she has of spying on people."

"Like her pet soothsayer?"

He nodded and grimaced.

"You want to know something silly?" she said, smiling.

"What's that?"

"I miss that Thyrusian brogue of yours."

He laughed, then flawlessly switched accents to say, "I could hardly take it to court with me."

"I know. But I loved it. Barra and Maireadd sound basically the same, but I always thought the way Thyrus twisted the words was the most beautiful." With her hands caressing the nape of his neck, her fingers encountered the cord there, and she tugged it out to reveal the light crystal she'd given him.

"Good for taking on the occasional hellhound," he quipped.

She smiled. "I'm glad you have it." She toyed with it thoughtfully for a moment.

"What?" he asked.

"Just thinking. There is a way to make a sort of a shield, for people who can't defend themselves against magic users. Humans, specifically. Elves have sort of discouraged that information from getting around, in case there's another war. They want to keep their advantage. But I bet I could make one. It might help when you... I mean it might give you a chance, anyway. I'll give it a try, and if it works, I'll find a way to get it to the priest here." She squeezed his arms. "I didn't know I was missing anything, till I met you."

"I know the feeling." He tilted her face up gently with his finger and kissed her. "I hope we both live through all this."

"Me too." She pulled his head back down to resume their kiss, lingering a few long moments before they were interrupted.

"Now you're kissing your human? That's going pretty far, even for you." Vasya stood at the door to the sanctuary, glaring at them.

"Stuff it, Elf boy."

Vasya continued to glower, but said nothing else, brushing past them and knocking into Sean's shoulder on the way by. He threw himself off balance, but Sean didn't budge. He waited by the door to the tunnel.

"I guess that means it's time to go," Rory whispered with her face in Sean's neck.

"Mmm." His arms tightened around her. "I wish..."

"Me too." She pulled away finally and kissed his cheek. "Till we meet again."

"God keep you."

Letting go and walking away was one of the hardest things she'd ever done. She passed Vasya without a word and entered the tunnel, and it was all she could do to keep it together and not let him see her break down as they walked.

God keep you, Sean.

27

A GIFT AND A WARNING

Sean kept his head down as the weeks passed, working, working out, blending in with the social scene as much as possible. He planned a hundred ways he might kill Dianthe, from long-range sniper hits to poison blow-darts, and everything in between. But no matter how the isolation and inactivity grated on him, the timing wasn't right. Not yet. Calla's standing with the court was still too precarious. Gaelan was still missing. One wrong move and the whole country could ignite into war. If he killed the queen too soon, it would be pinned on the elves, and then Maireadd could be dragged into the war. So he waited. Summer dragged on and turned into fall, fall began to fade, and with the restless change of season he grew more paranoid. But they were playing the long game now, and he could do nothing but wait.

Gossip continued to circulate about the missing crown prince, but so far there was no real news, and Sean didn't dare contact Princess Calla to find out whether she'd heard anything.

Dylan's promised article in the newspaper came out, and then his book, two months later. Calla announced her engagement to Jamie and caused a near riot at court. But slowly, subtly, public perception started to shift. Not enough, but it was something, anyway.

Dianthe no longer held absolute sway over popular opinion. And she wasn't happy about it. She was getting paranoid too, even worse than usual, worried about the unidentified assassin and spy in her court. She tried to have Calla assassinated again, and soon after, another article appeared in the papers about how the princess's werewolf protector and fiance had saved her. It was a good article. Dylan's work again, no doubt.

Sean quit checking in with Colonel Jacobs every week, talking to him only once or twice a month, and he almost never called Rory anymore. That hurt the worst, because he never stopped thinking about her. He began to make his plans, to look for opportunities. And every day he went in to work half expecting to be arrested, or detained. But nothing happened, until the day that it did.

He was starting to think the head chef was either dying, or else was taking advantage of him to a disgraceful extent. The man called in sick for days at a time, several times a month, leaving Sean to work long days, late evenings, and pick up the slack of ordering and planning, which he seemed to always contrive to leave undone. With the Midwinter Ball coming up, that workload was even more intense. This year's ball was to be a masquerade, and it was whispered that this was a nod to the rash of masked sorcerers that had been terrorizing the city—people Queen Dianthe supported rather than bringing to justice.

It was after midnight that night when Sean got home and parked the bike. The front porch light welcomed him back like his only friend. The house was dark and peaceful when he let himself in, so it took him a moment to realize why he suddenly tensed as he closed the door. It was a scent.

Just the faintest whiff of soap or cologne that wasn't his lingered in the air.

The light that he'd left on above the stove still illuminated the small kitchen, dining and living area. By its soft glow he searched the room, keeping his back to the wall. Nothing. Reaching around the corner, he flicked on the bedroom light without entering. Nothing happened, so he cautiously checked that room as well. Then the bathroom. He found nothing but that faint whiff of unbelonging fragrance, yet he couldn't shake the unsettled feeling that something wasn't right. So he started a more careful search.

He found the listening devices. Three of them. They were planted right where he would have put them himself if he was the one trying to catch a spy—one in each room. For now he would leave them there. But he wouldn't be able to make any more calls on his mirror from the house. Probably he shouldn't keep it around at all, in case they came through next time and made a sweep for magical items. He assumed that they hadn't discovered it this time, since they'd only left listening devices for him, and not a welcoming party.

Unable to settle down in the house, eventually he took his pillow and a couple of blankets outside and climbed onto the roof. It was cold up there, the shingles icy with frost, but he fell asleep watching the glittering stars, and rested better than he had in weeks.

The next day he took his magic mirror, left Colonel Jacobs a message, and threw it into the river. He watched it flash dully underwater before it sank out of sight. He was on his own now, and he would either succeed and kill the queen, or die. Either way, there really wasn't anything more to report.

Things were beginning to shift, but was it enough? If there was no Gaelan, and Calla was engaged to a werewolf, would the court accept her, if the queen were to die? He was going to have to risk it.

After dumping his mirror, Sean climbed back on his bike and drove out to the little stone church further down river. For once he arrived while the service was in session, and slipped into a seat in the back. The priest's kindly voice filled the small sanctuary, urging his people to "Love one another, as God has loved you... regardless of race or convenience or popular opinion. Love in spite of differences and disagreements, and across all the lines that have been drawn. Love even unto death."

For some reason his words left an ache in Sean's heart.

When the last parishioner had filed out the priest beckoned him into his office. They sat down where he, Rory, and the others had had their meeting several months ago.

"I'm glad you're here. I have something for you." The priest pulled a tiny package from his desk drawer. Wrapped in brown paper, it was flat and smaller than the palm of his hand. "A friend dropped it off a few days ago. She couldn't stay, and didn't dare seek you out, but said it was urgent that you get this."

Sean's heart leapt, and then instantly fell. Rory had been here, and he'd missed her. He took the little parcel and untied the string around it, letting the paper fall away to reveal a pendant on a leather cord. It looked to be several different materials somehow fused together. Crystal, like the light crystal he still wore, bone, wood, stone, and metal. All in an intricately woven pattern over a convex circle, like an actual tiny shield. She had written a few words on the inside of the wrapping paper.

Sean, this is the shield we talked about. It will guard you from direct magical attacks only. God keep you and light your way till we meet again. Love, Rory.

He brushed his fingers across the strong, beautiful script.

"I'm afraid, after this, you shouldn't come here again, my friend," said the priest, interrupting his thoughts.

Sean looked up sharply. "What's happened?"

The priest reached into his drawer again and dumped a handful of broken metal, plastic pieces, and tiny wires onto the desk. The remains of several listening devices.

"Don't worry. These were recent, and I had one of my magically inclined friends make sure there were no others. But I'm afraid they're watching me now, too. So if you come, best do so during regular services."

Sean stared in wordless dismay at the little pile of broken pieces and gulped. It was like feeling the noose fall over his head. If Dianthe's bugs had been destroyed, she would likely have sent someone to watch the church in person. He stood slowly and tied Rory's shield around his neck, then handed the note to the priest.

"Burn this please. And I guess this is goodbye."

The other man pulled a lighter out of his desk drawer and set it to the corner of the paper at once. "Goodbye, my friend. I hope you succeed where others have failed."

"I hope so too. If I don't... tell grandfather what happened, okay? That I still want Rory under the Family's protection."

The priest nodded. "Knowing Jack, he'll send his own people to avenge you."

"He's wanted to send help for months, I think. But the situation has been ticklish. Anyway, if this goes south, tell him... everything. He needs to know who the good guys are." Sean moved to stand up, but at that moment a soft rap came on the door. He froze, his panicked gaze going to the priest, who looked just as wide-eyed. Another knock. At Sean's nod, the priest got up, smoothing his rumpled corduroy jacket, and went to the door while Sean slipped out of his chair and went to stand in the corner where he wouldn't be visible until their uninvited guest was fully in the room.

"Oh! It's you!" the priest sounded relieved, but Sean remained tensed until a young man with a familiar blond cowlick poked his head around the door and grinned at him.

"Dylan?" he said in disbelief.

The empath stepped into the room while the priest closed the door.

"Good to see you," Dylan said. "I was hoping I'd get here in time."

"In time for what?"

"To catch you before you left." He turned to the priest. "Hey, can we have a minute?"

The priest nodded and ducked out. Once they were alone, Dylan sank into one of the rolling office chairs with a sigh and ran his hand over his cowlick. He looked good, if tired. Last time Sean had seen him, he'd still carried the bruises and cuts inflicted by Dianthe. Now, his nose had a slight crook to it, and a thin white scar crossed his cheek below his eye, but those were the only visible reminders of what he'd suffered.

Sean took the other chair. "What's this about?"

"I'm not sure," said Dylan. "I just talked with a mutual friend of ours. Gaelan. He's still alive. And having visions, apparently."

"What, like the Seer?"

"Something like that."

"Is Beck still chasing him?"

Dylan shook his head, but didn't elaborate. Instead he said, "Gaelan is worried."

"Ha!" Sean snorted, leaning back in his chair. "So am I."

The empath nodded, but didn't speak again for a moment, instead staring at his hands, which were folded casually in front of him as he leaned forward, elbows on knees. He rocked the chair back and forth like an antsy toddler. At length he said, "Gaelan wanted me to give you a message. He said that once you bleed on the altar, it will have to be destroyed, otherwise the curse will fall."

Sean sat back, dread blooming in his guts like blood from a wound. "Once I bleed on the altar."

Dylan didn't respond. He stared at his hands and rocked some more.

Sean touched his string tie, painfully aware that his fear and loneliness were an open book to the other man. They sat there in uncomfortable silence until, with sudden insight, Sean realized that this conversation might actually be harder for Dylan than himself. Dylan switched to rubbing the scar under his eye. He had bled in this fight, too. And he'd been alone. He'd faced Dianthe and her whole court alone, and been tortured in front of hundreds of people.

A thread of shame wormed its way through Sean. "When you were goading Dianthe in front of the court last summer—did you know she wasn't going to kill you?"

Dylan snorted. "At that point I was wishing she would. I had stage fright." He glanced up, flashing a grin.

"You hid it well." Sean returned his grin, but quickly let it slide from his face. "So Gaelan says I have to destroy the altar after I bleed on it. Any ideas on how to do that? Or, uh, how much blood we're talking about? Or what altar?"

"No. He's turned into a typical seer. All cryptic warnings and nothing actually helpful."

"Hm. He must mean Dianthe's altar somewhere in the palace?"

Dylan lifted a hand in a shrug. "I imagine he would have been more specific if he could."

"You ever wonder why God would grant visions and give information, but leave it vague and confusing all the time?"

At first the empath didn't look like he was going to respond. His chair quit swinging back and forth and he stared at the wall as though he could see through it. Then finally said, "I think He gives us as much information as we can handle. Sometimes the only way to get through something is to walk into it blind and trust Him as you go." He touched the scar on his face again briefly. "Sometimes knowing too much would paralyze us, or make us bitter. Or knowing too much could unwittingly turn us from the path we would have followed."

"What would you have done differently, if you'd known?" Sean asked.

Dylan shook his head, keeping his eyes averted. "I don't know. Made sure my family and everyone was out of danger before I went on the run, maybe? But... if I hadn't been there, then Beck would still be Dianthe's puppet. Gaelan wouldn't have turned against the queen..."

"You wouldn't have challenged Dianthe and inspired everyone at court."

"The thing is," Dylan went on, "I wasn't really alone. Even when the soothsayer and his hellhounds came. I had Kiah." He opened his hand and a tiny greenish light flickered to life above it, glowing like the bioluminescent creatures found deep under the ocean. A selkie light. "Her magic," he explained. "Since she gave me her coat, I can do little things like this. And God was with me too."

"Can you feel Him, too?" Sean asked curiously.

"Usually, if I'm trying to. Look at it like this—you can turn the lights out and make the room dark, but the furniture is still there for you to walk into. Just because you can't see something, or Someone, doesn't mean you can't stub your toe on it."

"Comforting."

"I will hold vigil for you. That's what you'd say in Thyrus, right? Gaelan said the curse is coming soon. Before Midwinter."

"Tomorrow is Midwinter's Eve."

Dylan nodded.

"He really is as mysterious as the old Seer. And you're pretty good at the mysterious shtick yourself."

"Yeah, sorry. Blame the prince. He didn't give me much to work with, and he definitely didn't pass along any helpful details for you. He just said you needed to know that. And that you're not alone."

"Well... thanks, I guess. What about you? You'll be okay here in the city?"

A shadow passed over Dylan's face again. "Yeah. I hate this place, but I'll be fine. Watch your back. I'll hang out here till after you leave."

Sean nodded. "Till we meet again."

"God lights your way."

Sean noted how he'd changed the wording of the farewell blessing slightly, but didn't comment. He slipped out, nodded to the priest as he passed through the sanctuary, and stepped out into the night.

* * * * *

Now that he was looking, Sean spotted Dianthe's spy right away when he stepped out of the church. The man stood two blocks up, leaning against the side of a building smoking a cigar and trying to look nonchalant. Nothing Sean could do about that now. He glanced in that direction and then away. Had the watcher been reaching for something? Sean's bike started with a roar then settled into its deep, comforting purr, and he pulled away from the curb, aware that he was still watched.

Tomorrow night was the masquerade. With suspicion closing in around him, and now that he had Rory's shield, he didn't dare wait any longer.

It had been flurrying when he went into the church earlier. Now, fat white flakes danced in front of his headlight, reminding him that Midwinter was only a few days away, and forcing him to slow his bike so he wouldn't spin out as the road turned white in front of him. It was colder now, too. A lot colder. Good thing this mission was almost over, or he'd have to find himself a different mode of transportation for the winter. Even going slow the wind cut through his leather jacket and set him shivering by the time he pulled off and waited for the iron gate to swing open at his uncle's estate.

Nearing midnight, and the lights were already off in the main house, even in Lina's room on the second floor. The porch light of the guest house twinkled through the snow as he pulled up. Snowflakes hit the bike and instantly melted from the warmth of the engine as he set the kickstand. He sat there staring up at the darkened windows and had the niggling feeling that something wasn't right. Lina never turned her lights out before one in the morning. And his uncle never turned the television off at all. Yet there was no blue flicker from the den.

Reaching into the bike's saddlebag, he withdrew the camp knife he kept there and pulled it from its sheath. He weighed it in his hand as he surveyed the grounds. Nothing appeared out of place. Maybe he was just extra paranoid after his talk with the priest. But better paranoid than dead—or being tortured for information. An image of Dylan's battered face popped into his mind.

There was no place that offered concealment around the guest house. It was surrounded by open lawn on one side and nothing but the walkway around the in-ground pool on the other. A lone rosebush adorned the corner of the building. The manor, on the other hand, had some shrubbery that filled the gaps between the decorative columns out front. It was out of sight from where he sat now, but he'd passed it on his way in. Making up his mind suddenly, he slid off the bike and ran for the front of the manor, keeping to a half crouch and following the wall.

The porch light gleamed oddly on the rifle scope sticking out around the corner of the building. Sean grabbed the rifle by the barrel and gave it a forward yank, pulling the surprised would-be attacker with it. His camp knife slid into the side of the man's throat and back out with sickening ease and no more than the whisper of caught breath and gurgle of blood. He shoved the body backward into a second attacker, who was just coming out of his shock to surge forward. His dying friend hit him with the dull thump of colliding body armor and he stumbled back into a big stone planter. Sean followed, stepping in with a short, upward jab to the nose with his open palm. The man's head snapped back, then when he reflexively leaned forward, reaching for his face, Sean slid the knife between the vertebrae at the back of his neck. He fell without a sound.

Sean straightened, huffing white clouds in the frosty air. Now what? They would have people in both the guest house, waiting for him to come in, and the manor, keeping an eye on his uncle and his family, provided they hadn't already been killed. And everyone would have heard his bike pull up, so they knew he was here. Only a matter of minutes before they got suspicious. He could run, or he could make sure his uncle's family was safe, and run the risk of getting killed, arrested, or seriously wounded before he could kill Dianthe.

28
SURPRISE AND GRAB

Sean ran along the front of the manor. There was a big sunroom on the far side. Lots of windows. If anyone was in the house, they would not be hiding out in that room. And a few of the floor-to-ceiling-windows were usually unlocked because Lina used them to get outside sometimes instead of the door.

The second window he tried slid open and he ducked inside. The house was silent.

Make it quick, he chided himself. Even now the waiting strike team was probably getting antsy over in the guest house. It had only been two or three minutes, tops, but how long would they expect someone to sit on their motorcycle in the snow in the driveway? Not long.

He passed through the library and parlor, moving silently but fast. The den was dark, the television with Uncle's precious news broadcasts turned off.

Dining room. That was where they'd be. It was central to the back of the house, with a view of the back yard, pool, and the back corner of the guest house. He took a back hallway into the kitchen, where he sidled up to the open doorway leading to the dining room. Sure enough. The heavy oak table and chairs had been pushed back. Sean's uncle and aunt sat on the floor, hands tied behind them, with their backs to the wall that divided the dining room from the kitchen. He couldn't see beyond them without sticking his head into the room, but assumed that Lina and at least one or two of the staff must be there as well. Two men guarded them, paying more attention to the window than to their prisoners. Their guns were held loosely pointed at the floor.

Sean needed to keep at least one of these guys alive to see if he could get any information out of them, if he could do it without things getting messy. And he'd have to move fast enough that none of the captives along the wall cried out and gave him away.

Someone's radio crackled softly. "Anyone have eyes on the target?"

One of them reached to depress his mic. "Negative."

Sean moved while they were distracted. In three quick strides he was across the room, and before the man on the radio had lowered his hand he had Sean's camp knife embedded in his neck. It took about two seconds. Sean left the knife there and spun to the other man, knocking the gun to the side with his arm, then continuing the motion, whipping his arm around until the rifle was hooked in his elbow. He jerked the gun butt up, which yanked the other man forward by the gun strap around his shoulders. Sean popped him in the jaw, half spinning him around—he had to let go of the gun—then grabbed him in a choke hold.

The radio crackled again. "Jones? Erricksen? See anything?"

Jones and Erricksen must have been the two men outside, because there was no answer. The radios went silent. Sean strained against the bucking, writhing attacker, but after a moment his struggles grew weak, and then he went limp. Sean eased him to the ground.

"Took you long enough," Uncle Arden said from his place by the wall.

"Sorry," Sean panted, stooping to retrieve his knife. He wiped it off on the dead man's clothes, then hastily searched him until he found a couple spare zip ties, which he used to tie the man he'd choked out.

How many were left? The guest house was small, so he guessed no more than three, but there might be backup nearby. A few men left with the vehicles, anyway, wherever they were hidden.

He stood and turned to face his uncle and the others, suddenly aware of several people crying. One of them was his aunt. The cook who lived in one of the apartments in the old servant's wing had been rounded up as well. She was in her pajamas and kept whimpering. The groundskeeper sat next to her making little shushing noises, though he looked as shocked as she was. Sean was glad he couldn't see their faces well in the dim light filtering through the window. Lina was there. She looked mad. And she had her werewolf-hating friend over. The other girl stared at him open-mouthed.

"Sorry," Sean apologized again, moving to cut the zip ties they had been restrained with. "Didn't mean for this to happen. Is everyone alright?"

"Fine," said Uncle Arden, rubbing his wrists. "You didn't clean up over at the guest house yet?"

"Came here first. You have any idea how many are over there?"

"There were seven altogether when they busted in here. They left these two to keep an eye on us."

Four down, three to go, then. The radio had been silent. They might be on the move by now.

"You got blood on me," Lina said, her voice shaky.

Sean looked down. He had wiped the knife off, but a good bit of blood still covered his hands and arms, slick and black in the dim light. "Sorry."

He hastily cut the others loose, glancing out the window every second. Lina's friend, when she got free, threw herself at him, wrapping her arms around his waist and sobbing.

"Thank you. That was amazing."

"I wouldn't thank me—they were here for me." He pried her off and stepped away, taking another look through the window. No movement. No radio chatter.

"You should go," Uncle Arden said.

Sean glanced at him, then nodded to the man he'd left alive. He was starting to stir. "I have questions."

Arden stooped to pick up the other rifle.

Sean snatched it away, looking at him askance. "What are you doing? You can't be involved in this. Take everyone and hide in the cellar or something."

Arden looked like he was going to argue, but his wife was hanging on his arm, pleading incoherently and sending Sean dirty looks. The two staff seemed shell shocked still. Lina and her friend stood quietly together. Finally he nodded.

"Take care of yourself. Probably won't see you after this."

"Not unless you visit Thyrus."

He reached over and slapped Sean's shoulder. "Give your mother a kiss for me if you make it home. She was always a lovely lady."

With that he herded the others into the hall and toward the basement, leaving Sean alone with the soldier who'd just woken up and started quietly cursing. Sean nudged him with his boot.

"Shut up."

He checked the rifle he'd swiped. Time to go hunting again. He had no desire to get cornered, and by now at least one of the remaining men would be sneaking around to see what was going on.

The house was still clear as he made his way back to the sunroom's open window and stepped out. The snow had stopped and the night grown colder. His boots squeaked faintly in the inch of snow that had fallen, until he stepped into the shelter of the colonnade where he ran silently back toward the first two men he'd killed. He slowed as he approached.

"Jones and Erricksen are down," someone said. The man sent out to scout. This was followed by a quiet round of swearing from around the corner.

Sean stepped out and smashed the rifle butt into the guy's face. He crumpled.

"Five down, two to go."

The last two would still be waiting in the guest house, and they'd be nervous. Sean could settle in right here and wait for them to do something stupid, but he was getting impatient, and even if he took out the whole strike team, there would be others. Either waiting with the vehicles or back at command. Someone would come looking before too long, and he needed to pry some information out of that guy inside yet.

He crouched next to the rapidly cooling bodies of the men he'd killed earlier and searched them, coming up with a couple grenades.

"Overkill much? You'd think you idiots were after some overpowered sorcerer, or an assassin or something." He snorted.

Taking his new arsenal, he reversed directions again, running silently back around the manor. This time he passed by the sunroom and continued to the far side of the building where he skirted around the pool, approaching the guest house from the back where there were no windows.

Sean assumed they were holed up in the big main room facing the door, which was really the only logical option. He left the pool walkway and went out around the back of the house and peered around the corner along the far wall. The stove light glowed faintly through the kitchen window. The house was small—just three rooms. Bedroom, bathroom, and main room, which included the kitchen, dining, and living area. So if he tossed a grenade through the kitchen window, that should do the trick. He just had to do it without getting shot, which meant not standing directly in line with that whole wall when he shot the window out.

That in mind, he paced away from the house till he was at a roughly forty-five degree angle from the window, then put a dozen rounds from the assault rifle through it, shattering both the glass and the stillness of the night. As expected, they opened fire from inside, spraying bullets back out the window and through the wall, ripping apart the siding. He waited a moment till there was a pause in the firing, then pulled the pin on one of the grenades and tossed it through the window. Inside, it clattered across the stove's glass cooktop, accompanied by panicked curses and scrambling.

That's gonna hurt.

The rest of the windows shattered with the ensuing whump. Someone screamed. Sean sprinted around to the front of the house and tossed the other grenade through a different window.

"Sorry, Uncle," he muttered.

The second explosion took out the front door, blowing it across the small porch in a rush of flames. Good enough. Jogging back toward the manor, he didn't hear sirens yet, so hopefully he had a few minutes to question the last man.

The attacker whom he'd choked out was awake and glared at him balefully when he came back and flicked on the lights in the dining room. The other man still lay in a pool of blood under the window.

"Did you kill them all?" his prisoner asked.

"Not sure." Sean grunted as he hefted the soldier up and onto a chair. His name patch read 'R. Bidden', and though the uniform was standard Barran military, Sean was betting he was one of Dianthe's pets, if he was participating in a strike against a noble in the royal court, within the capital.

Sean patted down his pockets and found another grenade as well as a stun gun. "So which were you planning on using on me?" he asked, holding them up for an instant before setting them on the table.

"It was just supposed to be a surprise and grab. No one was supposed to get hurt."

"You were all packing a lot of heat if that's true."

Bidden stared over at his dead comrade. "Yeah, well. Always best to be prepared."

"How did that work out for you?" Sean snorted.

Bidden turned back to him. "Look. I'm not an idiot. I know I'm only alive so you can question me. So what is it you want to know? And if I tell you, will you let me live?"

Sean shrugged. "Probably."

29

CUSHY ASSASSIN TITLE

Sean woke up that morning cold and hungry in a sleeping bag that smelled like old cabbage. It had to be nearly noon. He lay there for a moment watching his breath fog in front of his face and studying the faded logo on a long-ago discarded gym bag sitting a couple feet away. Presently he rolled over to see if the rest of his surroundings were just as glorious. Mounds of garbage shifted around him.

"Good morning, human!" called a cheerful, rumbling voice.

"Nigel. Is that... coffee?" Sean sat up, shivering as the sleeping bag slid down. He reached for his jacket, draped over a broken chair nearby, and pulled it on. Last night's dried blood cracked and flaked off along the creases.

"Coffee, sandwiches, hot dough-nuts." Nigel the troll held the brown paper bag over Sean's head and shook it. His mane of gray hair—or fur—was flecked with snow, as was his checkered flannel shirt. He wasn't wearing a coat, but didn't seem to mind.

"Thanks," Sean croaked, reaching for it.

They sat together among the piles of refuse beneath the bridge and ate the surprisingly fresh, hot meal. Sean's bike leaned against the underside of the bridge arch nearby.

"Last night you promised the story of how you killed the queen's men," Nigel reminded him presently.

"Right." Sean stared in disgust at his hands. They still had patches of dried blood on them. He'd been so hungry he didn't care, but now his stomach twisted a little. Monsters, he could fight all day, but humans... as good as he was at killing, he didn't like it. He forced himself to pop the last bite of the doughnut into his mouth, then launched into the story, sparing none of the gritty details. He'd bargained a night's refuge from the troll in exchange for a good, bloody tale, and a bargain was a bargain.

"This man that you questioned. What did he say?" Nigel asked when he concluded.

Sean brooded over his coffee for a moment. "He said Dianthe is making her move, and there's nothing I can do about it. She arrested a dozen or more people yesterday, and even planned to raid the church after I left it. Her people started rounding up magicals, too. Something bad is going down tonight."

"But you must do something about it," Nigel said simply.

Sean nodded. "I was sent here to kill her. All these months and the time just hasn't been right. But now it is."

"What do you need to do this?"

"Heh. An army, maybe, or a mage of my own? Short of that, I could use a shower. Can't sneak up on anyone smelling like death and dirty socks."

"Dirty socks are an honorable smell," Nigel said soberly.

Sean blinked. "Well, I'm a spy. I'm not supposed to be honorable."

Nigel considered that for a moment, his craggy face thoughtful, then nodded. "Different honor. I know a place. Come with me."

Sean rolled up the sleeping bag and crumpled the napkins and wrappers from breakfast, tucking them into a nearby garbage bag. Nigel might live in a pile of junk under a bridge, but it was still his home. Best to respect that. Then he followed the troll out into the weak winter light.

A storm was brewing. The air had a bitter, evil feel to it as they left the meager shelter of the bridge. Nigel led him away from the river into a maze of dilapidated houses and apartments. Some of them were boarded up and looked on the verge of collapse, though of these, several seemed to be home to squatters. He was a bit relieved when the troll lumbered into one of the better-looking apartment buildings and led the way up a dingy flight of stairs that smelled like cigars and wet dog. He stopped in front of a door that stood out from the rest because it was painted like a sunrise in bright yellow, pink, orange, and blue. It even had some swirls of glitter. Sean raised an eyebrow at it.

Nigel pounded on the obnoxious door with a fist that looked like a lump of rock, rattling it on the hinges. Nothing happened for a long moment. Even Nigel shifted on his big feet and started to say something. But then a shadow passed underneath the door and a couple of deadbolts snicked. A chain rattled.

The door jerked open, bringing them face-to-face with the last person Sean expected to see. Almond eyes narrowed, pointy incisors gleaming, and dressed in the most hideous green and red homemade sweater Sean had ever seen, Beck stood there grinning at them. The kind of grin that looked like he was thinking about eating them.

"Uh..." said Sean.

Nigel gave him a friendly shove forward, which was like getting a nudge from a battering ram. "My friend needs a shower so he can kill the queen."

Beck's eyes narrowed even further. "Took you long enough. I thought you were dead."

"I'm... not. Yet. Is this your place?"

"It's my girlfriend's. She had to get out of the city and hasn't been able to come back, since the assassin that was *supposed* to kill Dianthe hasn't yet."

"Hey, don't look at me. I'm not the only one here that can pull a trigger or throw a knife."

Beck scoffed, but he stepped aside and waved them in. The rest of the apartment was just as... unique... as the front door, with bright colors, bright, homemade throw rugs, and bright lace curtains. There were polka dots and stripes everywhere, and nothing matched anything else. It kind of hurt to look at. And there were about a hundred light crystals embedded in the ceiling. Thankfully only a dozen of them were lit. There were houseplants everywhere, too, and a miniature lemon tree in the corner, loaded with fruit.

"Are you actually going to kill her this time, now that you've waited till it's almost too late?"

"Gonna try. And there was more going on than just Dianthe's evil. If you didn't notice, Gaelan was on the run from *you*, and Calla was one wrong sneeze away from getting strung up by her nobles. The king is a vegetable. If I'd have killed Dianthe before, Barra would have gone into civil war."

Beck grumbled, but didn't argue. "So what do you need? I take it you didn't get anything out of your house before you tossed a grenade in the window?"

How the assassin knew that, Sean wasn't going to ask. He said, "A shower would be nice. Clothes if you have them." He eyed Beck's ugly sweater anxiously.

Beck saw his look and scowled. "Prissy made this for me." He ran a hand defensively over his chest.

"Prissy... the fairy?"

"Half fairy."

"Right. I always heard they have an eye for color."

"She's special. You need weapons?"

Sean shook his head. He'd scavenged a couple handguns and extra knives from the dead strike team last night, and pilfered the twin rapiers from his uncle's collection. They were with the bike, hidden behind a pile of garbage under the bridge.

Nigel shifted toward the door. "I'm going home. You'll come back for your machine?"

"Yeah. Thanks."

The troll nodded and lumbered out, ducking to get through the door and leaving Sean and Beck eyeing each other warily.

"You're a friend of Dylan's?" Beck asked after an uncomfortable silence.

"Yeah. Dragon fire, but I wish I had him to watch my back tonight. Then I know I'd win." Sean scratched at the back of his head sheepishly. "No chance you'd want to take on a witch with me tonight?"

Beck recoiled a little. "I can't fight Dianthe. You know what would happen if...? Never mind. Besides, I have other things that need doing tonight." Which Sean took to mean "other people that need killing."

The assassin disappeared into another room and came back with a pile of clean clothes, then led Sean to the tiny bathroom, which was just as colorful as the rest of the house.

Once Sean was alone, he puffed out a sigh and allowed himself half a minute to deflate. Now, even more than before, he had a bad feeling about tonight. He touched the shield and light crystal hanging at his neck and wished fervently that Rory was there to watch his back. Or Dylan. Or even Jamie or Beck. For once, he didn't want to work alone.

After a scalding hot shower he pulled on the clothes Beck had given him—a black, long-sleeved T-shirt that was a bit snug, and black trousers that looked like they were custom made from soft suede leather. They were utterly silent when he moved, fit surprisingly well, and had pockets everywhere.

"Must be nice to be able to advertise what you do," he muttered, admiring them. Maybe someday he'd land a nice cushy assassin's title where he could walk around looking all deadly and intimidating people. He chuckled.

Beck was in the kitchen slapping together sandwiches when he came back out. "Help yourself."

"Thanks." Sean surveyed the array of cold cuts and cheese spread out. "I heard a rumor that Dianthe was rounding up magicals in the city. Any idea what that's about?"

Beck popped a slice of pickle in his mouth and glanced over. "She'll sacrifice them. You know what tonight is? Midwinter's eve. Darkest night of the year. Big mojo for black magic."

Sean felt some of the blood drain out of his face. "What's she hoping to accomplish? She's already powerful."

"There's always more. Soothsayers are like seers' evil counterparts. But they offer big sacrifices to the spirits in exchange for their power. Maybe she's trying to do that. Then there's shadow walkers, which are an evil counterpart to my people. They... you don't want to know. Anyhow. Bad stuff." He took his plate of sandwiches and went back into the living room, leaving Sean standing in the kitchen feeling queasy.

He reluctantly finished putting his own sandwiches together, stacking cold cuts, cheese, pickles, and mustard. Outside, the wind howled around the old building like a living beast, rattling ill-fitting windows in their frames. Dread knotted in his stomach, but he forced himself to join Beck in the other room and eat. The food Nigel had brought earlier had worn off already, and he had to keep his energy up. It was going to be a long night.

"The Midwinter masquerade ball is tonight," Beck said without looking up when Sean sat down.

"Yeah." Sean wondered idly if the head chef had been forced to come back to work since he was on the run.

Beck turned a critical eye on him, studying him from top to bottom. He smirked.

His mouth full of sandwich, Sean asked, "What?"

"You have an invitation to get in the door?"

"Yeah. I never took it off my bike. Not that it'll do me much good. I can't exactly flash my ID with it."

Beck nodded. He finished his meal in a few quick bites and left the room, returning a moment later with another stack of items. This time, a black dress shirt, black fedora, and black eye mask. Finally, a small ID card.

Sean looked at them dubiously. "You want me to go disguised as you?"

"No one will have the guts to question you. If they do... just tell them you want to see the queen. They'll let you in."

"I thought you were a fugitive too."

"I am, but I'm not a *spy*. Dianthe wants me back in her control. It's why I can't risk going near her. But you... they've got roadblocks in or out of the city, looking for you."

"Of course they do." Sean sighed. "And you're the last one anyone would try to impersonate. Or steal identification from." He fingered the hat thoughtfully. "Do you know what kind of personal wards Dianthe keeps on herself? She's paranoid about poison in her food and checks everything, I know that much."

Beck nodded. "She has spells woven into the jewels in that big gaudy ring she always wears. They'll turn aside blades and bullets. Either get rid of the ring first, or you'll have to get close enough to snap her neck."

That was what he'd been afraid of, and fully prepared to have to do. "And the magicals she's taken?"

"They'll be in the cells in her ritual chamber. Never been down there?"

"No. I couldn't have gone there without blowing my cover."

Beck nodded and briefly outlined how to get into the dungeons, and specifically the witch queen's ritual chamber.

"Just hope you don't have to chase her down there," he said. "That place is evil, even by my standards."

"Here's to hoping," said Sean, pulling on the dress shirt over top of his T-shirt.

30

WATCH FOR THE HELLHOUNDS

Bitter wind swirled fitfully around Rory, driving stinging snow pellets into her face and obscuring the horse and rider just a half dozen yards in front of her. It was a dark day, even for Midwinter's Eve, and a cheerless one, too. For perhaps the thousandth time she wondered what was happening to Sean, and whether he'd gotten the shield she had delivered to the priest. She hadn't heard anything from him since long before that, and the last time they had talked, he'd been afraid. He hadn't said it, but she caught it in the way he hunched close to the running shower in his bathroom and still talked so quietly she could hardly understand him. It had been evident too in the uncharacteristic hardness of his face and the clipped tone of his voice.

Rory fingered the lump of his signet ring under her coat and sent up another prayer for him.

"Eyes open, scout!" Tarha, Rory's scouting partner, called through the driving snow. She had stopped her horse and waited for Rory to catch up. She'd taken it upon herself to act as Rory's 'mentor' during their two-week patrol.

Rory thought ruefully that she would rather be paired with Vasya and his goading than Tarha with her condescending watchfulness. She muttered something unflattering under her breath.

"Is this your first Midwinter on the border?" Tarha asked, half shouting over the wind.

"No," said Rory shortly, hoping to divert another of her partner's long-winded stories. Whether it was that or the driving wind and snow, the other elf remained silent, riding abreast with Rory for a while, instead of taking the lead. Glancing over, Rory was surprised to see her looking pensive. Begrudgingly she asked, "What's wrong?"

"I don't know," said Tarha. "This storm feels evil, doesn't it? Or is Maireadd preying on my mind today?"

Rory gripped the ring under her coat a little tighter. "I feel it too."

"What say we stop at the next campsite and have a rest? Getting out of this wind will help us get our wits about us."

Rory agreed, and within an hour they were leading the horses into the shelter of a young thicket and activating the wards there. There had been storm damage in the area at one time that took out the heavy, old trees, and the young trees had grown up thick and tangled in their place till the elves carved out crisscrossing tunnels through them and placed their usual wards for refuge. It was always better to have as much natural shelter to build their wards around as possible, and cutting broad tunnels through the thick growth made a sturdier structure than simply carving out a clearing. Most of these refuge sites weren't meant to host a large company, simply to offer protection and meager comfort to the scouts on their ceaseless trails. They typically featured wards protecting against weather, physical attack, and monsters of the shadow realm, as well as a fire pit and a small cache of emergency supplies and feed for the horses. Larger scouting parties came through several times a year to replenish the various sites which were scattered throughout Maireadd.

Once the wards were activated, blocking the wind and stinging snow, Rory and Tarha both pulled their hats off to free their ears as they built a fire. Though it was only around noon, the storm made it unnaturally dark and had turned the trail treacherous, so by unspoken agreement they made camp and prepared to hunker down until tomorrow. Whatever evil was in the wind today was indefinable and directionless—nothing but a hunch, really. And nothing they could go blindly blundering through the storm to find. Even Tarha remained subdued as they unpacked their cooking gear and rations for a hot meal.

Happy Midwinter to us, Rory thought with a sigh as she poked the coals and threw another branch onto the fire.

Tarha settled a small pot of water among the coals. "Midwinter is always the worst tour of the year. Seems like there's always trouble. I just hope this storm is the worst of it."

She'd hardly finished speaking when the wards moaned and whispered under another onslaught of wind, and with the wind, a muffled shout.

Rory and Tarha looked at each other. Had it actually been a real voice? They sat there still as lumps of ice, straining their ears. Suddenly the magic in the atmosphere around them popped and rippled, like water in a pond reacting to a dropped rock. Something had struck the wards.

Rory leapt to her feet, heart pounding, calling magic to her fingertips. Beside her, Tarha had jumped up as well, drawing her longknife. A moment later the magic stirred again, though much more gently this time, as whoever was out there entered the shelter of the wards. They must have thrown themselves against them last time, to have activated them. But now whoever it was had been allowed by the magic to pass through. Not a beast then, or a shadow creature. Definitely a person.

"Hello?" a man's voice called from one of the tree tunnels. "Rory?"

Rory and Tarha exchanged startled looks. Rory nodded silently toward the dense wall of saplings behind Tarha, who acknowledged with her own nod before disappearing into the uncut thicket. Rory did the same, slipping between tree trunks no thicker than her arms and then crouching down where she could watch their camping area. Once there, she went totally still, listening.

The rustle of footsteps through fallen leaves and long grasses preceded the figure that came into view a moment later, stumbling down the cleared path through the saplings. He looked a little wild, his shaggy blond hair a tousled mess, his clothes torn and dirty. He wasn't dressed for this kind of storm, with only hiking boots, jeans, and a winter coat. He fumbled to a stop before the fire and dropped to his knees beside it, stretching out reddened hands to the warmth. But his attention didn't stay on the fire for long. He closed his eyes for a moment, then turned his head and looked right at Rory's hiding place.

"Rory? Auralie Agent? Are you there?"

Rory rose slowly from her crouch, feeling her magic still sparking at her fingertips as she eased her way back out through the saplings to the cleared path. She stepped softly into the open. "I'm here."

The stranger wilted with relief. He looked vaguely familiar, but she couldn't place him, even as she drew nearer and gained a better view.

"Thank God I found you. You don't know me, do you?"

"No," she said, noting how his red ears were turning white with the beginnings of frostbite at the tips.

"I'm Gaelan, of Barra."

"Crown Prince Gaelan?" she chirped in surprise, even though she remembered as soon as he said it that she had, indeed, glimpsed him at court during her brief visit with Erinn Ambassador. No wonder she hadn't been able to place him.

"I'm not so sure about the crown part anymore, but yes." He touched the tips of his ears and grimaced. "They're numb. But they hurt."

Rory stepped closer, letting her magic fade away, and rubbed the pale patch on the ear closest to her. "If you can still feel them, they'll be fine. Why are you here?"

"The curse is coming on my country. Tonight. I saw it." He swiped viciously at the melted snow on his face. "I went to your elf council to beg for help, but they refused to get involved. Sean Leigh is going to kill the queen, but he will lose his life, and the curse will come anyway, and they wouldn't do *anything*."

At mention of Sean, Rory's heart kicked her in the ribs, then went on pounding dully. She felt her face go cold, and horror clenched her stomach till she thought she would be sick. "What can I do?"

"Dianthe is coming here, to Maireadd, to make her sacrifices for more power. There's a place... it has these standing stones..."

"I know it," Rory said, with a fresh wave of terror shuddering through her. "It's near one of the tunnel exits just across the border, but it's at least four or five hours' ride from here. Longer in this storm. Did you tell the council that Dianthe was coming here?"

"Of course." Gaelan moved to sit on a rock beside the fire and began pulling his boots off. "They said that they didn't dare get involved. Especially since *I* was the one asking for help. They didn't want to get caught up in a civil war, or meddle with another country's ruler. 'The elves will not risk another war with humans.' I quote. Worthless cowards. No offense." He peeled off wet socks and stretched his feet out to the fire, wincing. They were splotched red and white, like his ears.

"I'm offended on your behalf," said Rory, gathering up the supplies and gear she'd just unpacked and shoving it back into her pack.

Tarha, who'd been waiting and listening through their conversation, stepped out of hiding just then. "Where do you think you're going?" she said to Rory, shooting Gaelan a dirty look.

"To help my friend."

"Your *human*. I should have known. And what about your duties here?"

"Duties to *what*?" Rory shrieked, turning on her. "To sitting by this fire all night listening to you talk down to me? Duties to protect our borders and watch for monster activity? Well guess what? We've got monster activity on the border here. Are you going to sit back and watch? Just who is neglecting their duties, Tarha Scout? These *are our duties*!" she was roaring by the time she finished. "If the elves are too stupid—too crazed by their fear—to know where their danger lies, and what Dianthe will do to us if she isn't stopped, then by God, *someone* had better step up and do something."

"I won't go against the wishes of the elf council!" Tarha cried, half whining, half accusing.

"Well, if you're really that blind and useless, then maybe you should be on the council yourself." Rory turned her back on Tarha's sputtering and went to her horse, leading it back to the campsite where she began saddling it back up. To Gaelan she asked, "Are you coming with me?"

His roguish face grew pensive. "No. There's something else I need to do tonight. I can't stay here long either."

"Okay. Tarha will get you dry boots and something to eat before you go."

"How dare you?!" Tarha stalked round the fire toward Rory.

"How dare I? Do you really want to let the crown prince of Barra lose his toes to frostbite while he's here? Even your precious council must agree that *that* would be a monumentally bad idea." She turned back to Gaelan. "What else can you tell me?"

"If there's blood on the altar, then Dianthe's ritual has already begun, and you'll have to destroy the altar itself to stop the curse. I saw..." his eyes slid away. "Just go as quickly as you can. Watch for the hounds. And pray."

Rory's horse balked at leaving the shelter of the wards and companionship of the other horse. One sniff of the wind and the ridiculous mare was bunching up and trying to back her way back into the shelter. Rory spun her in a tight circle and then set her heels to her flanks, and they burst out of the wards' protection with a startled leap. The storm hit them with the fury of an attacking enemy, howling its rage that they had escaped it, even for a short time. Hard ice pellets battered and sliced at Rory's face, and the horse hunched up again, tucking her ears back.

Rory dismounted, walking around to the horse's head, where she murmured a few commands and cupped her hands over the animal's face and ears. She felt the shielding air cushion form beneath her hands, a warm resistance that turned away the wind and stinging snow. The mare calmed. Though still sullen, she agreed to continue once Rory mounted up again and urged her forward. Soon Rory was forced to work a similar spell for herself so she could see the path in the dim, gray light.

She pushed on through the afternoon, coaxing the horse to a quicker pace than was safe for either of them. Thankfully, though it continued to snow ice pellets, the fitful, angry wind kept the trail mostly clear, so the footing wasn't as bad as it could have been, but it was increasingly hard to see through the storm and Maireadd's natural gloom. Nightfall came early on Midwinter. Only a few hours past noon the light faded, and soon Rory was forced to dismount and lead the horse over a difficult section of trail. It was while she was picking her way around rocks and boulders that she heard the first howl in the wind.

All the blood seemed to freeze inside her veins and her scalp prickled under her hat as she stopped in the trail. The mare threw her head up and chuffed nervously.

Watch for the hellhounds, Gaelan had said.

"Can't watch for what you can't see," said Rory through bloodless lips. She tugged her hat down tighter and forced herself to take another step. Then another. Then she started to jog. She was still miles from the standing stones and from helping Sean. She didn't have time for hellhounds.

31

THE MASQUERADE

It was already getting late in the afternoon when Sean pulled his jacket back on, settled the fedora on his head, and slunk out of the apartment. The mask he shoved in his pocket for later. When he stepped out onto the street the wind nearly took the hat off his head. He caught it and mashed it down tight. The sky had grown dark while he was inside—far too dark even for late afternoon on Midwinter's Eve. Fine pellets of snow stung his face and bounced off his coat. They hit the ground and were instantly blown away into slithering white snakes that neither melted nor stuck to the pavement.

"This is going to be a sucky ride," he muttered, turning his collar up. He should have taken his uncle's car when he ran last night. Cars were harder to conceal though, and easier to recognize, when they were bright yellow sports cars. He just hoped this storm didn't get any worse.

Nigel had a fire going in a fifty-five gallon drum when he got back to the bridge. The troll was roasting chestnuts on a rusty wire rack over top of it, and singing carols.

"You're taking your machine in this storm?" he asked as Sean paused to warm his hands over the fire.

"I guess I have to."

"It's going to get worse. This isn't a natural snow," warned the troll.

"Great." Sean wheeled the bike out of the shelter of the bridge and stowed Beck's hat in the saddlebag. His helmet would at least keep his ears warm over top of the mask, the heated grips would keep his hands from stiffening and being unusable, and the seat warmer would help a bit, but the rest of him was going to be *cold* by the time he got to the palace. He hadn't exactly had a chance to grab his winter riding gear before he tossed that grenade in the window.

Thankfully, his *other* gear he tended to keep on his person at all times. The set of carbon-fiber blades in his boot, and the pointed, hollow tube that looked like an ink pen clipped in his pocket. He hadn't saved his lucky string tie though, unfortunately.

After thanking Nigel again for his hospitality, Sean pulled on his helmet and gloves and set off for the palace. Any fear or dread he might have had earlier he let go of now, forcing his emotions to be blank and empty. That was the only way he could kill, and the thing that made him good at it.

The big iron gates stood open, and Sean slowed to join a line of vehicles entering the palace grounds. One of the security guards hailed him. He was an older man with a white mustache and a paunch over his belt.

"Cold ride," he said, stepping out of the guard shack when Sean stopped and flipped up the visor of his helmet.

"Yeah."

He did a double-take of Sean and the motorcycle as he took his invitation and Beck's ID. "Isn't this Sean Leigh's bike?"

Sean did his best to imitate Beck's tone and manner of speech. "It might be."

The guard handed the cards back. "Her majesty will want to see you."

"I'm counting on it."

Sean let out a shivery breath and turned off onto the long drive around to the employee parking in back, rather than follow the others to the visitor's lot. He parked the bike and reluctantly took off his warm helmet to re-tie the mask around his head. It was a simple bandanna style with eye holes, but it wrapped around and over his head, tying in back and totally covering his red hair. He settled the fedora over it, then walked back around to the main entrance, trying to work some warmth back into his limbs before he got there. The palace security gave him no more trouble than the gate had, shying back from him when he stepped up to the metal detector, then waving him through without going near him.

"Cushy assassin title," Sean muttered as he walked away.

The ballroom glittered. Ice sculptures stood in every corner, the chandeliers sparkled with crystal icicles, and the nobles were a mass of shimmering colors and jewels. It was all slightly nauseating. Masked faces turned to stare at him as he entered, some decked in feathers and others in rhinestones or glass chips. They eased away from him as he passed, a dark blot against their rainbowed brilliance.

The queen was already there, seated on her dais in a white gown encrusted with sparkling crystals like sunshine on snow. She wore a scarlet feathered eye mask that turned to follow him as he eased along the edge of the crowd. Well, he had her attention.

The crowd in the center of the ballroom was starting to clear out to begin the evening with dancing, pressing back toward the walls, while in the corner a small orchestra started playing a waltz. Apparently he'd arrived just in time to miss the queen's welcome speech and for the dancing to begin. Nothing he could do now but blend in for a while... or not. He kept attracting stares while repelling contact. Until suddenly someone loomed in his way. The man was dressed in dark colors with a full-faced wolf mask in gray fur and brown leather. His dark hair had a single small braid in the side of it and was pulled back into a short tail. Jamie.

"You're not Beck," he said, stepping closer. His nostrils flared and he cocked his head to the side.

"That I'm not," replied Sean glibly, pitching his voice lower and allowing his native brogue to shine through the words. He'd hardly used a Thyrusian accent in over a year and the syllables sounded strange to him now. He was more worried about giving himself away with his normal voice to anyone who might be eavesdropping than by assuming an accent. Sean Leigh might be suspected as an assassin or as a spy, but there was nothing tying him to Thyrus, specifically, and never in the time he'd been in Barra had he spoken anything but the flawless dialect of the capital.

Jamie's mask gave away nothing, but he huffed a soft chuckle. "Good to know you're alive and well, after last night. We wondered."

"For now. Maybe not for long."

Jamie nodded his understanding. "I'll help if I can."

Calla swept up to them then, taking Jamie's arm as she surveyed Sean. She cocked her head at him, not unlike her fiance had, but she didn't have his werewolf sense of smell. "Good evening."

He offered her a slight bow, keeping his brogue. "Your highness."

She stared at him for a long moment, her brow wrinkling in confusion over her little pink jeweled eye mask. He gave her a small grin, flashing his dimples for just an instant. Her brow smoothed and she laughed in relief and delight, clapping silk-gloved hands.

"Brilliant. Oh, I love it." Her face, what he could see around her mask, fell. "But be careful tonight, please. I have such a horrible feeling."

He searched her face for a moment, half hidden though it was, then nodded. "Your Highness."

He slipped back into the crowd, but when he glanced over at the dais again, the queen was gone. Standing still, surrounded by strangers in masks, his heart pounded dully. Conversation around him quieted suddenly, and he felt the back of his neck prickle. He turned and came face to face with Queen Dianthe.

"Your majesty." He bowed.

She scrutinized him. "You're not Beck."

"No, your majesty." He kept his brogue, his voice pitched low, and didn't smile. If she recognized anything about him, it would be his dimples.

"Dance with me?" she asked, holding out a soft, bejeweled hand to him.

He bowed over her hand and led her onto the dance floor, where she signaled the musicians. They began the steps to another stately waltz.

"That is a daring costume," she said.

"Aye, your majesty. I'm a daring man."

"A man of Thyrus," she prompted. "Or perhaps you've perfected the accent in order to charm the ladies tonight."

He said nothing as they began a series of more complicated steps and he had to twirl his partner away and back. He dipped her backward, her auburn curls brushing the floor, her white throat long and exposed, then swept her back upright and into another twirl, to a smattering of applause. Her cheeks flushed a rosy pink below her crimson mask. The song ended to more applause.

"Is there nothing I could do to induce you to give me your name?" she asked, pouting her rosebud lips.

"Madam." He bowed to her again and eased back into the crowd. Spotting Jamie and Calla lingering not far away, he angled toward them. He didn't stop, but bumped Jamie's shoulder on the way through, using the motion to press Dianthe's enchanted ring of protection into his hand. She had been too busy twirling and cleverly trying to figure him out to notice when he slid it off her finger. As long as she also didn't notice its absence immediately....

Jamie looked after him sharply, but said nothing.

Beck's disguise came in handy again as Sean left the ballroom and headed toward the old palace dungeons. No one stopped or questioned him, or even looked in his direction for too long. He had no desire to face Dianthe in her ritual room, but he knew that was where she would eventually come, and even if he waited for her in the passageway, he'd need to take care of the guard, or else he'd likely end up with a bullet in his back. He didn't want this to be a suicide mission if it didn't need to be. He also didn't want to leave more of a trail of bodies than he needed to, so when he came to the guard stationed at the door at the head of the stairs leading down to the dungeon level, he decided on a small gamble. Instead of knifing the man, he tipped his hat, offered his best Beck-inspired feral grin, and walked right on past. Beck might be a wanted man, but he was wanted *back*, for the queen's purposes, not wanted dead, like Sean, who's neck prickled as he descended the narrow stone steps. The guard never said a word.

Bare light bulbs lit his way, strung along the wall on a black utility power cord. The cord was suspended by rusted nails driven into the brittle gray mortar between stones. That atmospheric lighting scheme continued through the maze of corridors down below, their low ceiling beams black with age and barely high enough for him to walk without ducking. He swiped a cobweb out of his face. *Cheery*. He passed ancient doors, black as the ceiling beams, their hinges mottled with rust. Some of them had barred windows in them, high up where he'd have to stand on his toes to look inside. Somewhere behind him a light blew out with a soft *pop* and the passage got just a bit darker. Dread slithered along his spine like a centipede. He paused to pull one of the carbon fiber blades from his boot, sliding it partway into his sleeve so it was hidden.

Another guard stood at the door to the ritual chamber, his gaze turned toward Sean as he came around the final corner. "You shouldn't be down here." He put his hand on his gun, ready to pull it from the holster.

Sean kept walking toward him without speaking.

"If Her Majesty sent you, she neglected telling me. Has she subverted you again?"

So that was Beck's secret, Sean thought. He'd been subverted by Dianthe, and escaped somehow. No wonder he wouldn't go near her.

"Stop where you are," the guard warned, drawing his gun. His brows creased as Sean continued toward him without speaking. "Are you Beck? Are you subverted? I know you're able to answer that. Tell me!"

Sean stopped when his chest bumped into the end of the pistol muzzle. He and the guard stared each other down for a drawn out second.

"No and no," Sean said suddenly, and swiped the gun aside with his forearm, twisting to the side as it went off. The bullet ricocheted down the corridor with a whining ping while Sean used his twisting motion to slide his knife into the guard's neck. The guard got off another wild shot before he dropped the gun and clutched at his throat. Ignoring his gurgles, Sean stepped around him and opened the door.

The first thing he saw in the center of the room was the altar. A massive stone slab, it was carved all around with wicked-looking runes and vile pictures, its top and sides so thickly stained with blood, both old and new, that it lay in dried layers like hardened candle wax. The room stank of death and rot. Sean gagged.

Beside the altar was a small wheeled table, like one might find in a hospital or laboratory, with an assortment of ornate knives and daggers laid out on it. To the right was a stone wall decorated with several sets of chains and shackles. To the left there were three cells, two of them with their barred doors standing open. The room appeared deserted, but for that single closed cell door. Where were all the magicals Dianthe was planning to sacrifice?

Sean double checked the hallway before stepping into the room. He had to suppress another gag as the stench of rotting blood enveloped him. With no desire to look too closely at the noisome altar or its collection of blades, he stepped over to the cells, glancing into the first two to confirm that they were empty before he got to the third, whose door was shut. As he came even with it he could see a lone figure through the bars, standing in the corner gazing out at him.

He and the prisoner stared at each other for a long, surreal moment before the other man said, "Sean?"

"Priest," Sean returned incredulously.

The priest tugged at his corduroy jacket, which was even more rumpled and bedraggled than usual, as he came up to the bars. "Well, praise God for His mercies. I didn't expect you to be here. Shouldn't you be... doing other things?"

"I am doing other things. Shouldn't there be more people here? Magicals for Dianthe's sacrifice? And when did they bring you in?"

"This morning," the priest answered. "They raided the church. The tunnel is still safe though—at least it was when they took me away. There were magicals here when they brought me in. At least a dozen. Dianthe and her people came and took them away though. That was hours ago. I heard them talking, and she's making her big sacrifice in Maireadd tonight."

"In Maireadd," Sean said, something close to panic blooming in his chest. It had been nearly seven o'clock when he left the ballroom. If Dianthe was going to Maireadd to make sacrifices at midnight, then she would need to leave immediately. She wouldn't be coming back down here. He swore, then apologized. "Why Maireadd, though?"

"I gathered that she was hoping for, well, a greater return on her blood sacrifice, I suppose. Big, evil mojo."

"Did you hear where, in Maireadd? It's got to be somewhere close, along the border, right? It would take almost an hour to drive out there from here, and then they'd have to go by foot or horseback. There's a storm going on, so it would be slow, and I don't see the queen being willing to hike very far."

"I'm so sorry. I just don't know. Nothing was said about it while they were here."

Sean drummed his fingers against the bars. "Well, is there anything you can think of, any place you remember hearing about, that might be likely?"

The priest began to shake his head, then paused. "Well, now, no... there may be something. I've heard rumors of a place. Something to do with the Curse War. I'm not sure just what it is, but anyone who goes through Maireadd seems to avoid it. It was near the tunnel entrance, I think. The one that begins in our chapel. I only remember because some of those who were fleeing the city, who'd been to Maireadd before, told me to warn others traveling through not to go near it."

"Okay. A place. That's good." Sean paced back over to the door to check the hallway, then dragged the dead guard inside. He began going through his pockets. "What kind of a place? What direction? Search that memory of yours, Priest. I know it's a good one."

The priest stood at the bars, gripping them as he watched Sean search the guard. "I always suspected, in theory, what it was that you did, but... to be honest, it's turning my stomach a bit. I'm not sure my conscience would ever allow me to take another person's life. Though that's not to say it isn't sometimes warranted."

"That's why you're a priest and I'm a killer," said Sean. "But I wouldn't feel too bad about this guy. He knew full well what he was guarding down here, and what went on in this room. Anyone who can listen to the screams of innocents being slaughtered like animals and guard their killer is someone who needs to be put down."

After a short pause the priest said, "Standing stones. There were standing stones around the place. And it's to the south of the tunnel exit. Ours was the southernmost entrance, and the standing stones were to the south of it, otherwise the other tunnels would have been in danger as well."

"Good. That's better. I can work with that, hopefully. The queen won't be taking the tunnel though." He found the guard's keys and stood, crossing to the cell. The doors in the upper palace had all been refitted with security locks that required key cards or biometric scanners, for certain of them, but the dungeons sported their original clunky iron locks with over-sized keys. It only took a moment to find the one that opened the priest's door.

"Sean," said the priest as he stepped out of the cell, "She has to be stopped tonight, before she can make that sacrifice."

"I know."

They left the ritual room together, backtracking through the maze of corridors. Since no one ever heard the screams of Dianthe's victims down there, Sean doubted that they had heard the two gunshots that the guard had gotten off, either, but he was still wary of every corner they turned. When they got to the stairs he left the priest at the bottom and ascended by himself, quickly and quietly. Once he'd choked out the guard he gave the priest a hushed call to come up.

"You didn't kill this one?" The priest asked, pausing for a moment to check the guard's pulse while Sean relieved him of his handcuffs, gun, and socks. The cuffs went on the guard's hands, the socks went in his mouth, and Sean kept the gun.

"I don't particularly like killing, even if I'm good at it. I *do* have a conscience."

"I know you do..."

"But you don't know whether my conscience is true, now that you've seen me spill blood?"

"Yes, I suppose that's part of it," the priest answered as they left the stairs behind and made their way through the deserted halls.

"Sometimes one person needs to die in order to save another, even if the one I'm saving is only myself. I am here to save lives, not take them. But sometimes that's not as clear cut as having a guard point their gun at you and knowing they'll kill you if you don't get them first. Sometimes it's killing a strike team so that you can go on with your mission, because if you don't, a whole lot more people are going to suffer and die for it."

"I understand. There needs to be someone who can do the hard things. And I'm glad it's you."

Sean stopped for a moment and looked at him as he caught up. They were almost back to the ballroom now, and could hear the murmur of voices and music.

"Because you have a conscience," said the priest.

"Thanks. Let's just hope those hard things aren't more than I'm good for tonight." He caught the priest's shoulder and stopped him. "Wait here. I need to look around the ballroom and make sure she isn't still in there. I'm not traipsing around Maireadd tonight if I don't have to."

Sean strolled back into the ballroom, but the priest was right. Queen Dianthe wasn't there. He didn't see Calla or Jamie either, so he rejoined the priest in the hallway and they made their way to the storeroom that opened into a loading bay at the back of the palace. The door was guarded, but not for long.

The wind lashed at them as soon as they stepped out of the shelter of the loading bay, hard ice pellets driving into their faces. They stepped back into the shelter of the bay for a moment.

"You be okay from here?" Sean said, raising his voice over the snarl of the wind.

"Yes. I'll be fine now, and you need to hurry. Thank you."

"Right. God keep you, then."

"God keep you. And Sean? I'll hold vigil for you tonight."

Sean nodded, then stepped back out into the wind and the snow and headed for his bike.

His jacket was freezing when he slipped it back on, but his helmet provided instant relief against the sound and wind. The bike started with a roar and he sat there for a moment, feeling the seat warmer slowly come to life and thinking. If he was going into Maireadd, the guns would do him no good, and he'd have to ditch his carbon fiber blades, too. They were a recent human technology. Whether they would trigger the curse or not Sean didn't know, but was it worth taking the chance? He had his camp knife in his saddlebags, and the twin rapiers that he'd taken from his uncle's stash.

"Lousy odds," he muttered as he pulled out. His mission had gone from long shot to desperate—to suicide. And what if he failed?

"By Your mercy, God."

Pulling around the side of the building, he caught sight of three sets of tail lights just disappearing out the front gate. Three armored SUVs.

"Dianthe!"

If he could get to her somehow before she got to Maireadd, then at least he'd have the use of his guns and other weapons. He gunned it and sped out after them, but was forced to slow down immediately as the bike fishtailed in the powdery snow and almost dumped him onto the road outside the guard shack. The road wasn't truly bad yet—not, at any rate, if you had a four-wheeled vehicle—but Sean, on his motorcycle, was forced to slow to a painful crawl, and soon lost sight of the queen's caravan. He swore. If he didn't start catching some breaks here, this really would be a loss.

As he got down into the city he weighed his options. He could stop and steal a car, but that would take precious minutes, and he was already too far behind to ever catch up with them before they reached Maireadd. Plus, if Beck was right, and they now had the roads set up with checkpoints, then the tunnels were the only safe and fast way out, and he couldn't take a car down there. But he could take the bike. He could, perhaps, make up some of the time he'd lost. On the other hand, he still didn't have any clear idea where he was going once he got out of the tunnel.

Suddenly, the bike lurched beneath him. It shot sideways, and he hit the ground before he could even react. He slid with the bike for a few yards along the patch of black ice that he hadn't seen before the tires hit the curb and they came to a stop. His breathing sounded ragged to his own ears within the helmet. Wind gusted, puffing snow over and around him as though it was laughing at him, obscuring the deserted road. His knee and leg started to ache.

Pushing the bike up, he slithered his leg out from underneath it and stood, his legs wobbly and breath still coming in short, shocked bursts. His knee throbbed, but it held his weight. He pulled his helmet off, gasping bitter wind into his lungs. The wind smelled like death.

"God above, keep my way tonight. Let Your creation turn to my protection. God Redeemer, buy back my soul from the forces of evil. God who is spirit, cleanse the paths before me that I walk unseeing." He stood in the street and prayed the ancient prayer of protection, the vile storm snatching away his frosty breaths with its shrieking rage. He pulled his helmet back on and heaved the bike upright, wheeling it beyond the patch of ice before he started it back up.

The city passed by in a blur of swirling snow, the minutes crawling on much faster than Sean was able to on the snowy road, though he knew, logically, that it wasn't taking as long as it felt like. He hadn't left the palace more than forty-five minutes ago. But it was still taking far longer than he could afford. Whether or not there were roadblocks, he'd have to chance the tunnels now, or he'd be too late.

The chapel loomed ahead, a black bulk against the street lamps, the graveyard around it nothing but indistinct grayness. Sean didn't see any sign of the guards that must have been left inside, but he had to assume they were there, someplace, waiting to see who might come to see the priest, not knowing he'd been taken into custody. He bumped the bike up onto the sidewalk and left it there for a moment, bounding up the two shallow steps to the door. It opened with a soft creak, spilling light and warmth out into the storm. No guards in sight yet. He grabbed a hymnal from the stack on its little table beside the entry so he could prop the door open. There were a couple offering plates there as well, beside the collection box. The plates wore a layer of dust because the priest so often forgot to have them sent round during services, but the collection box itself was burnished with use, from those who lovingly dropped offerings without being asked. Anger spiked through Sean as he went back for the bike. How dare Dianthe desecrate this holy place?

He revved the bike up the steps and through the door—and right into the two guards who'd come running from the back to investigate. Their eyes popped wide as he plowed into them. One was knocked into the pews, while the other tried to stumble back. Sean kicked him, and he bounced off the end of a pew, then recoiled forward and met Sean's fist. His head snapped back and he hit the pew again on his way down. He lay still. The other guard regained his balance, meanwhile, and brought his rifle up.

Sean kicked the bike into reverse and spun backward barely in time to miss a burst of bullets. He cut sideways behind the last pew and grabbed one of the dusty brass offering plates from the little table, chucking it at the gunman. It missed, but it distracted him from shooting long enough for Sean to grab the second plate and throw it. This one caught the shooter in the teeth and knocked him down between pews. Sean set the kickstand and leapt over the pew back, then used the next few backs as stepping stones, bounding across the tops to come down on the shooter as he was picking himself back up, his mouth a bloody mess. He grabbed the rifle and smashed it into the other man's face.

Sean stood over him, panting. It was getting foggy inside his helmet, plus it made it hard to hear, so he pulled it off. Other than the rumble of his motorcycle idling, the church was quiet. The two guards were both out cold, though he noted with disgust that this one had been a bit messier than the other. He bent down and wiped a trickle of blood off the man's cheek before it could drip onto the floor of the sanctuary.

"That's on you, bleeding on holy ground," he muttered, wiping his glove off on the man's jacket.

He returned to the bike and cruised carefully down the aisle and into the hallway, past the office, to the tapestry that covered the hidden door to the tunnel. As the priest had said, it was undisturbed, and slid open easily for him. The bike's headlight bounced wildly as he eased it down the steps. There he paused and reset the trip odometer. Twelve miles. That's how long this tunnel supposedly went, under the city and the fields and finally into Maireadd. He couldn't risk running it too close to the Maireadd opening, for fear of activating the curse, so he would have to keep a careful eye on the distance.

The throaty roar of the engine was deafening down here, even inside his helmet, and the ceiling and walls so close that he felt as though he was being funneled into a monster's gullet. With the glare of the headlight being swallowed up by the endless darkness ahead, it gave the impression that the tunnel would just narrow down and cease to exist—a choking, claustrophobic feeling that closed around Sean the further he went. Blackened ceiling beams flashed past altogether too close above his head. But at least there was no wind or snow down here, and he flew over the packed earth floor at heart-pounding speed, splitting the night ahead and feeling it close in sullenly behind.

Ten miles. Eleven. He slowed. Eleven and a half. He slowed the bike to a crawl, watching the ceiling and walls ahead. When dangling roots reached down into the beam of his headlight he stopped and killed the engine.

Silence sealed around him like it wanted to strangle him. Given his proximity to Maireadd and its curse, it probably did. He pulled his helmet off and left it, along with his guns, carbon fiber blades, and cell phone. He took his camp knife and the twin rapiers of his uncle's, and jogged toward the exit.

The blizzard greeted him with a vengeful roar the second he stepped out of the shelter of the tunnel, stealing his breath and blinding him all at once. The unfamiliar shapes of the forest loomed ominously through the driving snow as he turned to the left and started jogging, keeping his hand up in front of his face to avoid getting his eyes lashed by branches and brush. After a few paces he was forced to slow to a walk. Now that he was out here, his hope seemed even more foolish. How was he to find the queen in all this? He would have to be right on top of something to see it. He had no idea where this place with the standing stones actually was. All he had to go on was rumor and conjecture, and the fate of Barra and its neighboring countries depended on him.

With each step Sean took, the more convinced he became that he would die out here, tonight. Whether he found Dianthe and succeeded in killing her or not, he would surely perish. The wind took on the sound of ghastly voices shrieking and laughing at him. The snow bit at his face and ears. Even the rocks and trees seemed to reach out and trip him and snag his clothes.

"Stupid," he muttered as he walked. "Stupid to let it get this far. Should have killed her before." And he wracked his brain for when the right opportunity would have been. But he hadn't known when Dianthe would strike at him. He hadn't had any good opportunity to strike at her—queens weren't exactly easy to get close to—and he'd had to wait for the situation with Calla to stabilize. When should he have made his move before this?

Still, it's cutting it close, he chided himself. *Could have taken a chance before this. It might have been a long shot, but this is hopeless. You're going to die alone out here, without ever even seeing her.* And if he died out here, he'd never see Rory again. Dianthe would bring her curse down on Barra, which in turn could collapse the economy of the entire continent. Lives and homes would be lost... and he'd be the one to blame.

He stopped walking suddenly. Where were these thoughts coming from? They might be realistic, but they weren't *his* thoughts. He never let himself have an opinion about his odds, or even the possibility of his own death. Not while he was working. He could, and did, detach from any kind of emotional stakes when he was going into a fight—that's what made it possible for him to do this kind of work. So why was he getting emotional now? Cold sweat had broken out under his jacket.

The storm blasted around him, with its eerie voices and howls. The trees snapped and creaked and lashed together with their own voices. He'd been walking blind in the dark, hoping to spot a light from Dianthe's party, so all he could make out were the vaguest dark shapes of trees as they loomed nearby.

He took another step, and his foot and knee struck something—probably a rock he couldn't see. He stumbled to his knees.

"Tripping over things in the dark," he murmured, his voice lost to the roar of the storm, but he was thinking suddenly of Dylan Blaine's visit, just before Dianthe's attack. In everything that had happened since, he'd nearly forgotten it. *Just because you can't see something, or Someone, doesn't mean you can't stub your toe on it.* The empath had been talking about God. "Well, I doubt I just tripped over God," said Sean, reaching out to the rock to steady himself as he fought the wind to stand up. His hand closed around it and he felt, to his surprise, square edges and smooth sides.

Kneeling beside the stone, his heart started to pound as he pulled Rory's light crystal out from his collar. He cupped the little crescent-moon shape down beside the stone and whispered to it to shine. It's soft white glow filled his cupped hands like water and illuminated the stone, which was roughly hewn in the shape of an obelisk. An image of some kind had once been etched into it, but years and weather had worn it to little more than a few indents in the stone. Still, the obelisk had obviously been placed here purposefully. A standing stone.

Sean sat back on his heels and laughed.

32

AN UNEXPECTED ALLY

Rory felt like the afternoon dragged on forever. She had no idea what time it was, but she kept pushing along as quickly as she could. She stopped just long enough to pull out a ration bar from her pack so she could eat it as she walked, doing her best to ignore the voices of the hounds in the wind. After a while she mounted up again, casting a light out in front of them to see the path. She was reluctant to spend her energy on maintaining the moderately complex spell, but if she didn't get to Sean in time, it wouldn't matter whether she had any magical energy left or not.

The circle of standing stones had been built during the Curse War near the border between Maireadd and Barra by the elves who had delved into black magic. Knowledge of the forbidden rites they had performed there had since been outlawed, and mostly forgotten anyway, yet it remained a place of power and evil, and was one of the most dangerous locations on route for border patrolling scouts, because monsters and shadow creatures were still drawn there. Rory often wondered why it hadn't been torn down, though perhaps it wouldn't matter anyway. If the veil between their world and the shadow realm was thinner in Maireadd than in other places, then it must be hardly as sturdy as paper amid the standing stones.

The closer she came to that circle of stones, the more wary Rory became. Even miles away she could feel the shift in the air, perhaps even in the ambient magic around her. It felt danker, somehow, despite the freezing temperature. Like the murky, foul feeling of a wyrm den. Black shadows danced in the trees to either side of the trail, writhing away from her light. The shadows in the trees didn't bother her overmuch, but when more of them sprang up across and beside the trail itself, wriggling and bunching, she knew she was in trouble.

"Light!" she commanded, and the orb of light leading in front of them flared brighter, sending the shadows tumbling back as though they'd been struck. The horse shied, and then leapt forward, chasing the light, which stayed ahead and above them, as Rory had commanded it.

Looking back, Rory saw the shadows closing in behind them, and red lights of eyes springing up and following in their wake. The first hellhound sprang at her back. She jerked forward over the mare's neck, and the black claws raked open the back of her coat. The horse bunched up and shot forward, only to rear up when more hellhounds materialized in front of them, beyond the circle of Rory's light. Rory clung to its back, her heart up in her throat and threatening to choke her as one of the hounds dashed in, its jaws snapping toward her leg to pull her from the panicked horse.

"Light!" she screeched, thrusting her hand out toward the attacking hound. White light blazed to life around her hand at the inelegant command, and the monster scrambled back with a yelping snarl.

The hellhounds weren't interested in the horse. They might chase down a deer or even a wolf in the wild, if there was no more intelligent prey around, but they were far more interested in people, with their fear and rage and despair. But the horse didn't know that. It came down and sprang ahead again, kicking out at the hounds and nearly dumping Rory out of the saddle for a second time. She held on, struggling to draw her longknife.

Teeth closed around her boot, though they didn't punch through the hard leather. She got her knife free and stabbed at the hound's face while bringing up a light with her other hand, nearly blinding herself as well as the hounds who were closing in on the other side. There was no time to work any complex spells. Fire and light streaked from her hands at her brief commands, and her knife flashed as it plunged in and out whenever a hound came too close. She wouldn't be able to keep this up for long.

Suddenly a new voice broke through her panicked commands and the howling of the storm and the hellhounds. "Light!" it bellowed.

A new light blazed up in the trail, bright as a small sun, not a dozen yards off. The air pressure changed suddenly, making Rory's ears pop. Electricity arced around the new rider who'd appeared with the light. It snapped out at the hellhounds, who scattered away from it in panic.

Dizziness washed over Rory as adrenaline, relief, and exhaustion whirled through her. With a moment's reprieve, she used the energy from the storm and built her own lightning spell, snapping it out at the fleeing hounds like a whip. Within moments they had scattered back into the brush along the trail, leaving her and the newcomer alone in the storm. Rory leaned her arm across the saddle horn and panted, waiting for the other rider to approach. She looked up once he'd drawn closer, and another jolt went through her.

"Vasya?!"

"Are you hurt?" he asked, reining in beside her where they could shout over the storm.

She shook her head. "What are you doing here?"

Vasya's face looked grim and harsh in the white light of the orb he maintained above them. Rory let her own magical light fade away to give herself a rest.

"I heard Prince Gaelan's warning to the Council. When they sent him away, I asked him what he was going to do, and he said that you were his last hope."

Rory straightened in the saddle, watching him. "Why did you come, then? What do you care about any of this?"

"It doesn't matter. Let's go save your human."

"It does matter," she said, urging the horse on up the trail.

"What did Gaelan tell you?" Vasya asked instead.

"To save Sean and destroy the altar. Wretched thing should have been ripped down a hundred years ago. I don't know why we haven't done it," she grumbled.

"Because it repels regular magic?" he said, his tone condescending as he reiterated information they both knew.

"Well, that's what they make sledgehammers for."

Vasya might have grunted. He pursed his lips and shot her a sideways look. "How do you plan on destroying it now?"

"I'm not sure."

"But you at least have an idea?"

"I have an idea. It's not a very good one," she admitted.

Vasya swore suddenly. Apparently, he'd had the same idea. "That would be suicide. Or worse!"

"But if it's the only way to destroy the altar?"

"You think your little human boyfriend would want you after you taint yourself with black magic?"

"Would it matter, if we're both dead anyway?"

"You would stand before the Redeemer with that blot on your soul?"

Rory was silent for a long moment. "I pray He would forgive me. But I pray first that He would provide another way to carry out his command."

Without time, sledgehammers, and strong bodies to wield them, the only way she could see to destroy the altar was to activate Maireadd's own curse. And there were only two ways to do that. If either a human brought their own technology and used it in the forest, or if an elf were to wield forbidden black magic in the forest. Then Maireadd would do the rest.

Vasya was silent for a long time. Finally, "God provides a way for those who would try to follow His command."

"I am... prepared to pay the price," she said. "Either way."

33

THE ALTAR

Sean's neck crawled as he stepped around the standing stone and continued past it. The storm still raged around him, the trees roaring and the snow pellets biting into his face, but it seemed oddly muffled here. He became conscious of the breath in his lungs and his heart beating in his ears, which ached with the cold. The air felt thicker. He let his light go out, but kept glancing back and around in the dark for the telltale glow of red eyes.

The ground sloped down beyond the stone, and within a few fumbling strides he spotted the eerie glow of lights in the shallow bowl of land below. Despite the urgency that had driven him on all the way from the palace, now he slowed his steps and approached cautiously. The last thing he needed was to lose his footing in the snow and dead leaves and go rolling down into the midst of his enemies. As he drew closer he slowed even more, trying to understand what the source of the light was. It wasn't from a flame or a flashlight, nor a light crystal like the elves used. It wasn't colored, yet there was a putrid look to it in the way it seemed to bleach the world of color and vibrancy. More stone obelisks stood sentry down there in the basin, these ones taller than Sean by a foot, and thick as tree trunks at the base. They tapered to the width of his arm at their tops, and stood at intervals of maybe four or five yards, marking out a circle half the size of the palace ballroom. Maybe it was a trick of the storm, but it looked like the light was coming from the standing stones themselves. They made Sean's skin crawl.

There was little to no brush around the circle, and even the trees were sparse and stunted, providing no cover as Sean crept closer. At least he didn't have to worry about being quiet, with the wind blasting across the open space like a freight train. The fine, pelting snow obscured his view, and hopefully theirs, until he drew right up near one of the stones. He crouched down perhaps a couple of yards off to assess the situation again.

Half a dozen men stood guard around the circle of stones, but they faced inward, away from Sean, rather than outward. Convenient—Dianthe obviously didn't expect to be bothered—but ominous. He would rather risk being seen than whatever danger was implied coming from within the circle. The guards were armed with swords and crossbows. Effective, if you hit your target on the first try, but the bows were a single shot weapon, and reloading took precious seconds. Likewise, it would be awkward to toss the bow and bring the sword to position if one wasn't used to the motion.

Dianthe stood in the center of the circle, half bent over a huge square slab of stone with an orb of light suspended in the air over her shoulder, writing, or perhaps sketching patterns over the top of the altar. Nothing appeared to be happening yet. The dozen or so prisoners she'd brought with her for sacrifice huddled together off to the side, and so far there weren't any bodies. So he was in time. Barely.

With his twin rapiers secured to his belt and his camp knife in hand, he rose from his crouch and sprinted toward the nearest guard. Dianthe was the real threat here, and he kept half an eye on her as he moved up behind the guard. Sean's knife slid easily in and out of the man's neck, and he plucked the crossbow from his hands as he gurgled, taking careful aim at Dianthe's back. She made an easy target in white ski pants and a puffy pink coat. The eerie glow from the standing stone was more pronounced now that he was right next to it. It turned his hands and the snow around him a weird, yellowish-green color, and even seemed to leech the vibrant crimson out of the guard's blood.

Bad light. Bad wind. I hate crossbows so much. How did the guards expect to hit anything like this?

But then he realized as he steadied the bow that there was no wind against his hands and arms, which were within the circle of standing stones. The guards' coats and uniforms, and the prisoners' lighter clothes, were all unruffled.

The bow jerked in his hand right as his finger tightened on the trigger. His bolt flew wide, and he flinched as the other bolt, the one that had just struck his bow, bounced upward and slapped him across the face. He threw the crossbow away and dove back behind the stone without checking to see which of the other guards had spotted him and ruined his shot.

Outside the wards that protected the inner circle, the wind screamed and beat at him, and he could hear nothing over its fury, but risking a glance around the stone, he saw Dianthe gesturing his direction, presumably yelling at her men. No point in letting them regroup. He rose and drew his uncle's rapiers, then sprinted for the next standing stone and the guard there. Crossbow bolts whistled around him as he ran. One punched through his leather jacket sleeve before burying itself in the hill. The guard was reloading his crossbow as Sean ran toward him, and raised it as he drew near. Sean reacted without thought, flicking one of his blades up to bump the crossbow skywards just as it fired. The bolt passed over his shoulder, so close that it nicked his ear. With one blade momentarily tangled in the crossbow, he brought the other up and ran it through the guard's chest, twisting around at the same time to put the guard between himself and the four other crossbows aimed at him. One of the other men fired as Sean was moving, and the bolt struck the dying guard's back with such force that it pierced all the way through him and narrowly missed hitting Sean as well.

I hate crossbows. He shoved the guard away and dove for cover again.

Glancing around the stone, he saw the remaining four guards had converged. Two of them kept Sean covered with their bows, while the other two split off and jogged toward him, swords out. The wind still cut through his jacket like it wasn't there, and he could feel himself starting to shiver, which would make him clumsy if this fighting dragged on too long. He spared a glance at the queen, who was still gesturing and yelling at her guards. The two that were covering him with crossbows jogged toward the prisoners while still trying to watch him. Meanwhile, the other two men had caught up with Sean, who growled in frustration. He raised his rapiers and stepped out to meet them.

Of the two men he faced, only one of them had much experience with a long blade. The other was young, hardly more than an insolent kid whom Dianthe had chosen to fill her personal puppet guards. Perhaps she was short handed since she'd fired all the magicals working for her. At any rate, he posed little challenge. Within moments they'd both fallen. Sean turned his attention back to Dianthe.

She had commanded the remaining two guards to bring her first victim to the altar. The would-be sacrifice was a young elf man, bound and gagged and struggling as they dragged him over. Dianthe, meanwhile, was leaning over the altar, which had started glowing ominously. Sean couldn't tell exactly what she was doing, but she held her hand out over the center of the altar while the weird sickly glow increased. He jogged back toward the circle, but that unholy light above the altar seemed to reach out and twist something inside of him, turning his stomach and igniting the kind of gut-rolling dread he hadn't felt in years. His steps slowed the nearer he got.

The last two guards were still watching him, but they had their hands full with their unwilling sacrifice. Sean was more worried about Dianthe and the way the air seemed to be warping around the altar. His skin crawled as he reached the edge of the circle, and he realized he was panting, the wind snatching away the mist of his breath. He forced himself to step between the standing stones and into the circle. Instantly the wind ceased battering him, and the snow cleared. His aching ears rang in the stillness.

Dianthe turned from the altar and smiled at him. "So it is you, after all."

Sean needed to get in there and end this, but unnatural terror held him fast in its grip, and as Dianthe spoke, something moved on the altar.

Sean's eyes flicked to the prisoner and the two guards, but they'd stopped a couple yards off and were waiting. There came more dark movement, a rippling of the air over the altar, and red eyes appeared. A hellhound. The beast planted its paws on the altar and heaved itself up and out as though born from the rock itself. It jumped down and shook itself, and at once another head emerged from whatever portal Dianthe had created. She nodded to the beasts in greeting.

"My friends. A plaything for you," she said to them, and swept her arm toward Sean.

Sean forced himself to action past the unnatural fear, grabbing Rory's crystal crescent and yanking the cord over his head. He held it up with his left-hand rapier and shouted, "Light!"

Pure white brilliance burst across the clearing and everyone, including Dianthe and Sean himself, flinched. The hellhounds backpedaled, snarling their rage. Even the fear that had bound Sean where he stood seemed to rear back away from him like a physical force that had been checked. He leapt forward to meet the hounds, even as more of them pulled themselves out of the rift above the altar. Swords swinging, the light flashed across his vision, dazzling and nearly blinding, but it was far worse for the hounds, baffling and hurting them. They scrambled away from him and he dispatched several of them, working his way toward Dianthe.

The two remaining guards were wrestling the elf toward the altar. Sean was painfully aware that he needed to get there and stop the sacrifice, but that rift was still open, and the hounds, and other unidentifiable shadows, kept pouring through. No matter how many he killed, they just multiplied, blocking his way. They were getting bolder, too, even with his light. Snapping at his legs and lunging toward his back.

It was the guards themselves that bought Sean a few extra seconds when they finally dropped the struggling elf and fled from the shadows, leaving Dianthe to magic her sacrifice to the altar herself. Still, she was only moments away from murdering her first victim, and then all would be lost.

Sweat ran down Sean's face and glued his shirt to his back, despite the cold. Fear and frustration threatened to break through his cool mental space. He could feel the fear beating around him like a physical force again, barely held at bay by Rory's light. Dianthe chanted as the elf slid closer to that rift over the altar.

Sean did the only thing he could think of. He stabbed a hellhound and left the sword lodged in its flank. Then he threw his light crystal.

It landed on the altar with a bright little tinkle and slid right over the rift as if it wasn't there, then bumped into the elf. Pure white light washed over the elf, the altar, and Dianthe. The air stopped rippling, the stone altar stopped glowing, and the queen stopped chanting.

But the hellhounds didn't stop.

The instant Sean cast his light away, they were on him. Claws raked across his exposed left side, tearing through his jacket like paper and opening up four lines of fiery venomous pain across his ribs. He yelled and whipped his remaining blade around as the beast leapt for his throat, decapitating it in mid air. Another leapt toward his face and he punched it in the snout with his free hand. It fell back with a yelp, but then something struck him from behind. He stumbled and fell forward as more claws dug into his back. Dianthe hadn't been exaggerating about him being a plaything for the hounds. They loved to play with their prey, and that's what they were doing now, he realized, face-down in the snow. Otherwise the hellhound on his back would have gone for his neck instead of raking his back with its paw like it was doing. He rolled over with an effort, dislodging the beast, then stabbed it in the belly. It dissolved into a pile of smoking goo.

"Stop!" Dianthe's voice rang across the clearing.

The handful of remaining hounds paused, drooling and expectant, while Sean got to his feet. The agony of hellhound venom was already spreading from his wounds, setting him on fire from the inside, and he could feel blood dripping down his back and side.

"You are getting annoying," the queen said, pacing toward him, her eyes narrowed. "Who *are* you, Sean Leigh? And how are you so good at getting away from me? My soothsayer couldn't identify you, my strike team couldn't capture you, my guards couldn't kill you, and now you've sent an alarming number of my hounds back to their realm. You *are* human, aren't you?"

"As far as I know," he gasped, taking the opportunity to glance around. The elf, still bound and gagged on the altar, had wiggled around and grabbed Sean's light crystal and clutched it desperately in his hands. He couldn't work magic without speaking or gesturing, but the crystal seemed to respond to him anyway, for it shone more brilliantly than ever.

"Perhaps I should keep you alive after all. I could send you through to the spirits for my living sacrifice tonight. Perhaps they would appreciate your..." she twirled her hand in the air, searching for a word. "Tenacity." She nodded to herself, then spoke again, her voice deepening with magic. "Come here, Sean."

The magical compulsion washed over him and rolled away, deflected by Rory's shield, which warmed against his chest. He limped over—not to Dianthe, but to the near side of the altar, where she had spread out an assortment of ornate ceremonial knives.

Dianthe frowned. "I said come here, Sean." Again the magical compulsion passed over him.

"It's shocking how often that spell doesn't work for you, isn't it?" he murmured, eyeing the knives.

With an angry screech she flung her hands out toward him in a blast of magic that should have sent him tumbling, but instead merely hushed around him like a whisper of wind. Her arms dropped to her sides and they stood there for a moment in silence, staring at one another. She turned back to the altar.

Sean lunged, snatched one of the ceremonial daggers off the stone, and flung it at Dianthe. But his wounds pulled and he flinched when he threw, so it glanced off her arm instead of striking her in the neck where he was aiming. With her side to him, she didn't present many good targets. But it got her attention. She turned back, her face white.

"You took my ring."

"That I did." Sean said. He lunged toward her.

Dianthe flicked her wrist and one of the blades resting on the altar shot toward him. Reflexively he twisted mid-lunge and jerked his sword up to intercept it, but wasn't fast enough. It sank into his thigh just below his hip. He was shielded from magic, but not flying steel. He stumbled, but kept coming. Dianthe backpedaled and scurried around the side of the altar, putting the corner between them.

"Stop him!" she shrieked, scrambling along to the opposite side.

But the hounds were still stymied by the light of the crystal in the elf's hands on the altar at Sean's side. They nipped and sprang at him, but came up short, their red eyes squinting in the light.

Sean vaulted up onto the altar and grabbed a couple of the knives to throw at the queen. She deflected the first one with her magic, and the second. The third struck her shoulder, slicing through her puffy coat. She pulled it out with a squeal and hurled it back, directing it with magic. Sean flicked it out of the air with the rapier's tip.

Screaming in rage, Dianthe threw her hands up, and all of her ceremonial daggers, both on the altar and the ground, rose into the air. Sean dove off the altar a bare instant before they whistled over his head. He crouched for a second, his back against the stone, panting. This wasn't going well. The hellhound venom was taking effect, shooting fiery pain across his nerve endings, and the wound in his leg was bleeding more than he liked, even with the blade still lodged in it. Four or five hellhounds glowered at him, mere feet away, their red eyes furious and blinking in the light. Sweat prickled in his hair and ran down his face and his heart thudded against his ribs.

From the altar above him there came a scuffle, and Dianthe's enraged curses, and the light jerked and bounced, making the stark shadows around the circle jerk wildly. Sean stood up with a grimace to face her. She was leaning over, struggling with the elf prisoner, fighting over the light crystal. Her eyes widened when Sean reappeared. Backing away hastily, she thrust out her hands with another blast of magic. This time it struck the bound elf and sent him flying off the altar and right into Sean, who narrowly missed stabbing him as they tumbled to the ground together, rolling over in a pile of limbs and blades and flashing light. The dagger blade in Sean's leg shifted and drove deeper, drawing a grunt of pain as he finally came to rest half on top of the elf. The light had gone out, either broken or buried under the elf, who lay face down and unmoving in the snow.

Sean started to push himself up, but something clamped around his boot and jerked, and he landed on his face again.

"Bring him!" Dianthe called.

Something else clamped around his sword arm. It wasn't teeth, rather something soft and cold and ticklish, but under the velvety, many-fingered exterior, it was hard as steel. It squeezed tighter and tighter, making the bones in his arm creak, until he gasped and let go of the sword.

It felt like something inside him shattered when the blade left his hand.

His hopes, his duties, his faith, his very identity seemed to crack and fracture as darkness closed over the clearing and the shadow creatures dragged him back toward the altar.

Snow, leaves, and rocks scraped under him. The knife in the side of his leg caught on something and wrenched free, drawing an involuntary cry. Even the poisoned wounds in his back and side intensified their agony. The calculated detachment with which he always fought finally ripped away and left his soul open and raw, and utterly alone.

Except for echoes of Dylan's words, not long ago. *You're not alone.*

The pressure on his foot and arm released and the ground fell away suddenly beneath Sean as he levitated into the air. He struggled and squirmed, but whatever held him now didn't care how much he thrashed. It tumbled him over onto his back and slammed him down on the cold stone altar, rattling his teeth and sending a shock through his wounds. The shadows slithered around him, whispering, chittering quietly among themselves. These weren't hounds, or even whatever slithery thing had grabbed him before. They must be Dianthe's spirits from the shadow world that she planned on sacrificing to tonight—ones that hadn't taken on a physical form. Yet somehow they held him with a slow, pulsing pressure that kept him paralyzed on the altar.

Dianthe stood over him, holding her bleeding shoulder. "Finally," she panted, then laughed. "What's the matter, Leigh? Are you afraid? You were just so eager to take the place of the elf here, how could I say no? My first sacrifice tonight was going to be a living one, and for that, you don't need to have magic." She removed her hand from her own wound and held it over the altar next to Sean, letting a few drops of her blood splash down onto the stone. The air, or perhaps the stone itself, began to ripple there. The forces that held Sean in place let him at least move his head so he could watch as a sickly glowing wrinkle appeared, swelling like a boil and elongating until it split open into a long tear in reality. Shadows moved against the glowing lips of the tear, pulling it apart, widening it, spilling out into the world and crowding around him.

Sean's heart hammered, his wounds burned like fire, and the icy calm he'd held during battle had shattered, leaving him bleeding and raw, open to the whispers and chitters of the shadows around him.

Failure. At least he wouldn't be around to face the fallout. He'd be... what? Eternally fed upon by shadows and monsters? Ripped apart and lost forever in a realm no human was meant to wander? Would his spirit cease to exist? Would he be damned?

He closed his eyes. *God the Redeemer. Mercy.*

"Stop. Praying!" Dianthe struck him across the face. She began to chant in some language Sean had never heard before, and he started moving again, dragged an inch at a time toward the rift. His right foot fell through, then his left.

White light like lightning flashed from across the circle, and someone shouted.

Sean's gaze jerked toward the interruption. Two riders had crested the hill. Haloed in light, with electricity crackling around them and elven longknives in their hands, they swept down toward the standing stones.

Rory?

Sean's heart leapt in sudden hope. But then his body lurched and slid across the stone altar. His legs went through the rift, and he felt the change in air brush his hands. Then the world fell away, the last flickers of lightning flashing in the sky overhead before being suddenly cut off. Gone.

Only it was Sean that was gone.

34

LIVING SACRIFICE

Sean instinctively held his breath as he tumbled through the rift, as though he was falling into a lake instead of into another world. He couldn't see, or there was nothing to see here, surrounded by utter black emptiness. But he wasn't alone. He could hear the whispers and chitters of the demon creatures holding him, feel their cold grip on his wrists and ankles, their trailing fingers brushing his face and clothing.

I'm in hell, he thought, betrayal and horror freezing the breath in his lungs. His heart clamored, begging to stop and end his life. Was he still alive?

One of the creatures laughed. Hot breath rushed across his hand as two sharp points of pressure came to rest against his skin. Teeth? Fangs? Claws? Another chuckle, so deep it was more an uncomfortable vibration in his chest rather than a sound. The teeth tore into his hand and wrist. He yelled, but at the same instant, blinding light flashed around him. The creature that had bitten him released his hand with a scream that sounded like it had been forcibly flung backward. In fact all the monsters groping and holding him fell away. Dazzled, he had a confused glimpse of the evil beings tumbling away. Sean's own blood, dripping down his hand, flashed white. It was the only thing he could actually see.

Then his boots struck stone and he gasped as color and sound and *being* exploded around him. He crumpled onto the cold stone and ended up laying mostly on his back, like he'd been back in his own world, so the first thing he got a clear look at was the sky. If it was a sky. Stars and moons and planets blazed overhead, nothing like he was used to seeing at night. These were clear and close, startlingly detailed. Galaxies swept across his vision like great, sparkling clouds, haloed in blue and gold and glorious purple. Comets streaked past, following their own misty white trails.

For an instant he lay there staring, shuddering in terror and pain and awe, even as a jumble of shouts and screeches intruded on his awareness. Movement flashed in his peripheral vision.

Still disoriented, he rolled onto his side and nearly fell off the rock on which he lay. With his face inches from the surface, he dazedly recognized the chiseled edge and evil carvings in the stone surface. It wasn't a rock. It was the altar. The very same altar he'd just been sacrificed on.

With a panicked shout he jerked his face back from the stone and rolled off the side, half falling, half scrambling away from it. Now that he was upright and looking around, the clamor around him came together with the flashes of movement and he realized, still frantic with confusion and pain, that he'd landed in the middle of a battle. Chaos raged around him, the altar, and the standing stones, which he recognized fleetingly as his eyes jumped around, trying to process what he was seeing.

His gaze rested on the unicorns, first, latching onto them as something familiar and identifiable, and because they stood out, flashing white amid the seething mass of movement. There must be hundreds of creatures gathered around him. Some of them his gaze didn't like to settle on, like it was somehow hard to focus on creatures that appeared... not right. He forced himself to be still and understand. Then, with a jolt, he realized what he was seeing. These were hellhounds and shadow rats and other creatures he couldn't name, pitted against the unicorns. But they were different here. In his own world they were rightly called shadow creatures, because they manifested out of shadows, and the darkness clung to them. They were far more terrifying on this side of the rift. Here, the red glow that lit their eyes shone through their bodies and their joints, fractured like badly-cut prisms. Their jaws opened wider. Their teeth and claws were like splintering glass, breaking off with every bite or slash and then instantly growing back. Worst of all, they almost seemed more human here. Something in the shape of their eyes and faces, though still canine, also bore the cruel expressions that only humans could wear. Like Dianthe.

Something warm and solid bumped into Sean from behind. He whirled, his heart crashing with fresh panic, but stumbled to his knees as his weakened leg refused the motion. Dizziness washed over him. His pant leg was saturated in blood. He'd nearly forgotten about the dagger wound, with the far greater pain of the hellhound venom. But the pain wouldn't kill him. Blood loss might. A whiskery, velvet muzzle bumped against his face.

Be calm, child. I won't hurt you. The words were clear, though not audible.

He raised his head to look into the face of the unicorn. Its pink muzzle was only inches from his face, and its beautiful, spiraled horn glittering like an opal was bent over him.

"What's happening here? Where am I? Where *was* I?"

The unicorn bent its head further and rested its horn across the top of his head. Warmth and peace radiated from it, trickling into him. He hadn't realized until that moment how cold he was, or how weak he was growing. He pressed a trembling hand over the wound in his leg.

You are in what your kind refers to the Shadow Realm. The place beyond your own. You had to pass through the Between to get here, and that is where the Corrupted ones attacked you. I am sorry for that, little one. Their poison is still in you.

"Yes," said Sean, looking down at his hand, which had been bitten moments ago. It hurt less than the slashes to his ribs and back, but as he looked at it, he realized he could see the glassy shards of broken teeth still in the wound. Was that what hellhound venom truly looked like? Did he have fragments lodged in all his injuries? His stomach churned and he forced himself to look away. To focus on the gleaming golden eyes of the unicorn watching him. Around them, the battle raged on, drawing nearer every moment. "What's happening here? I need to get back."

You will. Until then, I was sent to protect you. The battle you see is because of you and your friends. We fight for you, and for the fate of Barra.

"Why?" still bewildered, he looked around again, feeling like he should help, somehow. But with the unicorn's horn still radiating warmth and calm through him, all he could do was sag further to the ground, shifting to ease his leg.

Because our God and yours commands it. Your prayers are heard. Even now, your friends hold vigil for you. They ask that you be allowed to accomplish your mission, that Barra and your life will be spared.

Sean opened his mouth to ask another question, but found he couldn't speak. He bowed his head and shuddered, his eyes suddenly burning. Presently, when he could get his throat to work, he said, "I don't know if I can go on."

You must, said the unicorn, moving to stand over Sean, its forelegs planted on either side of him.

The fight had reached them, sweeping down the hill and closing them in. Sean gripped his leg and ducked as the unicorn swung its head to skewer a charging hellhound. Working with one blood-slicked hand, he unfastened his belt and pulled it loose, then hastily shrugged out of his jacket and the shirt Beck had loaned him. While his unicorn protector fended off another attack, he wadded the torn shirt and pressed it over the stab wound, then used the belt to cinch it in place—not too tightly lest he lose use of his leg altogether. Shivering, he pulled his jacket back on, biting his cheek against the fiery pain of the claw marks in his side and back. There was nothing he could do about them, except to endure.

I will burn the poison from your wounds, said the unicorn, as if in answer to his thoughts. *But we must wait for the help that's coming. Otherwise, you would not be able to finish your task.*

"That sounds ominous." Sean rested his head against one of the unicorn's white forelegs. Why he trusted this beast so implicitly was a question that tickled the back of his mind, but he was in too much pain, and too weary, to bother with it. Injured and without weapons, he didn't really have a choice at the moment. What would he find waiting for him back across the rift? And how was he even getting back?

He noticed that the thick of the fight had moved back from them again, and realized that another unicorn had joined them, standing nose-to-tail with the first. While his unicorn menaced and slashed at anything that came near, the other unicorn's tail whipped through the air, crackling with lightning that sparked from the ends.

"Dianthe sent me through as a living sacrifice, for the..." he watched one of the hellhounds leap onto a unicorn's back and tear at its flesh, leaving jagged wounds filled with slivers of its broken claws. The unicorn tossed its head around, trying to reach it with teeth and horn, but the hound just kept ripping at it, till another unicorn dashed past, slowing just long enough to skewer the hound. "They were supposed to devour me, I think," Sean finished. "Why didn't they?"

You are already a living sacrifice, little one. You belong to Another. Did you think, all these years, that you were just casting your faith and your prayers into the void—that God would not accept you? He hears your prayers for mercy, and he sees your sleepless nights as you watch over your friends. He knows that you've been broken and weary and alone. You've already made yourself a living sacrifice.

Once again, Sean's throat ached, but he forced words out. "Will you answer another question?"

You may ask, said the unicorn.

"My friend—he was a training partner—was dragged through a rift by hellhounds years ago. Do you know what happened to him?"

That is easy, came the reply. *The hounds of hell cannot keep their prey when the person belongs to God the Redeemer. If the person rejected the Redeemer, then he would have had no protection. He would have been torn apart here and then the hounds would have dragged his spirit to the next world.*

"He never came back..." Sean ventured. "Would he have come back if—if he was safe?"

Perhaps, perhaps not. That would be between him and God.

"What about me, then? How will I get back, since you say I must?" Sean leaned wearily against the unicorn, fighting the desire to curl up in the dirt and pass out as the hellhound venom seemed to burn hotter every moment. He watched the ebb and swell of the battle around them, but here in the eye of the storm it was quiet.

Instead of answering his question, the unicorn said, *Listen to me, little one.*

Sean looked up into the beast's golden eye. It had lowered and turned its head so it could see him. "Yes?"

To prevent the curse from falling, you must destroy the altar when you get back. It already has your and the witch's blood on it, thus setting her ritual in motion.

With a start, he remembered Dylan's warning. He raised his head to peer through a gap in the battle. The altar where he'd landed when he came through did have blood on it. It trickled down the side, shimmering faintly. How was he going to destroy it, without any tools? Even if he had a sledgehammer, the thought of beating away at it in his current state was sickening. He could barely hold himself upright.

"How do I do that?"

The unicorn merely looked at him. *Your help is here.*

At almost the same instant, the atmosphere in front of them seemed to solidify and darken into a solid wall of shadow. Then the shadow split with a flash and a crack like thunder, and two figures dropped out of it—none other than Beck and Dylan.

Beck was in his panther form, coal-black and deadly, and Dylan clung to the scruff of his neck, his eyes squeezed shut and his face looking slightly green. At once, Beck shook off Dylan's grip and his form blurred, then became human. He grabbed the disoriented empath and shoved him toward Sean. The two of them crouched on either side of him, within the circle of protection provided by his two guardian unicorns.

"What are you two doing here?" Sean nearly laughed with relief.

"Having your back," said Dylan, offering a wobbly smile. He still looked like he might throw up.

"Where are we at?" Beck asked, all business.

Sean gestured to his leg. Even that simple motion made black spots flash across his vision. "The queen isn't dead, the altar isn't destroyed, and here we are. Rory and another elf showed up right before I got dragged through. Don't know what's happening with them."

"You reek of hellhound venom."

"Can't imagine why." He leaned back against the unicorn again and closed his eyes.

Dylan asked, "What's the plan for destroying the altar?"

"I have no idea. Suggestions?"

Silence. Sean didn't open his eyes. Had they lost anyway? After everything? Even with the help of Beck and Dylan and Rory?

Do not give in to the hellhounds' despair yet. Remember their poison is in your mind. We must burn it out before you go back. Once it is gone, you'll be able to continue, if only for a short time.

"I hope you're right," said Sean.

"Who's right?" Beck asked, giving him a suspicious squint.

Dylan answered before Sean, who hadn't realized that his friends hadn't heard the other half of that conversation. "I think he's talking to the unicorn." Dylan looked up at the unicorn and addressed it. "Will you tell me what to do?" He paused as though listening, his face losing a few shades of its color that had just begun to return.

While this conversation was going on, the rush of battle between the unicorns and hellhounds drew near them again. Beck took his panther shape and bounded into the action, helping to drive back anything that came near.

"He doesn't feel anything, even when he's fighting," Dylan remarked. "That should probably scare the socks off me, but it's kind of refreshing." The empath changed position, moving to sit cross-legged, facing Sean. He rested his elbow on his knee and opened his hand, like he was preparing to arm-wrestle. "Let's get this over with."

Sean looked from him to the unicorn, who explained, *He will help ease your pain.*

Already burning with venom and weak from that and blood loss, Sean nodded wearily and clasped the empath's hand. Instantly, the pain and weakness drained away and his head cleared. He drew a deep breath for the first time since he'd fallen through the rift, and with the moment of clarity, noticed a few things that he hadn't earlier.

For one thing, he realized that this world seemed very similar, if not identical to his own. The colors were different, the light was all wrong, with that spectacular, impossible sky, and there was no storm here. Yet the shape of the land was the same. They sat within the bowl of land around the altar, between it and the ring of standing stones, which also appeared to exist in both worlds. Back in his own world, the stones had glowed with an eerie light. Here, they almost looked like they were alive, their surfaces writhing as though they were covered in maggots. Wisps of cloudy magic stretched between them and the altar like the spokes of a ghostly wheel.

Another thing he noticed was that some of the battle he'd assumed was happening here, in this world, was actually insubstantial. Shapes and shadows of things that were not physically present, as though ghosts fought alongside the unicorns and hellhounds. Some of them were shadowed, like the hounds themselves, others were luminous white. There were flickers of lightning and ripples in the air, as though whatever fought did so while brushing against the veil that separated them from this world.

Sean wanted to ask what he was seeing. Was there another realm, still? One that was neither his own world nor this shadow realm? But Dylan's face had gone gray and he nodded to the unicorn who stood over them. The beast lowered its horn and touched the tip of it to Sean's forehead.

White fire erupted across Sean's skin, blazing without burning him, except where it touched the wounds from the hellhounds, which ignited in searing agony. Sean clenched his teeth around a yell, while Dylan groaned and slumped forward a bit farther. The fire spread inward, scorching its way through Sean's veins, burning and cleansing away the hellhound venom as it went. It hit the stab wound in his leg, eliciting another jolt of pain, though with Dylan taking much of it into himself, and compared to the fire and venom, it felt mild.

With that last flare of pain, the fire extinguished, leaving Sean sweating and weak. Dylan released his grip, his own hand trembling and slick with sweat. Sean felt like he had a high fever, though his head was clearer. His wounds still burned, but not like before. Now, his leg hurt the worst. He touched it with a wince.

It's been cauterized, said the unicorn.

"I feel like *I've* been cauterized," Sean complained. He met Dylan's gaze for a moment and gave him a nod of both thanks and respect.

The empath flashed a pained grin. "Let's not do that again right away."

It's time to go back, little one. They need your help. But remember, you must destroy the altar.

"I still have no idea how to do that!"

But the unicorn had already turned its gaze toward Beck, who extricated himself from the battle and bounded over to them, resuming his man-shape.

During that brief moment though, an idea burned itself into Sean's mind, now that it was clear of poison. His thoughts flashed over reports about Maireadd's curse, what could trigger it, how it would react. The localized raw destruction that took place each time it activated. He knew how to destroy the altar.

When Beck came up beside them Sean said, "Please tell me you have a gun."

The assassin's eyebrows shot up. "I always have a gun. What do you want with it?"

"To destroy the altar."

Beck's face was a blank question mark for a moment. Then understanding dawned. He swore. "That's suicide."

"Not if you keep the rift open, right? Will the curse happen here, too?"

Beck looked doubtful. "Perhaps... but not in the same way." He twitched one shoulder in a shrug and pulled out a sleek little pistol that had been tucked into the small of his back, handing it to Sean. "Go knock yourself out."

Sean checked the clip and chambered a round. "Perfect."

35

MAIREADD'S CURSE

Hellhounds had dogged Rory and Vasya's trail as they pushed on toward the cursed standing stones. Despite the lights they kept aloft in front and behind them, the hounds grew bolder the closer they came to the evil place, and attacked again and again. Dread created a sick, cold feeling in Rory's stomach as she thought about Sean, alone in the midst of this pit of swarming evil. Her imagination kept furnishing her with images of his blood smeared across the altar, with Dianthe's knife through his heart. But when they finally broke out into the open, what she saw was almost worse.

A dark haze hung in the bowl of land before them, lit eerily by the glow coming from the standing stones and the altar itself. No wonder it had resisted all their magic for all these years. But Rory had never actually seen it lit up like this before. Bodies littered the ground around the circle, little more than dark blots against the snow. And there were dark shapes moving down there. Hellhounds, shadow rats, a wendigo, and some slithering, worm-like things that even she couldn't name. A small band of prisoners huddled off to one side.

But the thing that momentarily stopped her heart was when she spotted Sean upon the altar, with Dianthe leaning over him, and an open rift in space at his feet. He wasn't struggling. Red blood smeared across the stone slab, just like she'd imagined, but as she watched, Dianthe reached out and slapped him across the face. Then his body lurched and started sliding toward the rift.

Rory screamed. Magic leapt to her fingertips, and she lashed out with it at the nearest hellhounds, who were rushing up the hill toward them. She and Vasya kicked their horses into motion, rushing down the hill. But they were too late. Sean slipped through the rift and was gone. In his place, more dark shapes poured into the clearing from the shadow realm. Was there no end to them?

The otherworldly creatures gathered around Dianthe, who threw back her head and laughed. Rory and Vasya had just reached the circle of standing stones, but already Rory could feel the rising pressure of magical energy building up around them.

"Get the prisoners, and get them out of here," Rory shouted.

Vasya nodded, lashing out with another stroke of lightning that splintered and branched out, reaching another wave of hounds and leaping from one to the next until half a dozen of them had fallen.

Rory urged her horse on toward the altar, numb to the danger and her exhaustion. She felt like she'd been physically stabbed through the heart. Though somehow, in the back of her mind, beneath the storm of action and magic there was a detached, logical point that wondered how Gaelan could have seen Sean kill Dianthe if he'd been dragged through a rift into the shadow realm.

The hellhounds surged around her plunging horse in wave after wave, while Vasya sent out his lightning in flashing blue fingers. More and more of them fell, creating a haze of ashy smoke as their bodies vanished. Meanwhile, the mare's hooves crunched over shadow rats and other crawling things. Rory reeled her magic back in, taking an instant to let go of the lightning she'd been flinging alongside Vasya, and switch to ice, which she gathered into a long, splintered blade.

Vasya split away, racing toward the prisoners, and instantly the hounds surrounded her in a leaping, snarling mass. Her sword flashed among them, its glittering edges splintering off and instantly renewing with every strike. But no matter how many of them she killed, more seemed to take their place. While she was busy with the sword, she dropped the reins from her other hand and used it to form a dozen small ice daggers which floated above her palm. Then with a scream of frustrated rage, she sent them flying out among the hounds. Next, she summoned the wind, mixing fire and ice together into it until it created a swirling vortex around her, sweeping away anything that came near. Her terrified horse quivered and pranced a circle in the calm middle of the tornado. Rory urged the animal forward once again, inching along with the wind a shield around them. Exhaustion clawed at her chest and limbs, but at last—at last!—she drew near Dianthe and the accursed altar.

It felt like ages since they'd arrived—since Sean had been dragged through the rift. Rory felt bleak despair creeping in past the raw pain of loss that lingered behind her intense focus. They weren't going to make it. It was too late. She would falter eventually—probably soon—and then she would be overrun. At least Vasya had made it to the huddle of prisoners, who were scattering away, so hopefully Dianthe would be deprived of more sacrifices. But the curse would still fall on Barra, if it hadn't already.

Rory's tornado was blasting against the altar itself now, unfortunately without doing it any harm. As Vasya had said, none of the elves' attempts to destroy it with their magic had ever succeeded. She let the wind spell go. At once the air cleared of flying snow and debris and Dianthe appeared, not two yards away. The instant they caught sight of one another, the queen flung her hand out in a blast of magic that caught Rory wholly unprepared and tumbled her off the back of the horse. The spooked animal bolted away, leaving Rory to clamber to her feet and face the witch-queen, while hellhounds closed in at her back.

Rory's ice sword slowly reformed in her right hand, and electricity sparked in her left. Dianthe smirked at her. Rory willed the electrical charge in her hand to grow, spreading along a path of static that she guided with whispered words of command until it formed a trailing, sparking whip in her hand, flashing with pure electric and magic. Dianthe flung another wave of her black magic, and this time Rory was ready for her. She flung her whip up and out, its sizzling tip cutting through the wave of magic, then she whirled, her ice blade extended to meet the hounds that leapt toward her back. The blade splintered in the first hellhound and she commanded it to reform as she dodged the second one. Her sparking whip took out a third, and then she had to deflect half a dozen ceremonial daggers that Dianthe sent flying toward her.

Everything was a blur of motion. Rory had never been so physically and magically exhausted, yet she burned with righteous rage, determined to fight her losing battle to the last breath. And then her whip sputtered and went out. The sword splintered in another hound, but wouldn't reform. She screamed the elven words of command, but her magic was sluggish and flowed to her hands like cold honey. Dianthe laughed and flung another knife, which Rory had to duck, and in her exhaustion, she stumbled to one knee. Grabbing one of Dianthe's scattered daggers, she pushed to her feet and faced the queen again.

"Give up, little elf. My business here doesn't concern you," said the queen.

"You're in my country, and you just sacrificed my friend," Rory panted. Cold, listless magic pooled into her hands, and she thought of the words that would shape it into a curse. A forbidden spell that would stop Dianthe's heart with nothing more than a touch. Her own heart thudded dully in her ears.

"It seems like my chef really got around." Dianthe started to say something else, but at that moment the air above the altar split open in a black gash.

Rory's breath stuck in her throat. What now? More shadow beasts?

Instead, Sean himself tumbled through the rift and landed on the altar with a grunt.

Rory and Dianthe both stared at him blankly. For an instant Rory wondered if he was actually Sean, and not instead some abomination of a reanimated corpse that the queen had contrived to create. He looked like one. Tattered and smeared with blood, his face ghastly in the glow of the altar, he looked nearly as horrifying as the monsters she'd been fighting.

He looked around, focused first on Dianthe, then on Rory, and grinned. For once his dimpled smile didn't light up his face. Instead, it made him look haggard and somehow even more gruesome. "It looks like you're without your sacrifices, Dianthe," he said.

Glancing around quickly, Rory saw that Vasya had gathered the prisoners and disappeared from the clearing.

"But I have a fine elf here that will do nicely," said the queen. "And I can always sacrifice you a second time. Perhaps not as a living sacrifice this time." She stared at him. "How are you here?"

He shrugged, then winced. "Turns out you can't be a living sacrifice to more than one God." With that he pulled a gun out of his jacket pocket. "Goodbye, your majesty. I doubt you will find as gracious guardians for your journey to the shadows as I did."

The shot rang out into the night.

Rory's heart crashed against her ribs, but all around them, everything else seemed to just *stop*. The storm snuffed out. The hellhounds went still. Dianthe looked down at the crimson stain spreading across her puffy coat, her face all confusion and disbelief. Even the hellhounds and shadow rats stood still, watching. The feeling of magic pressing all around them grew nearly unbearable, like the pressure before a lightning strike.

And then something snapped. The air crackled. Thunder cracked overhead. The trees nearby shuddered.

"Rory!" Sean called, crouched upon the altar.

But Rory stood frozen, watching Dianthe. A look of dawning horror had come into the witch's eyes, which darted frantically, watching something that Rory couldn't see. Her own hellhounds padded toward her, brushing past Rory as though she wasn't there. At the side of the altar, below where Sean crouched with his hand outstretched, the air bubbled and warped and then split into a black crack, opening into some formless abyss. The atmosphere wavered in front of it, like heat rolling off a fire. Dianthe lurched toward the new rift suddenly, clutching her chest.

"No, no, no," she murmured, panting. "This isn't the power you promised me." Blood flowed over her hands. The hellhounds closed in around her, grinning wide, crowding her toward the lower rift below the altar.

"Rory!" Sean shouted.

She jerked, as though waking from a horrified trance, and ran toward him. The last she saw of Dianthe, the witch-queen had fallen to her knees, and one of her hellhounds was dragging her into the rift.

Maireadd roared. Branches snapped together, trees groaned in great, creaking, crashing voices. The forest was on the move, drawing in around them, nearer and nearer, like the hellhounds around Dianthe. The ground itself heaved under Rory's feet as she ran to the other side of the altar—away from Dianthe and that lower rift. Sean grabbed her hand and hauled her up, where she felt the altar shaking. The stone snapped under them, and a spiderweb of thin cracks spread down its center. One of the standing stones crashed down in the midst of a writhing nest of roots that boiled across the earth toward them. Another stone obelisk toppled. It snapped in two, its eerily glow visible among the tree roots for an instant before it disappeared, dragged down into the earth. Shadow rats squealed, trying to scurry away from the groping roots, while the remaining hellhounds slipped quietly into the rift after Dianthe.

Within seconds the forest was upon them.

Sean wrapped his arms around Rory—he smelled of blood and ozone—and leapt for the open rift. The last thing Rory saw were tree roots shooting up around the stone where they'd just stood, wooden fingers groping over the surface of the altar.

Panic gripped her as darkness closed around them, and she went rigid in Sean's arms. Whispers, chitters of voices without words surrounded them. Sean's breath caught, and she whimpered into his shoulder. Then they were out of the dark and tumbling into someone, who grunted and cursed as they bowled him over. Some kind of tumult was raging around them here, wherever they were. She didn't have time to see much, let alone comprehend what was happening, when someone grabbed her and picked her up off the ground.

"Let's go!" called a second man who was hefting Sean to his feet. "Time to run."

"What—?" Rory got fleeting glimpses of unicorns and other creatures like hellhounds battling around them. A couple feet away stood an altar identical to the one they'd just left behind. Cracks ran through it, with chinks opening up, gaping wider.

Whoever had picked her up gave her a swift but gentle shove, pulling her away. Sean was at her other side and scrambled along with her, up the hill away from the altar.

"Gah! Never again!" Exclaimed the man who'd pulled her up as they ran.

Rory glanced over and stuttered in surprise. "D-Dylan?"

The empath had one hand to his head as they ran, but he flashed her a grin. "Sorry. This place is trippy."

"Shut up and run!" said the other man. He looked familiar, but Rory couldn't place him.

"What—are we running from?" she panted.

In answer, the altar behind them gave a great crack like thunder, and then exploded. Chunks of rock flew around them, some of the smaller ones striking them as they ran. With the explosion came a blast of foul magic like a bomb. It swept outward, howling, blotting out the light. Rory was flung off her feet and hurled to ground, tumbling and somersaulting along like a leaf in a gale.

When she finally rolled to a stop she simply lay there for a moment, her ears ringing, shocked and disoriented. Quiet settled around her. Everything had gone still. The clamor of battle was gone. Had her eardrums blown out?

But then she heard the soft thuds of footsteps over the ground. Something nudged her, and cool, calming magic flashed through her system for a moment, clearing her head. She peeled her eyes open and picked her face up out of soft grass to look around. Grass? Wherever they were, it obviously didn't follow Maireadd's seasons. She rolled over and looked up into the golden eyes of a unicorn.

"Oh," she said simply.

It's finished, said the unicorn telepathically. *Well done.*

Slowly she sat up and looked around. The third man, whom she still couldn't place, was also sitting up, and they'd been joined by another unicorn, who nudged Dylan with its horn. The empath startled and shot upright, then swayed, looking around with a wince. Sean hadn't stirred yet. He lay face-down in the grass, quiet as a corpse. Still shaky, Rory crawled over to him.

"Sean?"

He didn't respond. She leaned down and rotated an ear to listen to his breathing, which was coming fast and shallow. Now that she had time to see his blood-soaked pants and shredded, stained jacket, her heart stuttered with fresh panic.

He lost much blood earlier, before we got it stopped, said the unicorn. *And endured much pain. He needs rest and warmth, and to return to your own world. This place is not good for most mortals to be in for long.*

"Tell me about it," muttered Dylan, who'd scooted over to them. He put his hand over Sean's, and grew paler than he had been. But Sean's breathing deepened, and he stirred, his eyelids fluttering.

Rory sat beside him and touched his face. He felt clammy and feverish.

"I can take you to the nearest warded shelter," said the third man, picking himself up off the ground.

Rory looked up at him and still couldn't identify his bland features, though she knew she'd seen him before. "I'm not sure we should move him."

"'M fine," mumbled Sean into the ground. "Just give me a minute."

Rory looked at Dylan, who, with his hand still touching Sean's, shook his head and looked dubious.

The unicorn leaned down, gently resting the tip of its horn against Sean's temple. Sean didn't even stir.

Humans never cease to amaze us, the beast said. *They have such capacity for evil, and yet also such capacity for loving service, to empty themselves completely for the sake of their friends. Or even their enemies.* Here, it glanced at Dylan as well. *It's no wonder the Redeemer chose this form to perform His own sacrifice.*

"Will he be okay?" Rory asked.

Yes, little one. He is tired and broken and empty, but he will live. If Beck will open the portal for us again, I will carry you both to your shelter, to make the crossing easier.

Rory pushed to her feet. "Thank you," she said to the unicorn, then looked around at Dylan, and the bland-faced Beck. "All of you." She looked down at Sean as well, and thought of the terrible spell she'd been about to utter when he dropped through the portal with his gun and set off the curse himself. *And thank you, God, for providing another way,* she thought silently.

The two men helped Sean to his feet, and from there onto the unicorn. Once he was up, he seemed to steady a bit, though he drooped with weariness and clung to the unicorn's mane. Rory scrambled up behind him, and Beck slashed open a rift in the air.

"Will you both come with us?" she asked.

Beck shook his head. "My girlfriend is waiting for me."

"Wife," said Dylan, grinning. "She's got some surprise she's been trying to keep secret for the past two weeks, waiting for Midwinter. If I have to go on any longer pretending to be oblivious, my acting skills just won't hold up."

Rory laughed, suddenly light with relief and joy. It was Midwinter's eve, after all. Or more likely Midwinter's day, by now. Time to celebrate the light. "A merry Midwinter to you, then," she called.

Dylan grinned, and even Beck raised a hand in farewell, and then the unicorn plunged through the rift. Darkness closed around them again, but this time there were no whispers.

36

YOUR HUMAN

Afterward, Sean vaguely remembered the darkness of the Between, and how the unicorn's horn shed soft light over them. And he remembered Rory's exclamation of surprise when they stepped out into a stone courtyard surrounded by crumbling ruins.

"This wasn't the nearest warded campsite."

No, said the unicorn. *But it is the nearest that isn't overrun with shadow creatures. You will not have to feel their eyes on you tonight from outside your wards, or their rage. Your human needs to be away from their influence until he can rest.*

Rory thanked the unicorn, and steadied Sean as he slid down from its back. The beast slipped away once they were clear of it. Sean rested against an age-pocked stone bench in what used to be a great, circular room, or maybe a courtyard, while Rory activated the sheltering wards and threw some of the gathered wood into the fire ring in the center of the yard. Once the fire was lit, the space around them began to warm at once. It was only then that Sean realized he was shivering.

Rory found the elves' cache of supplies and dragged them over to the fire, where she collapsed beside him. She looked exhausted, but she dug through the supplies for food and blankets, and the medical kit.

"Are you hurt?" he asked, his words slurred with pain and weariness. His leg still burned from the unicorn's cauterizing fire, and the hellhound's gashes across his side and back, though they'd been cleared of venom, throbbed angrily.

"No, you are. Get that jacket off for me."

Sean obediently shrugged out of his ruined jacket, allowing warm air to brush across his skin. Rory sucked in a sharp breath.

"Is it that bad?" he mumbled.

But she only remarked, "I always wondered where that tattoo was that you mentioned."

"That was a long time ago. You must have been really curious if you remembered." He winced as she dabbed blood from the wounds across his back.

"How could I forget that conversation? You gave me your freaking signet ring. Me. An elf."

Sean was silent for a few minutes as she worked. The cool, spicy scent of nymph healing salve wafted over his shoulder when she opened the jar that had been among the medical supplies. It was a calming smell, and soothed away most of the pain almost instantly. "You weren't like any elf or human woman I'd ever met before. You were—are—special."

Her hands stilled for an instant. Then she moved to work on his side. "You should lie down. You're barely upright anyway, and it would make this easier."

He pulled one of the blankets over and eased down onto it, resting his head on his rolled-up jacket. Rory's hands were cool and feather-soft, and his eyelids drooped, until something hot and wet splashed onto his arm. He peeled his eyes back open to see her working over him, her huge, mercury eyes overflowing with tears.

"I never realized how lonely this job would be," she said. "Or how much I would miss having friends, or a partner to work with. Till I met you, with your stupid, dragon-fighting grin. Every time we were together, we were *good* together. The fighting, the banter, the food, the... kisses. But this is no way to have a relationship." She finished with his side and smoothed a thick gauze pad over it, taping it into place.

"I'm not taking my pants off," said Sean.

"*What*?!"

"My leg. You'll have to cut the pant leg open, cause I'm not taking them off."

"Oh." Rory's face flushed deep crimson. "We'll make it work."

"We'll make the other thing work, too," he said. "Somehow." His eyes drooped shut again, and before she'd finished he was asleep.

He woke several times that night to nightmares full of glowing red eyes and evil whispers, but each time he startled and looked around, there was just the yellow, cheerful light of the fire flickering over worn flagstones, and Rory's gentle breathing at his back, where she huddled against him in her sleep, as though they had been lovers. There were no hellhounds, nor other monsters, nor even any unicorns. Toward morning his wounds began to ache again, and kept him from going back to sleep. So he lay there and watched the fire and listened to Rory breathing, and let the thoughts chase each other drowsily through his mind. Longing blushed through him, painful as quiet tears, when she shifted in her sleep and nuzzled her face into his shoulder. As long as they both lived the lives they did, they would never be able to have this. They'd never be more to each other than friends, passing and occasionally meeting, perhaps to dress one another's wounds, until eventually one of them was killed. He realized in that instant that he would gladly give up his duties for her, to spend more moments like this, feeling her soft touch, waking with her beside him. But did she feel the same? And what if he did give up his work to marry his elf girl? What if another Dianthe came along?

"Sean?" Her voice sounded drowsy, but the blankets shifted and rustled as she pushed herself upright.

"Hm?"

"How do you feel?"

"Everything hurts." It wasn't a lie, though he didn't necessarily mean his injuries.

She got up and tossed more wood on the fire, then gathered her supplies and went to work redressing his wounds. This time he was painfully aware of her nearness and the way her fingers lingered longer than they needed to.

"What is this place?" he asked.

"It's Tristini Castle—what's left of it. It belonged to the last king of the elves, during the Curse War. The king was one of the ones who used forbidden spells in the fight against humans, and they say he still haunts the place." She looked around at the crumbling stone arches and the remnants of walls and towers, her face suddenly pensive. But then her expression cleared when her gaze found him again, and she smiled. "Maybe that's why hellhounds never come here. It's one of the best emergency shelters we have, but it's a terror to get here, unless you're riding a unicorn through the shadow realm, that is." She bent back to her work, taping the last of the fresh bandages in place beneath his torn pant leg.

"Rory..."

He was interrupted by the chime of her magic mirror. She gave him an apologetic grimace as she slapped her pockets and finally pulled out the mirror. It was Princess Calla.

"No curse?" Rory questioned after their initial excited greeting.

"No curse!" Calla confirmed. "Dianthe?"

"Gone," said Rory. "And we're okay. Or, we will be."

"Thank God! I'm... not looking forward to taking her place, but Gaelan won't take the crown, after everything that's happened."

"You will make a great queen, your Highness," said Rory, smiling.

"Calla. Just Calla. Look, Rory, I'm going to make some changes as soon as I can, but I wanted to make sure you'll be okay with them. Barra and Maireadd have always been on shaky ground with each other, and that needs to change. Dianthe did a lot of damage to both our countries. But you're the only elf I trust, who serves a higher calling than just to look out for your own interests. That's what we need here, on both sides. I'm going to ask your council to send you to Barra as our new ambassador. If you're willing."

Rory flushed. "I'm not so sure they'll go along with that."

"I'm not going to give them a choice."

Sean watched her excited conversation, feeling the pain of longing building in his chest. Everything was changing now. Fear, paranoia, and dread had been a part of him for so long, and now suddenly it was all over. All that remained of the darkness was inside him, in his nightmares, and the pain of his wounds, and the feeling of displacement, wondering if he could go back to his old life, his regular assignments, even if he wanted to.

Rory ended the call and came over and sat beside him, her eyes shining, but with a question behind the excitement. He knew the question, he just wasn't sure how to answer it yet. So he gave her a crooked smile and lay back down. He didn't have to pretend to still be sick and in pain. She went through the dried food supplies that the elves kept stocked in each of their shelters, and soon had a pot of stew bubbling over the fire.

She had just offered him a bowl of the thick, salty soup, when someone called from outside the ruins. Rory startled, and Sean reached for weapons that were no longer there.

"Vasya?" she said.

A moment later the surly elf appeared, leading a small band of magicals that Sean recognized as Dianthe's prisoners from the night before. Vasya grumbled a greeting and all but collapsed in front of the fire.

"You hiked all this way?" Rory asked incredulously.

"Took us all night," he said as the others settled in and converged on Rory's small pot of stew like a flock of vultures. It was gone within minutes.

"But why not stay at one of the closer shelters?" Rory asked, already digging out more food. Thank goodness for the elves' habit of always being over prepared.

"Hellhounds. They're everywhere, and they're *mad*. We tried to stop, but dozens of them would just gather around the shelter and howl and beat against the wards until they started to fail. So we kept coming." He looked between her and Sean. "I see you two have had an easy night of it. How did you escape? We were barely away when the curse triggered, and I was afraid it would catch up with us."

Sean finished eating and dozed off again while they were exchanging stories.

He'd had injuries before—even ones that had nearly killed him. Those were always the times, when he slept and slept, waiting for his body to heal, that the nightmares crowded in. But this time when they started, Rory was there, whispering soothing words in elvish that chased away the disquiet.

He woke a while later to Rory's mirror chiming again. This time, after she answered it, she brought it over and handed it to him, her eyebrows raised. He pushed himself upright and took the mirror. It was Grandpa Jack.

"You are still alive, boy. Good. I was thinking I'd have to send some people over to avenge you."

"Not this time." He grinned. "Did you hear the news? Barra is getting a new queen."

Grandpa waved that off, as of no consequence. "You look terrible."

"I feel terrible. Is that the only reason you called? To tell me I look bad?"

"No!" The bushy eyebrows descended as Grandpa glared. "I'm recalling you from military service. The Family needs you." As a member of one of the Families, Sean's first duty had always been to them. His service to the Thyrus government was secondary, a fact which the government loathed.

Stunned, Sean could only blink. His heart started to pound. "What's happened?"

"Nothing, yet. But I'm hearing things from my spies. Barra is weak. That witch wrung her out and divided her, and now there's a new, young queen without experience, and Barra's enemies have noticed. War is coming."

Sean's heart dropped into his stomach. "What do you need?"

"A point man inside Barra. Someone who knows the country and knows what he's doing. I've named you my heir as Family head, but I want you over there for now."

"I...That's..."

"A lot to saddle you with, I know. I'm sorry for that. But you won't be alone. I want you to work with that little elf of yours. You still sweet on her?"

"Uh..." Sean's gaze flew to Rory, who he discovered was watching him, her eyes round. "Ye-es. You could say that. But she's going to be busy. Calla is requesting her as Barra's new ambassador from Maireadd."

"Even better. I've been trying to get my people into Maireadd for years. You can go with her when she reports to her council. She's a pretty little thing, if she's who I just talked to, so at least that part of your assignment won't be a trial."

Sean felt himself flush, and looked up to see Rory blushing as well. "That's—why are we having this conversation?"

"If you're worried about her honor, then marry her. Remember, you're the one that brought her into the Family."

Sean cleared his throat. "And the war situation?"

"Will wait till you're healed up. Get some rest, boy. We'll talk in a few days."

The mirror went blank.

Sean hung his head, groaning. "The thing about Grandpa Jack is, he always gets what he wants, and can't imagine it any other way."

"I gathered."

"We don't have to get married. Or, we could..." he trailed off. *Troll's turds!* "I mean, the Family doesn't control that. Not even Grandpa Jack."

She nodded, still pink-faced. But instead of pressing the issue, she said, "War? And you're going to be Family head."

Sean puffed out a breath, his mind already racing ahead. He still felt so weary, bruised down to his soul. Neither the possibility of looming war, nor the massive responsibility his grandfather wanted to put on him were things he could face at the moment, with the wind whistling outside the wards, and the quiet conversation and soft snores of Vasya and his little band of magicals, who had all but collapsed after breakfast. He still heard the echoing whispers of voices in the dark, and felt the ripping agony of phantom teeth and venom whenever he closed his eyes. The paranoia of a year of solitude, cut off from friends and allies. It would get better. He knew that. He'd always been good at bouncing back, not letting himself dwell on the wounds of the past. But healing took time, and his hurts were still fresh. Now he wondered how much time he would have.

Rory's cool hands reached out and covered his fists, which he didn't realize he'd clenched together. He looked up and met her gaze. The blush had gone out of her face, and now she seemed composed and utterly self-assured.

"You're not alone." As though she'd read his thoughts. She worked his hand open and wove her fingers through his. "You never were. I talked to that priest, you know. He told me how you were always coming in and lighting a candle, holding vigil for your friends. Do you think we weren't praying and holding vigil for you, even when we couldn't talk to you? And when you needed help..."

"You were there," he said, flashing her a grin to cover the way his voice wavered. "You and Dylan and even Beck, and the unicorns. And that wretched, jealous dragon-turd of an elf." He glanced over at Vasya, who was snoring into his arm.

"You knew he was jealous?" Rory asked in surprise.

"Of course he was," said Sean, a little surprised in his turn. How could Vasya not have been jealous? Rory was...everything. Clever, gracious, principled, dangerous and powerful. And lovely.

She was watching him, her other-worldly eyes narrowed in suspicion. Wisps of her fine, black hair had escaped her usual braided crown and floated around her ears. He dared reach out and touch one of the pointed tips of her ears. Then, even more daring, let his fingers slide down her ear's edge to the wisps of loose hair at her neck. She shivered.

"Everything's changed," he said thoughtfully. She tilted her head into his hand, so that he was cupping her jaw. "Last night you said this was no way to have a relationship—two agents of different countries, always on the run. But maybe as an ambassador and a Family head, we could make it work."

"We'd still be terribly busy," she pointed out.

"And maybe at cross-purposes sometimes."

At that she shook her head. "No. Remember the unicorn? I mean, that first one we saw together, and what I asked you then? As long as we serve a higher authority than governments or Families, we would never be very seriously at odds."

"So do you think we could make it work?"

"Only one way to find out." She leaned in and kissed him, mumbling against his lips. "Cute human."

"Your human."

"You were always my human."

Look for more titles in the Seer's Gambit series.

Sea and Soul

Seer's Gambit #1

Doom and Destiny await empath Dylan Blaine on the Isle of Selkies. Accidentally married, can he and Kiah escape the witch's hands long enough to fall in love?

Fate and Fang

A Seer's Gambit novella

A cursed man and a suicidal werewolf become vigilante protectors in this standalone companion to the Seer's Gambit series.

Coming soon!

Crown and Claw

Seer's Gambit #3

Princess Calla was never supposed to inherit the crown, but with her father under the sorceress queen's thrall and her brother missing, she may not have a choice. Meanwhile, her forbidden love for a werewolf might topple the country under her, if the queen doesn't destroy it first.

ABOUT THE AUTHOR

Shari Branning is the author of several speculative fiction novels and a lifelong lover of words. She's a stay at home mom, married to her sweetheart, and lives in the beautiful countryside of Northeast Pennsylvania. You can find more of her books through her website https://sharibranning.wixsite.com/mysite

Or follow her author page on Facebook.

https://www.facebook.com/shari.branning/

Made in the USA
Monee, IL
14 November 2024

70133902R00233